6 What a very, very
LUCKY
person you are.

Spread out before you are the
FINEST and **FUNNIEST**
words from the finest and funniest writer
the past century ever knew. *9*

Stephen Fry

Pelham Grenville Wodehouse (always known as 'Plum') wrote more than ninety novels and some three hundred short stories over 73 years. He is widely recognised as the greatest 20th century writer of humour in the English language.

Wodehouse mixed the high culture of his classical education with the popular slang of the suburbs in both England and America, becoming a 'cartoonist of words'. Drawing on the antics of a near-contemporary world, he placed his Drones, Earls, Ladies (including draconian aunts and eligible girls) and Valets, in a recently vanished society, whose reality is transformed by his remarkable imagination into something timeless and enduring.

Perhaps best known for the escapades of Bertie Wooster and Jeeves, Wodehouse also created the world of Blandings Castle, home to Lord Emsworth and his cherished pig, the Empress of Blandings. His stories include gems concerning the irrepressible and disreputable Ukridge; Psmith, the elegant socialist; the ever-so-slightly-unscrupulous Fifth Earl of Ickenham, better known as Uncle Fred; and those related by Mr Mulliner, the charming raconteur of The Angler's Rest, and the Oldest Member at the Golf Club.

Wodehouse collaborated with a variety of partners on straight plays and worked principally alongside Guy Bolton on providing the lyrics and script for musical comedies with such composers as George Gershwin, Irving Berlin and Cole Porter. He liked to say that the royalties for 'Just My Bill', which Jerome Kern incorporated into Showboat, were enough to keep him in tobacco and whisky for the rest of his life.

In 1936 he was awarded The Mark Twain Medal for 'having made an outstanding and lasting contribution to the happiness of the world'. He was made a Doctor of Letters by Oxford University in 1939 and in 1975, aged 93, he was knighted by Queen Elizabeth II. He died shortly afterwards, on St Valentine's Day.

To have created so many characters that require no introduction places him in a very select group of writers, lead by Shakespeare and Dickens.

'You don't analyse such sunlit
PERFECTION
you just bask in it's warmth and splendour'

Stephen Fry

'Wodehouse is the
GREATEST
comic writer'

Douglas Adams

'**SUBLIME**
comic genius . . . light as a feather, but fabulous'

Ben Elton

'The
FUNNIEST
writer ever to put words on paper'

Hugh Laurie

'P.G. Wodehouse wrote
THE BEST
English comic novels of the century'

Sebastian Faulks

'**WITTY**
and effortlessly fluid. His books are laugh-out-loud funny'

Arabella Weir

'**THE HEAD**
of my profession'

Hilaire Belloc

'Wodehouse was quite simply
THE BEE'S KNEES.
And then some'

Joseph Connolly

'Mr Wodehouse's
IDYLLIC WORLD CAN NEVER STALE.
He will continue to release future generations from captivity
that may be more irksome than our own. He has made a
world for us to live in and delight in'

Evelyn Waugh

'**THE ULTIMATE IN COMFORT READING**
because nothing bad ever happens in P.G. Wodehouse land. Or
even if it does, it's always sorted out by the end of the book. For
as long as I'm immersed in a P.G. Wodehouse book, it's possible
to keep the real world at bay and live in a far, far nicer,
funnier one where happy endings are the order of the day'

Marian Keyes

'You should read Wodehouse when you're well
and when you're poorly; when you're travelling,
and when you're not; when you're feeling clever, and when
you're feeling utterly dim. Wodehouse
ALWAYS LIFTS YOUR SPIRITS,
no matter how high they happen to be already'

Lynne Truss

'P. G. Wodehouse remains the greatest chronicler of
A CERTAIN KIND OF ENGLISHNESS,
that no one else has ever captured quite so sharply, or with
quite as much wit and affection'

Julian Fellowes

'Not only the funniest English novelist who
ever wrote but one of our finest stylists.
His world is **PERFECT**, his stories are
PERFECT, his writing is **PERFECT**.
What more is there to be said?'

Susan Hill

'One of my (few) proud boasts is that I once spent a day interviewing P. G. Wodehouse at his home in America. He was exactly as I'd expected: a lovely, modest man. He could have walked out of one of his own novels. It's dangerous to use the word

GENIUS

to describe a writer, but I'll risk it with him'

John Humphrys

'The

INCOMPARABLE AND TIMELESS

genius – perfect for readers of all ages, shapes and sizes!'

Kate Mosse

'**COMPULSORY READING**

for anyone who has a pig, an aunt – or a sense of humour!'

Lindsey Davis

'A genius . . .

ELUSIVE, DELICATE BUT LASTING.

He created such a credible world that, sadly, I suppose, never really existed but what a delight it always is to enter it and the temptation to linger there is sometimes almost overwhelming'

Alan Ayckbourn

'I've recorded all the Jeeves books, and I can tell you this: it's like singing Mozart. The perfection of the phrasing is

A PHYSICAL PLEASURE.

I doubt if any singer in the English language has more perfect music'

Simon Callow

'I constantly find myself drooling with admiration at the

SUBLIME

way Wodehouse plays with the English language'

Simon Brett

'To pick up a Wodehouse novel is to find oneself in the presence of genius – no writer has ever given me so much
PURE ENJOYMENT'

John Julius Norwich

'P. G. Wodehouse is
THE GOLD STANDARD OF ENGLISH WIT'

Christopher Hitchens

'Wodehouse is so
UTTERLY, PROPERLY, SIMPLY FUNNY'

Adele Parks

'To dive into a Wodehouse novel is to swim in some of the most
ELEGANTLY TURNED PHRASES
in the english language'

Ben Schott

'P.G. Wodehouse should be prescribed to treat depression. Cheaper, more effective than valium and far, far more
ADDICTIVE'

Olivia Williams

'My only problem with Wodehouse is deciding which of his
ENCHANTING
books to take to my desert island'

Ruth Dudley Edwards

'Quite simply,
THE MASTER OF COMIC WRITING
at work'

Jane Moore

P.G. WODEHOUSE

Weekend Wodehouse

INTRODUCTION BY
Hilaire Belloc

ILLUSTRATIONS BY
Kerr

arrow books

Published by Arrow Books 2012

1 3 5 7 9 10 8 6 4 2

First published in Great Britain by Herbert Jenkins Ltd 1939
First published by Hutchinson 2011

Arrow Books
The Random House Group Limited
20 Vauxhall Bridge Road, London, SW1V 2SA

www.randomhouse.co.uk
www.wodehouse.co.uk

Addresses for companies within The Random House Group Limited can be found at:
www.randomhouse.co.uk/offices.htm

The Random House Group Limited Reg. No. 954009

A CIP catalogue record for this book
is available from the British Library

ISBN 9780099558149

The Random House Group Limited supports The Forest
Stewardship Council (FSC®), the leading international forest
certification organisation. Our books carrying the FSC label are
printed on FSC® certified paper. FSC is the only forest certification
scheme endorsed by the leading environmental organisations,
including Greenpeace. Our paper procurement policy can be found at:
www.randomhouse.co.uk/environment

Printed and bound by CPI Group (UK) Ltd, Croydon, CR0 4YY

Weekend Wodehouse

INTRODUCTION

SOME two or three years ago I was asked in the United States to broadcast a few words on my own trade of writing—what I thought of it and why I disliked it.

I understand that this broadcast was heard by a very large number—some millions it seems. Now in the course of this broadcast I gave as the best writer of English now alive, Mr. P. G. Wodehouse.

It was not only a very sincere but a reasonable and well thought out pronouncement. Yet I got a vast number of communications asking me what I exactly meant. Not that those who had heard me doubted Mr. Wodehouse's genius. They had given proof of their perception of that genius by according him the very wide circulation which he enjoys on that side of the Atlantic, as I am glad to say he does elsewhere. No; their puzzlement was why I should call the author who was supreme in that particular line of country the "best" writer of our time: the best living writer of *English*: why I should have called him, as I did call him, "the head of my profession".

I cannot do better in such a brief introduction as this than take that episode as my text and explain why and how Mr. Wodehouse occupies this position.

Writing is a craft, like any other: playing the violin, skating, batting at cricket, billiards, wood-carving—anything you like; and mastership in any craft is attainment of the end to which that craft is devoted. A craftsman is excellent in his craft according to his degree of attainment towards its end, and his use of the means towards that end. Now the end of writing is the production in the reader's mind of a certain image and a certain emotion. And the means towards that end are the use of words in any particular language; and the complete use of that medium is the choosing of the right words and the putting of them into the right order. It is *this* which Mr. Wodehouse does better, in the English language, than anyone else alive; or at any rate than anyone else whom I have read for many years past.

His object is comedy in the most modern sense of that word: that is, his object is to present the laughable, and he does this with such mastery and skill that he nearly always approaches, and often reaches, perfection.

It is a test of power in this craft of writing that its object shall be attained by some method which the reader cannot directly perceive. To write prose so that your search for effect appears on the surface is to write bad prose. To write prose so that you get your effects by unusual words, deliberately chosen for their oddity, is to write bad prose. To write prose so that the reader thinks more of the construction than of the image conveyed is to write bad prose. So to write is not necessarily to write the worst prose nor even very bad prose, but it is to miss perfection.

There are various ways in which you may test the truth of what I here say about this master in my own craft of writing. One is to attempt an imitation. You will find you cannot do it. In all the various departments of his skill Mr. Wodehouse is unique for simplicity and exactitude, which is as much as to say that he is unique for an avoidance of all frills. He gets the full effect, bang! One may say of him as the traveller in the story, hearing Shakespeare for the first time, said of Hamlet: "Doesn't he pull it off?" Or again one may consider his inimitable use of parallelism. The use of parallelism is one of the special marks of leadership in English. For it has become one of the chief marks of English prose in its most sharp-edged form. Now in parallelism Mr. Wodehouse is again supreme. There is no one like him in this department. One may say of him what he might say of his own Jeeves, "There is none like you, none". Whether one quotes a single phrase such as "quaking like a jelly in a high wind" (for the effect of an aunt upon a young nephew), or of the laugh of another lady and its effect upon another young man: "it was like cavalry clatterir over a tin bridge"; or any one out of a hundred examples, it is always the same success. Mr. Wodehouse has done the trick. In every case the parallelism has enhanced to the utmost the value of the thing described. It appears not only in phrases, but in the use of one single metaphorical word, and especially in the use of passing vernacular slang.

Then you may consider the situations: the construction. Properly this does not concern the excellence of the writer as such. It is the art of the playwright more than of the prose-writer pure and simple. But observe how admirably it is used in these hands! The situation, the climax, general and particular, the interplay of character and circumstance are as exact as such arrangements can be. They produce the full effect and are always complete.

There is yet another perfection which I note in him. It is one which most moderns, I think, would not regard as a perfection at all. Well! I differ from them. It is the repeated use of one set of characters. The English country house and its setting, the aged absent-minded earl, the young ladies and gentlemen with too much leisure or too little, too much money, or (contrariwise) embarrassment—all these form one set of recurrent figures, one set of "property" scenes. Another is New York with its special characters and special situations—particularly the suddenly enriched and the vagaries of their young, more human than their mothers.

There is the club of the young, idle, and very-much-to-be-liked young Englishmen of the wealthier sort, the pageant of the Drones (and, by the way, talking of clubs, what more exact bullseye has ever been hit by any marksman than the casual remark about the man being shown all the sights of London, "ending up with Bucks"?). Then there are the immortal, vivid glimpses of suburban life, for example the glorious adventures of the uncle who breaks loose once a year and showers gold upon the young man who jellies eels and his devoted would-be spouse: a lovely pair of lovers, as vivid as a strong transparency concentrated on one small screen—yet not a dozen adjectives between them.

7

Everything this author has seen he has observed; everything he has observed he has engraved; but, what is more remarkable than observation (which is common to many), or even than the record of observation (which is, though rare in any excellent degree, yet fairly well known), is the presentation of the thing observed so that it rises almost violently before the eye to which it is presented. That is everywhere, in every style, in every manner of subject the very heart of prose; not only of imaginative prose but of all prose.

Those great masters of prose whom the foolish think dull possess that power, as may be proved by the way in which whatever they have written is retained in the memory of the reader. To quote an instance of which I am fond and which is little known: Newman's chapters on "The Arians of the Fourth Century".

Now my fellow-worshippers at this shrine which Mr. Wodehouse has raised to the glory of his country, that is, of English letters, may rightly complain that praise of a man's craftsmanship is arid praise. When you say that Brou (which I suppose is the finest sculpture in Europe) leaves you breathless, you do not want to add any long technical discussion of how the figures were modelled or how the chisel worked upon that stone. Let me end therefore with something that is not a mere hymn of praise to Mr. Wodehouse's style (which I repeat and still maintain to be the summit of his achievement); let me end with something about him which is intensely national—I mean the creation of one more figure in that long gallery of living figures which makes up the glory of English fiction.

For the English people, more than any other, have created in their literature living men and women rather than types—and Mr. Wodehouse has created Jeeves.

He has created others, but in his creation of Jeeves he has done something which may respectfully be compared to the work of the Almighty in Michelangelo's painting. He has formed a man filled with the breath of life. It is probable that the race of butlers will die even sooner than other modern

8

species. They rose to meet a need. They played a national role triumphantly. That role is now near extinction and they are ready to depart. You may say that Jeeves is not exactly a butler, but he is of the same rare divine metal from which butlers are made. He leads among those other butlers of Mr. Wodehouse's invention and indeed he leads all the gentlemen's gentlemen of the world. I should like the foreigner or posterity (much the same thing) to steep themselves in the living image of Jeeves and thus comprehend what the English character in action may achieve. Talk of efficiency!

I have just said that those of whom Jeeves is the prototype or the god are perhaps doomed, and this leads me to the last question which one always asks of all first-rate writing: will Mr. Wodehouse's work endure?

Pray note that literary work does not necessarily endure through its excellence. What is called "immortality" (whereas nothing mortal is immortal) is conferred upon a man's writing by external circumstances as much as by internal worth. I can show you whole societies of men for whom Keats would be meaningless and I know dozens of Englishmen well versed in the French language who find Racine merely dull. Whether the now famous P. G. Wodehouse will remain upon that level for as many generations as he deserves, depends, alas, upon what happens to England. For my part I would like to make it a test of that very thing—"What happens to England."

If in, say, 50 years Jeeves and any other of that great company—but in particular Jeeves—shall have faded, then what we have so long called England will no longer be.

H. BELLOC.

CONTENTS

CLASSIFIED CONTENTS

DRONES CLUB STORIES

MR. MULLINER STORIES

JEEVES STORIES

LORD EMSWORTH STORIES

UKRIDGE STORIES

THE OLDEST MEMBER STORIES

EXTRACTS FROM NOVELS

MISCELLANEOUS

UNCLE FRED FLITS BY

In order that they might enjoy their after-luncheon coffee in peace, the Crumpet had taken the guest whom he was entertaining at the Drones Club to the smaller and less frequented of the two smoking-rooms. In the other, he explained, though the conversation always touched an exceptionally high level of brilliance, there was apt to be a good deal of sugar thrown about.

The guest said he understood.

"Young blood, eh?"

"That's right. Young blood."

"And animal spirits."

"And animal, as you say, spirits," agreed the Crumpet. "We get a fairish amount of those here."

"The complaint, however, is not, I observe, universal."

"Eh?"

The other drew his host's attention to the doorway, where a young man in form-fitting tweeds had just appeared. The aspect of this young man was haggard. His eyes glared wildly and he sucked at an empty cigarette-holder. If he had a mind, there was something on it. When the Crumpet called to him to come and join the party, he merely shook his head in a distraught sort of way and disappeared, looking like a character out of a Greek tragedy pursued by the Fates.

The Crumpet sighed.

"Poor old Pongo!"

"Pongo?"

"That was Pongo Twistleton. He's all broken up about his Uncle Fred."

"Dead?"

"No such luck. Coming up to London again to-morrow. Pongo had a wire this morning."

"And that upsets him?"

"Naturally. After what happened last time."

"What was that?"

"Ah!" said the Crumpet.

"What happened last time?"

"You may well ask."

"I do ask."

"Ah!" said the Crumpet.

Poor old Pongo (said the Crumpet) has often discussed his Uncle Fred with me, and if there weren't tears in his eyes when he did so, I don't know a tear in the eye when I see one. In round numbers the Earl of Ickenham, of Ickenham Hall, Ickenham, Hants, he lives in the country most of the year, but from time to time has a nasty way of slipping his collar and getting loose and descending upon Pongo at his flat in the Albany. And every time he does so, the unhappy young blighter is subjected to some soul-testing experience. Because the trouble with this uncle is that, though sixty if a day, he becomes on arriving in the metropolis as young as he feels—which is, apparently, a youngish twenty-two. I don't know if you happen to know what the word "excesses" means, but those are what Pongo's Uncle Fred from the country, when in London, invariably commits.

It wouldn't so much matter, mind you, if he would confine his activities to the club premises. We're pretty broad-minded here, and if you stop short of smashing the piano, there isn't much that you can do at the Drones that will cause the raised eyebrow and sharp intake of breath. The snag is that he will insist on lugging Pongo out in the open and there, right in the public eye, proceeding to step high, wide and plentiful.

So when, on the occasion to which I allude, he stood pink and genial on Pongo's hearth-rug, bulging with Pongo's lunch and wreathed in the smoke of one of Pongo's cigars, and said: "And now, my boy, for a pleasant and instructive afternoon," you will readily understand why the unfortunate young clam gazed at him as he would have gazed at two-penn'orth of dynamite, had he discovered it lighting up in his presence.

18

"A what?" he said, giving at the knees and paling beneath the tan a bit.

"A pleasant and instructive afternoon," repeated Lord Ickenham, rolling the words round his tongue. "I propose that you place yourself in my hands and leave the programme entirely to me."

Now, owing to Pongo's circumstances being such as to necessitate his getting into the aged relative's ribs at intervals and shaking him down for an occasional much-needed tenner or what not, he isn't in a position to use the iron hand with the old buster. But at these words he displayed a manly firmness.

"You aren't going to get me to the dog-races again."

"No, no."

"You remember what happened last June."

"Quite," said Lord Ickenham, "quite. Though I still think that a wiser magistrate would have been content with a mere reprimand."

"And I won't——"

"Certainly not. Nothing of that kind at all. What I propose to do this afternoon is to take you to visit the home of your ancestors."

Pongo did not get this.

"I thought Ickenham was the home of my ancestors."

"It is one of the homes of your ancestors. They also resided rather nearer the heart of things, at a place called Mitching Hill."

"Down in the suburbs, do you mean?"

"The neighbourhood is now suburban, true. It is many years since the meadows where I sported as a child were sold and cut up into building lots. But when I was a boy Mitching Hill was open country. It was a vast, rolling estate belonging to your great-uncle, Marmaduke, a man with whiskers of a nature which you with your pure mind would scarcely credit, and I have long felt a semtimental urge to see what the hell the old place looks like now. Perfectly foul, I expect. Still, I think we should make the pious pilgrimage."

Pongo absolutely-ed heartily. He was all for the scheme.

A great weight seemed to have rolled off his mind. The way he looked at it was that even an uncle within a short jump of the looney bin couldn't very well get into much trouble in a suburb. I mean, you know what suburbs are. They don't, as it were, offer the scope. One follows his reasoning, of course.

"Fine!" he said. "Splendid! Topping!"

"Then put on you hat and rompers, my boy," said Lord Ickenham, "and let us be off. I fancy one gets there by omnibuses and things."

Well, Pongo hadn't expected much in the way of mental uplift from the sight of Mitching Hill, and he didn't get it. Alighting from the bus, he tells me, you found yourself in the middle of rows and rows of semi-detached villas, all looking exactly alike, and you went on and you came to more semi-detached villas, and those all looked exactly alike, too. Nevertheless, he did not repine. It was one of those early spring days which suddenly change to mid-winter and he had come out without his overcoat, and it looked like rain and he hadn't an umbrella, but despite this his mood was one of sober ecstasy.

The hours were passing and his uncle had not yet made a goat of himself. At the dog-races the other had been in the hands of the constabulary in the first ten minutes.

It began to seem to Pongo that with any luck he might be able to keep the old blister pottering harmlessly about here till nightfall, when he could shoot a bit of dinner into him and put him to bed. And as Lord Ickenham had specifically stated that his wife, Pongo's Aunt Jane, had expressed her intention of scalping him with a blunt knife if he wasn't back at the Hall by lunch time on the morrow, it really looked as if he might get through this visit without perpetrating a single major outrage on the public weal. It is rather interesting to note that as he thought this Pongo smiled, because it was the last time he smiled that day.

All this while, I should mention, Lord Ickenham had been stopping at intervals like a pointing dog and saying that it must have been just about here that he plugged the gardener in the trousers seat with his bow and arrow and that over there he had been sick after his first cigar, and he now paused in front of a villa which for some unknown reason called itself The Cedars. His face was tender and wistful.

"On this very spot, if I am not mistaken," he said, heaving a bit of a sigh, "on this very spot, fifty years ago come Lammas Eve, I . . . Oh, blast it!"

The concluding remark had been caused by the fact that the rain, which had held off until now, suddenly began to buzz down like a shower-bath. With no further words, they leaped into the porch of the villa and there took shelter, exchanging glances with a grey parrot which hung in a cage in the window.

Not that you could really call it shelter. They were protected from above all right, but the moisture was now falling with a sort of swivel action, whipping in through the sides of the porch and tickling them up properly. And it was just after Pongo had turned up his collar and was huddling against the door that the door gave way. From the fact that a female of general-servant aspect was standing there he gathered that his uncle must have rung the bell.

This female wore a long mackintosh, and Lord Ickenham beamed upon her with a fair spot of suavity.

"Good afternoon," he said.

The female said good afternoon.

"The Cedars?"

The female said yes, it was The Cedars.

"Are the old folks at home?"

The female said there was nobody at home.

"Ah? Well, never mind. I have come," said Lord Ickenham, edging in, "to clip the parrot's claws. My assistant, Mr. Walkinshaw, who applies the anæsthetic," he added, indicating Pongo with a gesture.

"Are you from the bird shop?"

"A very happy guess."

"Nobody told me you were coming."

"They keep things from you, do they?" said Lord Ickenham, sympathetically. "Too bad."

Continuing to edge, he had got into the parlour by now, Pongo following in a sort of dream and the female following Pongo.

"Well, I suppose it's all right," she said. "I was just going out. It's my afternoon."

"Go out," said Lord Ickenham cordially. "By all means go out. We will leave everything in order."

And presently the female, though still a bit on the dubious side, pushed off, and Lord Ickenham lit the gasfire and drew a chair up.

"So here we are, my boy," he said. "A little tact, a little address, and here we are, snug and cosy and not catching our deaths of cold. You'll never go far wrong if you leave things to me."

"But, dash it, we can't stop here," said Pongo.

Lord Ickenham raised his eyebrows.

"Not stop here? Are you suggesting that we go out into that rain? My dear lad, you are not aware of the grave issues involved. This morning, as I was leaving home, I had a rather painful disagreement with your aunt. She said the weather was treacherous and wished me to take my woolly muffler. I replied that the weather was not treacherous and that I would be dashed if I took my woolly muffler. Eventually, by the exercise of an iron will, I had my way, and I ask you, my dear boy, to envisage what will happen if I return with a cold in the head. I shall sink to the level of a fifth-class power. Next time I came to London, it would be with a liver pad and a respirator. No! I shall remain here, toasting my toes at this really excellent fire. I had no idea that a gas-fire radiated such warmth. I feel all in a glow."

So did Pongo. His brow was wet with honest sweat. He is reading for the Bar, and while he would be the first to admit that he hasn't yet got a complete toe-hold on the Law of Great Britain he had a sort of notion that oiling into a perfect stranger's semi-detached villa on the pretext of pruning the parrot was a tort or misdemeanour, if not actual barratry or soccage in fief or something like that. And apart from the legal aspect of the matter there was the embarrassment of the thing. Nobody is more of a whale on correctness and not doing what's not done than Pongo, and the situation in which he now found himself caused him to chew the lower lip and, as I say, perspire a goodish deal.

"But suppose the blighter who owns this ghastly house comes back?" he asked. "Talking of envisaging things, try that one over on your pianola."

And, sure enough, as he spoke, the front door bell rang.

"There!" said Pongo.

"Don't say 'There!' my boy," said Lord Ickenham reprovingly. "It's the sort of thing your aunt says. I see no reason for alarm. Obviously this is some casual caller. A ratepayer would have used his latchkey. Glance cautiously out of the window and see if you can see anybody."

"It's a pink chap," said Pongo, having done so.

"How pink?"

"Pretty pink."

"Well, there you are, then. I told you so. It can't be the big chief. The sort of fellows who own houses like this are pale and sallow, owing to working in offices all day. Go and see what he wants."

"You go and see what he wants."

"We'll both go and see what he wants," said Lord Ickenham.

So they went and opened the front door, and there, as Pongo had said, was a pink chap. A small young pink chap, a bit moist about the shoulder-blades.

"Pardon me," said this pink chap, "is Mr. Roddis in?"

"No," said Pongo.

"Yes," said Lord Ickenham. "Don't be silly, Douglas—of course I'm in. I am Mr. Roddis," he said to the pink chap. "This, such as he is, is my son Douglas. And you?"

"Name of Robinson."

"What about it?"

"My name's Robinson."

23

"Oh, *your* name's Robinson? Now we've got it straight. Delighted to see you, Mr. Robinson. Come right in and take your boots off."

They all trickled back to the parlour, Lord Ickenham pointing out objects of interest by the wayside to the chap, Pongo gulping for air a bit and trying to get himself abreast of this new twist in the scenario. His heart was becoming more and more bowed down with weight of woe. He hadn't liked being Mr. Walkinshaw, the anæthetist, and he didn't like it any better being Roddis Junior. In brief, he feared the worst. It was only too plain to him by now that his uncle had got it thoroughly up his nose and had settled down to one of his big afternoons, and he was asking himself, as he had so often asked himself before, what would the harvest be?

Arrived in the parlour, the pink chap proceeded to stand on one leg and look coy.

"Is Julia here?" he asked, simpering a bit, Pongo says.

"Is she?" said Lord Ickenham to Pongo.

"No," said Pongo.

"No," said Lord Ickenham.

"She wired me she was coming here to-day."

"Ah, then we shall have a bridge four."

The pink chap stood on the other leg.

"I don't suppose you've ever met Julia. Bit of trouble in the family, she gave me to understand."

"It is often the way."

"The Julia I mean is your niece Julia Parker. Or, rather, your wife's niece Julia Parker."

"Any niece of my wife is a niece of mine," said Lord Ickenham heartily. "We share and share alike."

"Julia and I want to get married."

"Well, go ahead."

"But they won't let us."

"Who won't?"

"Her mother and father. And Uncle Charlie Parker and Uncle Henry Parker and the rest of them. They don't think I'm good enough."

24

"The morality of the modern young man is notoriously lax."

"Class enough, I mean. They're a haughty lot."

"What makes them haughty? Are they earls?"

"No, they aren't earls."

"Then why the devil," said Lord Ickenham warmly, "are they haughty? Only earls have a right to be haughty. Earls are hot stuff. When you get an earl, you've got something."

"Besides, we've had words. Me and her father. One thing led to another, and in the end I called him a perishing old——Coo!" said the pink chap, breaking off suddenly.

He had been standing by the window, and he now leaped lissomly into the middle of the room, causing Pongo, whose nervous system was by this time definitely down among the wines and spirits and who hadn't been expecting this *adagio* stuff, to bite his tongue with some severity.

"They're on the doorstep! Julia and her mother and father. I didn't know they were all coming."

"You do not wish to meet them?"

"No, I don't!"

"Then duck behind the settee, Mr. Robinson," said Lord Ickenham, and the pink chap, weighing the advice and finding it good, did so. And as he disappeared the door bell rang.

Once more, Lord Ickenham led Pongo out into the hall.

"I say!" said Pongo, and a close observer might have noted that he was quivering like an aspen.

"Say on, my dear boy."

"I mean to say, what?"

"What?"

"You aren't going to let these bounders in, are you?"

"Certainly," said Lord Ickenham. "We Roddises keep open house. And as they are presumably aware that Mr. Roddis has no son, I think we had better return to the old-lay-out. You are the local vet, my boy, come to minister to my parrot. When I return, I should like to find you by the cage, staring at the bird in a scientific manner. Tap your teeth from time to time with a pencil and try to smell of iodoform. It will help to add conviction."

So Pongo shifted back to the parrot's cage and stared so earnestly that it was only when a voice said "Well!" that he became aware that there was anybody in the room. Turning, he perceived that Hampshire's leading curse had come back, bringing the gang.

It consisted of a stern, thin, middle-aged woman, a middle-aged man and a girl.

You can generally accept Pongo's estimate of girls, and when he says that this one was a pippin one knows that he uses the term in its most exact sense. She was about nineteen, he thinks, and she wore a black beret, a dark-green leather coat, a shortish tweed skirt, silk stockings and high-heeled shoes. Her eyes were large and lustrous and her face like a dewy rosebud at daybreak on a June morning. So Pongo tells me. Not that I suppose he has ever seen a rosebud at daybreak on a June morning, because it's generally as much as you can do to lug him out of bed in time for nine-thirty breakfast. Still, one gets the idea.

"Well," said the woman, "you don't know who I am I'll be bound. I'm Laura's sister Connie. This is Claude, my husband. And this is my daughter Julia. Is Laura in?"

"I regret to say, no," said Lord Ickenham.

The woman was looking at him as if he didn't come up to her specifications.

"I thought you were younger," she said.

"Younger than what?" said Lord Ickenham.

"Younger than you are."

"You can't be younger than you are, worse luck," said Lord Ickenham. "Still, one does one's best, and I am bound to say that of recent years I have made a pretty good go of it."

The woman caught sight of Pongo, and he didn't seem to please her, either.

"Who's that?"

"The local vet, clustering round my parrot."

"I can't talk in front of him."

"It is quite all right," Lord Ickenham assured her. "The poor fellow is stone deaf."

And with an imperious gesture at Pongo, as much as to bid him stare less at girls and more at parrots, he got the company seated.

"Now, then," he said.

There was silence for a moment, then a sort of muffled sob, which Pongo thinks proceeded from the girl. He couldn't see, of course, because his back was turned and he was looking at the parrot, which looked back at him—most offensively, he says, as parrots will, using one eye only for the purpose. It also asked him to have a nut.

The woman came into action again.

"Although," she said, "Laura never did me the honour to invite me to her wedding, for which reason I have not communicated with her for five years, necessity compels me to cross her threshold to-day. There comes a time when differences must be forgotten and relatives must stand shoulder to shoulder."

"I see what you mean," said Lord Ickenham. "Like the boys of the old brigade."

"What I say is, let bygones be bygones. I would not have intruded on you, but needs must. I disregard the past and appeal to your sense of pity."

The thing began to look to Pongo like a touch, and he is convinced that the parrot thought so, too, for it winked and cleared its throat. But they were both wrong. The woman went on.

"I want you and Laura to take Julia into your home for a week or so, until I can make other arrangements for her. Julia is studying the piano, and she sits for her examination in two weeks' time, so until then she must remain in London. The trouble is, she has fallen in love. Or thinks she has."

"I know I have," said Julia.

Her voice was so attractive that Pongo was compelled to slew round and take another look at her. Her eyes, he says, were shining like twin stars and there was a sort of Soul's Awakening expression on her face, and what the dickens there was in a pink chap like the pink chap, who even as pink chaps go wasn't much of a pink chap, to make her look like that, was frankly, Pongo says, more than he could understand. The thing baffled him. He sought in vain for a solution.

"Yesterday, Claude and I arrived in London from our Bexhill home to give Julia a pleasant surprise. We stayed naturally, in the boarding-house where she has been living for the past six weeks. And what do you think we discovered?"

"Insects."

"Not insects. A letter. From a young man. I found to my horror that a young man of whom I knew nothing was arranging to marry my daughter. I sent for him immediately and found him to be quite impossible. He jellies eels!"

"Does what?"

"He is an assistant at a jellied-eel shop."

"But surely," said Lord Ickenham, "that speaks well for him. The capacity to jelly eel seems to me to argue intelligence of a high order. It isn't everybody who can do it, by any means. I know if someone came to me and said 'Jelly this eel!' I should be nonplussed. And so, or I am very mistaken, would Ramsay MacDonald and Winston Churchill."

The woman did not seem to see eye to eye.

"Tchah!" she said. "What do you suppose my husband's brother Charlie Parker would say if I allowed his niece to marry a man who jellies eels?"

"Ah!" said Claude, who, before we go any further, was a tall, drooping bird with a red soup-strainer moustache.

"Or my husband's brother, Henry Parker."

"Ah!" said Claude. "Or Cousin Alf Robbins, for that matter."

"Exactly. Cousin Alfred would die of shame."

The girl Julia hiccoughed passionately, so much so that Pongo says it was all he could do to stop himself nipping across and taking her hand in his and patting it.

"I've told you a hundred times, mother, that Wilberforce is only jellying eels till he finds something better."

"What is better than an eel?" asked Lord Ickenham, who had been following this discussion with the close attention it deserved. "For jellying purposes, I mean."

"He is ambitious. It won't be long," said the girl, "before Wilberforce suddenly rises in the world."

She never spoke a truer word. At this very moment up he came from behind the settee like a leaping salmon.

"Julia!" he cried.

"Wilby!" yipped the girl.

And Pongo says he never saw anything more sickening in his life than the way she flung herself into the blighter's arms and clung there like the ivy on the old garden wall. It wasn't that he had anything specific against the pink chap, but this girl had made a deep impression on him and he resented her gluing herself to another in this manner.

Julia's mother, after just that brief moment which a woman needs in which to recover from her natural surprise at seeing eel-jelliers pop up from behind sofas, got moving and plucked her away like a referee breaking a couple of welterweights.

"Julia Parker," she said, "I'm ashamed of you!"

"So am I," said Claude.

"I blush for you."

"Me, too," said Claude. "Hugging and kissing a man who called your father a perishing old bottle-nosed Gawd-help-us."

"I think," said Lord Ickenham, shoving his oar in, "that before proceeding any further we ought to go into that point. If he called you a perishing old bottle-nosed Gawd-help-us, it seems to me that the first thing to do is to decide whether he was right, and frankly, in my opinion . . ."

"Wilberforce will apologize."

"Certainly I'll apologize. It isn't fair to hold a remark passed in the heat of the moment against a chap. . . ."

"Mr. Robinson," said the woman, "you know perfectly well that whatever remarks you may have seen fit to pass don't matter one way or the other. If you were listening to what I was saying you will understand. . . ."

"Oh, I know, I know. Uncle Charlie Parker and Uncle Henry Parker and Cousin Alf Robbins and all that. Pack of snobs!"

29

"What!"

"Haughty, stuck-up snobs. Them and their class distinctions. Think themselves everybody just because they've got money. I'd like to know how they got it."

"What do you mean by that?"

"Never mind what I mean."

"If you are insinuating——"

"Well, of course, you know, Connie," said Lord Ickenham mildly, "he's quite right. You can't get away from that."

I don't know if you have ever seen a bull-terrier embarking on a scrap with an Airedale and just as it was getting down nicely to its work suddenly having an unexpected Kerry Blue sneak up behind it and bite it in the rear quarters. When this happens, it lets go of the Airedale and swivels round and fixes the butting-in animal with a pretty nasty eye. It was exactly the same with the woman Connie when Lord Ickenham spoke these words.

"What!"

"I was wondering if you had forgotten how Charlie Parker made his pile."

"What are you talking about?"

"I know it is painful," said Lord Ickenham, "and one doesn't mention it as a rule, but, as we are on the subject, you must admit that lending money at two hundred and fifty per cent interest is not done in the best circles. The judge, if you remember, said so at the trial."

"I never knew that!" cried the girl Julia.

"Ah," said Lord Ickenham. "You kept it from the child? Quite right, quite right."

"It's a lie!"

"And when Henry Parker had all that fuss with the bank it was touch and go they didn't send him to prison. Between ourselves, Connie, has a bank official, even a brother of your husband, any right to sneak fifty pounds from the till in order to put it on a hundred to one shot for the Grand National? Not quite playing the game, Connie. Not the straight bat. Henry, I grant you, won five thousand of the best and never looked back afterwards, but, though we applaud his judgment of form, we must surely look askance at his financial methods. As for Cousin Alf Robbins. . . ."

The woman was making rummy stuttering sounds. Pongo tells me he once had a Pommery Seven which used to express itself in much the same way if you tried to get it to take a hill on high. A sort of mixture of gurgles and explosions.

"There is not a word of truth in this," she gasped at length, having managed to get the vocal chords disentangled. "Not a single word. I think you must have gone mad."

Lord Ickenham shrugged his shoulders.

"Have it your own way, Connie. I was only going to say that, while the jury were probably compelled on the evidence submitted to them to give Cousin Alf Robbins the benefit of the doubt when charged with smuggling dope, everybody knew that he had been doing it for years. I am not blaming him, mind you. If a man can smuggle cocaine and get away with it, good luck to him, say I. The only point I am trying to make is that we are hardly a family that can afford to put on dog and sneer at honest suitors for our daughters' hands. Speaking for myself I consider that we are very lucky to have the chance of marrying even into eel-jellying circles."

"So do I," said Julia firmly.

"You don't believe what this man is saying?"

"I believe every word."

"So do I," said the pink chap.

The woman snorted. She seemed over-wrought.

"Well," she said, "goodness knows I have never liked Laura, but I would never have wished her a husband like you!"

"Husband?" said Lord Ickenham, puzzled. "What gives you the impression that Laura and I are married?"

There was a weighty silence, during which the parrot threw out a general invitation to the company to join it in a nut. Then the girl Julia spoke.

"You'll have to let me marry Wilberforce now," she said. "He knows too much about us."

"I was rather thinking that myself," said Lord Ickenham. "Seal his lips, I say."

"You wouldn't mind marrying into a low family would you, darling?" asked the girl, with a touch of anxiety.

"No family could be too low for me, dearest, if it was yours," said the pink chap.

"After all, we needn't see them."

"That's right."

"It isn't one's relations that matter: it's oneselves."

"That's right too."

"Wilby!"

"Julia!"

They repeated the old ivy on the garden wall act. Pongo says he didn't like it any better than the first time, but his distaste wasn't in it with the woman Connie's.

"And what, may I ask," she said, "do you propose to marry on?"

This seemed to cast a damper. They came apart. They looked at each other. The girl looked at the pink chap, and the pink chap looked at the girl. You could see that a jarring note had been struck.

"Wilberforce is going to be a very rich man some day."

"Some day!"

"If I had a hundred pounds," said the pink chap, "I could buy a half-share in one of the best milk walks in South London to-morrow."

"If!" said the woman.

"Ah!" said Claude.

"Where are you going to get it?"

"Ah!" said Claude.

"Where," repeated the woman, plainly pleased with the snappy crack and loath to let it ride without an encore, "are you going to get it?"

"That," said Claude, "is the point. Where are you going to get a hundred pounds?"

"Why, bless my soul," said Lord Ickenham jovially, "from me, of course. Where else?"

32

And before Pongo's bulging eyes he fished out from the recesses of his costume a crackling bundle of notes and handed it over. And the agony of realizing that the old bounder had had all that stuff on him all this time and that he hadn't touched him for so much as a tithe of it was so keen, Pongo says, that before he knew what he was doing he had let out a sharp, whinnying cry which rang through the room like the yowl of a stepped-on puppy.

"Ah," said Lord Ickenham. "The vet wishes to speak to me. Yes, vet?"

This seemed to puzzle the cerise bloke a bit.

"I thought you said this chap was your son."

"If I had a son," said Lord Ickenham, a little hurt, "he would be a good deal better-looking than that. No, this is the local veterinary surgeon. I may have said I *looked* on him as a son. Perhaps that was what confused you."

He shifted across to Pongo and twiddled his hands enquiringly. Pongo gaped at him, and it was not until one of the hands caught him smartly in the lower ribs that he remembered he was deaf and started to twiddle back. Considering that he wasn't supposed to be dumb, I can't see why he should have twiddled, but no doubt there are moments when twiddling is about all a fellow feels himself equal to. For what seemed to him at least ten hours Pongo had been undergoing great mental stress, and one can't blame him for being chatty. Anyway, be that as it may, he twiddled.

"I cannot quite understand what he says," announced Lord Ickenham at length, "because he sprained a finger this morning and that makes him stammer. But I gather that he wishes to have a word with me in private. Possibly my parrot has got something the matter with it which he is reluctant to mention even in sign language in front of a young unmarried girl. You know what parrots are. We will step outside."

"*We* will step outside," said Wilberforce.

"Yes," said the girl Julia. "I feel like a walk."

"And you?" said Lord Ickenham to the woman Connie,

who was looking like a female Napoleon at Moscow. "Do you join the hikers?"

"I shall remain and make myself a cup of tea. You will not grudge us a cup of tea, I hope?"

"Far from it," said Lord Ickenham cordially. "This is Liberty Hall. Stick around and mop it up till your eyes bubble."

Outside, the girl, looking more like a dewy rosebud than ever, fawned on the old buster pretty considerably.

"I don't know how to thank you!" she said. And the pink chap said he didn't either.

"Not at all, my dear, not at all," said Lord Ickenham.

"I think you're simply wonderful."

"No, no."

"You are. Perfectly marvellous."

"Tut, tut," said Lord Ickenham. "Don't give the matter another thought."

He kissed her on both cheeks, the chin, the forehead, the right eyebrow, and the tip of the nose, Pongo looking on the while in a baffled and discontented manner. Everybody seemed to be kissing this girl except him.

Eventually the degrading spectacle ceased and the girl and the pink chap shoved off, and Pongo was enabled to take up the matter of that hundred quid.

"Where," he asked, "did you get all that money?"

"Now, where did I?" mused Lord Ickenham. "I know your aunt gave it to me for some purpose. But what? To pay some bill or other, I rather fancy."

This cheered Pongo up slightly.

"She'll give you the devil when you get back," he said, with not a little relish. "I wouldn't be in your shoes for something. When you tell Aunt Jane," he said, with confidence, for he knew his Aunt Jane's emotional nature, "that you slipped her entire roll to a girl, and explain, as you will have to explain, that she was an extraordinarily pretty girl—a girl, in fine, who looked like something out of a beauty chorus of the better sort, I should think she would pluck down one of the ancestral battle-axes from the wall and jolly well strike you on the mazzard."

"Have no anxiety, my dear boy," said Lord Ickenham. "It is like your kind heart to be so concerned, but have no anxiety. I shall tell her that I was compelled to give the money to you to enable you to buy back some compromising letters from a Spanish *demi-mondaine*. She will scarcely be able to blame me for rescuing a fondly loved nephew from the clutches of an adventuress. It may be that she will feel a little vexed with you for a while, and that you may have to allow a certain time to elapse before you visit Ickenham again, but then I shan't be wanting you at Ickenham till the ratting season starts, so all is well."

At this moment, there came toddling up to the gate of The Cedars a large red-faced man. He was just going in when Lord Ickenham hailed him.

"Mr. Roddis?"

"Hey?"

"Am I addressing Mr. Roddis?"

"That's me."

"I am Mr. J. G. Bulstrode from down the road," said Lord Ickenham. "This is my sister's husband's brother, Percy Frensham, in the lard and imported-butter business."

The red-faced bird said he was pleased to meet them. He asked Pongo if things were brisk in the lard and imported-butter business, and Pongo said they were all right, and the red-faced bird said he was glad to hear it.

"We have never met, Mr. Roddis," said Lord Ickenham, "but I think it would be only neighbourly to inform you that a short while ago I observed two suspicious-looking persons in your house."

"In my house? How on earth did they get there?"

"No doubt through a window at the back. They looked to me like cat burglars. If you creep up, you may be able to see them."

The red-faced bird crept, and came back not exactly foaming at the mouth but with the air of a man who for two pins would so foam.

"You're perfectly right. They're sitting in my parlour as cool as dammit, swigging my tea and buttered toast."

"I thought as much."

"And they've opened a pot of my raspberry jam."

"Ah, then you will be able to catch them red-handed. I should fetch a policeman."

"I will. Thank you, Mr. Bulstrode."

"Only too glad to have been able to render you this little service, Mr. Roddis," said Lord Ickenham. "Well, I must be moving along. I have an appointment. Pleasant after the rain, is it not? Come, Percy."

He lugged Pongo off.

"So that," he said, with satisfaction, "is that. On these visits of mine to the metropolis, my boy, I always make it my aim, if possible, to spread sweetness and light. I look about me, even in a foul hole like Mitching Hill, and I ask myself—How can I leave this foul hole a better and happier foul hole than I found it? And if I see a chance, I grab it. Here is our omnibus. Spring aboard, my boy and on our way home we will be sketching out rough plans for the evening. If the old Leicester Grill is still in existence, we might look in there. It must be fully thirty-five years since I was last thrown out of the Leicester Grill. I wonder who is the bouncer there now."

Such (concluded the Crumpet) is Pongo Twistleton's Uncle Fred from the country, and you will have gathered by now a rough notion of why it is that when a telegram comes announcing his impending arrival in the great city Pongo blenches to the core and calls for a couple of quick ones.

The whole situation, Pongo says, is very complex. Looking at it from one angle, it is fine that the man lives in the country most of the year. If he didn't he would have him in his midst all the time. On the other hand, by living in the country he generates, as it were, a store of loopiness which expends itself with frightful violence on his rare visits to the centre of things.

What it boils down to is this—Is it better to have a loopy uncle whose loopiness is perpetually on tap but spread out thin, so to speak, or one who lies low in distant Hants for three hundred and sixty days in the year and does himself proud in London for the other five? Dashed moot, of course, and Pongo has never been able to make up his mind on the point.

Naturally, the ideal thing would be if someone would chain the old hound up permanently and keep him from Jan. one to Dec. thirty-one where he wouldn't do any harm—viz. among the spuds and tenantry. But this, Pongo admits, is a Utopian dream. Nobody could work harder to that end than his Aunt Jane, and she has never been able to manage it.

* * * * *

Freddie's views on babies are well defined. He resents their cold stare and the supercilious and up-stage way in which they dribble out of the corner of their mouths on seeing him. Eyeing them, he is conscious as to whether Man can really be Nature's last word.

GALAHAD ON TEA

A THOROUGHLY mis-spent life had left the Hon. Galahad Threepwood, contrary to the most elementary justice, in what appeared to be perfect, even exuberantly perfect physical condition. How a man who ought to have had the liver of the century could look and behave as he did was a constant mystery to his associates. His eye was not dimmed nor his natural force abated. And when, skipping blithely across the turf, he tripped over the spaniel, so graceful was the agility with which he recovered his balance that he did not spill a drop of the whisky and soda in his hand. He continued to bear the glass aloft like some brave banner beneath which he had often fought and won. Instead of the blot on the proud family, he might have been a teetotal acrobat.

Having disentangled himself from the spaniel and soothed the animal's wounded feelings by permitting it to sniff the whisky-and-soda, the Hon. Galahad produced a black-rimmed monocle, and, screwing it into his eye, surveyed the table with a frown of distaste.

"Tea?"

Millicent reached for a cup.

"Cream and sugar, Uncle Gally?"

He stopped her with a gesture of shocked loathing.

"You know I never drink tea. Too much respect for my inside. Don't tell me you are ruining your inside with that poison."

"Sorry, Uncle Gally. I like it."

"You be careful," urged the Hon. Galahad, who was fond of his niece and did not like to see her falling into bad habits. "You be very careful how you fool about with that stuff. Did I ever tell you about poor Buffy Struggles back in 'ninety-three? Some misguided person lured poor old Buffy into one of those temperance lectures illustrated with coloured slides, and he called on me next day ashen, poor old chap—ashen. 'Gally,' he said. 'What would you say the procedure was when a fellow wants to buy tea? How would a fellow set about it?' 'Tea?' I said. 'What do you want tea for?' 'To drink', said Buffy. 'Pull yourself together, dear boy,' I said. 'You're talking wildly. You can't drink tea. Have a brandy and soda.' 'No more alcohol for me,' said Buffy. 'Look what it does to the common earthworm.' 'But you're not a common earthworm,' I said, putting my finger on the flaw in his argument right away. 'I dashed soon shall be if I go on drinking alcohol,' said Buffy. Well, I begged him with tears in my eyes not to do anything rash, but I couldn't move him. He ordered in ten pounds of the muck and was dead inside the year."

"Good heavens! Really?"

The Hon. Galahad nodded impressively.

"Dead as a door-nail. Got run over by a hansom cab, poor dear old chap, as he was crossing Piccadilly."

Extract from "Summer Lightning."

MY GENTLE READERS [1]

I HAVE often felt a little sorry for writers like Cicero or Diogenes Laertius, or, for the matter of that, Pliny the Elder, who operated in the days before the post office came into existence. They could never tell for certain when they had pushed their stuff across and made a solid hit with the great public. For, as everybody knows, an author's success can be estimated by the number of letters he receives from readers: It is the acid test.

Pliny, of course, had a few old school friends who thought he was a wonder—or, at any rate, told him so when they had made quite sure that he was going to pay for the last round of Falernian wine; and sometimes a kindly Senator would pat Cicero on the shoulder in the Campus Martius and say, "Stick at it, boy. You're doing fine!" But, looking at the thing in a broad way, they were simply working in the dark, and it must have been discouraging for them.

There is no point on which your modern author is more touchy than this business of testimonials from the public. You will see Gibbs stroll up to Maugham in the club and yawn with an ill-assumed carelessness.

"You don't happen to know of a good secretary, do you, Willie?" he says. "I have been caught short, confound it. Mine has just got typist's cramp, answering letters from admirers of my books, and more pouring in by every post."

"Phil," says Maugham, "you know me. If I could help you, I would do it like a shot. But I'm in just the same fix myself. Both my secretaries collapsed this morning and are in hospital with ice-packs on their heads. I've never known the fan-mail heavier."

[1]*Reproduced from the book "Louder and Funnier" by kind permission of Messrs. Faber and Faber.*

"Look here," says Gibbs abruptly, "how many fan-letters did you get last week?"

"How many did you?"

"I asked you first," says Gibbs, and they part on bad terms. And, over in a corner, Hugh Walpole rising and walking away in a marked manner from H. G. Wells.

As far as I, personally, am concerned, if I am to submit to this test, I should describe myself as a sort of fair-to-medium —not, on the one hand, a definite wam, and yet not, on the other, a total bust. Something about half-way in between. The books which I write seem to appeal to a rather specialized public. Invalids like me. So do convicts. And I am all right with the dog-stealers. As regards Obuasie, I am not so sure.

From Obuasie (wherever that is) there arrived a short while ago the following letter, rather flatteringly addressed to "P. G. Wodehouse, England":

"Dear Sir,

"I have heard your name and address highly have been recommended to me by a certain friend of mine that you are the best merchant in your city London. So I want you to send me one of your best catalogue and I am ready to deal with you until I shall go into the grave.

"Soon as possible send me early.

"I remain,

"Yours very good truly."

Now, it is difficult to know just what to make of a letter like that. At first glance, of course, it would seem as if the old boy had clicked in Obuasie on rather an impressive scale. But there is also the possibility that some mistake or confusion has arisen. If I get my publishers to flood Obuasie with my books, will they command a ready sale, or is Obuasie under the impression that I deal in something quite different from veritable masterpieces of absorbing fiction? Misunderstandings so easily occur at a distance. You remember the story of the traveller in

41

cement docks, who would often rush half-way across the world on hearing that there was a demand for his wares in Pernambuco or Spitzbergen, only to discover, after he had dragged his bag of samples all that weary way, that what the natives really wanted was not docks but socks.

Better, perhaps, then, for the moment, to give Obuasie a miss and stick to the invalids and convicts, who, with the dog-stealers, surely make up a public quite large enough for any author who is not utterly obsessed by the lust for gold.

My popularity with invalids puts me in something of a quandary. Naturally, I like my stories to be read as widely as possible; but, kind-hearted by nature, I do not feel altogether happy when I think that some form of wasting sickness is an essential preliminary to their perusal. And such seems to be the case.

I can understand it, of course. You know how it is. When you are fit and strong and full of yeast and all that sort of thing, you go about with your chin up and your chest out, without a single morbid tendency. "I feel great," you say, "so why should I deliberately take the sunshine out of my life by reading Wodehouse?" And you don't.

So far, so good. But comes a day when the temperature begins to mount, the tonsils to ache, and dark spots to float before the eyes. Then, somehow or other, you find one of my books by your bedside, and a week later you are writing to me to the following effect:

"*Dear Sir,*

"*I have never read anything of yours before, as I have always enjoyed robust health from a boy. But recently, owing to drinking unfiltered water, I became covered with pink spots and my brain-power was temporarily affected. A friend lent me your latest story, and I read it with great enjoyment. Kindly send me your photograph and autographed copies of all your other books.*

"*Thanking you in anticipation,*

"*I remain,*
"*Yours truly.*"

42

You see the dilemma this places me in? On the one hand, I am rejoiced that the sufferer is now convalescent. On the other, I feel that until he contracts some other ailment I have lost a reader. If you want to see a mind in a ferment of doubt and indecision, take a look at mine when the papers announce that another epidemic has broken out and hundreds collapsing daily.

But, you will say, why bother about the invalids if the heart of the dog-stealers remains sound? And here I am faced by a somewhat embarrassing confession. When I said I was read by dog-stealers I was swanking. It is not dog-stealers who enjoy my work, but a (one) solitary dog-stealer, and—a galling thought—a rotten dog-stealer, at that, for he specifically admits to having been arrested. And, further, his motives in writing to me are mixed. It was not simply a clean, flame-like admiration for a great artist that caused him to take pen in hand, but also a desire to know whether I would give him a sum of money sufficient to enable him to start a street book-maker's business. In fact, the more I think over this letter, the less confident do I feel that the man is going to be anything in the nature of a steady income to me down the long years.

One has got to face the facts. The way I figure it out is that in order to buy my books he is obliged to steal dogs, and in order to steal dogs in anything like the necessary quantity he will have to develop considerably more skill than he possesses at present. As a commercial proposition, therefore, I can only write him down as shaky. He might have a good year, when the dogs came briskly in and he felt himself in a position not only to buy his own copy but to send others as birthday presents to his friends. But the chances are far greater that his bungling methods will lead to another arrest, and what use will he be to me, shut off from the book-stores just at the moment when my new novel needs support to make it go?

For he is a London dog-stealer, and in English prisons they tend to give the inmate nothing to read but things like the first volume of *Waverley* and *Marvels of Pond Life*. My convict public is entirely American. I have had so many letters recently from American penitentiaries that I am beginning to think that the American criminal must look on one or more of my works as an essential part of his kit.

I seem to see the burglar's mother sending him off for the night shift.

"Another cup of cocoa, Clarence?"

"No, thank you, mother. I must be off."

"Yes, it is getting late. Are you well wrapped up?"

"Yes, mother."

"Wearing your warm underclothing?"

"Yes, mother."

"Have you everything you need? Revolver? Brass knucks? Oxy-acetylene blow-pipe? Wodehouse novel? Black-jack? Skeleton keys? Mask?"

"Yes, mother."

"Then Heaven speed you, boy, and always remember what your dear father used to say: Tread lightly, read your Wodehouse, and don't fire till you see the whites of their eyes."

There was a gunman in Chicago last year who, in a fit of preoccupation caused by business worries, imprudently took with him by mistake a copy of Harold Bell Wright. The shock of discovering his blunder, when he opened the volume to go on with Chapter Eleven, so unnerved him that he missed the policeman at three yards and was expelled from his gang in disgrace. He was formally stripped of his machine-gun at the next general meeting, and is now a soda-jerker in a small town in Kansas.

You cannot be too careful if you wish to succeed in a difficult and overcrowded profession.

Yes, I go like a breeze in the prisons of America; and, as I say, I am much read by those whose minds have been temporarily unhinged by physical suffering. And yet, at the risk of seeming ungracious, I must own that I am not entirely satisfied. Apart from the uncomfortable thought that the study of my books may be a part of an American prison-sentence, I cannot restrain a wistful yearning for a few readers of sound health who do not belong to the criminal classes. It is nice, of course, to be looked on as a valuable counter-irritant in cases of mumps, measles, or tertiary fever. And it is pleasant to feel that the tedium of drilling a safe has been mitigated for many a conscientious workman by an occasional glance at a story of mine.

Nevertheless, I do have this yearning: and it would be a great pleasure to me if I could somehow manage to interest a few blameless and robust persons in my books.

I thought I had found one the other day. She sat next to me at dinner, one of those delightful, intelligent old ladies from whom the years have not taken their keenness of mind and their ability to spot a good man when they see one.

"This is a great moment for me," she said. "I can't tell you how proud I am. I think I have read everything you have ever written."

I looked at her closely. Her features were not worn with suffering. If there had been an Old Ladies' Marathon event at the Olympic Games, I would have expected to see her win in a canter.

"Had much sickness in your family lately?" I asked, to make sure.

"None," she said. "We are an extraordinarily healthy family. We all love your books. My eldest son reads nothing else. He is in America now."

This sounded suspicious.

"Joliet?" I said. "Or Sing-Sing?"

"He is at the Embassy in Washington."

"Has *he* been pretty fit lately?"

"He is never ill."

"And he reads my books?"

"Every one of them. And so do my grandsons. The table in their room is piled with them. And when I go home to-night," she added, "and tell them that I have actually been sitting at dinner next to Edgar Wallace, I don't know what they will say."

*   *   *   *   *

45

"It was as if Nature had intended to make a gorilla, and had changed its mind at the last moment. Close to, what you noticed more was his face, which was square and powerful and slightly moustached towards the centre.

"I don't know if you have ever seen those pictures of Dictators with tilted chins and blazing eyes, inflaming the populace with fiery words on the occasion of the opening of a new skittle alley, but that was what he reminded me of."

*　　*　　*　　*　　*

This whole business of jacking up the soul is one that varies according to what Jeeves calls the psychology of the individual, some being all for it, others not. You take me, for instance. I don't say I have got much of a soul, but, such as it is, I'm perfectly satisfied with the little chap. I don't want people feeling about with it. "Leave it alone," I say. "Don't touch it. I like it the way it is."

THE SALVATION OF GEORGE MACKINTOSH

THE young man came into the club-house. There was a frown on his usually cheerful face, and he ordered a ginger-ale in the sort of voice which an ancient Greek would have used when asking the executioner to bring on the hemlock.

Sunk in the recesses of his favourite settee the Oldest Member had watched him with silent sympathy.

"How did you get on?" he inquired.

"He beat me."

The Oldest Member nodded his venerable head.

"You have had a trying time, if I am not mistaken. I feared as much when I saw you go out with Pobsley. How many a young man have I seen go out with Herbert Pobsley exulting in his youth, and crawl back at eventide looking like a toad under the harrow! He talked?"

"All the time, confound it! Put me right off my stroke."

The Oldest Member sighed.

"The talking golfer is undeniably the most pronounced pest of our complex modern civilisation," he said, "and the most difficult to deal with. It is a melancholy thought that the noblest of games should have produced such a scourge. I have frequently marked Herbert Pobsley in action. As the crackling of thorns under a pot. . . . He is almost as bad as poor George Mackintosh in his worst period. Did I ever tell you about George Mackintosh?"

"I don't think so."

"His," said the Sage, "is the only case of golfing garrulity I have ever known where a permanent cure was effected. If you would care to hear about it——?"

.   .   .   .   .

George Mackintosh (said the Oldest Member), when I first knew him, was one of the most admirable young fellows I have ever met. A handsome, well-set-up man, with no vices except a tendency to use the mashie for shots which should have been made with the light iron. And as for his positive virtues, they were too numerous to mention. He never swayed his body, moved his head, or pressed. He was always ready to utter a tactful grunt when his opponent foozled. And when he himself achieved a glaring fluke, his self-reproachful click of the tongue was music to his adversary's bruised soul. But of all his virtues the one that most endeared him to me and to all thinking men was the fact that, from the start of a round to the finish, he never spoke a word except when absolutely compelled to do so by the exigencies of the game. And it was this man who subsequently, for a black period which lives in the memory of all his contemporaries, was known as Gabby George and became a shade less popular than the germ of Spanish Influenza. Truly, *corruptio optimi pessima!*

One of the things that sadden a man as he grows older and reviews his life is the reflection that his most devastating deeds were generally the ones which he did with the best motives. The thought is disheartening. I can honestly say that, when George Mackintosh came to me and told me his troubles, my sole desire was to ameliorate his lot. That I might be starting on the downward path a man whom I liked and respected never once occurred to me.

One night after dinner when George Mackintosh came in, I could see at once that there was something on his mind, but what this could be I was at a loss to imagine, for I had been playing with him myself all the afternoon, and he had done an eighty-one and a seventy-nine. And, as I had not left the links till dusk was beginning to fall, it was practically impossible that he could have gone out again and done badly. The idea of financial trouble seemed equally out of the question. George had a good job with the old-established legal firm of Peabody, Peabody, Peabody, Peabody, Cootes, Toots, and Peabody. The third alternative, that he might be in love, I rejected at once. In all the time I had known him I had never seen a sign that George Mackintosh gave a thought to the opposite sex.

48

Yet this, bizarre as it seemed, was the true solution. Scarcely had he seated himself and lit a cigar when he blurted out his confession.

"What would you do in a case like this?" he said.

"Like what?"

"Well——" He choked, and a rich blush permeated his surface. "Well, it seems a silly thing to say and all that, but I'm in love with Miss Tennant, you know!"

"You are in love with Celia Tennant?"

"Of course I am. I've got eyes, haven't I? Who else is there that any sane man could possibly be in love with? That," he went on, moodily, "is the whole trouble. There's a field of about twenty-nine, and I should think my place in the betting is about thirty-three to one."

"I cannot agree with you there," I said. "You have every advantage, it appears to me. You are young, amiable, good-looking, comfortably off, scratch——"

"But I can't talk, confound it!" he burst out. "And how is a man to get anywhere at this sort of game without talking?"

"You are talking perfectly fluently now."

"Yes, to you. But put me in front of Celia Tennant, and I simply make a sort of gurgling noise like a sheep with the botts. It kills my chances stone dead. You know these other men. I can give Claude Mainwaring a third and beat him. I can give Eustace Brinkley a stroke a hole and simply trample on his corpse. But when it comes to talking to a girl, I'm not in their class."

"You must not be diffident."

"But I *am* diffident. What's the good of saying I mustn't be diffident when I'm the man who wrote the words and music, when Diffidence is my middle name and my telegraphic address? I can't help being diffident."

"Surely you could overcome it?"

"But how? It was in the hope that you might be able to suggest something that I came round to-night."

And this was where I did the fatal thing. It happened that, just before I took up "Braid on the Push-Shot," I had been

49

dipping into the current number of a magazine, and one of the advertisements, I chanced to remember, might have been framed with a special eye to George's unfortunate case. It was that one, which I have no doubt you have seen, which treats of "How to Become a Convincing Talker." I picked up this magazine now and handed it to George.

He studied it for a few minutes in thoughtful silence. He looked at the picture of the Man who had taken the course being fawned upon by lovely women, while the man who had let this opportunity slip stood outside the group gazing with a wistful envy.

"They never do that to me," said George.

"Do what, my boy?"

"Cluster round, clinging cooingly."

"I gather from the letterpress that they will if you write for the booklet."

"You think there is really something in it?"

"I see no reason why eloquence should not be taught by mail. One seems to be able to acquire every other desirable quality in that manner nowadays."

"I might try it. After all, it's not expensive. There's no doubt about it," he murmured, returning to his perusal, "that fellow does look popular. Of course, the evening dress may have something to do with it."

"Not at all. The other man, you will notice, is also wearing evening dress, and yet he is merely among those on the out-skirts. It is simply a question of writing for the booklet."

"Sent post free."

"Sent, as you say, post free."

"I've a good mind to try it."

"I see no reason why you should not."

"I will, by Duncan!" He tore the page out of the magazine and put it in his pocket. "I'll tell you what I'll do. I'll give this thing a trial for a week or two, and at the end of that time I'll go to the boss and see how he reacts when I ask for a rise of salary. If he crawls, it'll show there's something in this. If he flings me out, it will prove the thing's no good."

We left it at that, and I am bound to say—owing, no doubt, to my not having written for the booklet of the Memory Training Course advertised on the adjoining page of the magazine—the matter slipped from my mind. When, therefore, a few weeks later, I received a telegram from young Mackintosh which ran:

Worked like magic,

I confess I was intensely puzzled. It was only a quarter of an hour before George himself arrived that I solved the problem of its meaning.

．　　　．　　　．　　　．　　　．　　　．

"So the boss crawled?" I said, as he came in.

He gave a light, confident laugh. I had not seen him, as I say, for some time, and I was struck by the alteration in his appearance. In what exactly this alteration consisted I could not at first have said; but gradually it began to impress itself on me that his eye was brighter, his jaw squarer, his carriage a trifle more upright than it had been. But it was his eye that struck me most forcibly. The George Mackintosh I had known had had a pleasing gaze, but, though frank and agreeable, it had never been more dynamic than a fried egg. This new George had an eye that was a combination of a gimlet and a searchlight. Coleridge's Ancient Mariner, I imagine, must have been somewhat similarly equipped. The Ancient Mariner stopped a wedding guest on his way to a wedding; George Mackintosh gave me the impression that he could have stopped the Cornish Riviera express on its way to Penzance. Self-confidence—aye, and more than self-confidence—a sort of sinful, overbearing swank seemed to exude from his very pores.

"Crawled?" he said. "Well, he didn't actually lick my boots, because I saw him coming and side-stepped; but he did everything short of that. I hadn't been talking an hour when——"

"An hour!" I gasped. "Did you talk for an hour?"

"Certainly. You wouldn't have had me be abrupt, would

you? I went into his private office and found him alone. I think at first he would have been just as well pleased if I had retired. In fact, he said as much. But I soon adjusted that outlook. I took a seat and a cigarette, and then I started to sketch out for him the history of my connection with the firm. He began to wilt before the end of the first ten minutes. At the quarter of an hour mark he was looking at me like a lost dog that's just found its owner. By the half-hour he was making little bleating noises and massaging my coat-sleeve. And when, after perhaps an hour and a half, I came to my peroration and suggested a rise, he choked back a sob, gave me double what I had asked, and invited me to dine at his club next Tuesday. I'm a little sorry now I cut the thing so short. A few minutes more, and I fancy he would have given me his sock-suspenders and made over his life-insurance in my favour."

"Well," I said, as soon as I could speak, for I was finding my young friend a trifle overpowering, "this is most satisfactory."

"So-so," said George. "Not un-so-so. A man wants an addition to his income when he is going to get married."

"Ah!" I said. "That, of course, will be the real test."

"What do you mean?"

"Why, when you propose to Celia Tennant. You remember you were saying when we spoke of this before——"

"Oh, that!" said George, carelessly. "I've arranged all that."

"What!"

"Oh, yes. On my way up from the station. I looked in on Celia about an hour ago, and it's all settled."

"Amazing!"

"Well, I don't know. I just put the thing to her, and she seemed to see it."

"I congratulate you. So now, like Alexander, you have no more worlds to conquer."

"Well, I don't know so much about that," said George. "The way it looks to me is that I'm just starting. This elo-quence is a thing that rather grows on one. You didn't hear about my after-dinner speech at the anniversary banquet of the firm, I suppose? My dear fellow, a riot! A positive stampede. Had 'em laughing and then crying and then laughing again and then crying once more till six of 'em had to be led out and the rest down with hic-coughs. Napkins waving . . . three tables broken . . . waiters in hysterics. I tell you, I played on them as on a stringed instrument. . . . "

"Can you play on a stringed instrument?"

"As it happens, no. But as I would have played on a stringed instrument if I could play on a stringed instrument. Wonderful sense of power it gives you. I mean to go in pretty largely for that sort of thing in future."

"You must not let it interfere with your golf."

He gave a laugh which turned my blood cold.

"Golf!" he said. "After all, what is golf? Just pushing a small ball into a hole. A child could do it. Indeed, children have done it with great success. I see an infant of fourteen has just won some sort of championship. Could that stripling convulse a roomful of banqueters? I think not! To sway your fellow-men with a word, to hold them with a gesture . . . that is the real salt of life. I don't suppose I shall play much more golf now. I'm making arrangements for a lecturing-tour, and I'm booked up for fifteen lunches already."

Those were his words. A man who had once done the lake-hole in one. A man whom the committee were grooming for the amateur championship. I am no weakling but I confess they sent a chill shiver down my spine.

George Mackintosh did not, I am glad to say, carry out his mad project to the letter. He did not altogether sever himself from golf. He was still to be seen occasionally on the links. But now—and I know of nothing more tragic that can befall a man—he found himself gradually shunned, he who in the days of his sanity had been besieged with more offers of games than he could manage to accept. Men simply would not stand his incessant flow of talk. One by one they dropped off, until the only person he could find to go round with him was old Major Moseby, whose hearing completely petered out as long ago as the year '98. And, of course, Celia Tennant would play with him occasionally; but it seemed to me that even she, greatly as no doubt she loved him, was beginning to crack under the strain.

So surely had I read the pallor of her face and the wild look of dumb agony in her eyes that I was not surprised when, as I sat one morning in my garden reading Ray On Taking Turf, my man announced her name. I had been half expecting her to come to me for advice and consolation, for I had known her ever since she was a child. It was I who had given her her first driver and taught her infant lips to lisp "Fore!" It is not easy to lisp the word "Fore!" but I had taught her to do it, and this constituted a bond between us which had been strengthened rather than weakened by the passage of time.

She sat down on the grass beside my chair, and looked up at my face in silent pain. We had known each other so long that I know that it was not my face that pained her, but rather some unspoken *malaise* of the soul. I waited for her to speak, and suddenly she burst out impetuously as though she could hold back her sorrow no longer.

"Oh, I can't stand it! I can't stand it!"

"You mean. . . ?" I said, though I knew only too well.

"This horrible obsession of poor George's," she cried passionately. "I don't think he has stopped talking once since we have been engaged."

"He *is* chatty," I agreed. "Has he told you the story about the Irishman?"

"Half a dozen times. And the one about the Swede oftener than that. But I would not mind an occasional anecdote. Women have to learn to bear anecdotes from the men they love. It is the curse of Eve. It is his incessant easy flow of chatter on all topics that is undermining even my devotion."

"But surely, when he proposed to you, he must have given you an inkling of the truth. He only hinted at it when he spoke to me, but I gather that he was eloquent."

"When he proposed," said Celia dreamily, "he was wonderful. He spoke for twenty minutes without stopping.

He said I was the essence of his every hope, the tree on which the fruit of his life grew; his Present, his Future, his Past . . . oh, and all that sort of thing. If he would only confine his conversation now to remarks of a similar nature, I could listen to him all day long. But he doesn't. He talks politics and statistics and philosophy and . . . oh, and everything. He makes my head ache."

"And your heart also, I fear," I said gravely.

"I love him!" she replied simply. "In spite of everything, I love him dearly. But what to do? What to do? I have an awful fear that when we are getting married instead of answering 'I will,' he will go into the pulpit and deliver an address on Marriage Ceremonies of All Ages. The world to him is a vast lecture-platform. He looks on life as one long after-dinner, with himself as the principal speaker of the evening. It is breaking my heart. I see him shunned by his former friends. Shunned! They run a mile when they see him coming. The mere sound of his voice outside the club-house is enough to send brave men diving for safety beneath the sofas. Can you wonder that I am in despair? What have I to live for?"

"There is always golf."

"Yes, there is always golf," she whispered bravely.

"Come and have a round this afternoon."

"I had promised to go for a walk. . . . " She shuddered, then pulled herself together. " . . . for a walk with George."

I hesitated for a moment.

"Bring him along," I said, and patted her hand. "It may be that together we shall find an opportunity of reasoning with him."

She shook her head.

"You can't reason with George. He never stops talking long enough to give you time."

"Nevertheless, there is no harm in trying. I have an idea that this malady of his is not permanent and incurable. The very violence with which the germ of loquacity has attacked him gives me hope. You must remember that before this seizure he was rather a noticeably silent man. Sometimes I think that it is just Nature's way of restoring the average, and that soon the fever may burn itself out. Or it may be that a sudden shock. . . . At any rate, have courage."

"I will try to be brave."

"Capital! At half-past two on the first tee, then."

"You will have to give me a stroke on the third, ninth, twelfth, fifteenth, sixteenth and eighteenth," she said, with a quaver in her voice. "My golf has fallen off rather lately."

I patted her hand again.

"I understand," I said gently. "I understand."

.   .   .   .   .

The steady drone of a baritone voice as I alighted from my car and approached the first tee told me that George had not forgotten the tryst. He was sitting on the stone seat under the chestnut-tree, speaking a few well-chosen words on the Labour Movement.

"To what conclusion, then, do we come?" he was saying. "We come to the foregone and inevitable conclusion that . . ."

"Good afternoon, George," I said.

He nodded briefly, but without verbal salutation.

He seemed to regard my remark as he would have regarded the unmannerly heckling of some one at the back of the hall. He proceeded evenly with his speech, and was still talking when Celia addressed her ball and drove off. Her drive, coinciding with a sharp rhetorical question from George, wavered in mid-air, and the ball trickled off into the rough half-way down the hill. I can see the poor girl's tortured face even now. But she breathed no word of reproach. Such is the miracle of woman's love.

"Where you went wrong there," said George, breaking off his remarks on Labour, "was that you have not studied the dynamics of golf sufficiently. You did not pivot properly. You allowed your left heel to point down the course when you were at the top of your swing. This makes for instability and loss of distance. The fundamental law of the dynamics of golf is that the left foot shall be solidly on the ground at the moment of impact. If you allow your heel to point down the course, it is almost impossible to bring it back in time to make the foot a solid fulcrum."

I drove, and managed to clear the rough and reach the fairway. But it was not one of my best drives. George Mackintosh, I confess, had unnerved me. The feeling he gave me resembled the self-conscious panic which I used to experience in my childhood when informed that there was One Awful Eye that watched my every movement and saw my every act. It was only the fact that poor Celia appeared even more affected by his espionage that enabled me to win the first hole in seven.

On the way to the second tee George discoursed on the beauties of Nature, pointing out at considerable length how exquisitely the silver glitter of the lake harmonized with the vivid emerald turf near the hole and the duller green of the rough beyond it. As Celia teed up her ball, he directed her attention to the golden glory of the sandpit to the left of the flag. It was not the spirit in which to approach the lake-hole, and I was not surprised when the unfortunate girl's ball fell with a sickening plop half-way across the water.

"Where you went wrong there," said George, "was that you made the stroke a sudden heave instead of a smooth, snappy flick of the wrists. Pressing is always bad, but with the mashie——"

"I think I will give you this hole," said Celia to me, for my shot had cleared the water and was lying on the edge of the green. "I wish I hadn't used a new ball."

"The price of golf-balls," said George, as we started to round the lake, "is a matter to which economists should give some attention. I am credibly informed that rubber at the present time is exceptionally cheap. Yet we see no decrease in the price of golf-balls, which, as I need scarcely inform you, are rubber-cored. Why should this be so? You will say that the wages of skilled labour have gone up. True. But——"

"One moment, George, while I drive," I said. For we had now arrived at the third tee.

"A curious thing, concentration," said George, "and why certain phenomena should prevent us from focusing our attention—— This brings me to the vexed question of sleep. Why is it that we are able to sleep through some vast convulsion of Nature when a dripping tap is enough to keep us awake? I am told that there were people who slumbered peacefully through the San Francisco earthquake, merely stirring drowsily from time to time to tell an imaginary person to leave it on the mat. Yet these same people——"

Celia's drive bounded into the deep ravine which yawns some fifty yards from the tee. A low moan escaped her.

"Where you went wrong there——" said George.

"I know," said Celia. "I lifted my head."

I had never heard her speak so abruptly before. Her manner, in a girl less noticeably pretty, might almost have been called snappish. George, however, did not appear to have noticed anything amiss. He filled his pipe and followed her into the ravine.

"Remarkable," he said, "how fundamental a principle of golf is this keeping the head still. You will hear professionals tell their pupils to keep their eye on the ball. Keeping the eye on the ball is only a secondary matter. What they really mean is that the head should be kept rigid, as otherwise it is impossible to——"

His voice died away. I had sliced my drive into the woods on the right, and after playing another had gone off to try to find my ball, leaving Celia and George in the ravine behind me. My last glimpse of them showed me that her ball had fallen into a stone-studded cavity in the side of the hill, and she was drawing her niblick from her bag as I passed out of sight. George's voice, blurred by distance to a monotonous murmur, followed me until I was out of earshot.

I was just about to give up the hunt for my ball in despair, when I heard Celia's voice calling to me from the edge of the undergrowth. There was a sharp note in it which startled me.

I came out, trailing a portion of some unknown shrub which had twined itself about my ankle.

"Yes?" I said, picking twigs out of my hair.

"I want your advice," said Celia.

"Certainly. What is the trouble? By the way," I said, looking round, "where is your *fiancé?*"

"I have no *fiancé*," she said, in a dull, hard voice.

"You have broken off the engagement?"

"Not exactly. And yet—well, I suppose it amounts to that."

"I don't quite understand."

"Well, the fact is," said Celia in a burst of girlish frankness, "I rather think I've killed George."

"Killed him, eh?"

It was a solution that had not occurred to me, but now that it was presented for my inspection I could see its merits. In these days of national effort, when we are all working together to try to make our beloved land fit for heroes to live in, it was astonishing that nobody before had thought of a simple, obvious thing like killing George Mackintosh. George Mackintosh was undoubtedly better dead, but it had taken a woman's intuition to see it.

"I killed him with my niblick," said Celia.

I nodded. If the thing was to be done at all, it was unquestionably a niblick shot.

"I had just made my eleventh attempt to get out of that ravine," the girl went on, "with George talking all the time about the recent excavations in Egypt, when suddenly—you know what it is when something seems to snap——"

"I had the experience with my shoe-lace only this morning."

"Yes, it was like that. Sharp—sudden—happening all in a moment. I suppose I must have said something, for George stopped talking about Egypt and said that he was reminded by a remark of the last speaker's of a certain Irishman——"

I pressed her hand.

"Don't go on if it hurts you," I said, gently.

"Well, there is very little more to tell. He bent his head to light his pipe, and well—the temptation was too much for me. That's all."

"You were quite right."

"You really think so?"

"I certainly do. A rather similar action, under far less provocation, once made Jael the wife of Heber the most popular woman in Israel."

"I wish I could think so too," she murmured. "At the moment, you know, I was conscious of nothing but an awful elation. But—but—oh, he was such a darling before he got this dreadful affliction. I can't help thinking of G-George as he used to be."

She burst into a torrent of sobs.

"Would you care for me to view the remains?" I said.

"Perhaps it would be as well."

She led me silently into the ravine. George Mackintosh was lying on his back where he had fallen.

"There!" said Celia.

And, as she spoke, George Mackintosh gave a kind of snorting groan and sat up. Celia uttered a sharp shriek and sank on her knees before him. George blinked once or twice and looked about him dazedly.

"Save the women and children!" he cried. "I can swim."

"Oh, George!" said Celia.

"Feeling a little better?"

"A little. How many people were hurt?"

"Hurt?"

"When the express ran into us." He cast another glance around him. "Why, how did I get here?"

"You were here all the time," I said.

"Do you mean after the roof fell in or before?"

Celia was crying quietly down the back of his neck.

"Oh, George!" she said, again.

He groped out feebly for her hand and patted it.

"Brave little woman!" he said. "Brave little woman! She stuck by me all through. Tell me—I am strong enough to bear it—what caused the explosion?"

It seemed to me a case where much unpleasant explanation might be avoided by the exercise of a little tact.

"Well, some say one thing and some another," I said. "Whether it was a spark from a cigarette——"

Celia interrupted me. The woman in her made her revolt against this well-intentioned subterfuge.

"I hit you, George!"

"Hit me?" he repeated, curiously. "What with? The Eiffel Tower?"

"With my niblick."

"You hit me with your niblick? But why?"

She hesitated. Then she faced him bravely.

"Because you wouldn't stop talking."

He gaped.

"Me!" he said. "*I* wouldn't stop talking! But I hardly talk at all. I'm noted for it."

Celia's eye met mine in agonised inquiry. But I saw what had happened. The blow, the sudden shock, had operated on George's brain-cells in such a way as to effect a complete cure. I have not the technical knowledge to be able to explain it, but the facts were plain.

"Lately, my dear fellow," I assured him, "you have dropped into the habit of talking rather a good deal. Ever since we started out this afternoon you have kept up an incessant flow of conversation!"

"Me! On the links! It isn't possible."

"It is only too true, I fear. And that is why this brave girl hit you with her niblick. You started to tell her a funny story just as she was making her eleventh shot to get her ball out of this ravine, and she took what she considered the necessary steps."

"Can you ever forgive me, George?" cried Celia.

George Mackintosh stared at me. Then a crimson blush mantled his face.

"So I did! It's all beginning to come back to me. Oh, heavens!"

"*Can* you forgive me, George?" cried Celia again.

He took her hand in his.

"Forgive you?" he muttered. "Can *you* forgive *me*? Me—a tee-talker, a green-gabbler, a prattler on the links, the lowest form of life known to science! I am unclean, unclean!"

"It's only a little mud, dearest," said Celia, looking at the sleeve of his coat. "It will brush off when it's dry."

"How can you link your lot with a man who talks when people are making their shots?"

"You will never do it again."

"But I have done it. And you stuck to me all through! Oh, Celia!"

"I loved you, George!"

The man seemed to swell with a sudden emotion. His eyes lit up, and he thrust one hand into the breast of his coat while he raised the other in a sweeping gesture. For an instant he appeared on the verge of a flood of eloquence. And then, as if he had been made sharply aware of what it was that he intended to do, he suddenly sagged. The gleam died out of his eyes. He lowered his hand.

"Well, I must say that was rather decent of you," he said.

A lame speech, but one that brought an infinite joy to both his hearers. For it showed that George Mackintosh was cured beyond possibility of relapse.

"Yes, I must say you are rather a corker," he added.

"George!" cried Celia.

I said nothing, but I clasped his hand; and then, taking my clubs, I retired. When I looked round she was still in his arms. I left them there, alone together in the great silence.

.   .   .   .   .

And so (concluded the Oldest Member) you see that a cure is possible, though it needs a woman's gentle hand to bring it about. And how few women are capable of doing what Celia Tennant did. Apart from the difficulty of summoning up the necessary resolution, an act like hers requires a straight eye and a pair of strong and supple wrists. It seems to me that for the ordinary talking golfer there is no hope. And the race seems to be getting more numerous every day. Yet the finest golfers are always the least loquacious. It is related of the illustrious Sandy McHoots that when, on the occasion of his winning the British Open Championship, he was interviewed by reporters from the leading daily papers as to his views on Tariff Reform, Bimetallism, the Trial by Jury System, and the Modern Craze for Dancing, all they could extract from him was the single word "Mphm!" Having uttered which, he shouldered his bag and went home to tea. A great man. I wish there were more like him.

*   *   *   *   *

BERTIE, JEEVES AND BARTHOLOMEW

I was standing there, hoping for the best, when my meditations were broken in upon by an odd, gargling sort of noise, something like static and something like distant thunder, and to cut a long story short this proved to proceed from the larynx of the dog Bartholomew.

He was standing on the bed, stropping his front paws on the coverlet, and so easy was it to read the message in his eyes that we acted like two minds with but a single thought. At the exact moment when I soared like an eagle on to the chest of drawers, Jeeves was skimming like a swallow on to the top of the cupboard. The animal hopped from the bed and, advancing into the middle of the room, took a seat, breathing through the nose with a curious, whistling sound, and looking at us from under his eyebrows like a Scottish elder rebuking sin from the pulpit.

THE ARTISTRY
OF ARCHIBALD

ARCHIBALD's imitation of a hen laying an egg was conceived on broad and sympathetic lines. Less violent than Salvini's "Othello," it had in it something of the poignant wistfulness of Mrs. Siddons in the sleep-walking scene of *Macbeth*. The rendition started quietly, almost inaudibly, with a sort of soft, liquid crooning—the joyful yet half-incredulous murmur of a mother who can scarcely believe as yet that her union has really been blessed, and that it is indeed she who is responsible for the oval mixture of chalk and albumen which she sees lying beside her in the straw.

Then, gradually, conviction comes.

"It looks like an egg," one seems to hear her say. "It feels like an egg. It's shaped like an egg. Damme, it *is* an egg!"

And at that, all doubting resolved, the crooning changes; takes on a firmer note; soars into the upper register; and finally swells into a maternal pæan of joy—a "Charawk-chawk-chawk-chawk-chawk" of such a calibre that few have ever been able to listen to it dry-eyed. Following which, it was Archibald's custom to run round the room, flapping the sides of his coat, and then, leaping onto a sofa or some convenient chair, to stand there with his arms at right angles, crowing himself purple in the face.

Mr. Mulliner Speaking.

OLD BILL TOWNEND

It is with some diffidence that I take typewriter in hand to inscribe these few words. The position of an author—call him Author A.— who writes an introduction to a book by another author--call him Author B.—must always be a little embarrassing. He inevitably runs the risk of seeming to claim for himself an importance and a right to speak which may be resented by a public consisting largely of cold-eyed men with tight lips and sneering eyebrows. In one way, however, he is unquestionably on velvet. He cannot be interrupted or heckled.

If I were to try to introduce these short stories of W. Townend verbally, the scene would run more or less as follows:—

MYSELF (*starting well*): It has been frequently said, gentlemen, that there is no public for a volume of short stories. I venture to think, however, that an exception will be made in favour of the book which I am presenting to your notice. The sea, gentlemen, is our heritage, and a writer who, like Mr. Townend, can bring home to us the glamour of the sea, can fill our nostrils with the salt breath of the sea, can put on paper the splendour, the mystery, the tragedy of the sea . . .

A VOICE: One moment. Just one moment.

MYSELF: Sir?

A VOICE: Did you say the splendour, the mystery, the tragedy of the sea?

MYSELF: I did.

A VOICE: What do you know about the splendour, the mystery, the tragedy of the sea?

MYSELF (*weakly*): That's all right what I know about the splendour, the mystery, the tragedy of the sea. Gentlemen, I venture to say . . .

A VOICE: Is it not a fact that, when you go to America, you travel first-class on the *Majestic*?

MYSELF: ... venture to say, gentlemen ...

A VOICE: And have breakfast in bed?

MYSELF: ... to say, gentlemen ...

A VOICE: And the only time anything tragic ever happened to you at sea was when the boat was so full you couldn't get a table at the Ritz Café?

MYSELF (*wisely changing the subject*): But not all the stories in this volume are set among the leaping billows and flying scud of perilous seas. What, in my opinion, is the gem of the collection—I allude to the story entitled "Bolshevik"— is a tale of London's submerged—a gripping, biting tale that reveals in a few short pages the Soul of England. ...

A VOICE: Just one moment.

MYSELF: ... That England, gentlemen, which never did or never shall lie at the proud foot ...

A VOICE: What do you know about London's submerged?

MYSELF: I ...

A VOICE: Is it not a fact that for years you have made your living writing about younger sons of dukes tripping over door-mats? I appeal to this audience to tear up the benches and throw them at the speaker.

(*The crowd rush the platform, and I am roughly handled before being rescued by the police.*)

In print, of course, one is safe from this sort of thing. Nevertheless, it is difficult not to be conscious of that Voice floating somewhere in the background and, realising my inadequacy as an introducer of a book like Townend's, I think it best to scamp the task and hurry on. I could say—but will not—that I think "Bolshevik" one of the greater short stories written in the last few years. I will refrain from giving my opinion of "Overseas For Flanders" and "In the Stokehold." I will go on at once to the part of this introduction where I am on safe ground, the personal details about the author.

Bill Townend shared a study with me at school. We brewed tea together, shoved in the same scrum, and on one occasion put on eighty-seven together for the fourth wicket in a final house match. (I must tell you all about that innings of mine one of these days when I have more time.) Shortly after this feat, our school career ended, and Townend started out in life as a black-and-white artist, in which capacity he contributed intermittently to *Punch* and other papers, and illustrated one of my books.

But all this while the writer in him was popping its head out at intervals. I was doing the "By-the-Way" column on the old *Globe* in those days, and could always rely on him to pitch in for a day or two when a holiday seemed imperative. For several weeks, till a directors' meeting was called and we were thrown out simultaneously, we wrote the "Answers to Correspondents" in *Tit-Bits* together. Everything that is any good in a novel entitled "Love Among the Chickens" was supplied by Townend. And we also collaborated—under a pseudonym—in a lurid serial in *Chums*. It was obviously only a question of time before a man capable of helping English Literature along to that extent would feel the urge to get going on his own account. And this happened just after Townend went to sea.

He had been to sea before, of course. Having a father who was an Army chaplain, he had been taken about the world quite a good deal: but this time he went in a tramp steamer, was nearly wrecked off the coast of Wales, messed about in the engine-room, and came back, looking perfectly foul in a stained tweed suit and a celluloid collar, resolved to write stories about men of the deep waters. His first long sea-story was "A Light For His Pipe," and his best, "The Tramp," published by Messrs. Jenkins last year. He has also contributed largely to American magazines.

His connection with America came about through his being offered a job out there. Some years ago, after a long separation, I met him in the Strand and immediately noticed something peculiar in his appearance and bearing. "That man," I said to myself, "has been sorting lemons." And so it proved. He had just returned from a long stay on a ranch in Chula Vista, California, and the only thing you do on a California ranch is sort lemons. You get up at about five, breakfast, and go out and sort lemons. Lunch at twelve-thirty, followed by a long afternoon of lemon-sorting. Then dinner, and perhaps sort a few small ones before bed-time and the restful sleep. Next morning you get up at five, breakfast, and go out and sort lemons. Lunch at . . . But you have gathered the idea, and will understand why in some of the stories written by him at that time there is a strong lemon-motive. His heroes in those days were usually young lemon-sorters who fell in love with the daughters of their employers, and the big scene was where the villain rang in a bad lemon on them and got them sacked.

This phase lasted only a brief time, and he was soon back again in his proper element, the sea. I have hinted above that I am not the best man to come to for authoritative pronouncements on the sea, but I take it a fellow, however scanty his knowledge, can make a remark if he wants to, and I maintain that nobody to-day writes better sea-stories than Old Bill Townend. Read "The Tramp." And read the sea-stories in this book.

And, whether he is writing of sea or land, he writes as a man whose artist schooling has trained his eye to observe details. He can make you visualise a background.

Gentlemen, I trust I have not detained you over-long. We old buffers are a bit inclined to drool on when we get on a subject that interests us. What I have been trying to convey is that W. Townend, when he writes, writes with knowledge. If he lays the scene of a story in a stokehold, you may be sure that he has been in that stokehold personally, no doubt encouraging the stokers with word and gesture. When he writes of soldiers, remember that soldiers flocked about his cradle. And if lemons creep in, bear in mind that here speaks a man who was known all through California, from distant wherever-it-is to far-off I-forget-the-name-of-the-place, as "The Prince of Sorters."

Gentlemen, I have finished. Mr. Townend will now rise to reply.

A WORD IN ADVANCE

Being a Brief Résumé of Events Which Preceded the Episode Narrated in the Following Chapter.

Gussie Fink-Nottle is bowed down by a sea of troubles.

True love, steering its proverbially serpentine course, has lured Madeline Bassett from his loving grasp, and, to add to his misery, he is due to present the prizes at the Market Snodsbury Grammar School. Since he is incapable of uttering more than two consecutive words coherently, the thought of having to make a speech to a large number of small boys quite paralyses him.

Fortunately, however, Jeeves and Bertie Wooster are at hand in his hour of trial. Bertie, who has yet to meet the trouble that cannot be dispersed by a few drinks taken in quick succession, suggests that in alcohol lies the solution to Gussie's difficulties. But whether from some hereditary taint or because he has promised his mother he won't, Gussie has never in his life taken intoxicating liquor, and steadfastly refuses to listen to Bertie's all-embracing plan.

Nor is he the only one who does not take kindly to the idea. Jeeves is opposed to it: indeed, when Bertie unfolds his scheme for surreptitiously lacing Gussie's orange-juice with gin in order to imbue the poor fish with a little courage and sang froid, Jeeves respectfully declines to co-operate. It is a big blow to Bertie, of course, but it does not deter him from going ahead on his own. The Woosters are men of iron when a pal's honour is at stake.

GUSSIE PRESENTS THE PRIZES[1]

SUNSHINE was gilding the grounds of Brinkley Court and the
ear detected a marked twittering of birds in the ivy outside the
window when I woke next morning to a new day. But there
was no corresponding sunshine in Bertram Wooster's soul and
no answering twitter in his heart as he sat up in bed, sipping his
cup of strengthening tea. It could not be denied that to
Bertram, reviewing the happenings of the previous night, the
Tuppy-Angela situation seemed more or less to have slipped a
cog. With every desire to look for the silver lining, I could not
but feel that the rift between these two haughty spirits had
now reached such impressive proportions that the task of
bridging same would be beyond even my powers.

I am a shrewd observer, and there had been something in
Tuppy's manner as he booted that plate of ham sandwiches
that seemed to tell me that he would not lightly forgive.

In these circs., I deemed it best to shelve their problem for
the nonce and turn the mind to the matter of Gussie, which
presented a brighter picture.

With regard to Gussie, everything was in train. Jeeves's
morbid scruples about lacing the chap's orange juice had put
me to a good deal of trouble, but I had surmounted every
obstacle in the old Wooster way. I had secured an abundance
of the necessary spirit, and it was now lying in its flask in the
drawer of the dressing table. I had also ascertained that the
jug, duly filled, would be standing on a shelf in the butler's
pantry round about the hour of one. To remove it from that
shelf, sneak it up to my room, and return it, laced, in good
time for the midday meal would be a task calling, no doubt,
for address, but in no sense an exacting one.

It was with something of the emotions of one preparing a
treat for a deserving child that I finished my tea and rolled over

[1] (*An episode from the novel "Right-Ho Jeeves!"*) *see preceding page.*

for that extra spot of sleep which just makes all the difference when there is man's work to be done and the brain must be kept clear for it.

And when I came downstairs an hour or so later, I knew how right I had been to formulate this scheme for Gussie's bucking up. I ran into him on the lawn, and I could see at a glance that if ever there was a man who needed a snappy stimulant, it was he. All nature, as I have indicated, was smiling, but not Augustus Fink-Nottle. He was walking round in circles, muttering something about not proposing to detain us long, but on this auspicious occasion feeling compelled to say a few words.

"Ah, Gussie," I said, arresting him as he was about to start another lap. "A lovely morning, is it not?"

Even if I had not been aware of it already, I could have divined from the abruptness with which he damned the lovely morning that he was not in merry mood. I addressed myself to the task of bringing the roses back to his cheeks.

"I've got good news for you, Gussie."

He looked at me with a sudden sharp interest.

"Has Market Snodsbury Grammar School burned down?"

"Not that I know of."

"Have mumps broken out? Is the place closed on account of measles?"

"No, no."

"Then what do you mean you've got good news?"

I endeavoured to soothe.

"You mustn't take it so hard, Gussie. Why worry about a laughably simple job like distributing prizes at a school?"

"Laughably simple, eh? Do you realize I've been sweating for days and haven't been able to think of a thing to say yet, except that I won't detain them long. You bet I won't detain them long. I've been timing my speech, and it lasts five seconds. What the devil am I to say, Bertie? What do you say when you're distributing prizes?"

I considered. Once, at my private school, I had won a

prize for Scripture knowledge, so I suppose I ought to have been full of inside stuff. But memory eluded me.

Then something emerged from the mists.

"You say the race is not always to the swift."

"Why?"

"Well, it's a good gag. It generally gets a hand."

"I mean, why isn't it? Why isn't the race to the swift?"

"Ah, there you have me. But the nibs say it isn't."

"But what does it mean?"

"I take it it's supposed to console the chaps who haven't won prizes."

"What the good of that to me? I'm not worrying about them. It's the ones that have won prizes that I'm worrying about, the little blighters who will come up on the platform. Suppose they make faces at me."

"They won't."

"How do you know they won't? It's probably the first thing they'll think of. And even if they don't——Bertie, shall I tell you something?"

"What?"

"I've a good mind to take that tip of yours and have a drink."

I smiled subtly. He little knew, about summed up what I was thinking.

"Oh, you'll be all right," I said.

He became fevered again.

"How do you know I'll be all right? I'm sure to blow up in my lines."

"Tush!"

"Or drop a prize."

"Tut!"

"Or something. I can feel it in my bones. As sure as I'm standing here, something is going to happen this afternoon which will make everybody laugh themselves sick at me. I can hear them now. Like hyenas. . . . Bertie!"

"Hullo?"

"Do you remember that kid's school we went to before Eton?"

"Quite. It was there I won my Scripture prize."

"Never mind about your Scripture prize. I'm not talking about your Scripture prize. Do you recollect the incident?"

I did, indeed. It was one of the high spots of my youth.

"Major-General Sir Wilfred Bosher came to distribute the prizes at that school," proceeded Gussie in a dull, toneless voice. "He dropped a book. He stooped to pick it up. And, as he stooped, his trousers split up the back."

"How we roared!"

Gussie's face twisted.

"We did, little swine that we were. Instead of remaining silent and exhibiting a decent sympathy for a gallant officer at a peculiarly embarrassing moment, we howled and yelled with mirth. I loudest of any. That is what will happen to me this afternoon, Bertie. It will be a judgment on me for laughing like that at Major-General Sir Wilfred Bosher."

"No, no, Gussie, old man. Your trousers won't split."

"How do you know they won't? Better men than I have split their trousers. General Bosher was a D.S.O., with a fine record of service on the north-western frontier of India, and his trousers split. I shall be a mockery and a scorn. I know it. And you, fully cognizant of what I am in for, come babbling about good news. What news could possibly be good to me at this moment except the information that bubonic plague had broken out among the scholars of Market Snodsbury Grammar School, and that they were all confined to their beds with spots?"

The moment had come for me to speak. I laid a hand gently on his shoulder. He brushed it off. I laid it on again. He brushed it off once more. I was endeavouring to lay it on for the third time, when he moved aside and desired, with a certain petulance, to be informed if I thought I was a ruddy osteopath.

"I found his manner trying, but one has to make allowances. I was telling myself that I should be seeing a very different Gussie after lunch.

"When I said I had good news, old man, I meant about Madeline Bassett."

The febrile gleam died out of his eyes, to be replaced by a look of infinite sadness.

"You can't have good news about her. I've dished myself there completely."

"Not at all. I am convinced that if you take another whack at her, all will be well."

And, keeping it snappy, I related what had passed between the Bassett and myself on the previous night.

"So all you have to do is play a return date, and you cannot fail to swing the voting. You are her dream man."

He shook his head.

"No."

"What?"

"No use."

"What do you mean?"

"Not a bit of good trying."

"But I tell you she said in so many words——"

"It doesn't make any difference. She may have loved me once. Last night will have killed all that."

"Of course it won't."

"It will. She despises me now."

"Not a bit of it. She knows you simply got cold feet."

"And I should get cold feet if I tried again. It's no good, Bertie. I'm hopeless, and there's an end of it. Fate made me the sort of chap who can't say 'bo' to a goose."

"It isn't a question of saying 'bo' to a goose. The point doesn't arise at all. It is simply a matter of——"

"I know, I know. But it's no good. I can't do it. The whole thing is off. I am not going to risk a repetition of last night's fiasco. You talk in a light way of taking another whack at her, but you don't know what it means. You have not been through the experience of starting to ask the girl you love to marry you and then suddenly finding yourself talking about the plumlike external gills of the newly-born newt. It's not a thing you can do twice. No, I accept my destiny. It's all over. And now, Bertie, like a good chap, shove off. I want to compose my speech. I can't compose my speech with you muckingaround. If you are going to continue to muck around, at least give me a couple of stories. The little hell hounds are sure to expect a story or two."

"Do you know the one about——"

"No good. I don't want any of your off-colour stuff from the Drones' smoking-room. I need something clean. Something that will be a help to them in their after lives. Not that I care a damn about their after lives, except that I hope they'll all choke."

"I heard a story the other day. I can't quite remember it, but it was about a chap who snored and disturbed the neighbours, and it ended, 'It was his adenoids that adenoid them.'"

He made a weary gesture.

"You expect me to work that in, do you, into a speech to be delivered to an audience of boys, every one of whom is probably riddled with adenoids? Damn it, they'd rush the platform. Leave me, Bertie. Push off. That's all I ask you to do. Push off.... Ladies and gentlemen," said Gussie, in a low, soliloquizing sort of way, "I do not propose to detain this auspicious occasion long——"

It was a thoughtful Wooster who walked away and left him at it. More than ever I was congratulating myself on having had the sterling good sense to make all my arrangements so that I could press a button and set things moving at an instant's notice.

Until now, you see, I had rather entertained a sort of hope that when I had revealed to him the Bassett's mental attitude, Nature would have done the rest, bracing him up to such an extent that artificial stimulants would not be required. Because naturally, a chap doesn't want to have to sprint about country houses lugging jugs of orange juice, unless it is absolutely essential.

But now I saw that I must carry on as planned. The total absence of pep, ginger, and the right spirit which the man had displayed during these conversational exchanges convinced me that the strongest measures would be necessary. Immediately upon leaving him, therefore, I proceeded to the pantry, waited till the butler had removed himself elsewhere, and nipped in and secured the vital jug. A few moments later, after a wary passage of the stairs, I was in my room. And the first thing I saw there was Jeeves, fooling about with trousers.

He gave the jug a look which—wrongly as it was to turn out—I diagnosed as censorious. I drew myself up a bit. I intended to have no rot from the fellow.

"Yes, Jeeves?"

"Sir?"

"You have the air of one about to make a remark, Jeeves."

"Oh, no, sir. I note that you are in possession of Mr. Fink-Nottle's orange juice. I was merely about to observe that in my opinion it would be injudicious to add spirit to it."

"That is a remark, Jeeves, and it is precisely——"

"Because I have already attended to the matter, sir."

"What?"

"Yes, sir. I decided, after all, to acquiesce in your wishes."

I stared at the man, astounded. I was deeply moved. Well, I mean, wouldn't any chap who had been going about thinking that the old feudal spirit was dead and then suddenly found it wasn't have been deeply moved?

"Jeeves," I said, "I am touched."

"Thank you, sir."

"Touched and gratified."

"Thank you very much, sir."

"But what caused this change of heart?"

"I chanced to encounter Mr. Fink-Nottle in the garden, sir, while you were still in bed, and we had a brief conversation."

"And you came away feeling that he needed a bracer?"

"Very much so, sir. His attitude struck me as defeatist."

I nodded.

"I felt the same. 'Defeatist' sums it up to a nicety. Did you tell him his attitude struck you as defeatist?"

"Yes, sir."

"But it didn't do any good?"

"No, sir."

"Very well, then, Jeeves. We must act. How much gin did you put in the jug?"

"A liberal tumblerful, sir."

"Would that be a normal dose for an adult defeatist, do you think?"

"I fancy it should prove adequate, sir."

"I wonder. We must not spoil the ship for a ha'porth of tar. I think I'll add just another fluid ounce or so."

"I would not advocate it, sir. In the case of Lord Brancaster's parrot——"

"You are falling into your old error, Jeeves, of thinking that Gussie is a parrot. Fight against this. I shall add the oz."

"Very good, sir."

"And, by the way, Jeeves, Mr. Fink-Nottle is in the market for bright, clean stories to use in his speech. Do you know any?"

"I know a story about two Irishmen, sir."

"Pat and Mike?"

"Yes, sir."

"Who were walking along Broadway?"

"Yes, sir."

"Just what he wants. Any more?"

"No, sir."

"Well, every little helps. You had better go and tell it to him."

"Very good, sir."

He passed from the room, and I unscrewed the flask and tilted into the jug a generous modicum of its contents. And scarcely had I done so, when there came to my ears the sound of footsteps without. I had only just time to shove the jug behind the photograph of Uncle Tom on the mantelpiece before the door opened and in came Gussie, curvetting like a circus horse.

"What-ho, Bertie," he said. "What-ho, what-ho, what-ho, and again what-ho. What a beautiful world this is, Bertie. One of the nicest I ever met."

I stared at him, speechless. We Woosters are as quick as lightning, and I saw at once that something had happened.

I mean to say, I told you about him walking round in circles. I recorded what passed between us on the lawn. And if I portrayed the scene with anything like adequate skill, the picture you will have retained of this Fink-Nottle will have been that of a nervous wreck, sagging at the knees, green about the gills, and picking feverishly at the lapels of his coat in an ecstasy of craven fear. In a word, defeatist. Gussie, during that interview, had, in fine, exhibited all the earmarks of one licked to a custard.

Vastly different was the Gussie who stood before me now. Self-confidence seemed to ooze from the fellow's every pore. His face was flushed, there was a jovial light in his eyes, the lips were parted in a swashbuckling smile. And when with a genial hand he sloshed me on the back before I could sidestep, it was as if I had been kicked by a mule.

"Well, Bertie," he proceeded, as blithely as a linnet without a thing on his mind, "you will be glad to hear that you were right. Your theory has been tested and proved correct. I feel like a fighting cock."

My brain ceased to real. I saw all.

"Have you been having a drink?"

"I have. As you advised. Unpleasant stuff. Like medicine. Burns your throat, too, and makes one as thirsty as the dickens. How anyone can mop it up, as you do, for pleasure beats me. Still, I would be the last to deny that it tunes up the system. I could bite a tiger."

"What did you have?"

"Whisky. At least, that was the label on the decanter, and I have no reason to suppose that a woman like your aunt—staunch, true-blue, British—would deliberately deceive the public. If she labels her decanters Whisky, then I consider that we know where we are."

"A Whisky and soda, eh? You couldn't have done better."

"Soda?" said Gussie thoughtfully. "I knew there was something I had forgotten."

"Didn't you put any soda in it?"

"It never occurred to me. I just nipped into the dining-room and drank out of the decanter."

"How much?"

"Oh, about ten swallows. Twelve, maybe. Or fourteen. Say sixteen medium-sized gulps. Gosh I'm thirsty."

He moved over to the wash-hand stand and drank deeply out of the water bottle. I cast a covert glance at Uncle Tom's photograph behind his back. For the first time since it had come into my life, I was glad that it was so large. It hid its secret well. If Gussie had caught sight of that jug of orange juice, he would unquestionably have been on to it like a knife.

"Well, I'm glad you're feeling braced," I said.

He moved buoyantly from the wash-stand, and endeavoured to slosh me on the back again. Foiled by my nimble footwork, he staggered to the bed and sat down upon it.

"Braced? Did I say I could bite a tiger?"

"You did."

"Make it two tigers. I could chew holes in a steel door. What an ass you must have thought me out there in the garden. I see now you were laughing in your sleeve."

"No, no."

"Yes," insisted Gussie. "That very sleeve," he said, pointing. "And I don't blame you. I can't imagine why I made all that fuss about a potty job like distributing prizes at a rotten little country grammar school. Can you imagine, Bertie?"

"No."

"Exactly. Nor can I imagine. There's simply nothing to it. I just shin up on the platform, drop a few gracious words, hand the little blighters their prizes, and hop down again, admired by all. Not a suggestion of split trousers from start to finish. I mean, why should anybody split his trousers? I can't imagine. Can you imagine?"

"No."

"Nor can I imagine. I shall be a riot. I know just the sort of stuff that's needed—simple, manly, optimistic stuff straight from the shoulder. This shoulder," said Gussie, tapping.

"Why I was so nervous this morning I can't imagine. For anything simpler than distributing a few footling books to a bunch of grimy-faced kids I can't imagine. Still, for some reason I can't imagine, I was feeling a little nervous, but now I feel fine, Bertie—fine, fine, fine—and I say this to you as an old friend. Because that's what you are, old man, when all the smoke has cleared away—an old friend. I don't think I've ever met an older friend. How long have you been an old friend of mine, Bertie?"

"Oh, years and years."

"Imagine! Though, of course, there must have been a time when you were a new friend. . . . Hullo, the luncheon gong. Come on, old friend."

And, rising from the bed like a performing flea, he made for the door.

I followed rather pensively. What had occurred was, of course, so much velvet, as you might say. I mean, I had wanted a braced Fink-Nottle—indeed, all my plans had had a braced Fink-Nottle as their end and aim—but I found myself wondering a little whether the Fink-Nottle now sliding down the banister wasn't, perhaps, a shade too braced. His demeanour seemed to me that of a man who might easily throw bread about at lunch.

Fortunately, however, the settled gloom of those round him exercised a restraining effect upon him at the table. It would have needed a far more plastered man to have been rollicking at such a gathering. I had told the Bassett that there were aching hearts in Brinkley Court, and it now looked probable that there would shortly be aching tummies. Anatole, I learned, had retired to his bed with a fit of the vapours, and the meal now before us had been cooked by the kitchen maid —as C3 a performer as ever wielded a skillet.

This, coming on top of their other troubles, induced in the company a pretty unanimous silence—a solemn stillness, as you might say—which even Gussie did not seem prepared to break. Except, therefore, for one short snatch of song on his part, nothing untoward marked the occasion, and presently we rose, with instructions from Aunt Dahlia to put on festal raiment and be at Market Snodsbury not later than 3.30. This leaving me ample time to smoke a gasper or two in a shady bower beside the lake, I did so, repairing to my room round about the hour of three.

Jeeves was on the job, adding the final polish to the old topper, and I was about to apprise him of the latest developments in the matter of Gussie, when he forestalled me by observing that the latter had only just concluded an agreeable visit to the Wooster bed-chamber.

"I found Mr. Fink-Nottle seated here when I arrived to lay out your clothes, sir."

"Indeed, Jeeves? Gussie was in here, was he?"

"Yes, sir. He left only a few moments ago. He is driving to the school with Mr. and Mrs. Travers in the large car."

"Did you give him your story of the two Irishmen?"

"Yes, sir. He laughed heartily."

"Good. Had you any other contributions for him?"

"I ventured to suggest that he might mention to the young gentlemen that education is a drawing out, not a putting in. The late Lord Brancaster was much addicted to presenting prizes at schools, and he invariably employed this dictum."

"And how did he react to that?"

"He laughed heartily, sir."

"This surprised you, no doubt? This practically incessant merriment, I mean."

"Yes, sir."

"You thought it odd in one who, when you last saw him, was well up in Group A of the defeatists."

"Yes, sir."

"There is a real explanation, Jeeves. Since you last saw him, Gussie has been on a bender. He's as tight as an owl."

"Indeed, sir?"

"Absolutely. His nerve cracked under the strain, and he sneaked into the dining-room and started mopping the stuff up like a vacuum cleaner. Whisky would seem to be what he filled the radiator with. I gather that he used up most of the decanter. Golly, Jeeves, it's lucky he didn't get at that laced orange juice on top of that, what?"

"Extremely, sir."

I eyed the jug. Uncle Tom's photograph had fallen into the fender, and it was standing there right out in the open, where Gussie couldn't have helped seeing it. Mercifully, it was empty now.

"It was a most prudent act on your part, if I may say so, sir, to dispose of the orange juice."

I stared at the man.

"What? Didn't you?"

"No, sir."

"Jeeves, let us get this clear. Was it not you who threw away that o.j.?"

"No, sir. I assumed, when I entered the room and found the pitcher empty, that you had done so."

We looked at each other, awed. Two minds with but a single thought.

"I very much fear, sir——"

"So do I, Jeeves."

"It would seem almost certain——"

"Quite certain. Weigh the facts. Sift the evidence. The jug was standing on the mantelpiece, for all eyes to behold. Gussie had been complaining of thirst. You found him in here, laughing heartily. I think that there can be little doubt, Jeeves, that the entire contents of that jug are at this moment reposing on top of the existing cargo in that already brilliantly lit man's interior. Disturbing, Jeeves."

"Most disturbing, sir."

"Let us face the position, forcing ourselves to be calm. You inserted in that jug—shall we say a tumblerful of the right stuff?"

"Fully a tumblerful, sir."

"And I added of my plenty about the same amount."

"Yes, sir."

"And in two shakes of a duck's tail Gussie, with all that lapping about inside him, will be distributing the prizes at Market

Snodsbury Grammar School before an audience of all that is fairest and most refined in the county."

"Yes, sir."

"It seems to me, Jeeves, that the ceremony may be one fraught with considerable interest."

"Yes, sir."

"What, in your opinion, will the harvest be?"

"One finds it difficult to hazard a conjecture, sir."

"You mean imagination boggles?"

"Yes, sir."

I inspected my imagination. He was right. It boggled.

"And yet, Jeeves," I said, twiddling a thoughtful steering wheel, "there is always the bright side."

Some twenty minutes had elapsed, and having picked the honest fellow up outside the front door, I was driving in the two-seater to the picturesque town of Market Snodsbury. Since we had parted—he to go to his lair and fetch his hat, I to remain in my room and complete the formal costume—I had been doing some close thinking.

The results of this I now proceeded to hand on to him.

"However dark the prospect may be, Jeeves, however murkily the storm clouds may seem to gather, a keen eye can usually discern the blue bird. It is bad, no doubt, that Gussie should be going, some ten minutes from now, to distribute prizes in a state of advanced intoxication, but we must never forget that these things cut both ways."

"You imply, sir——"

"Precisely. I am thinking of him in his capacity of wooer. All this ought to have put him in rare shape for offering his hand in marriage. I shall be vastly surprised if it won't turn him into a sort of caveman. Have you ever seen James Cagney in the movies?"

"Yes, sir."

"Something on those lines."

I heard him cough, and sniped him with a sideways glance. He was wearing that informative look of his.

"Then you have not heard, sir?"

"Eh?"

"You are not aware that a marriage has been arranged and will shortly take place between Mr. Fink-Nottle and Miss Bassett?"

"What?"

"Yes, sir."

"When did this happen?"

"Shortly after Mr. Fink-Nottle had left your room, sir."

"Ah! In the post-orange-juice era?"

"Yes, sir."

"But are you sure of your facts? How do you know?"

"My informant was Mr. Fink-Nottle himself, sir. He appeared anxious to confide in me. His story was somewhat incoherent, but I had no difficulty in apprehending its substance. Prefacing his remarks with the statement that this was a beautiful world, he laughed heartily and said that he had become formally engaged."

"No details?"

"No, sir."

"But one can picture the scene."

"Yes, sir."

"I mean, imagination doesn't boggle."

"No, sir."

And it didn't. I could see exactly what must have happened. Insert a liberal dose of mixed spirits in a normally abstemious man, and he becomes a force. He does not stand round, twiddling his fingers and stammering. He acts. I had no doubt that Gussie must have reached for the Bassett and clasped her to him like a stevedore handling a sack of coals. And one could readily envisage the effect of that sort of thing on a girl of romantic mind.

"Well, well, well, Jeeves."

"Yes, sir."

"This is splendid news."

"Yes, sir."

"You see now how right I was."

"Yes, sir."

"It must have been a rather an eye-opener for you, watching me handle this case."

"Yes, sir."

"The simple, direct method never fails."

"No, sir."

"Whereas the elaborate does."

"Yes, sir."

"Right ho, Jeeves."

We had arrived at the main entrance of Market Snodsbury Grammar School. I parked the car, and went in, well content. True, the Tuppy-Angela problem still remain unsolved and Aunt Dahlia's five hundred quid seemed as far off as ever, but it was gratifying to feel that good old Gussie's troubles were over, at any rate.

The Grammar School at Market Snodsbury had, I understood, been built somewhere in the year 1416, and, as with so many of these ancient foundations, there still seemed to brood over its Great Hall, where the afternoon's festivities were to take place, not a little of the fug of the centuries. It was the hottest day of the summer, and though somebody had opened a tentative window or two, the atmosphere remained distinctive and individual.

In this hall the youth of Market Snodsbury had been eating its daily lunch for a matter of five hundred years, and the flavour lingered. The air was sort of heavy and languorous, if you know what I mean, with the scent of Young England and boiled beef and carrots.

Aunt Dahlia, who was sitting with a bevy of the local nibs in the second row, sighted me as I entered and waved to me to join her, but I was too smart for that. I wedged myself in among the standees at the back, leaning up against a chap who, from the aroma, might have been a corn chandler or something of that order. The essence of strategy on these occasions is to be as near the door as possible.

The hall was gaily decorated with flags and coloured paper, and the eye was further refreshed by the spectacle of a mixed drove of boys, parents, and what not, the former running a good deal to shiny faces and Eton collars, the latter stressing the black-satin note rather when female, and looking as if their coats were too tight, if male. And presently there was some applause—sporadic, Jeeves has since told me it was—and I saw Gussie being steered by a bearded bloke in a gown to a seat in the middle of the platform.

And I confess that as I beheld him and felt that there but for the grace of God went Bertram Wooster, a shudder ran through the frame. It all reminded me so vividly of the time I had addressed that girls' school.

Of course, looking at it dispassionately, you may say that for horror and peril there is no comparison between an almost human audience like the one before me and a mob of small girls with pigtails down their backs, and this, I concede, is true. Nevertheless, the spectacle was enough to make me feel like a fellow watching a pal going over Niagara Falls in a barrel, and the thought of what I had escaped caused everything for a moment to go black and swim before my eyes.

When I was able to see clearly once more, I perceived that Gussie was now seated. He had his hands on his knees, with his elbows out at right angles, like a nigger minstrel of the old school about to ask Mr. Bones why a chicken crosses the road, and he was staring before him with a smile so fixed and pebble-beached that I should have thought that anybody could have guessed that there sat one in whom the old familiar juice was plashing up against the back of the front teeth.

In fact, I saw Aunt Dahlia, who, having assisted at so many hunting dinners in her time, is second to none as a judge of the symptoms, give a start and gaze long and earnestly. And she was just saying something to Uncle Tom on her left when the bearded bloke stepped to the footlights and started making a speech. From the fact that he spoke as if he had a hot potato in his mouth without getting the raspberry from the lads in the ringside seats, I deduced that he must be the headmaster.

With his arrival in the spotlight, a sort of perspiring resignation seemed to settle on the audience. Personally, I snuggled up against the chandler and let my attention wander.

The speech was on the subject of the doings of the school during the past term, and this part of a prize-giving is always apt rather to fail to grip the visiting stranger. I mean, you know how it is. You're told that J. B. Brewster has won an Exhibition for Classics at Cats', Cambridge, and you feel that it's one of those stories where you can't see how funny it is unless you really know the fellow. And the same applies to G. Bullett being awarded the Lady Jane Wix Scholarship at the Birmingham College of Veterinary Science.

In fact, I and the corn chandler, who was looking a bit fagged I thought, as if he had had a hard morning chandling the corn, were beginning to doze lightly when things suddenly brisked up, bringing Gussie into the picture for the first time.

"To-day," said the bearded bloke, "we are all happy to welcome as the guest of the afternoon Mr. Fitz-Wattle——"

At the beginning of the address, Gussie had subsided into a sort of daydream, with his mouth hanging open. About half-way through, faint signs of life had begun to show. And for the last few minutes he had been trying to cross one leg over the other and failing and having another shot and failing again. But only now did he exhibit any real animation. He sat up with a jerk.

"Fink-Nottle," he said, opening his eyes.

"Fitz-Nottle."

"Fink-Nottle."

"I should say Fink-Nottle."

"Of course you should, you silly ass," said Gussie genially. "All right, get on with it."

And closing his eyes, he began trying to cross his legs again.

I could see that this little spot of friction had rattled the bearded bloke a bit. He stood for a moment fumbling at the fungus with a hesitating hand. But they make these head masters of tough stuff. The weakness passed. He came back nicely and carried on.

"We are all happy, I say, to welcome as the guest of the after-noon Mr. Fink-Nottle, who has kindly consented to award the prizes. This task, as you know, is one that should have devolved upon that well-beloved and vigorous member of our board of governors, the Rev. William Plomer, and we are all, I am sure, very sorry that illness at the last moment should have prevented him from being here to-day. But, if I may borrow a familiar metaphor from the—if I may employ a homely metaphor familiar to you all—what we lose on the swings we gain on the roundabouts."

He paused, and beamed rather freely, to show that this was comedy. I could have told the man it was no use. Not a ripple. The corn chandler leaned against me and muttered "Whoddidesay?" but that was all.

It's always a nasty jar to wait for the laugh and find that the gag hasn't got across. The bearded bloke was visibly discomposed. At that, however, I think he would have got by, had he not, at this juncture, unfortunately stirred Gussie up again.

"In other words, though deprived of Mr. Plomer, we have with us this afternoon Mr. Fink-Nottle. I am sure that Mr. Fink-Nottle's name is one that needs no introduction to you. It is, I venture to assert, a name that is familiar to us all."

"Not to you," said Gussie.

And the next moment I saw what Jeeves had meant when he had described him as laughing heartily. "Heartily" was absolutely the *mot juste*. It sounded like a gas explosion.

"You didn't seem to know it so dashed well, what, what?" said Gussie. And, reminded apparently by the word "what" of the word "Wattle," he repeated the latter some sixteen times with a rising inflection.

"Wattle, Wattle, Wattle," he concluded. "Right-ho. Push on."

But the bearded bloke had shot his bolt. He stood there, licked at last; and, watching him closely, I could see that he was now at the crossroads. I could spot what he was thinking as clearly as if he had confided it to my personal ear. He wanted to sit down and call it a day, I mean, but the thought that gave him pause was that, if he did, he must then either uncork Gussie or take the Fink-Nottle speech as read and get straight on to the actual prize-giving.

It was a dashed tricky thing, of course, to have to decide on the spur of the moment. I was reading in the paper the other day about those birds who are trying to split the atom, the nub being that they haven't the foggiest as to what will happen if they do. It may be all right. On the other hand, it may not be all right. And pretty silly a chap would feel, no doubt, if, having split the atom, he suddenly found the house going up in smoke and himself torn limb from limb.

So with the bearded bloke. Whether he was abreast of the inside facts in Gussie's case, I don't know, but it was obvious to him by this time that he had run into something pretty hot. Trial gallops had shown that Gussie had his own way of doing things. Those interruptions had been enough to prove to the perspicacious that here seated on the platform at the big binge of the season, was one who, if pushed forward to make a speech, might let himself go in a rather epoch-making manner.

On the other hand, chain him up and put a green-baize cloth over him, and where were you? The proceedings would be over about half an hour too soon.

It was, as I say, a difficult problem to have to solve, and, left to himself, I don't know what conclusion he would have come to. Personally, I think he would have played it safe. As it happened, however, the thing was taken out of his hands, for at this moment, Gussie, having stretched his arms and yawned a bit, switched on that pebble-beached smile again and tacked down to the edge of the platform.

"Speech," he said affably.

He then stood with his thumbs in the armholes of his waistcoat, waiting for the applause to die down.

It was some time before this happened, for he had got a very fine hand indeed. I suppose it wasn't often that the boys of Market Snodsbury Grammar School came across a man public-spirited enough to call their head master a silly ass, and they showed their appreciation in no uncertain manner. Gussie may have been one over the eight, but as far as the majority of those present were concerned he was sitting on top of the world.

"Boys," said Gussie, "I mean ladies and gentlemen and boys,

I do not detain you long, but I propose on this occasion to feel compelled to say a few auspicious words. Ladies—and boys and gentlemen—we have all listened with interest to the remarks of our friend here who forgot to shave this morning—I don't know his name, but then he didn't know mine—Fitz-Wattle, I mean, absolutely absurd—which squares things up a bit—and we are all sorry that the Reverend What-ever-he-was-called should be dying of adenoids, but after all, here to-day, gone to-morrow, and all flesh is as grass, and what not, but that wasn't what I wanted to say. What I wanted to say was this—and I say confidently—without fear of contradiction—I say, in short, I am happy to be here on the auspicious occasion and I take much pleasure in kindly awarding the prizes, consisting of the handsome books you see laid out on the table. As Shakespeare says, there are sermons in books, stones in the running brooks, or, rather, the other way about, and there you have it in a nutshell."

It went well, and I wasn't surprised. I couldn't quite follow some of it, but anybody could see that it was real ripe stuff, and I was amazed that even the course of treatment he had been taking could have rendered so normally tongue-tied a dumb brick as Gussie capable of it.

It just shows, what any member of Parliament will tell you, that if you want real oratory, the preliminary noggin is essential. Unless pie-eyed, you cannot hope to grip.

"Gentlemen," said Gussie, " I mean ladies and gentlemen and, of course, boys, what a beautiful world this is. A beautiful world, full of happiness on every side. Let me tell you a little story. Two Irishman, Pat and Mike, were walking along Broadway, and one said to the other, 'Begorrah, the race is not always to the swift,' and the other replied, 'Faith and begob, education is a drawing out, not a putting in.' "

I must say it seemed to me the rottenest story I had ever heard, and I was surprised that Jeeves should have considered it worth while shoving into a speech. However, when I taxed him with this later, he said that Gussie had altered the plot a good deal, and I dare say that accounts for it.

At any rate, that was the *conte* as Gussie told it, and when I say that it got a very fair laugh, you will understand what a popular favourite he had become with the multitude. There might be a bearded bloke or so on the platform and a small section in the second row who were wishing the speaker would conclude his remarks and resume his seat, but the audience as a whole was for him solidly.

There was applause, and a voice cried: "Hear, hear!"

"Yes," said Gussie, "it is a beautiful world. The sky is blue, the birds are singing, there is optimism everywhere. And why not, boys and ladies and gentlemen? I'm happy, you're happy, we're all happy, even the meanest Irishman that walks along Broadway. Though, as I say, there were two of them— Pat and Mike, one drawing out, the other putting in. I should like you boys, taking the time from me, to give three cheers for this beautiful world. All together now."

Presently the dust settled down and the plaster stopped falling from the ceiling, and he went on.

"People who say it isn't a beautiful world don't know what they are talking about. Driving here in the car to-day to award the kind prizes, I was reluctantly compelled to tick off my host on this very point. Old Tom Travers. You will see him sitting there on the second row next to the large lady in beige."

He pointed helpfully, and the hundred or so Market Snodsburians who craned their necks in the direction indicated were able to observe Uncle Tom blushing prettily.

"I ticked him off properly, the poor fish. He expressed the opinion that the world was in a deplorable state. I said, 'Don't talk rot, old Tom Travers.' 'I am not accustomed to talk rot,' he said. 'Then, for a beginner,' I said, 'you do it dashed well.' And I think you will admit boys and ladies and gentlemen, that that was telling him."

The audience seemed to agree with him. The point went big. The voice that had said, "Hear, hear" said "Hear, hear" again, and my corn chandler hammered the floor vigorously with a large-size walking-stick.

"Well, boys," resumed Gussie, having shot his cuffs and smirked horribly, "this is the end of the summer term, and many of you, no doubt, are leaving the school. And I don't blame you, because there's a froust in here you could cut with with a knife. You are going out into the great world. Soon many of you will be walking along Broadway. And what I want to impress upon you is that, however much you may suffer from adenoids, you must all use every effort to prevent yourselves becoming pessimists and talking rot like old Tom Travers—there in the second row. The fellow with a face rather like a walnut."

He paused to allow those wishing to do so to refresh themselves with another look at Uncle Tom, and I found myself musing in some little perplexity. Long association with the members of the Drones has put me pretty well in touch with the various ways in which an overdose of the blushful Hippocrene can take the individual, but I had never seen anyone react quite as Gussie was doing.

There was a sort of snap about his work which I had never witnessed before, even in Barmy Fotheringay-Phipps on New Year's Eve.

Jeeves, when I discussed the matter with him later, said it was something to do with inhibitions, if I caught the word correctly, and the suppression of, I think he said, the ego. What he meant, I gathered, was that, owing to the fact that Gussie had just completed a five years' stretch of blameless seclusion among the newts, all the goofiness which ought to have been spread out thin over those five years and had been bottled up during that period came to the surface on this occasion in a lump—or, if you prefer to put it that way, like a tidal wave.

There may be something in this. Jeeves generally knows.

Anyway, be that as it may, I was dashed glad I had had the shrewdness to keep out of that second row. It might be unworthy of the prestige of a Wooster to squash in among the proletariat in the standing-room-only section, but at least, I felt, I was out of the danger zone. So thoroughly had Gussie got it up his nose by now that it seemed to me that had he sighted me he might have become personal about even an old school friend.

"If there's one thing in the world I can't stand," proceeded Gussie, "it's a pessimist. Be optimists, boys. You all know the difference between an optimist and a pessimist. An optimist is a man who—well, take the case of the Irishmen walking along Broadway. One is an optimist and one is a pessimist, just as one's name is Pat and the other's Mike. . . . Why, hullo, Bertie; I didn't know you were here."

Too late, I endeavoured to go to earth behind the chandler, only to discover that there was no chandler there. Some appointment, suddenly remembered—possibly a promise to his wife that he would be home to tea—had caused him to ooze away while my attention was elsewhere, leaving me right out in the open.

Between me and Gussie, who was now pointing in an offensive manner, there was nothing but a sea of interested faces looking up at me.

"Now, there," boomed Gussie, continuing to point, "is an instance of what I mean. Boys and ladies and gentlemen, take a good look at that object standing up there at the back— morning coat, trousers as worn, quiet grey tie, and carnation in buttonhole—you can't miss him. Bertie Wooster, that is, and as foul a pessimist as ever bit a tiger. I tell you I despise that man. And why do I despise him? Because, boys and ladies and gentlemen, he is a pessimist. His attitude is defeatist. When I told him I was going to address you this afternoon, he tried to dissuade me. And do you know why he tried to dissuade me? Because he said my trousers would split up the back."

The cheers that greeted this were the loudest yet. Anything about splitting trousers went straight to the simple hearts of the young scholars of Market Snodsbury Grammar School. Two in the row in front of me turned purple, and a small lad with freckles seated beside them asked me for my autograph.

"Let me tell you a story about Bertie Wooster."

A Wooster can stand a good deal, but he cannot stand having his name bandied in a public place. Picking my feet up softly, I was in the very process of executing a quiet sneak for the door, when I perceived that the bearded bloke had at last decided to apply the closure.

Why he hadn't done so before is beyond me. Spellbound, I take it. And, of course, when a chap is going like a breeze with the public, as Gussie had been, it's not so dashed easy to chip in. However, the prospect of hearing another of Gussie's anecdotes seemed to have done the trick. Rising rather as I had risen from my bench at the beginning of the painful scene with Tuppy on the twilight, he made a leap for the table, snatched up a book and came bearing down on the speaker.

He touched Gussie on the arm, and Gussie, turning sharply and seeing a large bloke with a beard apparently about to bean him with a book, sprang back in an attitude of self-defence.

"Perhaps, as time is getting on, Mr. Fink-Nottle, we had better——"

"Oh, ah," said Gussie, getting the trend. He relaxed. "The prizes, eh? Of course, yes. Right-ho. Yes, might as well be shoving along with it. What's this one?"

"Spelling and dictation—P. K. Purvis," announced the bearded bloke.

"Spelling and dictation—P. K. Purvis," echoed Gussie, as if he were calling coals. "Forward, P. K. Purvis."

Now that the whistle had been blown on his speech, it seemed to me that there was no longer any need for the strategic retreat which I had been planning. I had no wish to tear myself away unless I had to. I mean, I had told Jeeves that this binge would be fraught with interest, and it was fraught with interest. There was a fascination about Gussie's methods which gripped and made one reluctant to pass the thing up provided personal innuendoes were steered clear of. I decided, accordingly, to remain, and presently there was a musical squeaking and P. K. Purvis climbed the platform.

The spelling-and-dictation champ was about three foot six in his squeaking shoes, with a pink face and sandy hair. Gussie patted this hair. He seemed to have taken an immediate fancy to the lad.

"You P. K. Purvis?"

"Sir, yes, sir."

"It's a beautiful world, P. K. Purvis."

"Sir, yes, sir."

"Ah, you've noticed it, have you? Good. You married, by any chance?"

"Sir, no, sir."

"Get married, P. K. Purvis," said Gussie earnestly. "It's the only life. . . . Well, here's your book. Looks rather bilge to me from a glance at the title page, but, such as it is, here you are."

P. K. Purvis squeaked off amidst sporadic applause, but one could not fail to note that the sporadic was followed by a rather strained silence. It was evident that Gussie was striking something of a new note in Market Snodsbury scholastic circles. Looks were exchanged between parent and parent. The bearded bloke had the air of one who had drained the bitter cup. As for Aunt Dahlia, her demeanour now told only too clearly that her last doubts had been resolved and her verdict was in. I saw her whisper to the Bassett, who sat on her right, and the Bassett nodded sadly and looked like a fairy about to shed a tear and add another star to the Milky Way.

Gussie, after the departure of P. K. Purvis, had fallen into a sort of day-dream and was standing with his mouth open and his hands in his pockets. Becoming abruptly aware that a fat kid in knickerbockers was at his elbow, he started violently.

"Hullo!" he said, visibly shaken. "Who are you?"

"This," said the bearded bloke, "is R. V. Smethurst."

"What's he doing here?" asked Gussie suspiciously.

"You are presenting him with the drawing prize, Mr. Fink-Nottle."

This apparently struck Gussie as a reasonable explanation. His face cleared.

"That's right too," he said. . . . "Well, here it is, cocky. You off?" he said, as the kid prepared to withdraw.

"Sir, yes, sir."

"Wait, R. V. Smethurst. Not so fast. Before you go, there is a question I wish to ask you."

But the bearded bloke's aim now seemed to be to rush the ceremonies a bit. He hustled R. V. Smethurst off stage rather like a chucker-out in a pub regretfully ejecting an old and respected customer, and started paging G. G. Simmons. A moment later the latter was up and coming, and conceive my emotion when it was announced that the subject on which he clicked was Scripture knowledge. One of us, I mean to say.

G. G. Simmons was an unpleasant, perky-looking stripling, mostly front teeth and spectacles, but I gave him a big hand. We Scripture-knowledge sharks stick together.

Gussie, I was sorry to see, didn't like him. There was in his manner, as he regarded G. G. Simmons, none of the chumminess which had marked it during his interview with P. K. Purvis or, in a somewhat lesser degree, with R. V. Smethurst. He was cold and distant.

"Well, G. G. Simmons."

"Sir, yes, sir."

"What do you mean—sir, yes, sir? Dashed silly thing to say. So you've won the Scripture-knowledge prize, have you?"

"Sir, yes, sir."

"Yes," said Gussie, "you look just the sort of little tick who would. And yet," he said, pausing and eyeing the child keenly, "how are we to know that this has all been open and above board? Let me test you, G. G. Simmons. Who was What's-His-Name—the chap who begat Thingummy? Can you answer me that, Simmons?"

"Sir, no, sir."

Gussie turned to the bearded bloke.

"Fishy," he said. "Very fishy. This boy appears to be totally lacking in Scripture knowledge."

The bearded bloke passed a hand across his forehead.

"I can assure you, Mr. Fink-Nottle, that every care was taken to insure a correct marking and that Simmons out distanced his competitors by a wide margin."

"Well, if you say so," said Gussie doubtfully. "All right, G. G. Simmons, take your prize."

"Sir, thank you, sir."

"But let me tell you that there's nothing to stick on side about in winning a prize for Scripture knowledge. Bertie Wooster——"

I don't know when I've had a nastier shock. I had been going on the assumption that, now that they had stopped him making his speech, Gussie's fangs had been drawn, as you might say. To duck my head down and resume my edging toward the door was with me the work of a moment.

"Bertie Wooster won the Scripture-knowledge prize at a kids' school we were at together, and you know what he's like. But, of course, Bertie frankly cheated. He succeeded in scrounging that Scripture-knowledge trophy over the heads of better men by means of some of the rawest and most brazen swindling methods ever witnessed even at a school where such things were common. If that man's pockets, as he entered the examination-room, were not stuffed to bursting point with lists of the kings of Judah——"

I heard no more. A moment later I was out in God's air, fumbling with a fevered foot at the self-starter of the old car.

"A short, stout comfortable man of middle age, and the thing that struck me first about him was the extraordinary childlike candour of his eyes. They were large and round and honest. I would have bought oil stocks from him without a tremor."

GOOD NEWS FROM DENMARK

The *Berlingske Tidende* Speaks Its Mind

NY WODEHOUSE

DEN VERDENSKENDTE engelsk-amerikanske humoristiske Institution, *P. G. Wodehouse*, har udsendt en ny Bog, hvis Titel paa Dansk er „ Unge Mænd med hvide Gamacher ", og som ifølge sit gule vebælte er „ The Drones Club Book of the Month ". Der fik Book Guild og Book Society den Stikpille, —og den er vel anbragt.

Skont Wodehouse læses af Millioner Verden over, betyder det dog ikke, at alle har det i sig, at de er i Stand til at goutere ham. Jeg véd, at der er dannede Mennesker, som ikke vil spilde deres kostbare Tid paa hans Bøger. Hvis man ikke er for Wodehouse, er man nødvendigvis imod ham, for der er kun een Undskyldning for at læse ham, og det er, at man kan klukle over ham.

Man skal lede efter Sludder, som er mere tosset, usandsynligt, skrupskørt end det, Wodehouse serverer i „ Unge Mennesker i hvide Gamacher ", men hvis man er stillet ind paa den rigtige Bølgelængde, vil man ikke kunne bare sig for at le. Der er elleve Historier, hvoraf de tre tilhører den noksom bekendte Mr. Mulliner (ham med de utallige Slægtninge!) og Resten fordeler sig blandt diverse, for ikke at skrive de værste „ Eggs, Beans and Crumpets ", Medlemmer af „ The Drones Club ", med Freddie Widgeon „ in the chair ". Hvis De ikke véd, om Wodehouse er for Dem eller ej, saa prøv at læse Historien af „ Good-bye to all Cats ". Hvis De stadig er lige stiv i Ansigtet efter at have læst den, er der ingen Tvivl mulig. De er uhelbredelig—og De har Lov at se ned paa os andre.

H. K.

INSIDE INFORMATION

"Girls' Open Egg and Spoon Race," read Bingo.

"I am told," said Jeeves, "it is a certainty for last year's winner, Sarah Mills, who will doubtless start an odds-on favourite."

"Good, is she?"

"They tell me in the village that she carries a beautiful egg, sir."

"Then there's the Obstacle Race," said Bingo. . . . "That's all, except the Choir Boys' Hundred Yards Handicap, for a pewter mug presented by the vicar—open to all whose voices have not broken before the second Sunday in Epiphany."

THE
FEUDAL SPIRIT

A BIT of dialogue now unshipped itself in the upper regions. The butler started it.

"Good morning, m'lord. Shall I assist your lordship to a little egg and bacon?"

The table shook as the aged peer shuddered strongly.

"Don't try to be funny, Gascoigne. There is a time to speak of eggs and a time not to speak of eggs. At the moment, I would prefer to try to forget that there are such things in the world."

The butler coughed in rather an unpleasant and censorious manner.

"Did your lordship exceed last night?"

"Certainly not."

"Did your lordship imbibe champagne?"

"The merest spot."

"A bottle?"

"It may have been a bottle."

"Two bottles?"

"Yes. Possibly two bottles."

The butler coughed again.

"I shall inform Doctor Spelvin."

"Don't be a cad, Gascoigne."

"He has expressly forbidden your lordship champagne."

"Tchah!"

"I need scarcely remind your lordship that champagne brings your lordship out in spots."

To
My Daughter
LEONORA

without whose never-failing
sympathy and encouragement
this book
would have been finished
in
half the time

Author's Dedication, "Heart of a Goof."

GOLFING TIGERS AND LITERARY LIONS

BEFORE LEADING the reader out on this little nine-hole course, I should like to say a few words on the club-house steps with regard to the criticisms of my earlier book of Golf stories, *The Clicking of Cuthbert*. In the first place, I noticed with regret a disposition on the part of certain writers to speak of Golf as a trivial theme, unworthy of the pen of a thinker. I can only say that right through the ages the mightiest brains have occupied themselves with this noble sport, and that I err, therefore, if I do err, in excellent company.

Apart from the works of such men as James Braid, John Henry Taylor and Horace Hutchinson, we find Publius Syrius not disdaining to give advice on the back-swing ("He gets through too late who goes too fast"); Diogenes describing the emotions of a cheery player at the water-hole ("Be of good cheer. I see land"); and Doctor Watts, who, watching one of his drives from the tee, jotted down the following couplet on the back of his score-card:

> "Fly, like a youthful hart or roe,
> Over the hills where spices grow."

And, when we consider that Chaucer, the father of English poetry, inserted in his Squire's Tale the line

> "Therefore behoveth him a ful long spoone"

(though, of course, with the modern rubber-covered ball an iron would have got the same distance) and that Shakespeare himself, speaking querulously in the character of a weak player who held up an impatient foursome, said:

> "Four rogues in buckram let drive at me"

we may, I think, consider these objections answered.

A far more serious grievance which I have against my critics is that many of them confessed to the possession of but the slightest knowledge of the game, and one actually stated in cold print that he did not know what a niblick was. A writer on golf is certainly entitled to be judged by his peers—which, in my own case, means men who do one good drive in six, four reasonable approaches in an eighteen-hole round, and average three putts per green: and I think I am justified in asking of editors that they instruct critics of this book to append their handicaps in brackets at the end of their remarks. By this

means the public will be enabled to form a fair estimate of the worth of the volume, and the sting in such critiques as "We laughed heartily while reading these stories—once—at a misprint" will be sensibly diminished by the figures (36) at the bottom of the paragraph. While my elation will be all the greater should the words "A genuine masterpiece" be followed by a simple (scr.).

One final word. The thoughtful reader, comparing this book with *The Clicking of Cuthbert* will no doubt, be struck by the poignant depth of feeling which pervades the present volume like the scent of muddy shoes in a locker-room: and it may be that he will conclude that, like so many English writers, I have fallen under the spell of the great Russians.

This is not the case. While it is, of course, true that my style owes much to Dostoievsky, the heart-wringing qualities of such stories as *The Awakening of Rollo Podmarsh* and *Keeping in with Vosper* are due entirely to the fact that I have spent much time recently playing on the National Links at Southampton, Long Island, U.S.A. These links were constructed by an exiled Scot who conceived the dreadful idea of assembling on one course all the really foul holes in Great Britain. It cannot but leave its mark on a man when, after struggling through the Sahara at Sandwich and the Alps at Prestwick, he finds himself faced by the Station-master's Garden hole at St. Andrew's and knows that the Redan and the Eden are just round the corner. When you turn in a medal score of a hundred and eight on two successive days, you get to know something about Life.

And yet it may be that there are a few gleams of sunshine in the book. If so, it is attributable to the fact that some of it was written before I went to Southampton and immediately after I had won my first and only trophy—an umbrella in a hotel tournament at Aiken, South Carolina, where, playing to a handicap of sixteen, I went through a field consisting of some of the fattest retired business-men in America like a devouring flame. If we lose the Walker Cup this year, let England remember that.

Author's Preface, "*Heart of a Goof.*"

THE SOUPINESS OF MADELINE

I CAN well imagine that a casual observer, if I had confided to him my qualms at the idea of being married to this girl, would have raised his eyebrows and been at a loss to understand. "Bertie," he would probably have said, "you don't know what's good for you," adding, possibly, that he wished he had half my complaint. For Madeline Bassett was undeniably of attractive exterior—slim, svelte, if that's the word, and bountifully equipped with golden hair and all the fixings.

But where the casual observer would have been making his bloomer was in overlooking that squashy soupiness of hers, that subtle air she had of being on the point of talking baby-talk. It was that that froze the blood. She was definitely the sort of girl who puts her hands over a husband's eyes, as he is crawling in to breakfast with a morning head, and says: "Guess who!"

LORD EMSWORTH AND THE GIRL FRIEND

THE day was so warm, so fair, so magically a thing of sunshine and blue skies and bird-song that anyone acquainted with Clarence, ninth Earl of Emsworth, and aware of his liking for fine weather, would have pictured him going about the place on this summer morning with a beaming smile and an uplifted heart. Instead of which, humped over the breakfast table, he was directing at a blameless kippered herring a look of such intense bitterness that the fish seemed to sizzle beneath it. For it was August Bank Holiday, and Blandings Castle on August Bank Holidays became, in his lordships' opinion, a miniature Inferno.

This was the day when his park and grounds broke out into a noisome rash of swings, roundabouts, marquees, toy balloons and paper bags; when a tidal wave of the peasantry and its squealing young engulfed those haunts of immemorial peace. On August Bank Holiday he was not allowed to potter pleasantly about his gardens in an old coat: forces beyond his control shoved him into a stiff collar and a top hat and told him to go out and be genial. And in the cool of the quiet evenfall they put him on a platform and made him make a speech. To a man with a day like that in front of him fine weather was a mockery.

His sister, Lady Constance Keeble, looked brightly at him over the coffee-pot.

"What a lovely morning!" she said.

Lord Emsworth's gloom deepened. He chafed at being called upon—by this woman of all others—to behave as if everything was for the jolliest in the jolliest of all possible worlds. But for his sister Constance and her hawk-like vigilance, he might, he thought, have been able at least to dodge the top-hat.

"Have you got your speech ready?"

106

"Yes."

"Well, mind you learn it by heart this time and don't stammer and dodder as you did last year."

Lord Emsworth pushed the plate and kipper away. He had lost his desire for food.

"And don't forget you have to go to the village this morning to judge the cottage gardens."

"All right, all right, all right," said his lordship testily. "I've not forgotten."

"I think I will come to the village with you. There are a number of those Fresh Air London children staying there now, and I must warn them to behave properly when they come to the Fête this afternoon. You know what London children are. McAllister says he found one of them in the gardens the other day, picking his flowers."

At any other time the news of this outrage would, no doubt, have affected Lord Emsworth profoundly. But now, so intense was his self-pity, he did not even shudder. He drank coffee with the air of a man who regretted that it was not hemlock.

"By the way, McAllister was speaking to me again last night about that gravel path through the yew alley. He seems very keen on it."

"Glug!" said Lord Emsworth—which, as any philologist will tell you, is the sound which peers of the realm make when stricken to the soul while drinking coffee.

Concerning Glasgow, that great commercial and manufacturing city in the county of Lanarkshire in Scotland, much has been written. So lyrically does the Encyclopædia Britannica deal with the place that it covers twenty-seven pages before it can tear itself away and go on to Glass, Glastonbury, Glauber and Glatz. The only aspect of it, however, which immediately concerns the present historian is the fact that the citizens it breeds are apt to be grim, dour, persevering, tenacious men; men with red whiskers who know what they want and mean to get it. Such a one was Angus McAllister, head-gardener at Blandings Castle.

For years Angus McAllister had set before himself as his

earthly goal the construction of a gravel path through the Castle's famous yew alley. For years he had been bringing the project to the notice of his employer, though in anyone less whiskered the latter's unconcealed loathing would have caused embarrassment. And now, it seemed, he was at it again.

"Gravel path!" Lord Emsworth stiffened through the whole length of his stringy body. Nature, he had always maintained, intended a yew alley to be carpeted with a mossy growth. And, whatever Nature felt about it, he personally was dashed if he was going to have men with Clydeside accents and faces like dissipated potatoes coming along and mutilating that lovely expanse of green velvet. "Gravel path, indeed! Why not asphalt? Why not a few hoardings with advertisements of liver pills and a filling station? That's what the man would really like."

Lord Emsworth felt bitter, and when he felt bitter he could be terribly sarcastic.

"Well, I think it is a very good idea," said his sister. "One could walk there in wet weather then. Damp moss is ruinous to shoes."

Lord Emsworth rose. He could bear no more of this. He left the table, the room and the house and, reaching the yew alley some minutes later, was revolted to find it infested by Angus McAllister in person. The head-gardener was standing gazing at the moss like a high priest of some ancient religion about to stick the gaff into the human sacrifice.

"Morning, McAllister," said Lord Emsworth coldly.

"Good morrrrning, your lorrudsheep."

There was a pause. Angus McAllister, extending a foot that looked like a violin-case, pressed it on the moss. The meaning of the gesture was plain. It expressed contempt, dislike, a generally anti-moss spirit: and Lord Emsworth, wincing, surveyed the man unpleasantly through his pince-nez. Though not often given to theological speculation, he was wondering why Providence, if obliged to make head-gardeners, had found it necessary to make them so Scotch. In the case of Angus McAllister, why, going a step farther, have made him a human being at all? All the ingredients of a first-class mule simply thrown away. He felt that he might have liked Angus McAllister if he had been a mule.

"I was speaking to her leddyship yesterday."

"Oh?"

"About the gravel path I was speaking to her leddyship."

"Oh?"

"Her leddyship likes the notion fine."

"Indeed! Well..."

Lord Emsworth's face had turned a lively pink, and he was about to release the blistering words which were forming themselves in his mind when suddenly he caught the head-gardener's eye and paused. Angus McAllister was looking at him in a peculiar manner, and he knew what that look meant. Just one crack, his eye was saying—in Scotch, of course—just one crack out of you and I tender my resignation. And with a sickening shock it came home to Lord Emsworth how completely he was in this man's clutches.

He shuffled miserably. Yes, he was helpless. Except for that kink about gravel paths, Angus McAllister was a head-gardener in a thousand, and he needed him. He could not do without him. That, unfortunately, had been proved by experiment. Once before, at the time when they were grooming for the Agricultural Show that pumpkin which had subsequently romped home so gallant a winner, he had dared to flout Angus McAllister. And Angus had resigned, and he had been forced to plead—yes, plead—with him to come back. An employer cannot hope to do this sort of thing and still rule with an iron hand. Filled with the coward rage that dares to burn but does not dare to blaze, Lord Emsworth coughed a cough that was undisguisedly a bronchial white flag.

"I'll—er—I'll think it over, McAllister."

"Mphm."

"I have to go to the village now. I will see you later."

"Mphm."

"Meanwhile, I will—er—think it over."

"Mphm."

The task of judging the floral displays in the cottage gardens of the little village of Blandings Parva was one to which Lord Emsworth had looked forward with pleasurable anticipation. It was the sort of job he liked. But now, even though he had managed to give his sister Constance the slip and was free from her threatened society, he approached the task with a downcast spirit. It is always unpleasant for a proud man to realize that he is no longer captain of his soul; that he is to all intents and purposes ground beneath the number twelve heel of a Glaswegian head-gardener; and, brooding on this, he judged the cottage gardens with a distrait eye. It was only when he came to the last on his list that anything like animation crept into his demeanour.

This, he perceived, peering over its rickety fence, was not at all a bad little garden. It demanded closer inspection. He unlatched the gate and pottered in. And a dog, dozing behind a water-butt, opened one eye and looked at him. It was one of those hairy, nondescript dogs, and its gaze was cold, wary and suspicious, like that of a stock-broker who thinks someone is going to play a confidence trick on him.

Lord Emsworth did not observe the animal. He had pottered to a bed of wallflowers and now, stooping, he took a sniff at them.

As sniffs go, it was an innocent sniff, but the dog for some reason appeared to read into it criminality of a high order. All the indignant householder in him woke in a flash. The next moment the world had become full of hideous noises, and Lord Emsworth's preoccupation was swept away in a passionate desire to save his ankles from harm.

As these chronicles of Blandings Castle have already shown, he was not at his best with strange dogs. Beyond saying "Go away, sir!" and leaping to and fro with an agility surprising in one of his years, he had accomplished little in the direction of a reasoned plan of defence when the cottage door opened and a girl came out.

"Hoy!" cried the girl.

And on the instant, at the mere sound of her voice, the

mongrel, suspending hostilities, bounded at the newcomer and writhed on his back at her feet with all four legs in the air. The spectacle reminded Lord Emsworth irresistibly of his own behaviour when in the presence of Angus McAllister.

He blinked at his preserver. She was a small girl, of uncertain age—possibly twelve or thirteen, though a combination of London fogs and early cares had given her face a sort of wizened motherliness which in some odd way caused his lordship from the first to look on her as belonging to his own generation. She was the type of girl you see in back streets carrying a baby nearly as large as herself and still retaining sufficient energy to lead one little brother by the hand and shout recrimination at another in the distance. Her cheeks shone from recent soaping, and she was dressed in a velveteen frock which was obviously the pick of her wardrobe. Her hair, in defiance of the prevailing mode, she wore drawn tightly back into a short pigtail.

"Er—thank you," said Lord Emsworth.

"Thank you, sir," said the girl.

For what she was thanking him, his lordship was not able to gather. Later, as their acquaintance ripened, he was to discover that this strange gratitude was a habit with his new friend. She thanked everybody for everything. At the moment, the mannerism surprised him. He continued to blink at her through his pince-nez.

Lack of practice had rendered Lord Emsworth a little rusty in the art of making conversation to members of the other sex. He sought in his mind for topics.

"Fine day."

"Yes, sir. Thank you, sir."

"Are you"—Lord Emsworth furtively consulted his list—"are you the daughter of—ah—Ebenezer Sprockett?" he asked, thinking, as he had often thought before, what ghastly names some of his tenantry possessed.

"No, sir. I'm from London, sir."

"Ah? London, eh? Pretty warm it must be there." He

paused. Then, remembering a formula of his youth: "Er—been out much this season?"

"No, sir."

"Everybody out of town now, I suppose? What part of London?"

"Drury Line, sir."

"What's your name? Eh, what?"

"Gladys, sir. Thank you, sir. This is Ern."

A small boy had wandered out of the cottage, a rather hard-boiled specimen with freckles, bearing surprisingly in his hand a large and beautiful bunch of flowers. Lord Emsworth bowed courteously and with the addition of this third party to the *tête-à-tête* felt more at his ease.

"How do you do," he said. "What pretty flowers!"

With her brother's advent, Gladys, also, had lost diffidence and gained conversational aplomb.

"A treat, ain't they?" she agreed eagerly. "I got 'em for 'em up at the big 'ahse. Coo! The old josser the plice belongs to didn't arf chase me. 'E found me picking 'em and 'e sharted somefin at me and come runnin' after me, but I copped 'im on the shin wiv a stone and 'e stopped to rub it and I come away."

Lord Emsworth might have corrected her impression that Blandings Castle and its gardens belonged to Angus McAllister, but his mind was so filled with admiration and gratitude that he refrained from doing so. He looked at the girl almost reverently. Not content with controlling savage dogs with a mere word, this super-woman actually threw stones at Angus McAllister—a thing which he had never been able to nerve himself to do in an association which had lasted nine years—and, what was more, copped him on the shin with them. What nonsense, Lord Emsworth felt, the papers talked about the Modern Girl. If this was a specimen, the Modern Girl was the highest point the sex had yet reached.

"Ern," said Gladys, changing the subject, "is wearin' 'air-oil todiy."

Lord Emsworth had already observed this and had, indeed, been moving to windward as she spoke.

"For the Feet," explained Gladys.

"For the feet?" It seemed unusual.

"For the Feet in the park this afternoon."

"Oh, you are going to the Fête?"

"Yes, sir, thank you, sir."

For the first time, Lord Emsworth found himself regarding the grisly social event with something approaching favour.

"We must look out for one another there," he said cordially. "You will remember me again? I shall be wearing"—he gulped—"a top hat."

"Ern's going to wear a stror penamaw that's been give 'em."

Lord Emsworth regarded the lucky young devil with frank envy. He rather fancied he knew that panama. It had been his constant companion for some six years and then had been torn from him by his sister Constance and handed over to the vicar's wife for her rummage-sale.

He sighed.

"Well, good-bye."

"Good-bye, sir. Thank you, sir."

Lord Emsworth walked pensively out of the garden and, turning into the little street, encountered Lady Constance.

"Oh, there you are, Clarence."

"Yes," said Lord Emsworth, for such was the case.

"Have you finished judging the gardens?"

"Yes."

"I am just going into this end cottage here. The vicar tells me there is a little girl from London staying there. I want to warn her to behave this afternoon. I have spoken to the others."

Lord Emsworth drew himself up. His pince-nez were slightly askew, but despite this his gaze was commanding and impressive.

"Well, mind what you say," he said authoritatively. "None of your district-visiting stuff, Constance."

"What do you mean?"

"You know what I mean. I have the greatest respect for the

young lady to whom you refer. She behaved on a certain recent occasion—on two recent occasions—with notable gallantry and resource, and I won't have her ballyragged. Understand that!"

The technical title of the orgy which broke out annually on the first Monday in August in the park of Blandings Castle was the Blandings Parva School Treat, and it seemed to Lord Emsworth, wanly watching the proceedings from under the shadow of his top hat, that if this was the sort of thing schools looked on as pleasure he and they were mentally poles apart. A function like the Blandings Parva School Treat blurred his conception of Man as Nature's Final Word.

The decent sheep and cattle to whom this park normally belonged had been hustled away into regions unknown, leaving the smooth expanse of turf to children whose vivacity scared Lord Emsworth and adults who appeared to him to have cast aside all dignity and every other noble quality which goes to make a one hundred per cent British citizen. Look at Mrs. Rossiter over there, for instance, the wife of Jno. Rossiter, Provisions, Groceries and Home-Made Jams. On any other day of the year, when you met her, Mrs. Rossiter was a nice, quiet, docile woman who gave at the knees respectfully as you passed. To-day, flushed in the face and with her bonnet on one side, she seemed to have gone completely native. She was wandering to and fro drinking lemonade out of a bottle and employing her mouth, when not so occupied, to make a devastating noise with what he believed was termed a squeaker.

The injustice of the thing stung Lord Emsworth. This park was his own private park. What right had people to come and blow squeakers in it? How would Mrs. Rossiter like it if one afternoon he suddenly invaded her neat little garden in the High Street and rushed about over her lawn, blowing a squeaker?

And it was always on these occasions so infernally hot. July might have ended in a flurry of snow, but directly the first

Monday in August arrived and he had to put on a stiff collar out came the sun, blazing with tropic fury.

Of course, admitted Lord Emsworth, for he was a fair-minded man, this cut both ways. The hotter the day, the more quickly his collar lost its starch and ceased to spike him like a javelin. This afternoon, for instance, it had resolved itself almost immediately into something which felt like a wet compress. Severe as were his sufferings, he was compelled to recognize that he was that much ahead of the game.

A masterful figure loomed at his side.

"Clarence!"

Lord Emsworth's mental and spiritual state was now such that not even the advent of his sister Constance could add noticeably to his discomfort.

"Clarence, you look a perfect sight."

"I know I do. Who wouldn't in a rig-out like this? Why in the name of goodness you always insist. . . ."

"Please don't be childish, Clarence. I cannot understand the fuss you make about dressing for once in your life like a reasonable English gentleman and not like a tramp."

"It's this top hat. It's exciting the children."

"What on earth do you mean, exciting the children?"

"Well, all I can tell you is that just now, as I was passing the place where they're playing football—Football! In weather like this!—a small boy called out something derogatory and threw a portion of a coco-nut at it."

"If you will identify the child," said Lady Constance warmly, "I will have him severely punished."

"How the dickens," replied his lordship with equal warmth, "can I identify the child? They all look alike to me. And if I did identify him, I would shake him by the hand. A boy who throws coco-nuts at top hats is fundamentally sound in his views. And stiff collars. . . ."

"Stiff! That's what I came to speak to you about. Are you aware that your collar looks like a rag? Go in and change it at once."

"But my dear Constance. . . ."

"At once, Clarence. I simply cannot understand a man having so little pride in his appearance. But all your life you have been like that. I remember when we were children . . ."

Lord Emsworth's past was not of such a purity that he was prepared to stand and listen to it being lectured on by a sister with a good memory.

"Oh, all right, all right, all right," he said. "I'll change it, I'll change it."

"Well, hurry. They are just starting tea."

Lord Emsworth quivered.

"Have I got to go into that tea-tent?"

"Of course you have. Don't be so ridiculous. I do wish you would realize your position. As master of Blandings Castle . . ."

A bitter, mirthless laugh from the poor peon thus ludicrously described drowned the rest of the sentence.

It always seemed to Lord Emsworth, in analysing these entertainments, that the August Bank Holiday Saturnalia at Blandings Castle reached a peak of repulsiveness when tea was served in the big marquee. Tea over, the agony abated, to become acute once more at the moment when he stepped to the edge of the platform and cleared his throat and tried to recollect what the deuce he had planned to say to the goggling audience beneath him. After that, it subsided again and passed until the following August.

Conditions during the tea hour, the marquee having stood all day under a blazing sun, were generally such that Shadrach, Meshach and Abednego, had they been there, could have learned something new about burning fiery furnaces. Lord Emsworth, delayed by the revision of his toilet, made his entry when the meal was half over and was pleased to find that his second collar almost instantaneously began to relax its grip. That, however, was the only gleam of happiness which was to be vouchsafed him. Once in the tent, it took his experienced eye but a moment to discern that the present feast was eclipsing in frightfulness all its predecessors.

Young Blandings Parva, in its normal form, tended rather to the stolidly bovine than the riotous. In all villages, of course, there must of necessity be an occasional tough egg—in the case of Blandings Parva the names of Willie Drake and Thomas (Rat-Face) Blenkiron spring to the mind—but it was seldom that the local infants offered anything beyond the power of a curate to control. What was giving the present gathering its striking resemblance to a reunion of *sans-culottes* at the height of the French Revolution was the admixture of the Fresh Air London visitors.

About the London child, reared among the tin cans and cabbage stalks of Drury Lane and Clare Market, there is a breezy insouciance which his country cousin lacks. Years of back-chat with annoyed parents and relatives have cured him of any tendency he may have had towards shyness, with the result that when he requires anything he grabs for it, and when he is amused by any slight peculiarity in the personal appearance of members of the governing classes he finds no difficulty in translating his thoughts into speech. Already, up and down the long tables, the curate's unfortunate squint was coming in for hearty comment, and the front teeth of one of the school-teachers ran it a close second for popularity. Lord Emsworth was not, as a rule, a man of swift inspirations, but it occurred to him at this juncture that it would be a prudent move to take off his top hat before his little guests observed it and appreciated its humorous possibilities.

The action was not, however, necessary. Even as he raised his hand a rock cake, singing through the air like a shell, took it off for him.

Lord Emsworth had had sufficient. Even Constance, unreasonable woman though she was, could hardly expect him to stay and beam genially under conditions like this. All civilized laws had obviously gone by the board and Anarchy reigned in the marquee. The curate was doing his best to form a provisional government consisting of himself and the two school-teachers, but there was only one man who could have coped adequately with the situation and that was King Herod, who

—regrettably—was not among those present. Feeling like some aristocrat of the old *régime* sneaking away from the tumbril, Lord Emsworth edged to the exit and withdrew.

Outside the marquee the world was quieter, but only comparatively so. What Lord Emsworth craved was solitude, and in all the broad park there seemed to be but one spot where it was to be had. This was a red-tiled shed, standing beside a small pond, used at happier times as a lounge or retiring-room for cattle. Hurrying thither, his lordship had just begun to revel in the cool, cow-scented dimness of its interior when from one of the dark corners, causing him to start and bite his tongue, there came the sound of a subdued sniff.

He turned. This was persecution. With the whole park to mess about in, why should an infernal child invade this one sanctuary of his? He spoke with angry sharpness. He came of a line of warrior ancestors and his fighting blood was up.

"Who's that?"

"Me, sir. Thank you, sir."

Only one person of Lord Emsworth's acquaintance was capable of expressing gratitude for having been barked at in such a tone. His wrath died away and remorse took its place. He felt like a man who in error has kicked a favourite dog.

"God bless my soul!" he exclaimed. "What in the world are you doing in a cow-shed?"

"Please, sir, I was put."

"Put? How do you mean, put? Why?"

"For pinching things, sir."

"Eh? What? Pinching things? Most extraordinary. What did you—er—pinch?"

"Two buns, two jem-sengwiches, two apples and a slicer cake."

The girl had come out of her corner and was standing correctly at attention. Force of habit had caused her to intone the list of the purloined articles in the sing-song voice in which she was wont to recite the multiplication-table at school, but Lord Emsworth could see that she was deeply moved. Tear-stains glistened on her face, and no Emsworth had ever been able to watch unstirred a woman's tears. The ninth Earl was visibly affected.

"Blow your nose," he said, hospitably extending his handkerchief.

"Yes, sir. Thank you, sir."

"What did you say you had pinched? Two buns . . ."

". . . Two jem-sengwiches, two apples and a slicer cake."

"Did you eat them?"

"No, sir. They wasn't for me. They was for Ern."

"Ern? Oh, ah, yes. Yes, to be sure. For Ern, eh?"

"Yes, sir."

"But why the dooce couldn't Ern have—er—pinched them for himself? Strong, able-bodied young feller, I mean."

Lord Emsworth, a member of the old school, did not like this disposition on the part of the modern young man to shirk the dirty work and let the woman pay.

"Ern wasn't allowed to come to the treat, sir."

"What! Not allowed? Who said he mustn't?"

"The lidy, sir."

"What lidy?"

"The one that come in just after you'd gorn this morning."

A fierce snort escaped Lord Emsworth. Constance! What the devil did Constance mean by taking it upon herself to revise his list of guests without so much as a . . . Constance, eh? He snorted again. One of these days Constance would go too far.

"Monstrous!" he cried.

"Yes, sir."

"High-handed tyranny, by Gad. Did she give any reason?"

"The lidy didn't like Ern biting 'er in the leg, sir."

"Ern bit her in the leg?"

"Yes, sir. Pliying 'e was a dorg. And the lidy was cross and Ern wasn't allowed to come to the treat, and I told 'im I'd bring 'im back somefing nice."

Lord Emsworth breathed heavily. He had not supposed that in these degenerate days a family like this existed. The sister copped Angus McAllister on the shin with stones, the brother bit Constance in the leg. . . . It was like listening to some grand old saga of the exploits of heroes and demigods.

"I thought if I didn't 'ave nothing myself it would make it all right."

"Nothing?" Lord Emsworth started. "Do you mean to tell me you have not had tea?"

"No, sir. Thank you, sir. I thought if I didn't 'ave none, then it would be all right Ern 'aving what I would 'ave 'ad if I 'ad 'ave 'ad."

His lordship's head, never strong, swam a little. Then it resumed its equilibrium. He caught her drift.

"God bless my soul!" said Lord Emsworth. "I never heard anything so monstrous and appalling in my life. Come with me immediately."

"The lidy said I was to stop 'ere, sir."

Lord Emsworth gave vent to his loudest snort of the afternoon.

"Confound the lidy!"

"Yes, sir. Thank you, sir."

Five minutes later Beach, the butler, enjoying a siesta in the housekeeper's room, was roused from his slumbers by the unexpected ringing of a bell. Answering its summons, he found his employer in the library, and with him a surprising young person in a velveteen frock, at the sight of whom his eyebrows quivered and, but for his iron self-restraint, would have risen.

"Beach!"

"Your lordship?"

"This young lady would like some tea."

"Very good, your lordship."

"Buns, you know. And apples, and jem—I mean jam-sandwiches, and cake, and that sort of thing."

"Very good, your lordship."

"And she has a brother, Beach."

"Indeed, your lordship?"

"She will want to take some stuff away for him." Lord

Emsworth turned to his guest. "Ernest would like a little chicken, perhaps?"

"Coo!"

"I beg your pardon?"

"Yes, sir. Thank you, sir."

"And a slice or two of ham?"

"Yes, sir. Thank you, sir."

"And—he has no gouty tendency?"

"No, sir. Thank you, sir."

"Capital! Then a bottle of that new lot of port, Beach. It's some stuff they've sent me down to try," explained his lordship. "Nothing special, you understand," he added apologetically, "but quite drinkable. I should like your brother's opinion of it. See that all that is put together in a parcel, Beach, and leave it on the table in the hall. We will pick it up as we go out."

A welcome coolness had crept into the evening air by the time Lord Emsworth and his guest came out of the great door of the castle. Gladys, holding her host's hand and clutching the parcel, sighed contentedly. She had done herself well at the tea-table. Life seemed to have nothing more to offer.

Lord Emsworth did not share this view. His spacious mood had not yet exhausted itself.

"Now, is there anything else you can think of that Ernest would like?" he asked. "If so, do not hesitate to mention it. Beach, can you think of anything?"

The butler, hovering respectfully, was unable to do so.

"No, your lordship. I ventured to add—on my own responsibility, your lordship—some hard-boiled eggs and a pot of jam to the parcel."

"Excellent! You are sure there is nothing else?"

A wistful look came into Gladys's eyes.

"Could he 'ave some flarze?"

"Certainly," said Lord Emsworth. "Certainly, certainly, certainly. By all means. Just what I was about to suggest my —er—what *is* flarze?"

Beach, the linguist, interpreted.

"I think the young lady means flowers, your lordship."

"Yes, sir. Thank you, sir. Flarze."

"Oh?" said Lord Emsworth. "Oh? Flarze?" he said slowly. "Oh, ah, yes. Yes. I see. H'm!"

He removed his pince-nez, wiped them thoughtfully, replaced them and gazed with wrinkling forehead at the gardens that stretched gaily out before him. Flarze! It would be idle to deny that those gardens contained flarze in full measure. They were bright with Achillea, Bignonia Radicans, Campanula, Digitalis, Euphorbia, Funkia, Gypsophila, Helianthus, Iris, Liatris, Monarda, Phlox Drummondi, Salvia, Thalictrum, Vinca and Yucca. But the devil of it was that Angus McAllister would have a fit if they were picked. Across the threshold of this Eden the ginger whiskers of Angus McAllister lay like a flaming sword.

As a general rule, the precedure for getting flowers out of Angus McAllister was as follows. You waited till he was in one of his rare moods of complaisance, then you led the conversation gently round to the subject of interior decoration, and then, choosing your moment, you asked if he could possibly spare a few to be put in vases. The last thing you thought of doing was to charge in and start helping yourself.

"I—er— . . ." said Lord Emsworth.

He stopped. In a sudden blinding flash of clear vision he had seen himself for what he was—the spineless, unspeakably unworthy descendant of ancestors who, though they may have had their faults, had certainly known how to handle employees. It was "How now, varlet!" and "Marry come up, thou malapert knave!" in the days of previous Earls of Emsworth. Of course, they had possessed certain advantages which he lacked. It undoubtedly helped a man in his dealings with the domestic staff to have, as they had had, the rights of the high, the middle and the low justice—which meant, broadly, that if you got annoyed with your head-gardener you could immediately divide him into four head-gardeners with a battle-axe and no questions asked—but even so, he realized that they were better men than he was and that, if he allowed craven fear of Angus McAllister to stand in the way of this delightful girl and her charming brother getting all the flowers they required, he was not worthy to be the last of their line.

Lord Emsworth wrestled with his tremors.

"Certainly, certainly, certainly," he said, though not without a qualm. "Take as many as you want."

And so it came about that Angus McAllister, crouched in his potting-shed like some dangerous beast in its den, beheld a sight which first froze his blood and then sent it boiling through his veins. Flitting to and fro through his sacred gardens, picking his sacred flowers, was a small girl in a velveteen frock. And—which brought apoplexy a step closer—it was the same small girl who two days before had copped him on the shin with a stone. The stillness of the summer evening was shattered by a roar that sounded like boilers exploding, and Angus McAllister came out of the potting-shed at forty-five miles per hour. Gladys did not linger. She was a London child, trained from infancy to bear herself gallantly in the presence of alarms and excursions, but this excursion had been so sudden that it momentarily broke her nerve. With a horrified yelp she scuttled to where Lord Emsworth stood and, hiding behind him, clutched the tails of his morning-coat.

"Oo-er!" said Gladys.

Lord Emsworth was not feeling so frightfully good himself. We have pictured him a few moments back drawing inspiration from the nobility of his ancestors and saying, in effect, "That for McAllister!" but truth now compels us to admit that this hardy attitude was largely due to the fact that he believed the head-gardener to be a safe quarter of a mile away among the swings and roundabouts of the Fête. The spectacle of the man charging vengefully down on him with gleaming eyes and bristling whiskers made him feel like a nervous English infantryman at the Battle of Bannockburn. His knees shook and the soul within him quivered.

And then something happened, and the whole aspect of the situation changed.

It was, in itself, quite a trivial thing, but it had an astoundingly stimulating effect on Lord Emsworth's morale. What happened was that Gladys, seeking further protection, slipped at this moment a small, hot hand into his.

It was a mute vote of confidence, and Lord Emsworth intended to be worthy of it.

"He's coming," whispered his lordship's Inferiority Complex agitatedly.

"What of it?" replied Lord Emsworth stoutly.

"Tick him off," breathed his lordship's ancestors in his other ear.

"Leave it to me," replied Lord Emsworth.

He drew himself up and adjusted his pince-nez. He felt filled with a cool masterfulness. If the man tendered his resignation, let him tender his damned resignation.

"Well, McAllister?" said Lord Emsworth coldly.

He removed his top hat and brushed it against his sleeve.

"What is the matter, McAllister?"

He replaced his top hat.

"You appear agitated, McAllister."

He jerked his head militantly. The hat fell off. He let it lie. Freed from its loathsome weight he felt more masterful than ever. It had just needed that to bring him to the top of his form.

"This young lady," said Lord Emsworth, "has my full permission to pick all the flowers she wants, McAllister. If you do not see eye to eye with me in this matter, McAllister, say so and we will discuss what you are going to do about it, McAllister. These gardens, McAllister, belong to me, and if you do not—er—appreciate that fact you will, no doubt, be able to find another employer—ah—more in tune with your views. I value your services highly, McAllister, but I will not be dictated to in my own garden, McAllister. Er—dash it," added his lordship, spoiling the whole effect.

A long moment followed in which Nature stood still, breathless. The Achillea stood still. So did the Bignonia Radicans. So did the Campanula, the Digitalis, the Euphorbia, the Funkia, the Gypsophila, the Helianthus, the Iris, the Liatris, the Monarda, the Phlox Drummondi, the Salvia, the Thalictrum, the Vinca and the Yucca. From far off in the direction of the park there sounded the happy howls of children who were probably breaking things, but even these seemed hushed. The evening breeze had died away.

Angus McAllister stood glowering. His attitude was that of one sorely perplexed. So might the early bird have looked if the worm ear-marked for its breakfast had suddenly turned and snapped at it. It had never occurred to him that his employer would voluntarily suggest that he sought another position, and now that he had suggested it Angus McAllister disliked the idea very much. Blandings Castle was in his bones. Elsewhere, he would feel an exile. He fingered his whiskers, but they gave him no comfort.

He made his decision. Better to cease to be a Napoleon than be a Napoleon in exile.

"Mphm," said Angus McAllister.

"Oh, and by the way, McAllister," said Lord Emsworth, "that matter of the gravel path through the yew alley. I've been thinking it over, and I won't have it. Not on any account. Mutilate my beautiful moss with a beastly gravel path? Make an eyesore of the loveliest spot in one of the finest and oldest gardens in the United Kingdom? Certainly not. Most decidedly not. Try to remember, McAllister, as you work in the gardens of Blandings Castle, that you are not back in Glasgow, laying out recreation grounds. That is all, McAllister. Er—dash it—that is all."

"Mphm," said Angus McAllister.

He turned. He walked away. The potting-shed swallowed him up. Nature resumed its breathing. The breeze began to blow again. And all over the gardens birds which had stopped on their high note carried on according to plan.

Lord Emsworth took out his handkerchief and dabbed with it at his forehead. He was shaken, but a novel sense of being a man among men thrilled him. It might seem bravado, but he almost wished—yes, dash it, he almost wished—that his sister

125

Constance would come along and start something while he felt like this.

He had his wish.

"Clarence!"

Yes, there she was, hurrying towards him up the garden path. She, like McAllister, seemed agitated. Something was on her mind.

"Clarence!"

"Don't keep saying 'Clarence!' as if you were a dashed parrot," said Lord Emsworth haughtily. "What the dickens is the matter, Constance?"

"Matter? Do you know what the time is? Do you know that everybody is waiting down there for you to make your speech?"

Lord Emsworth met her eye sternly.

"I do not," he said. "And I don't care. I'm not going to make any dashed speech. If you want a speech, let the vicar make it. Or make it yourself. Speech! I never heard of such dashed nonsense in my life." He turned to Gladys. "Now, my dear," he said, "if you will just give me time to get out of these infernal clothes and this ghastly collar and put on something human, we'll go down to the village and have a chat with Ern."

*　　*　　*　　*　　*

He looked like a bishop who had just discovered Schism and Doubt among the minor clergy.

126

ONE MOMENT!

Before my friend, Mr. Jenkins—wait a minute, Herbert—before my friend Mr. Jenkins formally throws this book open to the public I should like to say a few words. You, sir, and you, and you at the back, if you will kindly restrain your impatience. . . . There is no need to jostle. There will be copies for all. Thank you. I shall not detain you long.

I wish to clear myself of a possible charge of plagiarism. You smile. Ah! but you don't know. You don't realise how careful even a splendid fellow like myself has to be. You wouldn't have me go down to posterity as Pelham the Pincher,

would you? No! Very well, then. By the time this volume is in the hands of the customers, everybody will, of course, have read Mr. J. Storer Clouston's *The Lunatic at Large Again*. (Those who are chumps enough to miss it deserve no consideration.) Well, both the hero of *The Lunatic* and my *Sam Marlowe* try to get out of a tight corner by hiding in a suit of armour in the hall of a country-house. Looks fishy, yes? And yet I call on Heaven to witness that I am innocent, innocent. And, if the word of Northumberland Avenue Wodehouse is not sufficient, let me point out that this story and Mr. Clouston's appeared simultaneously in serial form in their respective magazines. This proves, I think, that at these cross-roads, at any rate, there has been no dirty work. All right, Herb., you can let 'em in now.

Author's Foreword, " The Girl on the Boat."

*　　*　　*　　*　　*

"Ye-e-es," said Cyprian. " 'Myes. Ha! H'm. Hrrmph! The thing has rhythm, undoubted rhythm, and to a certain extent, certain inevitable curves. And yet can one conscientiously say that one altogether likes it? One fears one cannot."

"No?" said Ignatius.

"No," said Cyprian. He toyed with his left whisker. He seemed to be massaging it for purposes of his own. "One quite inevitably senses at a glance that the patina lacks vitality."

"Yes?" said Ignatius.

"Yes," said Cyprian.

THE FIRST TIME I WENT TO NEW YORK[1]

THE OTHER day I received a letter from one of our youngest literati, who has gone to America with the idea of establishing personal contacts, as they call it, with American publishers and—if the good old racket has not turned blue by this time—doing a bit of lecturing. The bulk of the communication is not of any great interest, dealing as it does almost entirely with the subject of how good the writer is, but it ends with a—to me—intensely significant passage.

As follows:

> *"I have placed my affairs on this side in the hands of a man named Jake Skolsky. I have given him a novel and some short stories to sell. He seems very capable and full of enthusiasm."*

It electrified me.

"Sweet suffering soupspoons!" I thought. "Can it be that old Jake is still alive? He must be a hundred. And, if alive, how on earth does he come to be alive? Has no one shot him in all this long time? It seems incredible."

And, as I mused, the years fell away, hair sprouted on the vast bare steppes of my head, where never hair has been almost within the memory of man, and I was once more a piefaced lad paying my first visit to New York.

Most people bring back certain definite impressions from their first visit to New York. They may be of the serious-minded type that wags its head and says, "What is the future of this great country?" or they may belong to the whimsical, frivolous brigade and write light essays on the difficulty they had in getting their shoes cleaned at the hotel; but to whichever class they are affiliated they are sure to speak of towering skyscrapers, majestic skylines, and the American girl.

[1] *Reproduced by kind permission of Messrs. Chapman and Hall from the book entitled: "The First Time I . . ."*

When I came home, people asked me in vain about these things. I did not remember them. I suppose they were there. No doubt there was a skyline. Even in those days there must have been skyscrapers. And the place, I should imagine, was full of American girls. But I was too preoccupied to notice them. My whole attention throughout my visit was absorbed by Jake Skolsky, the capable and enthusiastic literary agent.

As Nicholas Boileau-Despreaux (1636–1711) says in Bartlett's well-known "Book of Familiar Quotations," "Every age has its pleasures, its style of wit, and its own ways." And, one might add, its own literary agents. It is one of the compensations of advancing years that time seems to bring with it bigger and better literary agents. When you arrive at the stage where the question of Japanese second serial rights crops up, you have generally got somebody looking after your affairs incapable of pocketing a yen. But in one's early days to get paid for the outright sale of a short story was a wonderful adventure. Especially in America, if you were represented by Jake Skolsky.

If this sketch had been written twenty-five years ago, when the blood was hot and the agony of being gypped out of most of one's microscopic income still fresh and raw, I should probably have begun it with the words, "I call on Heaven to judge between this man and me." Or would I? Perhaps not, even then. For all through our association I could never quite bring myself to regard Jake as a fellow human being. He was always just a sort of Thing wriggling on the prismatic surface of New York life.

An old actor once told me of a club which used to exist during Buckstone's days at the Haymarket. At the meetings of the club the members sat round a big barrel, which had a hole in the top. Through this hole they were wont to throw any scraps and odds and ends they did not want. Bits of tobacco, bread, marrow bones, the dregs of their glasses—anything and everything went into the barrel. "And," said my informant, "as the barrel became fuller and fuller, strange animals made their appearance—animals of peculiar shape and form crawled out of the barrel and attempted to escape across the floor. But we headed them off with our sticks, sir, and we chased them back again into the place where they had been born and bred. We poked them in, sir, with our sticks."

Many a time when he was handling my affairs, I used to feel that Jake would have gone back into that barrel. And no questions asked, either, by its inhabitants. Just another of the boys, they would have said to themselves.

My first dealings with Jake were through the medium of the post. It was a medium to which, as I shall show later, he did not always trust, but he did so on this occasion, and very charming letters he wrote. I have lost them now, but I remember them. I had sent the MS. of a novel of mine, "Love Among the Chickens," to an English friend living in New York. Pressure of business compelled him to hand it over to a regular agent. He gave it to Jake. That was the expression he used in writing to me—"I am giving it to Jake Skolsky"— and I think Jake must have taken the word "giving" literally. Certainly, when the book was published in America, it had on its title page, "Copyright by Jacob Skolsky," and a few years later, when the story was sold for motion pictures, I was obliged to pay Jake two hundred and fifty dollars to release it.

For the book was published in America. I will say that for Jake—he sold not only the book rights but the serial rights, and at a price which seemed to me fantastic. A thousand dollars it was, and to one who, like myself, had never got above fifty pounds for a serial and whose record royalties for a book were eighteen pounds eleven and fourpence, a thousand dollars was more than merely good. It was great gravy. It made the whole world seem different. A wave of gratitude towards my benefactor swept over me. I felt like a man who has suddenly got in touch with a rich and benevolent uncle.

There was just one flaw in my happiness. The money seemed a long time coming. In the letter (a delightful letter) in which he informed me of the sale, Jake said that a draft would arrive on October 1st. But October came and went. "These busy New Yorkers," I said to myself. "They have so little time. I must be patient." By Christmas I was inclined to restlessness. In March I cabled, and received a reply, "Letter explaining. Cheque immediately." Late in April the old restlessness returned, for no explaining letter had arrived. Towards the middle of May I decided to go to New York. In several of his letters Jake had told me I was the coming man. I came.

Jake entered my life heralded by a cloud of smoke and the penetrating aroma of one of the most spirited young cigars I have ever encountered; a little vulture-like man with green eyes, yellow hands, a blue suit, a red tie, and grey hair. Quite a colour scheme he presented that pleasant May morning.

"Say, listen," said Jake.

It was an interesting story that he told. Sad, too. It seemed that where he had gone wrong was in trying to kill two birds with one stone. There was a charming girl of his acquaintance whom he wanted me to meet, and he also wanted me to get my cheque. And as this girl was leaving for England, the happy idea struck him to give her the cheque to take to me. By doing this, he would avoid all chance of having the letter get lost in the post and would enable his friend to meet me in circumstances where she would catch me at my best and sunniest—viz., while fingering a cheque for a thousand dollars.

But what he had failed to take into account was that she would visit Monte Carlo on her way to England. . . .

There being no Southern route in those days, this surprised me a little.

"Monte Carlo?" I said.

"Monte Carlo," said Jake.

"Monte *Carlo*?" I said.

"Monte Carlo," said Jake.

"But I didn't know . . . "

"Say, listen," said Jake.

He resumed his story. Yes, she had stopped off at Monte Carlo *en route*. But even then, mind you, it would have been all right if she had been by herself. She was a nice girl, who would never have dreamed of cashing a stranger's cheque. But her brother was with her, and he had fewer scruples. He gambled at the tables and lost; borrowed his sister's jewellery and lost again. After that, there was nothing left for him to do but fall back on my cheque.

"But don't you worry," said Jake, so moved, I remember, that he forgot to begin, "Say, listen." "You shall be paid. I will pay you myself. Yessir!"

And he gave me ten dollars and told me to get my hat and come along and see editors.

Jake had magnetism. In his presence I was but as a piece of chewed string. There were moments before we separated when I almost believed that story and thought it rather decent of him to let me have ten dollars. Ten dollars, I meant to say . . . just like that . . . right out of his own pocket. Pretty square.

His generalship was, I admit, consummate. He never ceased to keep moving. All that day we were dashing into elevators, dashing out, plunging into editorial offices ("Shake hands with Mr. Wodehouse"), plunging out, leaping into street cars, leaping out, till anything like rational and coherent thought was impossible.

He made only one tactical error. That was when he introduced me to the man to whom he had given my cheque.

He was an author from Kentucky. His experience had been practically identical with mine. He had sent his stories from Kentucky to a friend in New York, and the friend had handed them on to Jake, and Jake had sold them with magical skill, and then there had occurred that painful stage-wait in the matter of the cashing up. Eventually, when he was about twelve hundred dollars down, the author, breathing hot Southern maledictions, packed a revolver and started for New York.

I think Jake must have been a little out of sorts the morning they met. The best he could do in the way of a story was to say he had lost the money on Wall Street. Later, he handed the Kentuckian the cheque he had received from the magazine for my novel, asserting that he had sent me another for the same amount.

I did not see that there was anything to be done. New York at that time was full of men who did not see that there was anything to be done about Jake. He was so friendly about it all. When unmasked, he betrayed none of the baffled fury of the stage villain. He listened to you, and considered the matter with his head on one side, like a vulture accused of taking an eyeball to which it was not entitled.

"Why, say, yes," he would observe at length. "Say, listen, I want to have a talk with you about that some time."

You then intimated that there was no time like the present. You pressed him. You were keen and resolute. And then somehow—for the life of you you could not say how—you found all of a sudden that the subject of your wrongs had been shelved and that you were accepting with every sign of good-fellowship a poisonous cigar from his waistcoat pocket.

Yes, Jake had magnetism. Clients might come in upon him like lions, but they always went out like lambs. Not till they had been out from under the influence for a good hour or so did the realisation of their imbecile weakness smite them, and then it was too late. His office, when they revisited it, was empty. He was out somewhere, dashing into elevators, dashing out, plunging into editorial offices, plunging out, leaping into street cars, leaping out. And if by some miracle you did get hold of him, he just stuck his head on one side.

"Why, say, yes . . ."

And all the weary round started again.

Only one man ever got the better of Jake. And he, oddly enough, was not one of the tough story-writers who were or had been reporters, but a poet. Those were the days when New York magazines had rather a weakness for short, crisp, uplift poems calling on the youth of America to throw out its chest and be up and doing. They would print these on their front page, facing the table of contents, accompanied by pictures of semi-nude men with hammers or hoes or whatever it might be, and a magician like Jake could get a hundred dollars out of them per poem.

He had got a hundred dollars for one of this man's poems, and he gave him his cheque for it, less the customary agent's fee. The poet presented the cheque, and it came back marked "Insufficient funds."

You would have said that there was nothing to be done. Nor, in the case of a prose writer, would there have been. Undoubtedly I or my Kentucky friend or any of the rest of Jake's stable would have treated the thing as a routine situation and handled it in the routine way, going round to see Jake—more as a matter of form than anything—and watching him put his head on one side and proceeding through the "Why, say, yes" to the orthodox cigar.

But not the poet. He gave Jake's office boy two dollars to nose about among Jake's papers and find out what his balance at the bank was. Having discovered that it was $73.50, he paid in $26.50 to Jake's account without delay, presented his cheque again, and cleaned Jake out. Jake never really got over that. He said it wasn't the money so much, it was the principle of the thing. It hurt him, the deceitfulness of it in a man on whom he had always looked almost as a son.

There are moments, when I am feeling particularly charitable, when I fancy that it was in that relationship that Jake regarded all of us bright young men. I think he meant well. He knew the temptations which New York holds for the young when they have money in their pockets, and he shielded us from them. What he would really have liked would have been to hold a sort of paternal patriarchal position to his clients. He owned at that time—perhaps he owns it still—what he called a farm down on Staten Island. It looked as if there had once been a house there and somebody had pulled it down and left the tool shed, and he was very urgent in inviting each new client to live at this curious residence.

His ideal, I believe, was to have the place full of eager young men, all working away at their stories and running to him when they wanted a little pocket money. He would have charge of all the cash accruing from their writings and would dole it out bit by bit as needed. Up to the moment when he and I parted for ever he had succeeded in inducing few authors to see eye to eye with him in this matter.

Just after I had written the above, another letter arrived from my friend in America.

"I am having a little trouble with Jake Skolsky," he writes. *"He is unquestionably an excellent man and has sold a number of my things, but I find it extraordinarily difficult to get the money from him. However, I have written him a note, informing him that unless he pays up I must place the matter in the hands of a lawyer, so I expect things will shortly adjust themselves."*

It sounds all right, I own. On the surface it has all the appearance of being a clincher. But, unless the years have played havoc with the old pep and reduced him to a mere shell of the man he used to be, Jake will wriggle out of it somehow. He will see that lawyer and bring his magnetism into play. He will talk to him. He will give him a near-cigar. I should not be surprised if, before the interview is over, he does not borrow money from him.

Sometimes I wonder if I ought to have warned my friend when I got that first letter of his. Thinking it over, I fancy not. He is a young man at the outset of his career, and there is no question of the value of an association with Jake in the formative years of an author's life. Mine was the making of me. Critics to-day sometimes say that my work would be improved by being less morbid, but nobody has ever questioned its depth. That depth I owe to Jake. (He owes me about two thousand dollars.)

THE FIERY WOOING OF MORDRED

THE pint of Lager breathed heavily through his nose.

"Silly fathead!" he said. "Ash-trays in every nook and cranny of the room—ash-trays staring you in the eye wherever you look—and he has to go and do a fool thing like that."

He was alluding to a young gentleman with a vacant, fishlike face who, leaving the bar-parlour of the Angler's Rest a few moments before, had thrown his cigarette into the wastepaper basket, causing it to burst into a cheerful blaze. Not one of the little company of amateur fire-fighters but was ruffled. A Small Bass with a high blood pressure had had to have his collar loosened, and the satin-clad bosom of Miss Postlethwaite, our emotional barmaid, was still heaving.

Only Mr. Mulliner seemed disposed to take a tolerant view of what had occurred.

"In fairness to the lad," he pointed out, sipping his hot Scotch and lemon, "we must remember that our bar-parlour contains no grand piano or priceless old walnut table, which to the younger generation are the normal and natural repositories for lighted cigarette-ends. Failing these, he, of course, selected the waste-paper basket. Like Mordred."

"Like who?" asked a Whisky and Splash.

"Whom," corrected Miss Postlethwaite.

The Whisky and Splash apologized.

"A nephew of mine. Mordred Mulliner, the poet."

"Mordred," murmured Miss Postlethwaite pensively. "A sweet name."

"And one," said Mr. Mulliner, "that fitted him admirably, for he was a comely, lovable sensitive youth with large, fawn-like eyes, delicately chiselled features and excellent teeth. I mention these teeth, because it was owing to them that the train of events started which I am about to describe."

"He bit somebody?" queried Miss Postlethwaite, groping.

"No. But if he had had no teeth he would not have gone to the dentist's that day, and if he had not gone to the dentist's he would not have met Annabelle."

"Annabelle whom?"

"Who," corrected Miss Postlethwaite.

"Oh, shoot," said the Whisky and Splash.

"Annabelle Sprockett-Sprockett, the only daughter of Sir Murgatroyd and Lady Sprockett-Sprockett of Smattering Hall, Worcestershire. Impractical in many ways," said Mr. Mulliner, "Mordred never failed to visit his dentist every six months, and on the morning on which my story opens he had just seated himself in the empty waiting-room and was turning the pages of a three-months-old copy of the *Tatler* when the door opened and there entered a girl at the sight of whom —or who, if our friend here prefers it—something seemed to explode on the left side of his chest like a bomb. The *Tatler* swam before his eyes, and when it solidified again he realized that love had come to him at last."

Most of the Mulliners (said Mr. Mulliner) have fallen in love at first sight, but few with so good an excuse as Mordred. She was a singularly beautiful girl, and for a while it was this beauty of hers that enchained my nephew's attention to the exclusion of all else. It was only after he had sat gulping for some minutes like a dog with a chicken-bone in its throat that he detected the sadness in her face. He could see now that her eyes, as she listlessly perused her four-months-old copy of *Punch*, were heavy with pain.

His heart ached for her, and as there is something about the atmosphere of a dentist's waiting-room which breaks down the barriers of conventional etiquette he was emboldened to speak.

"Courage!" he said. "It may not be so bad, after all. He may just fool about with that little mirror thing of his, and decide that there is nothing that needs to be done."

For the first time she smiled—faintly, but with sufficient breath to give Mordred another powerful jolt.

"I'm not worrying about the dentist," she explained. "My

trouble is that I live miles away in the country and only get a chance of coming to London about twice a year for about a couple of hours. I was hoping that I should be able to put in a long spell of window-shopping in Bond Street, but now I've got to wait goodness knows how long I don't suppose I shall have time to do a thing. My train goes at one-fifteen."

All the chivalry in Mordred came to the surface like a leaping trout.

"If you would care to take my place——"

"Oh, I couldn't."

"Please. I shall enjoy waiting. It will give me an opportunity of catching up with my reading."

"Well, if you really wouldn't mind——"

Considering that Mordred by this time was in the market to tackle dragons on her behalf or to climb the loftiest peak of the Alps to supply her with edelweiss, he was able to assure her that he did not mind. So in she went flashing at him a shy glance of gratitude which nearly doubled him up, and he lit a cigarette and fell into a reverie. And presently she came out and he sprang to his feet, courteously throwing his cigarette into the waste-paper basket.

She uttered a cry. Mordred recovered the cigarette.

"Silly of me," he said, with a deprecating laugh. "I'm always doing that. Absent-minded. I've burned two flats already this year."

She caught her breath.

"Burned to the ground?"

"Well, not to the ground. They were on the top floor."

"But you burned them?"

"Oh, yes. I burned them."

"Well, well!" She seemed to muse. "Well, good-bye, Mr.——"

"Mulliner. Mordred Mulliner."

"Good-bye, Mr. Mulliner, and thank you so much."

"Not at all, Miss——"

"Sprockett-Sprockett."

"Not at all, Miss Sprockett-Sprockett. A pleasure."

She passed from the room, and a few minutes later he was lying back in the dentist's chair, filled with an infinite sadness. This was not due to any activity on the part of the dentist, who had just said with a rueful sigh that there didn't seem to be anything to do this time, but to the fact that his life was now a blank. He loved this beautiful girl, and he would never see her more. It was just another case of ships that pass in the waiting-room. Conceive his astonishment, therefore, when by the afternoon post next day he received a letter which ran as follows:

> Smattering Hall,
>> Lower Smattering-on-the-Wissel,
>>> Worcestershire.
>
> DEAR MR. MULLINER,
> My little girl has told me how very kind you were to her at the dentist's to-day. I cannot tell you how grateful she was. She does so love to walk down Bond Street and breathe on the jewellers' windows, and but for you she would have had to go another six months without her little treat.
>
> I suppose you are a very busy man, like everybody in London, but if you can spare the time it would give my husband and myself so much pleasure if you could run down and stay with us for a few days—a long week-end, or even longer if you can manage it.
>> With best wishes,
>>> Yours sincerely,
>>>> AURELIA SPROCKETT-SPROCKETT.

Mordred read this communication six times in a minute and a quarter and then seventeen times rather more slowly in order to savour any *nuance* of it that he might have overlooked. He took it that the girl must have got his address from the dentist's secretary on her way out, and he was doubly thrilled—first, by this evidence that one so lovely was as intelligent as she was beautiful, and secondly because the whole thing seemed to him so frightfully significant. A girl, he meant to say, does not get her mother to invite fellows to her country home for long week-ends (or even longer if they can manage it) unless such fellows have made a pretty substantial hit with her. This, he contended, stood to reason.

He hastened to the nearest post-office, despatched a telegram to Lady Sprockett-Sprockett assuring her that he would be with her on the morrow, and returned to his flat to pack his effects. His heart was singing within him. Apart from anything else, the invitation could not have come at a more fortunate moment, for what with musing of his great love while smoking cigarettes he had practically gutted his little nest of the previous evening, and while it was still habitable in a sense there was no gain-saying the fact that all those charred sofas and things struck a rather melancholy note and he would be glad to be away from it all for a few days.

It seemed to Mordred, as he travelled down on the following afternoon, that the wheels of the train, clattering over the metals, were singing "Sprockett-Sprockett"—not "Annabelle," of course, for he did not yet know her name—and it was with a whispered "Sprockett-Sprockett" on his lips that he alighted at the little station of Smattering-cum-Blimpstead-in-the-Vale, which, as his hostess's notepaper had informed him, was where you got off for the Hall. And when he perceived that the girl herself had come to meet him in a two-seater car the whisper nearly became a shout.

For perhaps three minutes, as he sat beside her, Mordred remained in this condition of ecstatic bliss. Here he was, he reflected, and here she was—here, in fact, they both were—together, and he was just about to point out how jolly this was and—if he could work it without seeming to rush things too much—to drop a hint to the effect that he could wish this state of affairs to continue through all eternity, when the girl drew up outside a tobacconist's.

"I won't be a minute," she said. "I promised Biffy I would bring him back some cigarettes."

A cold hand seemed to lay itself on Mordred's heart.

"Biffy?"

"Captain Biffing, one of the men at the Hall. And Guffy wants some pipe-cleaners."

"Guffy?"

"Jack Guffington. I expect you know his name, if you are interested in racing. He was third in last year's Grand National."

"Is he staying at the Hall, too?"

"Yes."

"You have a large house-party?"

"Oh, not so very. Let me see. There's Billy Biffing, Jack Guffington, Ted Prosser, Freddie Boot—he's the tennis champion of the county, Tommy Mainprice, and—oh, yes, Algy Fripp—the big-game hunter, you know."

The hand on Mordred's heart, now definitely iced, tightened its grip. With a lover's sanguine optimism, he had supposed that this visit of his was going to be just three days of jolly sylvan solitude with Annabelle Sprockett-Sprockett. And now it appeared that the place was unwholesomely crowded with his fellow men. And what fellow men! Big-game hunters . . . Tennis champions. . . . Chaps who rode in Grand Nationals. . . . He could see them in his mind's eye —lean, wiry, riding-breeched and flannel-trousered young Apollos, any one of them capable of cutting out his weight in Clark Gables.

A faint hope stirred within him.

"You have also, of course, with you Mrs. Biffing, Mrs. Guffington, Mrs. Prosser, Mrs. Boot, Mrs. Mainprice and Mrs. Algernon Fripp?"

"Oh, no, they aren't married."

"None of them?"

"No."

The faint hope coughed quietly and died.

"Ah," said Mordred.

While the girl was in the shop, he remained brooding. The fact that not one of these blisters should be married filled him with an austere disapproval. If they had had the least spark of civic sense, he felt, they would have taken on the duties and responsibilities of matrimony years ago. But no. Intent upon their selfish pleasures, they had callously remained bachelors. It was this spirit of *laissez-faire*, Mordred considered, that was eating like a canker into the soul of England.

He was aware of Annabelle standing beside him.

"Eh?" he said, starting.

"I was saying: 'Have you plenty of cigarettes?'"

"Plenty, thank you."

"Good. And of course there will be a box in your room. Men always like to smoke in their bedrooms, don't they? As a matter of fact, two boxes—Turkish and Virginian. Father put them there specially."

"Very kind of him," said Mordred mechanically.

He relapsed into a moody silence, and they drove off.

It would be agreeable (said Mr. Mulliner) if, having shown you my nephew so gloomy, so apprehensive, so tortured with dark forebodings at this juncture, I were able now to state that the hearty English welcome of Sir Murgatroyd and Lady Sprockett-Sprockett on his arrival at the Hall cheered him up and put new life into him. Nothing, too, would give me greater pleasure than to say that he found, on encountering the dreaded Biffies and Guffies, that they were negligible little runts with faces incapable of inspiring affection in any good woman.

But I must adhere rigidly to the facts. Genial, even effusive, though his host and hostess showed themselves, their cordiality left him cold. And, so far from his rivals being weeds, they were one and all models of manly beauty, and the spectacle of their obvious worship of Annabelle cut my nephew like a knife.

And on top of all this there was Smattering Hall itself.

Smattering Hall destroyed Mordred's last hope. It was one of those vast edifices, so common throughout the countryside of England, whose original founders seem to have budgeted for families of twenty-five or so and a domestic staff of not less than a hundred. "Home isn't home," one can picture them

143

saying to themselves, "unless you have plenty of elbow room." And so this huge, majestic pile had come into being. Romantic persons, confronted with it, thought of knights in armour riding forth to the Crusades. More earthly individuals felt that it must cost a packet to keep up. Mordred's reaction on passing through the front door was a sort of sick sensation, a kind of settled despair.

How, he asked himself, even assuming that by some miracle he succeeded in fighting his way to her heart through all these Biffies and Guffies, could he ever dare to take Annabelle from a home like this? He had quite satisfactory private means, of course, and would be able, when married, to give up the bachelor flat and spread himself to something on a bigger scale—possibly, if sufficiently *bijou*, even a desirable residence in the Mayfair district. But after Smattering Hall would not Annabelle feel like a sardine in the largest of London houses?

Such were the dark thoughts that raced through Mordred's brain before, during and after dinner. At eleven o'clock he pleaded fatigue after his journey, and Sir Murgatroyd accompanied him to his room, anxious, like a good host, to see that everything was comfortable.

"Very sensible of you to turn in early," he said, in his bluff, genial way. "So many young men ruin their health with late hours. Now you, I imagine, will just get into a dressing-gown and smoke a cigarette or two and have the light out by twelve. You have plenty of cigarettes? I told them to see that you were well supplied. I always think the bedroom smoke is the best one of the day. Nobody to disturb you, and all that. If you want to write letters or anything, there is lots of paper, and here is the waste-paper basket, which is always so necessary. Well, good night, my boy, good night."

The door closed, and Mordred, as foreshadowed, got into a dressing-gown and lit a cigarette. But though, having done this, he made his way to the writing-table, it was not with any idea of getting abreast of his correspondence. It was his purpose to compose a poem to Annabelle Sprockett-Sprockett.

144

He had felt it seething within him all the evening, and sleep would be impossible until it was out of his system.

Hitherto, I should mention, my nephew's poetry, for he belonged to the modern fearless school, had always been stark and rhymeless and had dealt principally with corpses and the smell of cooking cabbage. But now, with the moonlight silvering the balcony outside, he found that his mind had become full of words like "love" and "dove" and "eyes" and "summer skies."

> *Blue eyes*, wrote Mordred . . .
>   *Sweet lips*, wrote Mordred . . .
> *Oh, eyes like skies of summer blue* . . .
> *Oh, love* . . .
> *Oh, dove* . . .
> *Oh, lips* . . .

With a muttered ejaculation of chagrin he tore the sheet across and threw it into the waste-paper basket.

Blue eyes that burn into my soul,
    Sweet lips that smile my heart away
Pom-pom, pom-pom, pom something whole (Goal?)
    And tiddly-iddly-umpty-ay (Gay? Say? Happy day?)

Blue eyes into my soul that burn,
    Sweet lips that smile away my heart,
Oh, something something turn or yearn
    And something something something part.

You burn into my soul, blue eyes,
You smile my heart away, sweet lips,
Short long short long of summer skies
    And something something something trips. (Hips?
Ships? Pips?)

He threw the sheet into the waste-paper basket and rose with a stifled oath. The waste-paper basket was nearly full now, and still his poet's sense told him that he had not achieved perfection. He thought he saw the reason for this. You can't just sit in a chair and expect inspiration to flow—you want to walk about and clutch your hair and snap your fingers. It had been his intention to pace the room, but the moonlight pouring in through the open window called to him. He went out on to the balcony. It was but a short distance to the dim, mysterious lawn. Impulsively he dropped from the stone balustrade.

The effect was magical. Stimulated by the improved conditions, his Muse gave quick service, and this time he saw at once that she had rung the bell and delivered the goods. One turn up and down the lawn, and he was reciting as follows:

TO ANNABELLE

Oh, lips that smile! Oh, eyes that shine
    Like summer skies, or stars above!
Your beauty maddens me like wine,
    Oh, umpty-pumpty-tumty love!

And he was just wondering, for he was a severe critic of his own work, whether that last line couldn't be polished up a bit, when his eye was attracted by something that shone like summer skies or stars above and, looking more closely, he perceived that his bedroom curtains were on fire.

Now, I will not pretend that my nephew Mordred was in every respect the cool-headed man of action, but this happened to be a situation with which use had familiarized him. He knew the procedure.

"Fire!" he shouted.

A head appeared in an upstairs window. He recognized it as that of Captain Biffing.

"Eh?" said Captain Biffing.

"Fire!"

"What?"

"Fire!" vociferated Mordred. "F for Francis, I for Isabel..."

"Oh, fire?" said Captain Biffing. "Right ho."

And presently the house began to discharge its occupants.

In the proceedings which followed, Mordred, I fear, did not appear to the greatest advantage. This is an age of specialization, and if you take the specialist off his own particular ground he is at a loss. Mordred's genius, as we have seen, lay in the direction of starting fires. Putting them out called for quite different qualities, and these he did not possess. On the various occasions of holocausts at his series of flats, he had never attempted to play an active part, contenting himself with going downstairs and asking the janitor to step up and see what he could do about it. So now, though under the bright eyes of Annabelle Sprockett-Sprockett he would have given much to be able to dominate the scene, the truth is that the Biffies and Guffies simply played him off the stage.

His heart sank as he noted the hideous efficiency of these young men. They called for buckets. They formed a line. Freddie Boot leaped lissomely on to the balcony, and Algy Fripp, mounted on a wheel-barrow, handed up to him the necessary supplies. And after Mordred, trying to do his bit, had tripped up Jack Guffington and upset two buckets over Ted Prosser he was advised in set terms to withdraw into the background and stay there.

It was a black ten minutes for the unfortunate young man. One glance at Sir Murgatroyd's twisted face as he watched the operations was enough to tell him how desperately anxious the fine old man was for the safety of his ancestral home and how bitter would be his resentment against the person who had endangered it. And the same applied to Lady Sprockett-Sprockett and Annabelle. Mordred could see the anxiety in their eyes, and the thought that ere long those eyes must be turned accusingly on him chilled him to the marrow.

Presently, Freddie Boot emerged from the bedroom to announce that all was well.

"It's out," he said, jumping lightly down. "Anybody know whose room it was?"

Mordred felt a sickening qualm, but the splendid Mulliner courage sustained him. He stepped forward, white and tense.

"Mine," he said.

He became the instant centre of attention. The six young men looked at him.

"Yours?"

"Oh, yours, was it?"

"What happened?"

"How did it start?"

"Yes, how did it start?"

"Must have started somehow, I mean," said Captain Biffing, who was a clear thinker. "I mean to say, must have, don't you know, what?"

Mordred mastered his voice.

"I was smoking, and I suppose I threw my cigarette into the waste-paper basket, and as it was full of paper . . ."

"Full of paper? Why was it full of paper?"

"I had been writing a poem."

There was a stir of bewilderment.

"A what?" said Ted Prosser.

"Writing a what?" said Jack Guffington.

"Writing a *poem*?" asked Captain Biffing of Tommy Mainprice.

"That's how I got the story," said Tommy Mainprice, plainly shaken.

"Chap was writing a poem," Freddie Boot informed Algy Fripp.

"You mean the chap writes poems?"

"That's right. Poems."

"Well, I'm dashed!"

"Well, I'm blowed!"

Their now unconcealed scorn was hard to bear. Mordred chafed beneath it. The word "poem" was flitting from lip to lip, and it was only too evident that, had there been an "s" in the word, those present would have hissed it. Reason told him that these men were mere clods, Philistines, fatheads

148

who would not recognize the rare and the beautiful if you handed it to them on a skewer, but that did not seem to make it any better. He knew that he should be scorning them, but it is not easy to go about scorning people in a dressing-gown, especially if you have no socks on and the night breeze is cool around the ankles. So, as I say, he chafed. And finally, when he saw the butler bend down with pursed lips to the ear of the cook, who was a little hard of hearing, and after a contemptuous glance in his direction speak into it, spacing his syllables carefully, something within him seemed to snap.

"I regret, Sir Murgatroyd," he said, "that urgent family business compels me to return to London immediately. I shall be obliged to take the first train in the morning."

Without another word he went into the house.

In the matter of camping out in devastated areas my nephew had, of course, become by this time an old hand. It was rarely nowadays that a few ashes and cinders about the place disturbed him. But when he had returned to his bedroom one look was enough to assure him that nothing practical in the way of sleep was to be achieved here. Apart from the unpleasant, acrid smell of burned poetry, the apartment, thanks to the efforts of Freddie Boot, had been converted into a kind of inland sea. The carpet was awash, and on the bed only a duck could have made itself at home.

And so it came about that some ten minutes later Mordred Mulliner lay stretched upon a high-backed couch in the library, endeavouring by means of counting sheep jumping through a gap in a hedge to lull himself into unconsciousness.

But sleep refused to come. Nor in his heart had he really thought that it would. When the human soul is on the rack, it cannot just curl up and close its eyes and expect to get its eight hours as if nothing had happened. It was all very well for Mordred to count sheep, but what did this profit him when each sheep in turn assumed the features and lineaments of Annabelle Sprockett-Sprockett and, what was more, gave him a reproachful glance as it drew itself together for the spring?

Remorse gnawed him. He was tortured by a wild regret for what might have been. He was not saying that with all these Biffies and Guffies in the field he had ever had more than a hundred to eight chance of winning that lovely girl, but at least his hat had been in the ring. Now it was definitely out. Dreamy Mordred may have been—romantic—impractical—but he had enough sense to see that the very worst thing you can do when you are trying to make a favourable impression on the adored object is to set fire to her childhood home, every stick and stone of which she has no doubt worshipped since they put her into rompers.

He had reached this point in his meditations, and was about to send his two hundred and thirty-second sheep at the gap, when with a suddenness which affected him much as an explosion of gelignite would have done, the lights flashed on. For an instant, he lay quivering, then, cautiously poking his head round the corner of the couch, he looked to see who his visitors were.

It was a little party of three that had entered the room. First came Sir Murgatroyd, carrying a tray of sandwiches. He was followed by Lady Sprockett-Sprockett with a syphon and glasses. The rear was brought up by Annabelle, who was bearing a bottle of whisky and two dry ginger ales.

So evident was it that they were assembling here for purposes of a family council that, but for one circumstance, Mordred, to whom anything in the nature of eavesdropping was as repugnant as it has always been to all the Mulliners, would have sprung up with a polite "Excuse me" and taken his blanket elsewhere. This circumstance was the fact that on lying down he had kicked his slippers under the couch, well out of reach. The soul of modesty, he could not affront Annabelle with the spectacle of his bare toes.

So he lay there in silence, and silence, broken only by the swishing of soda-water and the *whoosh* of opened ginger-ale bottles, reigned in the room beyond.

Then Sir Murgatroyd spoke.

"Well, that's that," he said, bleakly.

There was a gurgle as Lady Sprockett-Sprockett drank ginger ale. Then her quiet, well-bred voice broke the pause.

"Yes," she said, "it is the end."

"The end," agreed Sir Murgatroyd heavily. "No good trying to struggle on against luck like ours. Here we are and here we have got to stay, mouldering on in this blasted barrack of a place which eats up every penny of my income when, but for the fussy interference of that gang of officious, ugly nitwits, there would have been nothing left of it but a pile of ashes, with a man from the Insurance Company standing on it with his fountain-pen, writing cheques. Curse those imbeciles! Did you see that young Fripp with those buckets?"

"I did, indeed," sighed Lady Sprockett-Sprockett.

"Annabelle," said Sir Murgatroyd sharply.

"Yes, Father?"

"It has seemed to me lately, watching you with a father's eye, that you have shown signs of being attracted by young Algernon Fripp. Let me tell you that if ever you allow yourself to be ensnared by his insidious wiles, or by those of William Biffing, John Guffington, Edward Prosser, Thomas Mainprice or Frederick Boot, you will do so over my dead body. After what occurred to-night, those young men shall never darken my door again. They and their buckets! To think that we could have gone and lived in London . . ."

"In a nice little flat . . ." said Lady Sprockett-Sprockett.

"Handy for my club . . ."

"Convenient for the shops . . ."

"Within a stone's throw of the theatres . . ."

"Seeing all our friends . . ."

"Had it not been," said Sir Murgatroyd, summing up, "for the pestilential activities of these Guffingtons, these Biffings, these insufferable Fripps, men who ought never to be trusted near a bucket of water when a mortgaged country-house has got nicely alight. I did think," proceeded the stricken old man, helping himself to a sandwich, "that when Annabelle, with a ready intelligence which I cannot over-praise, realized this young Mulliner's splendid gifts and made us ask him down here, the happy ending was in sight. What Smattering Hall has needed for generations has been a man who throws his cigarette-ends into waste-paper baskets. I was convinced that here at last was the angel of mercy we required."

"He did his best, Father."

"No man could have done more," agreed Sir Murgatroyd cordially. "The way he upset those buckets and kept getting entangled in people's legs. Very shrewd. It thrilled me to see him. I don't know when I've met a young fellow I liked and respected more. And what if he is a poet? Poets are all right. Why, dash it, I'm a poet myself. At the last dinner of the Loyal Sons of Worcestershire I composed a poem which, let me tell you, was pretty generally admired. I read it out to the boys over the port, and they cheered me to the echo. It was about a young lady of Bewdley, who some-times behaved rather rudely . . ."

"Not before Mother, Father."

"Perhaps you're right. Well, I'm off to bed. Come along, Aurelia. You coming, Annabelle?"

"Not yet, Father. I want to stay and think."

"Do what?"

"Think."

"Oh, think? Well, all right."

"But, Murgatroyd," said Lady Sprockett-Sprockett, "is there no hope? After all, there are plenty of cigarettes in the house, and we could always give Mr. Mulliner another waste-paper basket. . . ."

"No good. You heard him say he was leaving by the first train to-morrow. When I think that we shall never see that splendid young man again . . . Why, hullo, hullo, hullo, what's this? Crying, Annabelle?"

"Oh, Mother!"

"My darling, what is it?"

A choking sob escaped the girl.

"Mother, I love him! Directly I saw him in the dentist's waiting-room, something seemed to go all over me, and I knew that there could be no other man for me. And, now . . ."

"Hi!" cried Mordred, popping up over the side of the couch like a jack-in-the-box.

He had listened with growing understanding to the conversation which I have related, but had shrunk from revealing his presence because, as I say, his toes were bare. But this was too much. Toes or no toes, he felt that he must be in this.

"You love me, Annabelle?" he cried.

His sudden advent had occasioned, I need scarcely say, a certain reaction in those present. Sir Murgatroyd had leaped like a jumping bean. Lady Sprockett-Sprockett had quivered like a jelly. As for Annabelle, her lovely mouth was open to the extent of perhaps three inches, and she was staring like one who sees a vision.

"You really love me, Annabelle?"

"Yes, Mordred."

"Sir Murgatroyd," said Mordred formally, "I have the honour to ask you for your daughter's hand. I am only a poor poet . . ."

"How poor?" asked the other, keenly.

"I was referring to my Art," explained Mordred. "Financially, I am nicely fixed. I could support Annabelle in modest comfort."

"Then take her, my boy, take her. You will live, of course"—the old man winced—"in London?"

"Yes. And so shall you."

Sir Murgatroyd shook his head.

"No, no, that dream is ended. It is true that in certain circumstances I had hoped to do so, for the insurance, I may mention, amounts to as much as a hundred thousand pounds, but I am resigned now to spending the rest of my life in this infernal family vault. I see no reprieve."

"I understand," said Mordred, nodding. "You mean you have no paraffin in the house?"

Sir Murgatroyd started.

"Paraffin?"

"If," said Mordred, and his voice was very gentle and winning, "there had been paraffin on the premises, I think it possible that to-night's conflagration, doubtless imperfectly quenched, might have broken out again, this time with more serious results. It is often this way with fires. You pour buckets of water on them and think they are extinguished, but all the time they have been smouldering unnoticed, to break out once more in—well, in here for example."

"Or the billiard-room," said Lady Sprockett-Sprockett.

"*And* the billiard-room," corrected Sir Murgatroyd.

"And the billiard-room," said Mordred. "And possibly —who knows?—in the drawing-room, dining-room, kitchen, servants' hall, butler's pantry and the usual domestic offices, as well. Still, as you say you have no paraffin . . ."

"My boy," said Sir Murgatroyd, in a shaking voice, "what gave you the idea that we have no paraffin? How did you fall into this odd error? We have gallons of paraffin. The cellar is full of it."

"And Annabelle will show you the way to the cellar—in case you thought of going there," said Lady Sprockett-Sprockett. "Won't you, dear?"

"Of course, Mother. You will like the cellar, Mordred, darling. Most picturesque. Possibly, if you are interested in paraffin, you might also care to take a look at our little store of paper and shavings, too."

"My angel," said Mordred, tenderly, "you think of everything."

He found his slippers, and hand in hand they passed down the stairs. Above them, they could see the head of Sir Murgatroyd, as he leaned over the banisters. A box of matches fell at their feet like a father's benediction.

LE VODEOUSE

THE QUESTION of how long an author is to be allowed to go on recording the adventures of any given character or characters is one that has frequently engaged the attention of thinking men. The publication of this book brings it once again into the foreground of national affairs.

It is now some fourteen summers since, an eager lad in my early thirties, I started to write Jeeves stories: and many people think this nuisance should now cease. Carpers say that enough is enough. Cavillers say the same. They look down the vista of the years and see these chronicles multiplying like rabbits, and the prospect appals them. But against this must be set the fact that writing Jeeves stories gives me a great deal of pleasure, and keeps me out of the public-houses.

At what conclusion, then, do we arrive? The whole thing is undoubtedly very moot.

From the welter of recrimination and argument, one fact emerges—that we have here the third volume of a series. And what I do feel very strongly is that, if a thing is worth doing, it is worth doing well and thoroughly. It is perfectly possible, no doubt, to read *Very Good, Jeeves!* as a detached effort—or, indeed, not to read it at all: but I like to think that this country contains men of spirit who will not rest content till they have dug down into the old oak chest and fetched up the sum necessary for the purchase of its two predecessors—*The Inimitable Jeeves* and *Carry On, Jeeves!* Only so can the best results be obtained. Only so will allusions in the present volume to incidents occurring in the previous volumes become intelligible, instead of mystifying and befogging.

We do you these two books at the laughable price of half-a-crown apiece, and the method of acquiring them is simplicity itself.

All you have to do is to go to the nearest bookseller, when the following dialogue will take place:

Yourself.   Good morning, Mr. Bookseller.
Bookseller.   Good morning, Mr. Everyman.
Yourself.   I want *The Inimitable Jeeves* and *Carry On, Jeeves!*
Bookseller.   Certainly, Mr. Everyman. You make the easy payment of five shillings, and they will be delivered at your door in a plain van.
Yourself.   Good morning, Mr. Bookseller.
Bookseller.   Good morning, Mr. Everyman.

Or take the case of a French visitor to London, whom, for want of a better name, we will call Jules St. Xavier Popinot. In this instance the little scene will run on these lines:

AU COIN DE LIVRES

Popinot.   Bon jour, Monsieur le marchand de livres.
Marchand.   Bon jour, Monsieur. Quel beau temps aujourd'hui, n'est-ce-pas?
Popinot.   Absolument. Eskervous avez le *Jeeves Inimitable* et le *Continuez, Jeeves!* du maître Vodeouse?
Marchand.   Mais certainement, Monsieur.
Popinot.   Donnez-moi les deux, s'il vous plaît.

Marchand.	Oui, par exemple, morbleu. Et aussi la plume, l'encre, et la tante du jardinier?
Popinot.	Je m'en fiche de cela. Je désire seulement le Vodeouse.
Marchand.	Pas de chemises, de cravats, ou le tonic pour les cheveux?
Popinot.	Seulement, le Vodeouse, je vous assure.
Marchand.	Parfaitement, Monsieur. Deux-et-six pour chaque bibelot—exactement cinq roberts.
Popinot.	Bon jour, Monsieur.
Marchand.	Bon jour, Monsieur.

As simple as that.

See that the name "Wodehouse" is on every label.

Author's Preface, "Very Good, Jeeves!"

"I never gaze into his eyes. Don't like his eyes. Wouldn't gaze into them if you paid me. I maintain his whole outlook on life is morbid and unwholesome. I like a man to be a clean, strong, upstanding Englishman who can look his gnu in the face and put an ounce of lead in it."

"Life," said Charlotte coldly, "is not all gnus."

"You imply that there are also wapiti, moose, zebus and mountain-goats?" said Sir Francis. "Well, maybe you're right. All the same, I'd give the fellow a wide berth, if I were you."

MR. BENNETT AND THE BULLDOG, SMITH

"THERE WAS the lake, shining through the trees, a mere fifty yards away. What could be more refreshing? He shed his pyjamas, and climbed into the bathing-suit. And presently, looking like the sun on a foggy day, he emerged from the house and picked his way with gingerly steps across the smooth surface of the lawn.

At this moment, from behind a bush where he had been thriftily burying a yesterday's bone, Smith, the bulldog, waddled out on to the lawn. He drank in the exhilarating air through an upturned nose which his recent excavations had rendered somewhat muddy. Then he observed Mr. Bennett, and moved gladly towards him. He did not recognise Mr. Bennett, for he remembered his friends principally by their respective bouquets, so he cantered silently across the turf to take a sniff at him. He was half-way across the lawn when some of the mud which he had inhaled when burying the bone tickled his lungs and he paused to cough.

Mr. Bennett whirled round; and then with a sharp exclamation picked up his pink feet from the velvet turf and began to run. Smith, after a momentary pause of surprise, lumbered after him, wheezing contentedly. This man, he felt, was evidently one of the right sort, a merry playfellow.

Mr. Bennett continued to run; but already he had begun to pant and falter, when he perceived looming upon his left the ruins of that ancient castle which had so attracted him on his first visit. On that occasion it had made merely an aesthetic appeal to Mr. Bennett; now he saw in a flash that its practical merits also were of a sterling order. He swerved sharply, took the base of the edifice in his stride, clutched at a jutting stone, flung his foot at another, and, just as his pursuer arrived and sat panting below, pulled himself on to a ledge, where he sat with his feet hanging well out of reach. The bulldog, Smith, gazed up at him expectantly. The game was a new one to Smith, but it seemed to have possibilities. He was a dog who was always perfectly willing to try anything once.

Mr. Bennett now began to address himself in earnest to the task of calling for assistance. His physical discomfort was acute. Insects, some winged, some without wings but—through Nature's wonderful law of compensation—equipped with a number of extra pairs of legs, had begun to fit out exploring expeditions over his body. They roamed about him as if he were some newly opened recreation ground, strolled in couples down his neck, and made up jolly family parties on his bare feet. And then, first dropping like the gentle dew upon the place beneath, then swishing down in a steady flood, it began to rain."

*   *   *   *   *

"The steward was a man in the middle forties, and time had robbed him of practically all his hair, giving him in niggardly exchange a pink pimple on the side of his nose."

GOOD-BYE TO ALL CATS

As the club kitten sauntered into the smoking-room of the Drones Club and greeted those present with a friendly miauw, Freddie Widgeon, who had been sitting in a corner with his head between his hands, rose stiffly.

"I had supposed," he said, in a cold, level voice, "that this was a quiet retreat for gentlemen. As I perceive that it is a blasted Zoo, I will withdraw."

And he left the room in a marked manner.

There was a good deal of surprise, not unmixed with consternation.

"What's the trouble?" asked an Egg, concerned. Such exhibitions of the naked emotions are rare at the Drones. "Have they had a row?"

A Crumpet, always well-informed, shook his head.

"Freddie has had no personal breach with this particular kitten," he said. "It is simply that since that week-end at Matcham Scratchings he can't stand the sight of a cat."

"Matcham what?"

"Scratchings. The ancestral home of Dahlia Prenderby in Oxfordshire."

"I met Dahlia Prenderby once," said the Egg. "I thought she seemed a nice girl."

"Freddie thought so, too. He loved her madly."

"And lost her, of course?"

"Absolutely."

"Do you know," said a thoughtful Bean, "I'll bet that if all the girls Freddie Widgeon has loved and lost were placed end to end—not that I suppose one could do it—they would reach half-way down Piccadilly."

"Further than that," said the Egg. "Some of them were pretty tall. What beats me is why he ever bothers to love them. They always turn him down in the end. He might just as well never begin. Better, in fact, because in the time saved he could be reading some good book."

"I think the trouble with Freddie," said the Crumpet, "is that he always gets off to a flying start. He's a good-looking sort of chap who dances well and can wiggle his ears, and the girl is dazzled for the moment, and this encourages him. From what he tells me, he appears to have gone very big with this Prenderby girl at the outset. So much so, indeed, that when she invited him down to Matcham Scratch-ings he had already bought his copy of *What Every Young Bridegroom Ought to Know*."

"Rummy, these old country-house names," mused the Bean. "Why Scratchings, I wonder?"

"Freddie wondered, too, till he got to the place. Then he tells me he felt it was absolutely the *mot juste*. This girl Dahlia's family, you see, was one of those animal-loving families, and the house, he tells me, was just a frothing maelstrom of dumb chums. As far as the eye could reach, there were dogs scratching themselves and cats scratching the furniture. I believe, though he never met it socially, there was even a tame chimpanzee somewhere on the premises, no doubt scratching away as assiduously as the rest of them. You get these conditions here and there in the depths of the country, and this Matcham place was well away from the centre of things being about six miles from the nearest station."

It was at this station (said the Crumpet) that Dahlia Prenderby met Freddie in her two-seater, and on the way to the house there occurred a conversation which I consider significant—showing, as it does, the cordial relations existing between the young couple at that point in the proceedings. I mean, it was only later that the bitter awakening and all that sort of thing popped up.

"I do want you to be a success, Freddie," said the girl, after talking a while of this and that. "Some of the men I've asked down here have been such awful flops. The great thing is to make a good impression on Father."

"I will," said Freddie.

"He can be a little difficult at times."

"Lead me to him," said Freddie. "That's all I ask. Lead me to him."

"The trouble is, he doesn't much like young men."

"He'll like me."

"He will, will he?"

"Rather!"

"What makes you think that?"

"I'm a dashed fascinating chap."

"Oh, you are?"

"Yes, I am."

"You are, are you?"

"Rather!"

Upon which, she gave him a sort of push and he gave her a sort of push, and she giggled and he laughed like a paper bag bursting, and she gave him a kind of shove and he gave her a kind of shove, and she said "You *are* a silly ass!" and he said "What ho!" All of which shows you, I mean to say, the stage they had got to by this time. Nothing definitely settled, of course, but Love obviously beginning to burgeon in the girl's heart.

Well, naturally, Freddie gave a good deal of thought during the drive to this father of whom the girl had spoken so feelingly, and he resolved that he would not fail her. The way he would suck up to the old dad would be nobody's business. He proposed to exert upon him the full force of his magnetic personality, and looked forward to registering a very substantial hit.

Which being so, I need scarcely tell you, knowing Freddie as you do, that his first act on entering Sir Mortimer Prenderby's orbit was to make the scaliest kind of floater, hitting him on the back of the neck with a tortoiseshell cat not ten minutes after his arrival.

His train having been a bit late, there was no time on reaching the house for any stately receptions or any of that "Welcome to Meadowsweet Hall" stuff. The girl simply

163

shot him up to his room and told him to dress like a streak, because dinner was in a quarter of an hour, and then buzzed off to don the soup and fish herself. And Freddie was just going well when, looking round for his shirt, which he had left on the bed, he saw a large tortoiseshell cat standing on it, kneading it with its paws.

Well, you know how a fellow feels about his shirt-front. For an instant, Freddie stood spellbound. Then with a hoarse cry he bounded forward, scooped up the animal, and, carrying it out on to the balcony, flung it into the void. And an elderly gentleman, coming round the corner at this moment, received a direct hit on the back of his neck.

"Hell!" cried the elderly gentleman.

A head popped out of a window.

"Whatever is the matter, Mortimer?"

"It's raining cats."

"Nonsense. It's a lovely evening," said the head, and disappeared.

Freddie thought an apology would be in order.

"I say," he said.

The old gentleman looked in every direction of the compass, and finally located Freddie on his balcony.

"I say," said Freddie, "I'm awfully sorry you got that nasty buffet. It was me."

"It was not you. It was a cat."

"I know. I threw the cat."

"Why?"

"Well . . ."

"Dam' fool."

"I'm sorry," said Freddie.

"Go to blazes," said the old gentleman.

Freddie backed into the room, and the incident closed.

Freddie is a pretty slippy dresser, as a rule, but this episode had shaken him, and he not only lost a collar-stud but made a mess of the first two ties. The result was that the gong went while he was still in his shirt-sleeves: and on emerging from his boudoir he was informed by a footman that the gang were already nuzzling their *bouillon* in the dining-room. He pushed straight on there, accordingly, and sank into a chair beside his hostess just in time to dead-heat with the final spoonful.

Awkward, of course, but he was feeling in pretty good form owing to the pleasantness of the thought that he was shoving his knees under the same board as the girl Dahlia: so, having nodded to his host, who was glaring at him from the head of the table, as much as to say that all would be explained in God's good time, he shot his cuffs and started to make sparkling conversation to Lady Prenderby.

"Charming place you have here, what?"

Lady Prenderby said that the local scenery was generally admired. She was one of those tall, rangy, Queen Elizabeth sort of women, with tight lips and cold, blanc-mange-y eyes. Freddie didn't like her looks much, but he was feeling, as I say, fairly fizzy, so he carried on with a bright zip.

"Pretty good hunting country, I should think."

"I believe there is a good deal of hunting near here, yes."

"I thought as much," said Freddie. "Ah, that's the stuff, is it not? A cracking gallop across good country with a jolly fine kill at the end of it, what, what? Hark for'ard, yoicks, tally-ho, I mean to say, and all that sort of thing."

Lady Prenderby shivered austerely.

"I fear I cannot share your enthusiasm," she said. "I have the strongest possible objection to hunting. I have always set my face against it, as against all similar brutalizing blood-sports."

This was a nasty jar for poor old Freddie, who had been relying on the topic to carry him nicely through at least a couple of courses. It silenced him for the nonce. And as he paused to collect his faculties, his host, who had now been glowering for six and a half minutes practically without cessation, put a hand in front of his mouth and addressed the girl Dahlia across the table. Freddie thinks he was under the impression that he was speaking in a guarded whisper, but, as a matter of fact, the words boomed through the air as if he had been a costermonger calling attention to his brussels sprouts.

"Dahlia!"

"Yes, Father?"

"Who's that ugly feller?"

"Hush!"

"What do you mean, hush? Who is he?"

"Mr. Widgeon."

"Mr. Who?"

"Widgeon."

"I wish you would articulate clearly and not mumble," said Sir Mortimer fretfully. "It sounds to me just like 'Widgeon.' Who asked him here?"

"I did."

"Why?"

"He's a friend of mine."

"Well, he looks a pretty frightful young slab of damnation to me. What I'd call a criminal face."

"Hush!"

"Why do you keep saying 'Hush'? Must be a lunatic, too. Throws cats at people."

"Please, Father!"

"Don't say 'Please, Father!' No sense in it. I tell you he does throw cats at people. He threw one at me. Half-witted, I'd call him—if that. Besides being the most offensive-looking young toad I've ever seen on the premises. How long's he staying?"

"Till Monday."

"My God! And to-day's only Friday!" bellowed Sir Mortimer Prenderby.

It was an unpleasant situation for Freddie, of course, and I'm bound to admit he didn't carry it off particularly well. What he ought to have done, obviously, was to have plunged into an easy flow of small-talk: but all he could think of was to ask Lady Prenderby if she was fond of shooting. Lady Prenderby having replied that, owing to being deficient in the savage instincts and wanton blood-lust that went to make up a

166

callous and cold-hearted murderess, she was not, he relapsed into silence with his lower jaw hanging down.

All in all, he wasn't so dashed sorry when dinner came to an end.

As he and Sir Mortimer were the only men at the table, most of the seats having been filled by a covey of mildewed females whom he had classified under the general heading of Aunts, it seemed to Freddie that the moment had now arrived when they would be able to get together once more, under happier conditions than those of their last meeting, and start to learn to appreciate one another's true worth. He looked forward to a cosy *tête-à-tête* over the port, in the course of which he would smooth over that cat incident and generally do all that lay within his power to revise the unfavourable opinion of him which the other must have formed.

But apparently Sir Mortimer had his own idea of the duties and obligations of a host. Instead of clustering round Freddie with decanters, he simply gave him a long, lingering look of distaste and shot out of the french window into the garden. A moment later, his head reappeared and he uttered the words: "You and your dam' cats!" Then the night swallowed him again.

Freddie was a good deal perplexed. All this was new stuff to him. He had been in and out of a number of country-houses in his time, but this was the first occasion on which he had ever been left flat at the conclusion of the evening meal, and he wasn't quite sure how to handle the situation. He was still wondering, when Sir Mortimer's head came into view again and its owner, after giving him another of those long, lingering looks, said: "Cats, forsooth!" and disappeared once more.

Freddie was now definitely piqued. It was all very well, he felt, Dahlia Prenderby telling him to make himself solid with her father, but how can you make yourself solid with a fellow who doesn't stay put for a couple of consecutive seconds? If it was Sir Mortimer's intention to spend the remainder of the night flashing past like a merry-go-round, there seemed little hope of anything amounting to a genuine *rapprochement*. It was a relief to his feelings when there suddenly appeared from nowhere his old acquaintance the tortoiseshell cat. It seemed to offer to him a means of working off his spleen.

Taking from Lady Prenderby's plate, accordingly, the remains of a banana, he plugged the animal neatly at a range of two yards. It yowled and withdrew. And a moment later, there was Sir Mortimer again.

"Did you kick that cat?" said Sir Mortimer.

Freddie had half a mind to ask this old disease if he thought he was a man or a jack-in-the-box, but the breeding of the Widgeons restrained him.

"No," he said, "I did not kick that cat."

"You must have done something to it to make it come charging out at forty miles an hour."

"I merely offered the animal a piece of fruit."

"Do it again and see what happens to you."

"Lovely evening," said Freddie, changing the subject.

"No, it's not, you silly ass," said Sir Mortimer. Freddie rose. His nerve, I fancy, was a little shaken.

"I shall join the ladies," he said, with dignity.

"God help them!" replied Sir Mortimer Prenderby in a voice instinct with the deepest feeling, and vanished once more.

Freddie's mood, as he made for the drawing-room, was thoughtful. I don't say he has much sense, but he's got enough to know when he is and when he isn't going with a bang. To-night, he realized, he had been very far from going in such a manner. It was not, that is to say, as the Idol of Matcham Scratchings that he would enter the drawing-room, but rather as a young fellow who had made an unfortunate first impression and would have to do a lot of heavy ingratiating before he could regard himself as really popular in the home.

He must bustle about, he felt, and make up leeway. And, knowing that what counts with these old-style females who have lived in the country all their lives is the exhibition of those little politenesses and attentions which were all the go in Queen Victoria's time, his first action, on entering, was to make a dive for one of the aunts who seemed to be trying to find a place to put her coffee-cup.

"Permit me," said Freddie, suave to the eyebrows.

And bounding forward with the feeling that this was the stuff to give them, he barged right into a cat.

"Oh, sorry," he said, backing and bringing down his heel on another cat.

"I say, most frightfully sorry," he said.

And, tottering to a chair, he sank heavily on to a third cat.

Well, he was up and about again in a jiffy, of course, but it was too late. There was the usual not-at-all-ing and don't-mention-it-ing, but he could read between the lines. Lady Prenderby's eyes had rested on his for only a brief instant, but it had been enough. His standing with her, he perceived, was now approximately what King Herod's would have been at an Israelite Mothers' Social Saturday Afternoon.

The girl Dahlia during these exchanges had been sitting on a sofa at the end of the room, turning the pages of a weekly paper, and the sight of her drew Freddie like a magnet. Her womanly sympathy was just what he felt he could do with at this juncture. Treading with infinite caution, he crossed to where she sat: and, having scanned the terrain narrowly for cats, sank down on the sofa at her side. And conceive his agony of spirit when he discovered that womanly sympathy had been turned off at the main. The girl was like a chunk of ice-cream with spikes all over it.

"Please do not trouble to explain," she said coldly, in answer to his opening words. "I quite understand that there are people who have this odd dislike of animals."

"But dash it. . . . " cried Freddie, waving his arm in a frenzied sort of way. "Oh, I say, sorry," he added, as his fist sloshed another of the menagerie in the short ribs.

Dahlia caught the animal as it flew through the air.

"I think perhaps you had better take Augustus, Mother," she said. "He seems to be annoying Mr. Widgeon."

"Quite," said Lady Prenderby. "He will be safer with me."

"But, dash it. . . . " bleated Freddie.

Dahlia Prenderby drew in her breath sharply.

"How true it is," she said, "that one never really knows a man till after one has seen him in one's own home."

"What do you mean by that?"

"Oh, nothing," said Dahlia Prenderby.

She rose and moved to the piano, where she proceeded to sing old Breton folk-songs in a distant manner, leaving Freddie to make out as best he could with a family album containing faded photographs with "Aunt Emily bathing at Llandudno, 1893", and "This is Cousin George at the fancy-dress ball" written under them.

And so the long, quiet, peaceful home evening wore on, till eventually Lady Prenderby mercifully blew the whistle and he was at liberty to sneak off to his bedroom.

You might have supposed that Freddie's thoughts, as he toddled upstairs with his candle, would have dwelt exclusively on the girl Dahlia. This, however, was not so. He did give her obvious shirtiness a certain measure of attention, of course, but what really filled his mind was the soothing reflection that at long last his path and that of the animal kingdom of Matcham Scratchings had now divided. He, so to speak, was taking the high road while they, as it were, would take the low road. For whatever might be the conditions prevailing in the dining-room, the drawing-room, and the rest of the house, his bedroom, he felt, must surely be a haven totally free from cats of all descriptions.

Remembering, however, that unfortunate episode before dinner, he went down on all fours and subjected the various nooks and crannies to a close examination. His eye could detect no cats. Relieved, he rose to his feet with a gay song on his lips: and he hadn't got much beyond the first couple of bars when a voice behind him suddenly started taking the bass: and, turning, he perceived on the bed a fine Alsatian dog.

Freddie looked at the dog. The dog looked at Freddie. The situation was one fraught with embarrassment. A glance at the animal was enough to convince him that it had got an entirely wrong angle on the position of affairs and was regarding him purely in the light of an intrusive stranger who had muscled in on its private sleeping quarters. Its manner was plainly resentful. It fixed Freddie with a cold, yellow eye and curled its upper lip slightly, the better to display a long, white tooth. It also twitched its nose and gave a *sotto-voce* imitation of distant thunder.

Freddie did not know quite what avenue to explore. It was impossible to climb between the sheets with a thing like that on the counterpane. To spend the night in a chair, on the other hand, would have been foreign to his policy. He did what I consider the most statesmanlike thing by sidling out on to the balcony and squinting along the wall of the house to see if there wasn't a lighted window hard by, behind which might lurk somebody who would rally round with aid and comfort.

There was a lighted window only a short distance away, so he shoved his head out as far as it would stretch, and said:

"I say!"

There being no response, he repeated:

"I say!"

And, finally, to drive his point home, he added:

"I say! I say! I say!"

This time he got results. The head of Lady Prenderby suddenly protruded from the window.

"Who," she enquired, "is making that abominable noise?"

It was not precisely the attitude Freddie had hoped for, but he could take the rough with the smooth.

"It's me. Widgeon, Frederick."

"Must you sing on your balcony, Mr. Widgeon?"

"I wasn't singing. I was saying 'I say'."

"What were you saying?"

" 'I say'."

"You say what?"

"I say I was saying 'I say'. Kind of a heart-cry, if you know what I mean. The fact is, there's a dog in my room."

"What sort of dog?"

" A whacking great Alsatian."

171

"Ah, that would be Wilhelm. Good night, Mr. Widgeon."

The window closed. Freddie let out a heart-stricken yip.

"But I say!"

The window reopened.

"Really, Mr. Widgeon!"

"But what am I to do?"

"Do?"

"About this whacking great Alsatian!"

Lady Prenderby seemed to consider.

"No sweet biscuits," she said. "And when the maid brings you your tea in the morning please do not give him sugar. Simply a little milk in the saucer. He is on a diet. Good night, Mr. Widgeon."

Freddie was now pretty well nonplussed. No matter what his hostess might say about this beastly dog being on a diet, he was convinced from its manner that its medical adviser had not forbidden it Widgeons, and once more he bent his brain to the task of ascertaining what to do next.

There were several possible methods of procedure. His balcony being not so very far from the ground, he could, if he pleased, jump down and pass a health-giving night in the nasturtium bed. Or he might curl up on the floor. Or he might get out of the room and doss downstairs somewhere.

This last scheme seemed about the best. The only obstacle in the way of its fulfilment was the fact that, when he started for the door, his room-mate would probably think he was a burglar about to loot silver of lonely country-house and pin him. Still, it had to be risked, and a moment later he might have been observed tiptoeing across the carpet with all the caution of a slack-wire artist who isn't any too sure he remembers the correct steps.

Well, it was a near thing. At the instant when he started, the dog seemed occupied with something that looked like a cushion on the bed. It was licking this object in a thoughtful way, and paid no attention to Freddie till he was half-way across No Man's Land. Then it suddenly did a sort of sitting high-jump in his direction, and two seconds later Freddie, with a draughty feeling about the seat of his trouserings, was on top of the wardrobe, with the dog underneath looking up. He tells me that if he ever moved quicker in his life it was only on the occasion when, a lad of fourteen, he was discovered by his uncle, Lord Blicester, smoking one of the latter's cigars in the library: and he rather thinks he must have clipped at least a fifth of a second off the record then set up.

It looked to him now as if his sleeping arrangements for the night had been settled for him. And the thought of having to roost on top of a wardrobe at the whim of a dog was pretty dashed offensive to his proud spirit, as you may well imagine. However, as you cannot reason with Alsatians, it seemed the only thing to be done: and he was trying to make himself as comfortable as a sharp piece of wood sticking into the fleshy part of his leg would permit, when there was a snuffling noise in the passage and through the door came an object which in the dim light he was at first not able to identify. It looked something like a pen-wiper and something like a piece of a hearth-rug. A second and keener inspection revealed it as a Pekinese puppy.

The uncertainty which Freddie had felt as to the newcomer's status was shared, it appeared, by the Alsatian: for after raising its eyebrows in a puzzled manner it rose and advanced enquiringly. In a tentative way it put out a paw and rolled the intruder over. Then, advancing again, it lowered its nose and sniffed.

It was a course of action against which its best friend would have advised it. These Pekes are tough eggs, especially when, as in this case, female. They look the world in the eye, and are swift to resent familiarity. There was a sort of explosion, and the next moment the Alsatian was shooting out of the room with its tail between its legs, hotly pursued. Freddie could hear the noise of battle rolling away along the passage, and it was music to his ears. Something on these lines was precisely what that Alsatian had been asking for, and now it had got it.

Presently, the Peke returned, dashing the beads of perspiration from its forehead, and came and sat down under the wardrobe, wagging a stumpy tail. And Freddie, feeling that the All Clear had been blown and that he was now at liberty to descend, did so.

His first move was to shut the door, his second to fraternize with his preserver. Freddie is a chap who believes in giving credit where credit is due, and it seemed to him that this Peke had shown itself an ornament of its species. He spared no effort, accordingly, to entertain it. He lay down on the floor and let it lick his face two hundred and thirty-three times. He tickled it under the left ear, the right ear, and at the base of the tail, in the order named. He also scratched its stomach.

All these attentions the animal received with cordiality and marked gratification: and as it seemed still in pleasure-seeking mood and had plainly come to look upon him as the official Master of the Revels, Freddie, feeling that he could not disappoint it but must play the host no matter what the cost to himself, took off his tie and handed it over. He would not have done it for everybody, he says, but where this life-saving Peke was concerned the sky was the limit.

Well, the tie went like a breeze. It was a success from the start. The Peke chewed it and chased it and got entangled in it and dragged it about the room, and was just starting to shake it from side to side when an unfortunate thing happened. Misjudging its distance, it banged its head a nasty wallop against the leg of the bed.

There is nothing of the Red Indian at the stake about a puppy in circumstances like this. A moment later, Freddie's blood was chilled by a series of fearful shrieks that seemed to ring through the night like the dying cries of the party of the second part to a first-class murder. It amazed him that a mere Peke, and a juvenile Peke at that, should have been capable of producing such an uproar. He says that a Baronet, stabbed in the back with a paper-knife in his library, could not have made half such a row.

Eventually, the agony seemed to abate. Quite suddenly, as if nothing had happened, the Peke stopped yelling and with an amused smile started to play with the tie again. And at the same moment there was a sound of whispering outside, and then a knock at the door.

"Hullo?" said Freddie.

"It is I, sir. Biggleswade."

"Who's Biggleswade?"

"The butler, sir."

"What do you want?"

"Her ladyship wishes me to remove the dog which you are torturing."

There was more whispering.

"Her ladyship also desires me to say that she will be reporting the affair in the morning to the Society for the Prevention of Cruelty to Animals."

There was another spot of whispering.

"Her ladyship further instructs me to add that, should you prove recalcitrant, I am to strike you over the head with the poker."

Well, you can't say this was pleasant for poor old Freddie, and he didn't think so himself. He opened the door, to perceive, without, a group consisting of Lady Prenderby, her daughter Dahlia, a few assorted aunts, and the butler, with poker. And he says he met Dahlia's eyes and they went through him like a knife.

"Let me explain. . ." he began.

"Spare us the details," said Lady Prenderby with a shiver. She scooped up the Peke and felt it for broken bones.

"But listen. . ."

"Good night, Mr. Widgeon."

The aunts said good night, too, and so did the butler. The girl Dahlia preserved a revolted silence.

"But, honestly, it was nothing, really. It banged its head against the bed . . ."

"What did he say?" asked one of the aunts, who was a little hard of hearing.

"He says he banged the poor creature's head against the bed," said Lady Prenderby.

"Dreadful!" said the aunt.

"Hideous!" said a second aunt.

A third aunt opened up another line of thought. She said that with men like Freddie in the house, was anyone safe? She mooted the possibility of them all being murdered in their beds. And though Freddie offered to give her a written guarantee that he hadn't the slightest intention of going anywhere near her bed, the idea seemed to make a deep impression.

"Biggleswade," said Lady Prenderby.

"M'lady?"

"You will remain in this passage for the remainder of the night with your poker."

"Very good, m'lady."

"Should this man attempt to leave his room, you will strike him smartly over the head."

"Just so, m'lady."

"But, listen . . ." said Freddie.

"Good night, Mr. Widgeon."

The mob scene broke up. Soon the passage was empty save for Biggleswade the butler, who had begun to pace up and down, halting every now and then to flick the air with his poker as if testing the lissomness of his wrist-muscles and satisfying himself that they were in a condition to ensure the right amount of follow-through.

The spectacle he presented was so unpleasant that Freddie withdrew into his room and shut the door. His bosom, as you may imagine, was surging with distressing emotions. That look which Dahlia Prenderby had given him had churned him up to no little extent. He realized that he had a lot of tense thinking to do, and to assist thought he sat down on the bed.

Or, rather, to be accurate, on the dead cat which was lying on the bed. It was this cat which the Alsatian had been licking just before the final breach in his relations with Freddie—the object, if you remember, which the latter had supposed to be a cushion.

He leaped up as if the corpse, instead of being cold, had been

176

piping hot. He stared down, hoping against hope that the animal was merely in some sort of coma. But a glance told him that it had made the great change. He had never seen a deader cat. After life's fitful fever it slept well.

You wouldn't be far out in saying that poor old Freddie was now appalled. Already his reputation in this house was at zero, his name mud. On all sides he was looked upon as Widgeon the Amateur Vivisectionist. This final disaster could not but put the tin hat on it. Before, he had had a faint hope that in the morning, when calmer moods would prevail, he might be able to explain that matter of the Peke. But who was going to listen to him if he were discovered with a dead cat on his person?

And then the thought came to him that it might be possible not to be discovered with it on his person. He had only to nip downstairs and deposit the remains in the drawing-room or somewhere and suspicion might not fall upon him. After all, in a super-catted house like this, cats must always be dying like flies all over the place. A housemaid would find the animal in the morning and report to G.H.Q. that the cat strength of the establishment had been reduced by one, and there would be a bit of tut-tutting and perhaps a silent tear or two, and then the thing would be forgotten.

The thought gave him new life. All briskness and efficiency, he picked up the body by the tail and was just about to dash out of the room when, with a silent groan, he remembered Biggleswade.

He peeped out. It might be that the butler, once the eye of authority had been removed, had departed to get the remainder of his beauty-sleep. But no. Service and Fidelity were evidently the watchwords at Matcham Scratchings. There the fellow was, still practising half-arm shots with the poker. Freddie closed the door.

And, as he did so, he suddenly thought of the window. There lay the solution. Here he had been, fooling about with doors and thinking in terms of drawing-rooms, and all the while there was the balcony staring him in the face. All he had to do was to shoot the body out into the silent night, and let gardeners, not housemaids, discover it.

He hurried out. It was a moment for swift action. He raised his burden. He swung it to and fro, working up steam. Then he let it go, and from the dark garden there came suddenly the cry of a strong man in his anger.

"Who threw that cat?"

It was the voice of his host, Sir Mortimer Prenderby.

"Show me the man who threw that cat!" he thundered.

Windows flew up. Heads came out. Freddie sank to the floor of the balcony and rolled against the wall.

"Whatever is the matter, Mortimer?"

"Let me get at the man who hit me in the eye with a cat."

"A cat?" Lady Prenderby's voice sounded perplexed. "Are you sure?"

"Sure? What do you mean sure? Of course I'm sure. I was just dropping off to sleep in my hammock, when suddenly a great beastly cat came whizzing through the air and caught me properly in the eyeball. It's a nice thing. A man can't sleep in hammocks in his own garden without people pelting him with cats. I insist on the blood of the man who threw that cat."

"Where did it come from?"

"Must have come from that balcony there."

"Mr. Widgeon's balcony," said Lady Prenderby in an acid voice. "As I might have guessed."

Sir Mortimer uttered a cry.

"So might I have guessed! Widgeon, of course! That ugly feller. He's been throwing cats all the evening. I've got a nasty sore place on the back of my neck where he hit me with one before dinner. Somebody come and open the front door. I want my heavy cane, the one with the carved ivory handle. Or a horsewhip will do."

"Wait, Mortimer," said Lady Prenderby. "Do nothing rash. The man is evidently a very dangerous lunatic. I will send Biggleswade to overpower him. He has the kitchen poker."

Little (said the Crumpet) remains to be told. At two-fifteen that morning a sombre figure in dress clothes without a tie limped into the little railway station of Lower Smattering on the Wissel, some six miles from Matcham Scratchings. At three-forty-seven it departed London-wards on the up milk-train. It was Frederick Widgeon. He had a broken heart and blisters on both heels. And in that broken heart was that loathing for all cats of which you recently saw so signal a manifestation. I am revealing no secrets when I tell you that Freddie Widgeon is permanently through with cats. From now on, they cross his path at their peril.

*   *   *   *   *

The town of Walsingford, though provided almost to excess with public-houses, possesses only one hotel of the higher class, the sort that can be considered a suitable pull-up for the nobility and gentry ... The fastidious find it a little smelly, for the rule against opening windows holds good here, as in all English country-town hotels, but it is really the only place where a motorist of quality can look in for a brush up and a cup of tea. Nowhere else will you find marble mantelpieces, armchairs, tables bearing bead ferns in brass pots and waiters in celluloid collars.

THE PENURIOUS ARISTOCRACY

"If you want to see real destitution, old boy, take a look at my family. I'm broke. My guv'nor's broke. My Aunt Vera's broke. It's a ruddy epidemic. I owe every tradesman in London. The guv'nor hasn't tasted meat for weeks. And, as for Aunt Vera, relict of the late Colonel Archibald Mace, C.V.O., she's reduced to writing Glad articles for evening papers. You know—things on the back page pointing out that there's always sunshine somewhere and that we ought to be bright, like the little birds in the trees. Why, I've known that woman's circumstances to become so embarrassed that she actually made an attempt to borrow money from me. Me, old boy! Lazarus in person."

I EXPLODE THE HAGGIS

WELL, boys, to-night's the night. St. Andrew's Day has come once again, and all over the world, from London to the remotest British colony, Scotsmen will soon be seated about dinner tables—waiting. They will have gathered together to do honour to their patron saint, but it will not be of him that they will be thinking at the moment. Their knives and forks clutched in their hands, their mouths watering, their eyes wolfish, they will be watching the door through which are about to enter, in the following order, bagpiper, the bearers of Atholl brose, and . . . the Haggis.

Incredible as it may seem, they will be looking forward to eating the beastly stuff. Yet do not think that I blame the honest fellows. I am broadminded. The fact that I, personally, have a stomach which shies like a startled horse and turns three handsprings at the mere thought of haggis, does not lead me to sneer at their simple enthusiasm. What I say to myself is that there must always be Dangerous Trades, that it takes all sorts to do the world's work, and that if these devoted men are willing to eat haggis, it ill becomes us to raise our eyebrows. A hearty, "*Well, best of luck,*" seems to me a more proper attitude.

It is never any use getting worked up about other people's food. You may not be able to understand why a cannibal chief, with all the advantages of an education at Balliol, should like to tuck into the fried missionary, but he does. The thing simply has to be accepted, just as we accept the fact that Americans enjoy Chicago potted-meat and Frenchmen *bouillabaisse*. In bouillabaisse you are likely to find almost anything, from a nautical gentleman's sea-boots to a small China mug engraved with the legend "*Un cadeau* (a present) *de* (from) *Deauville* (Deauville)", while Chicago potted-meat. . . . Well, we have all read Upton Sinclair's *The Jungle*, and are familiar with the poignant little story of the emotional packer named Young who once, when his nerves were unstrung, put his wife Josephine into the chopping machine and canned her and labelled her "Tongue."

Nevertheless, Frenchmen do go for this bouillabaisse in a big way, and so do Americans for potted-meat. It is the same with Scotsmen and haggis. They like it. It is no good trying any appeals to reason. I tell you they like it.

The fact that I am not a haggis addict is probably due to my having read Shakespeare. It is the same with many Englishmen. There is no doubt that Shakespeare has rather put us off the stuff. We come across that bit in *Macbeth* in our formative years and it establishes a complex.

You remember the passage to which I refer? Macbeth happens upon the three witches while they are preparing the evening meal. They are dropping things into the cauldron and chanting "Eye of newt and toe of frog, wool of bat and tongue of dog," and so on, and he immediately recognises the recipe. "How now, you secret, black and midnight haggis," he cries shuddering.

This has caused misunderstandings, and has done an injustice to haggis. Grim as it is, it is not as bad as that—or should not be. What the dish really consists of—or should consist of—is the more intimate parts of a sheep, chopped up fine and blended with salt, pepper, nutmeg, onions, oatmeal, and beef suet. But it seems to me that there is a grave danger of the cook going all whimsy and deciding not to stop there. When you reflect that the haggis is served up with a sort of mackintosh round it, concealing its contents, you will readily see that the temptation to play a practical joke on the boys must be almost irresistible.

Scotsmen have their merry moods, like all of us, and the thought must occasionally cross the cook's mind that it would be no end of a lark to shove in a lot of newts and frogs and bats and dogs and then stand in the doorway watching the poor simps wade into them.

Nor could the imposture be easily detected. That Athol brose, to which I have referred above as the junior partner of haggis, is a beverage composed of equal parts of whisky, cream, and honey. After a glass or two of this, you simply don't notice anything, not even if you are at the table or under it.

I must confess that if I were invited to a St. Andrew's night, I would insist on taking Sir Bernard Spilsbury with me, and turning my plate over to him before I touched a mouthful.

My caution might cast a damper on the party. Unpleasant looks might be directed at me. I would not care. "Just analyse this, Bernard," I would say, quietly, but firmly. And only when he had blown the All Clear would I consent to join the revels.

Haggis has another quality which I dislike. I asked a Scottish friend how you started in on it—what was the first move, as it were—and a dreamy, soulful look came into his face.

"*You give it a big cut with your knife,*" *he said,* "*and it smiles at you.*" I deprecate this. Heaven knows I am no snob, but there are social distinctions. A decent humility is what we expect in our food, not heartiness and familiarity. A haggis should know its place like a chop. Who ever saw a simpering chop?

An odd thing—ironical, you might say—in connection with haggis is that it is not Scottish. In an old cook book, published 1653, it is specifically mentioned as an English dish called haggas or haggus, while France claims it as her mince (hachis) going about under an alias. It would be rather amusing if it turned out one day that Burns was really a couple of Irish boys named Pat and Mike.

*   *   *   *   *

"Jeeves," I said, "those spats."

"Yes, sir?"

"You really dislike them?"

"Intensely, sir."

"You don't think time might induce you to change your views?"

"No, sir."

"All right, then. Very well. Say no more. You may burn them."

"Thank you very much. I have already done so. Before breakfast this morning. A quiet grey is far more suitable, sir. Thank you, sir."

To the
Immortal Memory
of
John Henrie and Pat Rogie
who
at Edinburgh, in the year A.D. 1593
were imprisoned for
"Playing of the gowff on the links of
Leith every Sabbath the time of the ser-
monses,"
also of
Robert Robertson
who got it in the neck in A.D. 1604
for the same reason.

Author's Dedication, "Clicking of Cuthbert."

DIET AND THE OMNIBUS

THIS TRACKLESS desert of print which we see before us, winding on and on into the purple distance, represents my first Omnibus Book: and I must confess that, as I contemplate it, I cannot overcome a slight feeling of chestiness, just the faint beginning of that offensive conceit against which we authors have to guard so carefully. I mean, it isn't everyone . . . I mean to say, an Omnibus Book. . . . Well, dash it, you can't say it doesn't mark an epoch in a fellow's career and put him just a bit above the common herd. P. G. Wodehouse, O.B. Not such a very distant step from P. G. Wodehouse, O.M.

Mingled with this pride there is a certain diffidence. Hitherto, I have administered Jeeves and Bertie to the public in reasonably small doses, spread over a lapse of time. (Fifteen years, to be exact.) How will my readers react to the policy of the Solid Slab?

There is, of course, this to be said for the Omnibus Book in general and this one in particular. When you buy it, you have got something. The bulk of this volume makes it almost the ideal paper-weight. The number of its pages assures its possessor of plenty of shaving paper on his vacation. Placed upon the waist-line and jerked up and down each morning, it will reduce embonpoint and strengthen the abdominal muscles. And those still at their public school will find that between—say Caesar's Commentaries in limp cloth and this Jeeves book there is no comparison as a missile in an inter-study brawl.

The great trouble with a book like this is that the purchaser is tempted to read too much of it at one time. He sees this hideous mass confronting him and he wants to get at it and have done with it. This is a mistake. I would not recommend anyone to attempt to finish this volume at a sitting.

It can be done—I did it myself when correcting the proofs—
but it leaves one weak, and is really not worth doing just
for the sake of saying you have done it.

Take it easy. Spread it out. Assimilate it little by little.
Here, for instance, is a specimen day's menu, as advocated
by a well-known West-end physician.

Breakfast

Toast.
Marmalade.
Coffee.
Soft-boiled egg.
Jeeves and the hard-boiled egg.

Luncheon

Hors d'œuvres.
Cauliflower au gratin.
Lamb cutlet.
Jeeves and the Kid Clementina.

Dinner

Clear soup.
Halibut.
Chicken en casserole.
Savoury.
Jeeves and the old school-friend.

Before Retiring

Liver pill.
Jeeves and the Impending Doom.

Should insomnia supervene, add ten minutes of one of the
other stories.

I find it curious, now that I have written so much about
him, to recall how softly and undramatically Jeeves first

entered my little world. Characteristically, he did not thrust himself forward. On that occasion, he spoke just two lines.

The first was:—

"Mrs. Gregson to see you, sir."

The second:—

"Very good, sir. Which suit will you wear?"

That was in a story in a volume entitled, "The Man With Two Left Feet." It was only some time later, when I was going into the strange affair which is related under the title of "The Artistic Career of Young Corky," that the man's qualities dawned upon me. I still blush to think of the off-hand way I treated him at our first encounter.

One great advantage in being historian to a man like Jeeves is that his mere personality prevents one selling one's artistic soul for gold. In recent years I have had lucrative offers for his services from theatrical managers, motion-picture magnates, the proprietors of one or two widely advertised commodities, and even the editor of the comic supplement of an American newspaper, who wanted him for a "comicstrip." But, tempting though the terms were, it only needed Jeeves's deprecating cough and his murmured "I would scarcely advocate it, sir," to put the jack under my better nature. Jeeves knows his place, and it is between the covers of a book.

A sudden thought comes to me at this point, and causes me a little anxiety. Never having been mixed up in this Omnibus Book business before, I am ignorant of the rules of the game. And what is worrying me is this,—Does the publication of an Omnibus Book impose a moral obligation on the author, a sort of gentleman's agreement that he will not write any more about the characters included in it? I hope not, for as regards Jeeves and Bertie all has not yet been told. The world at present knows nothing of Young Thos. and his liver-pad, of the curious affair of old Boko and the Captain Kidd costume, or of the cook Anatole and the unwelcome birthday present. Nor has the infamy wrought by Tuppy Glossop upon Bertie been avenged.

Before we go any further, I must have it distinctly understood that the end is not yet.

Author's Introduction, "Jeeves Omnibus."

UKRIDGE'S ACCIDENT SYNDICATE

"HALF A minute, laddie," said Ukridge. And, gripping my arm, he brought me to a halt on the outskirts of the little crowd which had collected about the church door.

It was a crowd such as may be seen any morning during the London mating-season outside any of the churches which nestle in the quiet squares between Hyde Park and the King's Road, Chelsea.

It consisted of five women of cooklike aspect, four nurse-maids, half a dozen men of the non-producing class who had torn themselves away for the moment from their normal task of propping up the wall of the Bunch of Grapes public-house on the corner, a costermonger with a barrow of vege-tables, divers small boys, eleven dogs, and two or three purposeful-looking young fellows with cameras slung over their shoulders. It was plain that a wedding was in progress—and, arguing from the presence of the camera-men and the line of smart motor-cars along the kerb, a fairly fashionable wedding. What was not plain—to me—was why Ukridge, sternest of bachelors, had desired to add himself to the spectators.

"What," I enquired, "is the thought behind this? Why are we interrupting our walk to attend the obsequies of some perfect stranger?"

Ukridge did not reply for a moment. He seemed plunged in thought. Then he uttered a hollow, mirthless laugh—a dreadful sound like the last gargle of a dying moose.

"Perfect stranger, my number eleven foot!" he responded, in his coarse way. "Do you know who it is who's getting hitched up in there?"

"Who?"

"Teddy Weeks."

"Teddy Weeks? Teddy Weeks? Good Lord!" I exclaimed.
"Not really?"

And five years rolled away.

It was at Barolini's Italian restaurant in Beak Street that
Ukridge evolved his great scheme. Barolini's was a favourite
resort of our little group of earnest strugglers in the days
when the philanthropic restaurateurs of Soho used to
supply four courses and coffee for a shilling and sixpence;
and there were present that night, besides Ukridge and
myself, the following men-about-town: Teddy Weeks, the
actor, fresh from a six-weeks' tour with the Number Three
"Only a Shop-Girl" Company; Victor Beamish, the artist,
the man who drew that picture of the O-So-Eesi Piano-
Player in the advertisement pages of the *Piccadilly Magazine;*
Bertram Fox, author of *Ashes of Remorse,* and other unpro-
duced motion-picture scenarios; and Robert Dunhill, who,
being employed at a salary of eighty pounds per annum by
the New Asiatic Bank, represented the sober, hard-headed
commercial element. As usual, Teddy Weeks had collared
the conversation, and was telling us once again how good he
was and how hardly treated by a malignant fate.

There is no need to describe Teddy Weeks. Under another
and a more euphonious name he has long since made his
personal appearance dreadfully familiar to all who read the
illustrated weekly papers. He was then, as now, a sickeningly
handsome young man, possessing precisely the same melting
eyes, mobile mouth, and corrugated hair so esteemed by the
theatre-going public to-day. And yet, at this period of his
career he was wasting himself on minor touring companies
of the kind which open at Barrow-in-Furness and jump to
Bootle for the second half of the week. He attributed this,
as Ukridge was so apt to attribute his own difficulties, to
lack of capital.

"I have everything," he said, querulously, emphasising his
remarks with a coffee-spoon. "Looks, talent, personality,
a beautiful speaking-voice—everything. All I need is a
chance. And I can't get that because I have no clothes fit to

wear. These managers are all the same, they never look below the surface, they never bother to find out if a man has genius. All they go by are his clothes. If I could afford to buy a couple of suits from a Cork Street tailor, if I could have my boots made to order by Moykoff instead of getting them ready-made and second-hand at Moses Brothers', if I could once contrive to own a decent hat, a really good pair of spats, and a gold cigarette-case, all at the same time, I could walk into any manager's office in London and sign up for a West-end production to-morrow."

It was at this point that Freddie Lunt came in. Freddie, like Robert Dunhill, was a financial magnate in the making and an assiduous frequenter of Barolini's; and it suddenly occurred to us that a considerable time had passed since we had last seen him in the place. We enquired the reason for this aloofness.

"I've been in bed," said Freddie, "for over a fortnight."

The statement incurred Ukridge's stern disapproval. That great man made a practice of never rising before noon, and on one occasion, when a carelessly-thrown match had burned a hole in his only pair of trousers, had gone so far as to remain between the sheets for forty-eight hours; but sloth on so majestic a scale as this shocked him.

"Lazy young devil," he commented severely. "Letting the golden hours of youth slip by like that when you ought to have been bustling about and making a name for yourself."

Freddie protested himself wronged by the imputation.

"I had an accident," he explained. "Fell off my bicycle and sprained an ankle."

"Tough luck," was our verdict.

"Oh, I don't know," said Freddie. "It wasn't bad fun getting a rest. And of course there was the fiver."

"What fiver?"

"I got a fiver from the *Weekly Cyclist* for getting my ankle sprained."

"You—*what?*" cried Ukridge, profoundly stirred—as ever—by a tale of easy money. "Do you mean to sit there and tell me that some dashed paper paid you five quid simply because you sprained your ankle? Pull yourself together, old horse. Things like that don't happen."

"It's quite true."

"Can you show me the fiver?"

"No; because if I did you would try to borrow it."

Ukridge ignored this slur in dignified silence.

"Would they pay a fiver to *anyone* who sprained his ankle?" he asked, sticking to the main point.

"Yes. If he was a subscriber."

"I knew there was a catch in it," said Ukridge, moodily.

"Lots of weekly papers are starting this wheeze," proceeded Freddie. "You pay a year's subscription and that entitles you to accident insurance."

We were interested. This was in the days before every daily paper in London was competing madly against its rivals in the matter of insurance and offering princely bribes to the citizens to make a fortune by breaking their necks. Nowadays papers are paying as high as two thousand pounds for a genuine corpse and five pounds a week for a mere dislocated spine; but at that time the idea was new and it had an attractive appeal.

"How many of these rags are doing this?" said Ukridge. You could tell from the gleam in his eyes that that great brain was whirring like a dynamo. "As many as ten?"

"Yes, I should think so. Quite ten."

"Then a fellow who subscribed to them all and then sprained his ankle would get fifty quid?" said Ukridge, reasoning acutely.

"More if the injury was more serious," said Freddie, the expert. "They have a regular tariff. So much for a broken arm, so much for a broken leg, and so forth."

Ukridge's collar leaped off its stud and his pince-nez wobbled drunkenly as he turned to us.

"How much money can you blokes raise?" he demanded.

"What do you want it for?" asked Robert Dunhill, with a banker's caution.

"My dear old horse, can't you see? Why, my gosh, I've got the idea of the century. Upon my Sam, this is the giltest-edged scheme that was ever hatched. We'll get together enough money and take out a year's subscription for every one of these dashed papers."

"What's the good of that?" said Dunhill, coldly unenthusiastic.

They train bank clerks to stifle emotion, so that they will be able to refuse overdrafts when they become managers. "The odds are we should none of us have an accident of any kind, and then the money would be chucked away."

"Good heavens, ass," snorted Ukridge, "you don't suppose I'm suggesting that we should leave it to chance, do you? Listen! Here's the scheme. We take out subscriptions for all these papers, then we draw lots, and the fellow who gets the fatal card or whatever it is goes out and breaks his leg and draws the loot, and we split it up between us and live on it in luxury. It ought to run into hundreds of pounds."

A long silence followed. Then Dunhill spoke again. His was a solid rather than a nimble mind.

"Suppose he couldn't break his leg?"

"My gosh!" cried Ukridge, exasperated. "Here we are in the twentieth century, with every resource of modern civilisation at our disposal, with opportunities for getting our legs broken opening about us on every side—and you ask a silly question like that! Of course he could break his leg. Any ass can break a leg. It's a little hard! We're all infernally broke—personally, unless Freddie can lend me a bit of that fiver till Saturday, I'm going to have a difficult job pulling through. We all need money like the dickens, and yet, when I point out this marvellous scheme for collecting a bit, instead of fawning on me for my ready intelligence you sit and make objections. It isn't the right spirit. It isn't the spirit that wins."

"If you're as hard up as that," objected Dunhill, "how are you going to put in your share of the pool?"

A pained, almost a stunned, look came into Ukridge's eyes.

He gazed at Dunhill through his lop-sided pince-nez as one who speculates as to whether his hearing has deceived him.

"Me?" he cried. "Me? I like that! Upon my Sam, that's rich! Why, damme, if there's any justice in the world, if there's a spark of decency and good feeling in your bally bosoms, I should think you would let me in free for suggesting the idea. It's a little hard! I supply the brains and you want me to cough up cash as well. My gosh, I didn't expect this. This hurts me, by George! If anybody had told me that an old pal would——"

"Oh, all right," said Robert Dunhill. "All right, all right, all right. But I'll tell you one thing. If you draw the lot it'll be the happiest day of my life."

"I sha'n't," said Ukridge. "Something tells me that I sha'n't."

Nor did he. When, in a solemn silence broken only by the sound of a distant waiter quarrelling with the cook down a speaking-tube, we had completed the drawing, the man of destiny was Teddy Weeks.

I suppose that even in the springtime of Youth, when broken limbs seems a lighter matter than they become later in life, it can never be an unmixedly agreeable thing to have to go out into the public highways and try to make an accident happen to one. In such circumstances the reflection that you are thereby benefiting your friends brings but slight balm. To Teddy Weeks it appeared to bring no balm at all. That he was experiencing a certain disinclination to sacrifice himself for the public good became more and more evident as the days went by and found him still intact. Ukridge, when he called upon me to discuss the matter, was visibly perturbed. He sank into a chair beside the table at which I was beginning my modest morning meal, and, having drunk half my coffee, sighed deeply.

"Upon my Sam," he moaned, "it's a little disheartening. I strain my brain to think up schemes for getting us all a bit of money just at the moment when we are all needing it most, and when I hit on what is probably the simplest and yet ripest notion of our time, this blighter Weeks goes and lets me down by shirking his plain duty. It's just my luck that a fellow like that should have drawn the lot. And the worst of it is, laddie, that, now we've started with him, we've got to keep on. We can't possibly raise enough money to pay yearly subscriptions for anybody else. It's Weeks or nobody."

"I suppose we must give him time."

"That's what he says," grunted Ukridge, morosely, helping himself to toast. "He says he doesn't know how to start about it. To listen to him, you'd think that going and having a trifling accident was the sort of delicate and intricate job that required years of study and special preparation. Why, a child of six could do it on his head at five minutes' notice. The man's so infernally particular. You make helpful suggestions, and instead of accepting them in a broad, reasonable spirit of co-operation, he comes back at you every time with some frivolous objection. He's so dashed fastidious. When we were out last night, we came on a couple of navvies scrapping. Good hefty fellows, either of them capable of putting him in hospital for a month. I told him to jump in and start separating them, and he said no; it was a private dispute which was none of his business, and he didn't feel justified in interfering. Finicky, I call it. I tell you, laddie, this blighter is a broken reed. He has got cold feet. We did wrong to let him into the drawing at all. We might have known that a fellow like that would never give results. No conscience. No sense of esprit de corps. No notion of putting himself out to the most trifling extent for the benefit of the community. Haven't you any more marmalade, laddie?"

"I have not."

"Then I'll be going," said Ukridge, moodily. "I suppose," he added, pausing at the door, "you couldn't lend me five bob?"

"How did you guess?"

"Then I'll tell you what," said Ukridge, ever fair and reasonable; "you can stand me dinner to-night." He seemed cheered up for the moment by this happy compromise, but gloom descended on him again. His face clouded. "When I think," he said, "of all the money that's locked up in that poor faint-hearted fish, just waiting to be released, I could sob. Sob, laddie, like a little child. I never liked that man—he has a bad eye and waves his hair. Never trust a man who waves his hair, old horse."

Ukridge's pessimism was not confined to himself. By the end of a fortnight, nothing having happened to Teddy Weeks worse than a slight cold which he shook off in a couple of days, the general consensus of opinion among his apprehensive colleagues in the Syndicate was that the situation had become desperate. There were no signs whatever of any return of the vast capital which we had laid out, and meanwhile meals had to be bought, landladies paid, and a reasonable supply of tobacco acquired. It was a melancholy task in these circumstances to read one's paper of a morning.

All over the inhabited globe, so the well-informed sheet gave one to understand, every kind of accident was happening every day to practically everybody in existence except Teddy Weeks. Farmers in Minnesota were getting mixed up with reaping-machines, peasants in India were being bisected by crocodiles; iron girders from skyscrapers were falling hourly on the heads of citizens in every town from Philadelphia to San Francisco; and the only people who were not down with ptomaine poisoning were those who had walked over cliffs, driven motors into walls, tripped over manholes, or assumed on too slight evidence that the gun was not loaded. In a crippled world, it seemed, Teddy Weeks walked alone, whole and glowing with health. It was one of those grim, ironical, hopeless, grey, despairful situations which the Russian novelists love to write about, and I could not find it in me to blame Ukridge for taking direct action in this crisis. My only regret was that bad luck caused so excellent a plan to miscarry.

My first intimation that he had been trying to hurry

matters on came when he and I were walking along the King's Road one evening, and he drew me into Markham Square, a dismal backwater where he had once had rooms.

"What's the idea?" I asked, for I disliked the place.

"Teddy Weeks lives here," said Ukridge. "In my old rooms." I could not see that this lent any fascination to the place. Every day and in every way I was feeling sorrier and sorrier that I had been foolish enough to put money which I could ill spare into a venture which had all the ear-marks of a wash-out, and my sentiments towards Teddy Weeks were cold and hostile.

"I want to enquire after him."

"Enquire after him? Why?"

"Well, the fact is, laddie, I have an idea that he has been bitten by a dog."

"What makes you think that?"

"Oh, I don't know," said Ukridge, dreamily. "I've just got the idea. You know how one gets ideas."

The mere contemplation of this beautiful event was so inspiring that for a while it held me silent. In each of the ten journals in which we had invested dog-bites were speci-fically recommended as things which every subscriber ought to have. They came about half-way up the list of lucrative accidents, inferior to a broken rib or a fractured fibula, but better value than an ingrowing toe-nail. I was gloating happily over the picture conjured up by Ukridge's words when an exclamation brought me back with a start to the realities of life. A revolting sight met my eyes. Down the street came ambling the familiar figure of Teddy Weeks, and one glance at his elegant person was enough to tell us that our hopes had been built on sand. Not even a toy Pomeranian had chewed this man.

"Hallo, you fellows!" said Teddy Weeks.

"Hallo!" we responded dully.

"Can't stop," said Teddy Weeks. "I've got to fetch a doctor."

"A doctor?"

"Yes. Poor Victor Beamish. He's been bitten by a dog."

Ukridge and I exchanged weary glances. It seemed as if Fate was going out of its way to have sport with us. What was the good of a dog biting Victor Beamish? What was the good of a hundred dogs biting Victor Beamish? A dog-bitten Victor Beamish had no market value whatever.

"You know, that fierce brute that belongs to my landlady," said Teddy Weeks. "The one that always dashes out into the area and barks at people who come to the front door." I remembered. A large mongrel with wild eyes and flashing fangs, badly in need of a haircut. I had encountered it once in the street, when visiting Ukridge, and only the presence of the latter, who knew it well and to whom all dogs were as brothers, had saved me from the doom of Victor Beamish. "Somehow or other he got into my bed-room this evening. He was waiting there when I came home. I had brought Beamish back with me, and the animal pinned him by the leg the moment I opened the door."

"Why didn't he pin you?" asked Ukridge, aggrieved.

"What I can't make out," said Teddy Weeks, "is how on earth the brute came to be in my room. Somebody must have put him there. The whole thing is very mysterious."

"Why didn't he pin you?" demanded Ukridge again.

"Oh, I managed to climb on to the top of the wardrobe while he was biting Beamish," said Teddy Weeks. "And then the landlady came and took him away. But I can't stop here talking. I must go and get that doctor."

We gazed after him in silence as he tripped down the street. We noted the careful manner in which he paused at the corner to eye the traffic before crossing the road, the wary way in which he drew back to allow a truck to rattle past.

"You heard that?" said Ukridge, tensely. "He climbed on to the top of the wardrobe!"

"Yes."

"And you saw the way he dodged that excellent truck?"

"Yes."

"Something's got to be done," said Ukridge, firmly. "The man has got to be awakened to a sense of his responsibilities."

Next day a deputation waited on Teddy Weeks.

Ukridge was our spokesman, and he came to the point with admirable directness.

"How about it?" asked Ukridge.

"How about what?" replied Teddy Weeks, nervously, avoiding his accusing eye.

"When do we get action?"

"Oh, you mean that accident business?"

"Yes."

"I've been thinking about that," said Teddy Weeks.

Ukridge drew the mackintosh which he wore indoors and out of doors and in all weathers more closely around him. There was in the action something suggestive of a member of the Roman Senate about to denounce an enemy of the State. In just such a manner must Cicero have swished his toga as he took a deep breath preparatory to assailing Clodius. He toyed for a moment with the ginger-beer wire which held his pince-nez in place, and endeavoured without success to button his collar at the back. In moments of emotion Ukridge's collar always took on a sort of temperamental jumpiness which no stud could restrain.

"And about time you *were* thinking about it," he boomed, sternly.

We shifted appreciatively in our seats, all except Victor Beamish, who had declined a chair and was standing by the mantelpiece. "Upon my Sam, it's about time you were thinking about it. Do you realise that we've invested an enormous sum on money in you on the distinct understanding that we could rely on you to do your duty and get immediate results? Are we to be forced to the conclusion that you are so yellow and few in the pod as to want to evade your honourable obligations? We thought better of you, Weeks. Upon my Sam, we thought better of you. We took you for a two-fisted, enterprising, big-souled, one hundred-per-cent, he-man who would stand by his friends to the finish."

"Yes, but——"

"Any bloke with a sense of loyalty and an appreciation of what it meant to the rest of us would have rushed out and found some means of fulfilling his duty long ago. You don't even grasp at the opportunities that come your way. Only yesterday I saw you draw back when a single step into the road would have had a truck bumping into you."

"Well, it's not so easy to let a truck bump into you."

"Nonsense. It only requires a little ordinary resolution. Use your imagination, man. Try to think that a child has fallen down in the street—a little golden-haired child," said Ukridge, deeply affected. "And a dashed great cab or something comes rolling up. The kid's mother is standing on the pavement, helpless, her hands clasped in agony. 'Dammit,' she cries, 'will no one save my darling?' 'Yes, by George,' you shout, '*I* will.' And out you jump and the thing's over in half a second. I don't know what you're making such a fuss about."

"Yes, but——" said Teddy Weeks.

"I'm told, what's more, it isn't a bit painful. A sort of dull shock, that's all."

"Who told you that?"

"I forget. Someone."

"Well, you can tell him from me that he's an ass," said Teddy Weeks, with asperity.

" All right. If you object to being run over by a truck there are lots of other ways. But, upon my Sam, it's pretty hopeless suggesting them. You seem to have no enterprise at all. Yesterday, after I went to all the trouble to put a dog in your room, a dog which would have done all the work for you—all that you had to do was stand still and let him use his own judgment—what happened? You climbed on to——"

Victor Beamish interrupted, speaking in a voice husky with emotion.

"Was it you who put that damned dog in the room?"

"Eh?" said Ukridge. "Why, yes. But we can have a good talk about all that later on," he proceeded, hastily. "The point at the moment is how the dickens we're going to persuade this poor worm to collect our insurance money for us. Why, damme, I should have thought you would have——"

"All I can say——" began Victor Beamish, heatedly.

"Yes, yes," said Ukridge; "some other time. Must stick to business now, laddie. I was saying," he resumed, "that I should have thought you would have been as keen as mustard to put the job through for your own sake. You're always beefing that you haven't any clothes to impress managers with. Think of all you can buy with your share of the swag once you have summoned up a little ordinary determination and seen the thing through. Think of the suits, the boots, the hats, the spats. You're always talking about your dashed career, and how all you need to land you in a West-end production is good clothes. Well, here's your chance to get them."

His eloquence was not wasted. A wistful look came into Teddy Weeks's eye, such a look as must have come into the eye of Moses on the summit of Pisgah. He breathed heavily. You could see that the man was mentally walking along Cork Street, weighing the merits of one famous tailor against another.

"I'll tell you what I'll do," he said, suddenly. "It's no use asking me to put this thing through in cold blood. I simply can't do it. I haven't the nerve. But if you fellows will give me a dinner to-night with lots of champagne I think it will key me up to it."

A heavy silence fell upon the room. Champagne! The word was like a knell.

"How on earth are we going to afford champagne?" said Victor Beamish.

"Well, there it is," said Teddy Weeks. "Take it or leave it."

"Gentlemen," said Ukridge, "it would seem that the company requires more capital. How about it, old horses?

Let's get together in a frank, business-like cards-on-the-table spirit, and see what can be done. I can raise ten bob."

"What!" cried the entire assembled company, amazed. "How?"

"I'll pawn a banjo."

"You haven't got a banjo."

"No, but George Tupper has, and I know where he keeps it."

Started in this spirited way, the subscriptions came pouring in. I contributed a cigarette-case, Bertram Fox thought his landlady would let him owe for another week, Robert Dunhill had an uncle in Kensington who, he fancied, if tactfully approached, would be good for a quid, and Victor Beamish said that if the advertisement-manager of the O-So-Eesi Piano-Player was churlish enough to refuse an advance of five shillings against future work he misjudged him sadly. Within a few minutes, in short, the Lightning Drive had produced the impressive total of two pounds six shillings, and we asked Teddy Weeks if he thought that he could get adequately keyed up within the limits of that sum."

"I'll try," said Teddy Weeks.

So, not unmindful of the fact that that excellent hostelry supplied champagne at eight shillings the quart bottle, we fixed the meeting for seven o'clock at Barolini's.

Considered as a social affair, Teddy Weeks's keying-up dinner was not a success. Almost from the start I think we all found it trying. It was not so much the fact that he was drinking deeply of Barolini's eight-shilling champagne while we, from lack of funds, were compelled to confine ourselves to meaner beverages; what really marred the pleasantness of the function was the extraordinary effect the stuff had on Teddy. What was actually in the champagne supplied to Barolini and purveyed by him to the public, such as were reckless enough to drink it, at eight shillings the bottle remains a secret between its maker and his Maker; but three glasses of it were enough to convert Teddy Weeks from a mild and rather oily young man into a truculent swashbuckler.

He quarrelled with us all. With the soup he was tilting at Victor Beamish's theories of Art; the fish found him ridiculing Bertram Fox's views in the future of the motion-picture; and by the time the leg of chicken with dandelion salad arrived—or, as some held, string salad—opinions varied on this point—the hell-brew had so wrought on him that he had begun to lecture Ukridge on his mis-spent life and was urging him in accents audible across the street to go out and get a job and thus acquire sufficient self-respect to enable him to look himself in the face in a mirror without wincing. Not, added Teddy Weeks, with what we all thought un-called-for offensiveness, that any amount of self-respect was likely to do that. Having said which, he called imperiously for another eight bob's worth.

We gazed at one another wanly. However excellent the end towards which all this was tending, there was no denying that it was hard to bear. But policy kept us silent. We recognised that this was Teddy Weeks's evening and that he must be humoured. Victor Beamish said meekly that Teddy had cleared up a lot of points which had been troubling him for a long time. Bertram Fox agreed that there was much in what Teddy had said about the future of the close-up. And even Ukridge, though his haughty soul was seared to its foundations by the latter's personal remarks, promised to take his homily to heart and act upon it at the earliest possible moment.

"You'd better!" said Teddy Weeks, belligerently, biting off the end of one of Barolini's best cigars. "And there's another thing—don't let me hear of your coming and sneaking people's socks again."

"Very well, laddie," said Ukridge, humbly.

"If there is one person in the world that I despise," said Teddy, bending a red-eyed gaze on the offender, "it's a snock-seeker—a seek-snocker—a—well, you know what I mean."

We hastened to assure him that we knew what he meant and he relapsed into a lengthy stupor, from which he emerged three-quarters of an hour later to announce that he didn't 'know what we intended to do, but that he was going. We said that we were going too, and we paid the bill and did so.

Teddy Weeks's indignation on discovering us gathered about him upon the pavement outside the restaurant was intense, and he expressed it freely. Among other things, he said—which was not true—that he had a reputation to keep up in Soho.

"It's all right, Teddy, old horse," said Ukridge, soothingly. "We just thought you would like to have all your old pals round you when you did it."

"Did it? Did what?"

"Why, had the accident."

Teddy Weeks glared at him truculently. Then his mood seemed to change abruptly, and he burst into a loud and hearty laugh.

"Well, of all the silly ideas!" he cried, amusedly. "I'm not going to have an accident. You don't suppose I ever seriously intended to have an accident, do you? It was just my fun." Then, with another sudden change of mood, he seemed to become a victim to an acute unhappiness. He stroked Ukridge's arm affectionately, and a tear rolled down his cheek. "Just my fun," he repeated. "You don't mind my fun, do you?" he asked, pleadingly. "You like my fun, don't you? All my fun. Never meant to have an accident at all. Just wanted dinner." The gay humour of it all overcame his sorrow once more. "Funniest thing ever heard," he said cordially. "Didn't want accident, wanted dinner. Dinner daxident, danner dixident," he added, driving home his point. "Well, good night all," he said, cheerily. And, stepping off the kerb on to a banana-skin, was instantly knocked ten feet by a passing lorry.

"Two ribs and an arm," said the doctor five minutes later, superintending the removal proceedings. "Gently with that stretcher."

It was two weeks before we were informed by the authorities of Charing Cross Hospital that the patient was in a condition to receive visitors. A whip-round secured the price of a basket of fruit, and Ukridge and I were deputed by the shareholders to deliver it with their compliments and kind enquiries.

"Hallo!" we said in a hushed, bedside manner when finally admitted to his presence.

"Sit down, gentlemen," replied the invalid.

I must confess even in that first moment to having experienced a slight feeling of surprise. It was not like Teddy Weeks to call us gentlemen. Ukridge, however, seemed to notice nothing amiss.

"Well, well, well," he said, buoyantly. "And how are you, laddie? We've brought you a few fragments of fruit."

"I am getting along capitally," replied Teddy Weeks, still in that odd precise way which had made his opening words strike me as curious. "And I should like to say that in my opinion England has reason to be proud of the alertness and enterprise of her great journals. The excellence of their reading-matter, the ingenuity of their various competitions, and, above all, the go-ahead spirit which has resulted in this accident insurance scheme are beyond praise. Have you got that down?" he enquired.

Ukridge and I looked at each other. We had been told that Teddy was practically normal again, but this sounded like delirium.

"Have we got that down, old horse?" asked Ukridge, gently.

Teddy Weeks seemed surprised.

"Aren't you reporters?"

"How do you mean, reporters?"

"I thought you had come from one of these weekly papers that have been paying me insurance money, to interview me," said Teddy Weeks.

Ukridge and I exchanged another glance. An uneasy glance this time. I think that already a grim forboding had begun to cast its shadow over us.

"Surely you remember me, Teddy, old horse?" said Ukridge, anxiously.

Teddy Weeks knit his brow, concentrating painfully.

"Why, of course," he said at last. "You're Ukridge, aren't you?"

"That's right. Ukridge."

"Of course. Ukridge."

"Yes. Ukridge. Funny your forgetting me!"

"Yes," said Teddy Weeks. "It's the effect of the shock I got when that thing bowled me over. I must have been struck on the head, I suppose. It has had the effect of rendering my memory rather uncertain. The doctors here are very interested. They say it is a most unusual case. I can remember some things perfectly, but in some ways my memory is a complete blank."

"Oh, but I say, old horse," quavered Ukridge. "I suppose you haven't forgotten about that insurance, have you?"

"Oh, no, I remember that."

Ukridge breathed a relieved sigh.

"I was a subscriber to a number of weekly papers," went on Teddy Weeks. "They are paying me insurance money now."

"Yes, yes, old horse," cried Ukridge. "But what I mean is you remember the Syndicate, don't you?"

Teddy Weeks raised his eyebrows.

"Syndicate? What Syndicate?"

"Why, when we all got together and put up the money to pay for the subscriptions to these papers and drew lots, to choose which of us should go out and have an accident and collect the money. And you drew it, don't you remember?"

Utter astonishment, and a shocked astonishment at that, spread itself over Teddy Weeks's countenance. The man seemed outraged.

"I certainly remember nothing of the kind," he said, severely. "I cannot imagine myself for a moment consenting to become a party to what from your own account would appear to have been a criminal conspiracy to obtain money under false pretences from a number of weekly papers."

"But, laddie——"

"However," said Teddy Weeks, "if there is any truth in this story, no doubt you have documentary evidence to support it."

Ukridge looked at me. I looked at Ukridge. There was a long silence.

"Shift-ho, old horse?" said Ukridge, sadly. "No use staying on here."

"No," I replied, with equal gloom. "May as well go."

"Glad to have seen you," said Teddy Weeks, "and thanks for the fruit."

The next time I saw the man he was coming out of a manager's office in the Haymarket. He had on a new Homburg hat of a delicate pearl grey, spats to match, and a new blue flannel suit, beautifully cut, with an invisible red twill. He was looking jubilant, and, as I passed him, he drew from his pocket a gold cigarette-case.

It was shortly after that, if you remember, that he made a big hit as the juvenile lead in that piece at the Apollo and started on his sensational career as a *matinée* idol.

Inside the church the organ had swelled into the familiar music of the Wedding March. A verger came out and opened the doors. The five cooks ceased their reminiscences of other and smarter weddings at which they had participated. The camera-men unshipped their cameras. The costermonger moved his barrow of vegetables a pace forward. A dishevelled and unshaven man at my side uttered a disapproving growl.

"Idle rich!" said the dishevelled man.

Out of the church came a beauteous being, leading attached to his arm another being, somewhat less beauteous.

There was no denying the spectacular effect of Teddy Weeks. He was handsomer than ever. His sleek hair gorgeously waved, shone in the sun, his eyes were large and bright; his lissom frame, garbed in faultless morning-coat and trousers, was that of an Apollo. But his bride gave the impression that Teddy had married money. They paused in the doorway, and the camera-men became active and fussy.

"Have you got a shilling, laddie?" said Ukridge, in a low, level voice.

"Why do you want a shilling?"

"Old horse," said Ukridge, tensely, "it is of the utmost vital importance that I have a shilling here and now."

I passed it over. Ukridge turned to the dishevelled man, and I perceived that he held in his hand a large rich tomato of juicy and over-ripe appearance.

"Would you like to earn a bob?" Ukridge said.

"Would I!" replied the dishevelled man.

Ukridge sank his voice to a hoarse whisper.

The camera-men had finished their preparations. Teddy Weeks, his head thrown back in that gallant way which has endeared him to so many female hearts, was exhibiting his celebrated teeth. The cooks, in undertones, were making adverse comments on the appearance of the bride.

"Now, please," said one of the camera-men.

Over the heads of the crowd, well and truly aimed, whizzed a large juicy tomato. It burst like a shell full between Teddy Weeks's expressive eyes, obliterating them in scarlet ruin. It spattered Teddy Weeks's collar, it dripped on Teddy Weeks's morning-coat. And the dishevelled man turned abruptly and raced off down the street.

Ukridge grasped my arm. There was a look of deep content in his eyes.

"Shift-ho?" said Ukridge.

Arm-in-arm we strolled off in the pleasant June sunshine.

*   *   *   *   *

Into the face of the young man who sat on the terrace of the hotel at Cannes there had crept a look of furtive shame, the shifty, hangdog look which announces that an Englishman is about to talk French.

HIGH STAKES

THE summer day was drawing to a close. Over the terrace outside the club-house the chestnut trees threw long shadows, and such bees as still lingered in the flower-beds had the air of tired business men who are about ready to shut up the office and go off to dinner and a musical comedy. The Oldest Member, stirring in his favourite chair, glanced at his watch and yawned.

As he did so, from the neighbourhood of the eighteenth green, hidden from his view by the slope of the ground, there came suddenly a medley of shrill animal cries, and he deduced that some belated match must just have reached a finish. His surmise was correct. The babble of voices drew nearer, and over the brow of the hill came a little group of men. Two, who appeared to be the ring-leaders in the affair, were short and stout. One was cheerful and the other dejected. The rest of the company consisted of friends and adherents; and one of these, a young man who seemed to be amused, strolled to where the Oldest Member sat.

"What," inquired the Sage, "was all the shouting for?"

The young man sank into a chair and lighted a cigarette.

"Perkins and Broster," he said, "were all square at the seventeenth, and they raised the stakes to fifty pounds. They were both on the green in seven, and Perkins had a two-foot putt to halve the match. He missed it by six inches. They play pretty high, those two."

"It is a curious thing," said the Oldest Member, "that men whose golf is of a kind that makes hardened caddies wince always do. The more competent a player, the smaller the stake that contents him. It is only when you get down into the submerged tenth of the golfing world that you find the big gambling. However, I would not call fifty pounds anything sensational in the case of two men like Perkins and

Broster. They are both well provided with the world's goods. If you would care to hear the story——"

The young man's jaw fell a couple of notches.

"I had no idea it was so late," he bleated. "I ought to be——"

"——of a man who played for really high stakes——"

"I promised to——"

"——I will tell it to you," said the Sage.

"Look here," said the young man, sullenly, "it isn't one of those stories about two men who fall in love with the same girl and play a match to decide which is to marry her, is it? Because if so——"

"The stake to which I allude," said the Oldest Member, "was something far higher and bigger than a woman's love. Shall I proceed?"

"All right," said the young man, resignedly. "Snap into it."

It has been well said—I think by the man who wrote the sub-titles for "Cage-Birds of Society" (began the Oldest Member)—that wealth does not always bring happiness. It was so with Bradbury Fisher, the hero of the story which I am about to relate. One of America's most prominent tainted millionaires, he had two sorrows in life—his handicap refused to stir from twenty-four and his wife disapproved of his collection of famous golf relics. Once, finding him crooning over the trousers in which Ouimet had won his historic replay against Vardon and Ray in the American Open, she had asked him why he did not collect something worth while, like Old Masters or first editions.

Worth while! Bradbury had forgiven, for he loved the woman, but he could not forget.

For Bradbury Fisher, like so many men who had taken to the game in middle age, after a youth misspent in the pursuits of commerce, was no half-hearted enthusiast. Although he still occasionally descended on Wall Street in order to pry the small investor loose from another couple of million, what he really lived for now was golf and his collection. He had begun the collection in his first year as a golfer, and he prized it dearly. And when he reflected that his wife had stopped him purchasing J. H. Taylor's shirt-stud, which he could have had for a few hundred pounds, the iron seemed to enter into his soul.

The distressing episode had occurred in London, and he was now on his way back to New York, having left his wife to continue her holiday in England. All through the voyage he remained moody and distrait; and at the ship's concert, at which he was forced to take the chair, he was heard to observe to the purser that if the alleged soprano who had just sung "My little Grey Home in the West" had the immortal gall to take a second encore he hoped that she would trip over a high note and dislocate her neck.

Such was Bradbury Fisher's mood throughout the ocean journey, and it remained constant until he arrived at his palatial home at Goldenville, Long Island, where, as he sat smoking a moody after-dinner cigar in the Versailles drawing-room, Blizzard, his English butler, informed him that Mr. Gladstone Bott desired to speak to him on the telephone.

"Tell him to go and boil himself," said Bradbury.

"Very good, sir."

"No, I'll tell him myself," said Bradbury. He strode to the telephone. "Hullo!" he said, curtly.

He was not fond of this Bott. There are certain men who seemed fated to go through life as rivals. It was so with Bradbury Fisher and J. Gladstone Bott. Born in the same town within a few days of one another, they had come to New York in the same week; and from that moment their careers had run side by side. Fisher had made his first million two days before Bott, but Bott's first divorce had got half a column and two sticks more publicity than Fisher's.

At Sing-Sing, where each had spent several happy years of early manhood, they had run neck and neck for the prizes which that institution has to offer. Fisher secured the position of catcher in the baseball nine in preference to Bott, but Bott just nosed Fisher out when it came to the choice of a tenor for the glee club. Bott was selected for the debating contest against Auburn, but Fisher got the last place on the crossword puzzle team, with Bott merely first reserve.

They had taken up golf simultaneously, and their handicaps had remained level ever since. Between such men it is not surprising that there was little love lost.

"Hullo!" said Gladstone Bott. "So you're back? Say, listen, Fisher. I think I've got something that'll interest you. Something you'll be glad to have in your golf collection."

Bradbury Fisher's mood softened. He disliked Bott, but that was no reason for not doing business with him. And though he had little faith in the man's judgment it might be that he had stumbled upon some valuable antique. There crossed his mind the comforting thought that his wife was three thousand miles away and that he was no longer under her penetrating eye—that eye which, so to speak, was always "about his bath and about his bed and spying out all his ways."

"I've just returned from a trip down South," proceeded Bott, "and I have secured the authentic baffy used by Bobby Jones in his first important contest—the Infants' All-In Championship of Atlanta, Georgia, open to those of both sexes not yet having finished teething."

Bradbury gasped. He had heard rumours that this treasure was in existence, but he had never credited them.

"You're sure?" he cried. "You're positive it's genuine?"

"I have a written guarantee from Mr. Jones, Mrs. Jones, and the nurse."

"How much, Bott, old man?" stammered Bradbury. "How much do you want for it, Gladstone, old top? I'll give you a hundred thousand dollars."

"Ha!"

"Five hundred thousand."

"Ha, ha!"

"A million."

"Ha, ha, ha!"

"Two million."

"Ha, ha, ha, ha!"

Bradbury Fisher's strong face twisted like that of a tortured fiend. He registered in quick succession rage, despair, hate, fury, anguish, pique, and resentment. But when he spoke again his voice was soft and gentle.

"Gladdy, old socks," he said, "we have been friends for years."

"No, we haven't," said Gladstone Bott.

"Yes, we have."

"No, we haven't."

"Well, anyway, what about two million five hundred?"

"Nothing doing. Say, listen. Do you really want that baffy?"

"I do, Botty, old egg, I do indeed."

"Then listen. I'll exchange it for Blizzard."

"For Blizzard?" quavered Fisher.

"For Blizzard."

It occurs to me that, when describing the closeness of the rivalry between these two men I may have conveyed the impression that in no department of life could either claim a definite advantage over the other. If that is so, I erred. It is true that in a general way, whatever one had, the other had something equally good to counterbalance it; but in just one matter Bradbury Fisher had triumphed completely over Gladstone Bott. Bradbury Fisher had the finest English butler on Long Island.

Blizzard stood alone. There is a regrettable tendency on the part of English butlers to-day to deviate more and more from the type which made their species famous. The modern butler has a nasty knack of being a lissom young man in perfect condition who looks like the son of the house. But Blizzard was of the fine old school. Before coming to the Fisher home he had been for fifteen years in the service of an earl, and his appearance suggested that throughout those fifteen years he had not let a day pass without its pint of port. He radiated port and pop-eyed dignity. He had splay feet and three chins,

215

and when he walked his curving waistcoat preceded him like the advance guard of some royal procession.

From the first, Bradbury had been perfectly aware that Bott coveted Blizzard, and the knowledge had sweetened his life. But this was the first time he had come out into the open and admitted it.

"Blizzard?" whispered Fisher.

"Blizzard," said Bott firmly. "It's my wife's birthday next week, and I've been wondering what to give her."

Bradbury Fisher shuddered from head to foot, and his legs wobbled like asparagus stalks. Beads of perspiration stood out on his forehead. The serpent was tempting him—tempting him grievously.

"You're sure you won't take three million—or four—or something like that?"

"No; I want Blizzard."

Bradbury Fisher passed his handkerchief over his streaming brow.

"So be it," he said in a low voice.

The Jones baffy arrived that night, and for some hours Bradbury Fisher gloated over it with the unmixed joy of a collector who has secured the prize of a lifetime. Then, stealing gradually over him, came the realisation of what he had done.

He was thinking of his wife and what she would say when she heard of this. Blizzard was Mrs. Fisher's pride and joy. She had never, like the poet, nursed a dear gazelle, but, had she done so, her attitude towards it would have been identical with her attitude towards Blizzard. Although so far away, it was plain that her thoughts still lingered with the pleasure she had left at home, for on his arrival Bradbury had found three cables awaiting him.

The first ran:

"How is Blizzard? Reply."

The second:

"How is Blizzard's sciatica? Reply."

216

The third:

"*Blizzard's hiccups. How are they? Suggest Doctor Murphy's Tonic Swamp-Juice. Highly spoken of. Three times a day after meals. Try for week and cable result.*"

It did not require a clairvoyant to tell Bradbury that, if on her return she found that he had disposed of Blizzard in exchange for a child's cut-down baffy, she would certainly sue him for divorce. And there was not a jury in America that would not give their verdict in her favour without a dissentient voice. His first wife, he recalled, had divorced him on far flimsier grounds. So had his second, third, and fourth. And Bradbury loved his wife. There had been a time in his life when, if he lost a wife, he had felt philosophically that there would be another along in a minute; but, as a man grows older, he tends to become set in his habits, and he could not contemplate existence without the company of the present incumbent.

What, therefore, to do? What, when you came right down to it, to do?

There seemed no way out of the dilemma. If he kept the Jones baffy, no other price would satisfy Bott's jealous greed. And to part with the baffy, now that it was actually in his possession, was unthinkable.

And then, in the small hours of the morning, as he tossed sleeplessly on his Louis Quinze bed, his giant brain conceived a plan.

On the following afternoon he made his way to the clubhouse, and was informed that Bott was out playing a round with another millionaire of his acquaintance. Bradbury waited, and presently his rival appeared.

"Hey!" said Gladstone Bott, in his abrupt, uncouth way. "When are you going to deliver that butler?"

"I will make the shipment at the earliest date," said Bradbury.

"I was expecting him last night."

"You shall have him shortly."

"What do you feed him on?" asked Gladstone Bott.

"Oh, anything you have yourselves. Put sulphur in his port in the hot weather. Tell me, how did your match go?"

"He beat me. I had rotten luck."

Bradbury Fisher's eye gleamed. His moment had come.

"Luck?" he said. "What do you mean, luck? Luck has nothing to do with it. You're always beefing about your luck. The trouble with you is that you play rottenly."

"What!"

"It is no use trying to play golf unless you learn the first principles and do it properly. Look at the way you drive."

"What's wrong with my driving?"

"Nothing, except that you don't do anything right. In driving, as the club comes back in the swing, the weight should be shifted by degrees, quietly and gradually, until, when the club has reached its top-most point, the whole weight of the body is supported by the right leg, the left foot being turned at the time and the left knee bent in toward the right leg. But, regardless of how much you perfect your style, you cannot develop any method which will not require you to keep your head still so that you can see your ball clearly."

"Hey!"

"It is obvious that it is impossible to introduce a jerk or a sudden violent effort into any part of the swing without disturbing the balance or moving the head. I want to drive home the fact that it is absolutely essential to——"

"Hey!" cried Gladstone Bott.

The man was shaken to the core. From the local pro, and from scratch men of his acquaintance, he would gladly have listened to this sort of thing by the hour, but to hear these words from Bradbury Fisher, whose handicap was the same as his own, and out of whom it was his unperishable conviction that he could hammer the tar any time he got him out on the links, was too much.

"Where do you get off," he demanded, heatedly, "trying to teach me golf?"

Bradbury Fisher chuckled to himself. Everything was working out as his subtle mind had foreseen.

"My dear fellow," he said, "I was only speaking for your good."

"I like your nerve! I can lick you any time we start."

"It's easy enough to talk."

"I trimmed you twice the week before you sailed to England."

"Naturally," said Bradbury Fisher, "in a friendly round, with only a few thousand dollars on the match, a man does not extend himself. You wouldn't dare to play me for anything that really mattered."

"I'll play you when you like for anything you like."

"Very well. I'll play you for Blizzard."

"Against what?"

"Oh, anything you please. How about a couple of railroads?"

"Make it three."

"Very well."

"Next Friday suit you?"

"Sure," said Bradbury Fisher.

It seemed to him that his troubles were over. Like all twenty-four handicap men, he had the most perfect confidence in his ability to beat all other twenty-four handicap men. As for Gladstone Bott, he knew that he could disembowel him any time he was able to lure him out of the clubhouse.

Nevertheless, as he breakfasted on the morning of the fateful match, Bradbury Fisher was conscious of an unwonted nervousness. He was no weakling. In Wall Street his phlegm in movements of stress was a by-word. On the famous occasion when the B. and G. crowd had attacked C. and D., and in order to keep control of L. and M. he had been compelled to buy so largely of S. and T., he had not turned a hair. And yet this morning, in endeavouring to prong up segments of bacon, he twice missed the plate altogether and on a third occasion speared himself in the cheek with his fork. The spectacle of Blizzard, so calm, so competent, so supremely the perfect butler, unnerved him.

"I am jumpy to-day, Blizzard," he said, forcing a laugh.

"Yes, sir. You do, indeed, appear to have the willies."

"Yes. I am playing a very important golf-match this morning."

"Indeed, sir?"

"I must pull myself together, Blizzard."

"Yes, sir. And, if I may respectfully make the suggestion, you should endeavour, when in action, to keep the head down and the eye rigidly upon the ball."

"I will, Blizzard, I will," said Bradbury Fisher, his keen eyes clouding under a sudden mist of tears. "Thank you, Blizzard, for the advice."

"Not at all, sir."

"How is your sciatica, Blizzard?"

"A trifle improved, I thank you, sir."

"And your hiccups?"

"I am conscious of a slight though possibly only a temporary relief, sir."

"Good," said Bradbury Fisher.

He left the room with a firm step; and, proceeding to his library, read for a while portions of that grand chapter in James Braid's "Advanced Golf" which deals with driving into the wind. It was a fair and cloudless morning, but it was as well to be prepared for emergencies. Then, feeling that he had done all that could be done, he ordered the car and was taken to the links.

Gladstone Bott was awaiting him on the first tee, in company with two caddies. A curt greeting, a spin of the coin, and Gladstone Bott, securing the honour, stepped out to begin the contest.

Although there are, of course, endless sub-species in their ranks, not all of which have yet been classified by science, twenty-four handicap golfers may be stated broadly to fall into two classes, the dashing and the cautious—those, that is to say, who endeavour to do every hole in a brilliant one and those who are content to win with a steady nine. Gladstone Bott was one of the cautious brigade. He fussed about for a few moments like a hen scratching gravel, then with a stiff quarter swing sent his ball straight down the fairway for a matter of seventy yards, and it was Bradbury Fisher's turn to drive.

Now, normally, Bradbury Fisher was essentially a dasher. It was his habit, as a rule, to raise his left foot some six inches from the ground, and having swayed forcefully back on to his right leg, to sway sharply forward again and lash out with sickening violence in the general direction of the ball. It was a method which at times produced excellent results, though it had the flaw that it was somewhat uncertain. Bradbury Fisher was the only member of the club, with the exception of the club champion, who had even carried the second green with his drive; but, on the other hand, he was also the only member who had ever laid his drive on the eleventh dead to the pin of the sixteenth.

But to-day the magnitude of the issues at stake had wrought a change in him. Planted firmly on both feet, he fiddled at the ball in the manner of one playing spillikins. When he swung, it was with a swing resembling that of Gladstone Bott; and, like Bott, he achieved a nice, steady, rainbow-shaped drive of some seventy yards straight down the middle. Bott replied with an eighty-yard brassie shot. Bradbury held him with another. And so, working their way cautiously across the prairie, they came to the green, where Bradbury, laying his third putt dead, halved the hole.

The second was a repetition of the first, the third and fourth repetitions of the second. But on the fifth green the fortunes of the match began to change. Here Gladstone Bott, faced with a fifteen-foot putt to win, smote his ball firmly off the line, as had been his practice at each of the preceding holes, and the ball, hitting a worm-cast and bounding off to the left, ran on a couple of yards, hit another worm-cast, bounded to the right, and finally, bumping into a twig, leaped to the left again and clattered into the tin.

"One up," said Gladstone Bott. "Tricky, some of these greens are. You have to gauge the angles to a nicety."

At the sixth a donkey in an adjoining field uttered a raucous bray just as Bott was addressing his ball with a mashie-niblick on the edge of the green. He started violently and, jerking his club with a spasmodic reflex action of the forearm, holed out.

"Nice work," said Gladstone Bott.

The seventh was a short hole, guarded by two large bunkers between which ran a narrow footpath of turf. Gladstone Bott's mashie-shot, falling short, ran over the rough, peered for a moment into the depths to the left, then, winding up the path, trickled on to the green, struck a fortunate slope, acquired momentum, ran on, and dropped into the hole.

"Nearly missed it," said Gladstone Bott, drawing a deep breath.

Bradbury Fisher looked out upon a world that swam and danced before his eyes. He had not been prepared for this sort of thing. The way things were shaping, he felt that it would hardly surprise him now if the cups were to start jumping up and snapping at Bott's ball like starving dogs.

"Three up," said Gladstone Bott.

With a strong effort Bradbury Fisher mastered his feelings. His mouth set grimly. Matters, he perceived, had reached a crisis. He saw now that he had made a mistake in allowing himself to be intimidated by the importance of the occasion into being scientific. Nature had never intended him for a scientific golfer, and up till now he had been behaving like an animated illustration out of a book by Vardon. He had taken his club back along and near the turf, allowing it to trend around the legs as far as was permitted by the movement of the arms. He had kept his right elbow close to the side, this action coming into operation before the club was allowed to describe a section of a circle in an upward direction, whence it was carried by means of a slow, steady, swinging movement. He had pivoted, he had pronated the wrists, and he had been careful about the lateral hip-shift.

And it had been all wrong. That sort of stuff might suit some people, but not him. He was a biffer, a swatter, and a slosher; and it flashed upon him now that only by biffing, swatting, and sloshing as he had never biffed, swatted, and sloshed before could he hope to recover the ground he had lost.

Gladstone Bott was not one of those players who grow careless with success. His drive at the eighth was just as steady and short as ever. But this time Bradbury Fisher made no attempt to imitate him. For seven holes he had been checking his natural instincts, and now he drove with all the banked-up fury that comes with release from long suppression.

For an instant he remained poised on one leg like a stork; then there was a whistle and a crack, and the ball, smitten squarely in the midriff, flew down the course and, soaring over the bunkers, hit the turf and gambolled to within twenty yards of the green.

He straightened out the kinks in his spine with a grim smile. Allowing himself the regulation three putts, he would be down in five, and only a miracle could give Gladstone Bott anything better than a seven.

"Two down," he said some minutes later, and Gladstone Bott nodded sullenly.

It was not often that Bradbury Fisher kept on the fairway with two consecutive drives, but strange things were happening to-day. Not only was his drive at the ninth a full two hundred and forty yards, but it was also perfectly straight.

"One down," said Bradbury Fisher, and Bott nodded even more sullenly than before.

There are few things more demoralising than to be consistently outdriven; and when he is outdriven by a hundred and seventy yards at two consecutive holes the bravest man is apt to be shaken. Gladstone Bott was only human. It was with a sinking heart that he watched his opponent heave and sway on the tenth tee; and when the ball once more flew straight and far down the course a strange weakness seemed to come over him. For the first time he lost his morale and topped. The ball trickled into the long grass, and after three fruitless stabs at it with a niblick he picked up, and the match was squared.

At the eleventh Bradbury Fisher also topped, and his tee-shot, though nice and straight, travelled only a couple of feet. He had to scramble to halve in eight.

The twelfth was another short hole; and Bradbury, unable to curb the fine, careless rapture which had crept into his game had the misfortune to overshoot the green by some sixty yards, thus enabling his opponent to take the lead once more.

The thirteenth and fourteenth were halved, but Bradbury, driving another long ball, won the fifteenth, squaring the match.

It seemed to Bradbury Fisher, as he took his stand on the sixteenth tee, that he now had the situation well in hand. At the thirteenth and fourteenth his drive had flickered, but on the fifteenth it had come back in all its glorious vigour and there appeared to be no reason to suppose that it had not come to stay. He recollected exactly how he had done that last colossal slosh, and he now prepared to reproduce the movements precisely as before. The great thing to remember was to hold the breath on the back-swing and not to release it before the moment of impact. Also, the eyes should not be closed until late in the down-swing. All great golfers have their little secrets, and that was Bradbury's.

With these aids to success firmly fixed in his mind, Bradbury Fisher prepared to give the ball the nastiest bang that a golf-ball had ever had since Edward Blackwell was in his prime. He drew in his breath and, with lungs expanded to their fullest capacity, heaved back on to his large, flat right foot. Then, clenching his teeth, he lashed out.

When he opened his eyes, they fell upon a horrid spectacle. Either he had closed those eyes too soon or else he had breathed too precipitately—whatever the cause, the ball, which should have gone due south, was travelling with great speed sou'-sou'-east. And, even as he gazed, it curved to earth and fell into as uninviting a bit of rough as he had ever penetrated. And he was a man who had spent much time in many roughs.

Leaving Gladstone Bott to continue his imitation of a spavined octogenarian rolling peanuts with a toothpick, Bradbury Fisher, followed by his caddie, set out on the long trail into the jungle.

Hope did not altogether desert him as he walked. In spite of its erratic direction, the ball had been so shrewdly smitten that it was not far from the green. Provided luck was with him and the lie not too desperate, a mashie would put him on the carpet. It was only when he reached the rough and saw what had happened that his heart sank. There the ball lay, half hidden in the grass, while above it waved the straggling tentacle of some tough-looking shrub. Behind it was a stone, and behind the stone, at just the elevation required to catch the back-swing of the club, was a tree. And, by an ironical stroke of fate which drew from Bradbury a hollow, bitter laugh, only a few feet to the right was a beautiful smooth piece of turf from which it would have been a pleasure to play one's second.

Dully, Bradbury looked round to see how Bott was getting on. And then suddenly, as he found that Bott was completely invisible behind the belt of bushes through which he had just passed, a voice seemed to whisper to him, "Why not?"

Bradbury Fisher, remember, had spent thirty years in Wall Street.

It was at this moment that he realised that he was not alone. His caddie was standing at his side.

Bradbury Fisher gazed upon the caddie, whom until now he had not had any occasion to observe with any closeness.

The caddie was not a boy. He was a man, apparently in the middle forties, with bushy eyebrows and a walrus moustache; and there was something in his appearance which suggested to

Bradbury that here was a kindred spirit. He reminded Bradbury a little of Spike Huggins, the safe-blower, who had been a fresher with him at Sing-Sing. It seemed to him that this caddie could be trusted in a delicate matter involving secrecy and silence. Had he been some babbling urchin, the risk might have been too great.

"Caddie," said Bradbury.

"Sir?" said the caddie.

"Yours is an ill-paid job," said Bradbury.

"It is indeed, sir," said the caddie.

"Would you like to earn fifty dollars?"

"I would prefer to earn a hundred."

"I meant a hundred," said Bradbury.

He produced a roll of bills from his pocket, and peeled off one of that value. Then, stooping, he picked up his ball and placed it on the little oasis of turf. The caddie bowed intelligently.

"You mean to say," cried Gladstone Bott, a few moments later, "that you were out with your second? With your second!"

"I had a stroke of luck."

"You're sure it wasn't about six strokes of luck?"

"My ball was right out in the open in an excellent lie."

"Oh!" said Gladstone Bott, shortly.

"I have four for it, I think."

"One down," said Gladstone Bott.

"And two to play," trilled Bradbury.

It was with a light heart that Bradbury Fisher teed up on the seventeenth. The match, he felt, was as good as over. The whole essence of golf is to discover a way of getting out of rough without losing strokes; and with this sensible, broad-minded man of the world caddying for him, he seemed to have discovered the ideal way. It cost him scarcely a pang when he saw his drive slice away into a tangle of long grass, but for the sake of appearances he affected a little chagrin.

"Tut, tut!" he said.

"I shouldn't worry," said Gladstone Bott. "You will

probably find it sitting upon an indiarubber tee which some-one has dropped there."

He spoke sardonically, and Bradbury did not like his manner. But then he never had liked Gladstone Bott's manner, so what of that? He made his way to where the ball had fallen. It was lying under a bush.

"Caddie," said Bradbury.

"Sir?" said the caddie.

"A hundred?"

"And fifty."

"And fifty," said Bradbury Fisher.

Gladstone Bott was still toiling along the fairway when Bradbury reached the green.

"How many?" he asked, eventually winning to the goal.

"On in two," said Bradbury. "And you?"

"Playing seven."

"Then let me see. If you take two putts, which is most unlikely, I shall have six for the hole and match."

A minute later Bradbury had picked up his ball out of the cup. He stood there, basking in the sunshine, his heart glowing with quiet happiness. It seemed to him that he had never seen the countryside looking so beautiful. The birds appeared to be singing as they had never sung before. The trees and the rolling turf had taken on a charm beyond anything he had ever encountered. Even Gladstone Bott looked almost bearable.

"A very pleasant match," he said, cordially, "conducted throughout in the most sporting spirit. At one time I thought you were going to pull it off, old man, but there—class will tell."

"I will now make my report," said the caddie with the walrus moustache.

"Do so," said Gladstone Bott, briefly.

Bradbury Fisher stared at the man with blanched cheeks. The sun had ceased to shine, the birds had stopped singing. The trees and the rolling turf looked pretty rotten, and Gladstone Bott perfectly foul. His heart was leaden with a hideous dread.

"Your report? Your—your report? What do you mean?"

"You don't suppose," said Gladstone Bott, "that I would play you an important match unless I had detectives watching you, do you? This gentleman is from the Quick Results Agency. What have you to report?" he said, turning to the caddie.

The caddie removed his bushy eyebrows, and with a quick gesture swept off his moustache.

"On the twelfth inst.," he began in a monotonous, sing-song voice, "acting upon instructions received, I made my way to the Goldenville Golf Links in order to observe the movements of the man Fisher. I had adopted for the occasion the Number Three disguise and——"

"All right, all right," said Gladstone Bott, impatiently. "You can skip all that. Come down to what happened at the sixteenth."

The caddie looked wounded, but he bowed deferentially.

"At the sixteenth hole the man Fisher moved his ball into what—from his actions and furtive manner—I deduced to be a more favourable position."

"Ah!" said Gladstone Bott.

"On the seventeenth the man Fisher picked up his ball and threw it with a movement of the wrist on to the green."

"It's a lie. A foul and contemptible lie," shouted Bradbury Fisher.

"Realising that the man Fisher might adopt this attitude, sir," said the caddie, "I took the precaution of snap-shotting him in the act with my miniature, wrist-watch camera, the detective's best friend."

Bradbury Fisher covered his face with his hands and uttered a hollow groan.

"My match," said Gladstone Bott, with vindictive triumph. "I'll trouble you to deliver that butler to me f.o.b. at my residence not later than noon to-morrow. Oh yes, and I was forgetting. You owe me three railroads."

Blizzard, dignified but kindly, met Bradbury in the Byzantine hall on his return home.

"I trust your golf-match terminated satisfactorily, sir?" said the butler.

A pang, almost too poignant to be borne, shot through Bradbury.

"No, Blizzard," he said. "No. Thank you for your kind inquiry, but I was not in luck."

"Too bad, sir," said Blizzard, sympathetically. "I trust the prize at stake was not excessive?"

"Well—er—well, it was rather big. I should like to speak to you about that a little later, Blizzard."

"At any time that is suitable to you, sir. If you will ring for one of the assistant-under-footmen when you desire to see me, sir, he will find me in my pantry. Meanwhile, sir, this cable arrived for you a short while back."

Bradbury took the envelope listlessly. He had been expecting a communication from his London agents announcing that they had bought Kent and Sussex, for which he had instructed them to make a firm offer just before he left England. No doubt this was their cable.

He opened the envelope, and started as if it had contained a scorpion. It was from his wife.

"*Returning immediately 'Aquitania,'*" (it ran) "*Docking Friday night. Meet without fail.*"

Bradbury stared at the words, frozen to the marrow. Although he had been in a sort of trance ever since that dreadful moment on the seventeenth green, his great brain had not altogether ceased to function; and, while driving home in the car, he had sketched out roughly a plan of action which, he felt, might meet the crisis. Assuming that Mrs. Fisher was to remain abroad for another month, he had practically decided to buy a daily paper, insert in it a front-page story announcing the death of Blizzard, forward the clipping to his wife, and then sell his house and move to another neighbourhood. In this way it might be that she would never learn of what had occurred.

But if she was due back next Friday, the scheme fell through and exposure was inevitable.

He wondered dully what had caused her change of plans and came to the conclusion that some feminine sixth sense must have warned her of peril threatening Blizzard. With a good deal of peevishness he wished that Providence had never endowed women with this sixth sense. A woman with merely five took quite enough handling.

"Sweet suffering soup-spoons!" groaned Bradbury.

"Sir?" said Blizzard.

"Nothing," said Bradbury.

"Very good, sir," said Blizzard.

For a man with anything on his mind, any little trouble calculated to affect the *joie de vivre*, there are few spots less cheering than the Customs shed of New York. Draughts whistle dismally there—now to, now fro. Strange noises are heard. Customs officials chew gum and lurk grimly in the shadows, like tigers awaiting the luncheon-gong. It is not surprising that Bradbury's spirits, low when he reached the place, should have sunk to zero long before the gang-plank was lowered and the passengers began to stream down it.

His wife was among the first to land. How beautiful she looked, thought Bradbury, as he watched her. And, alas, how intimidating. His tastes had always lain in the direction of spirited women. His first wife had been spirited. So had his second, third, and fourth. And the one at the moment holding office was perhaps the most spirited of the whole platoon. For one long instant, as he went to meet her, Bradbury Fisher was conscious of a regret that he had not married one of those meek, mild girls who suffer uncomplainingly at their husband's hands in the more hectic type of feminine novel. What he felt he could have done with at the moment was the sort of wife who thinks herself dashed lucky if the other half of the sketch does not drag her round the billiard-room by her hair, kicking her the while with spiked shoes.

Three conversational openings presented themselves to him as he approached her.

"Darling, there is something I want to tell you——"

"Dearest, I have a small confession to make——"

"Sweetheart, I don't know if by any chance you remember Blizzard, our butler. Well, it's like this——"

But, in the event, it was she who spoke first.

"Oh, Bradbury," she cried, rushing into his arms, "I've done the most awful thing, and you must try to forgive me!"

Bradbury blinked. He had never seen her in this strange mood before. As she clung to him, she seemed timid, fluttering, and—although a woman who weighed a full hundred and fifty-seven pounds—almost fragile.

"What is it?" he inquired, tenderly. "Has somebody stolen your jewels?"

"No, no."

"Have you been losing money at bridge?"

"No, no. Worse than that."

Bradbury started.

"You didn't sing 'My little Grey Home in the West' at the ship's concert?" he demanded, eyeing her closely.

"No, no! Ah, how can I tell you? Bradbury, look! You see that man over there?"

Bradbury followed her pointing finger. Standing in an attitude of negligent dignity beside a pile of trunks under the letter V was a tall, stout, ambassadorial man, at the very sight of whom, even at this distance, Bradbury Fisher felt an odd sense of inferiority. His pendulous cheeks, his curving waistcoat, his protruding eyes, and the sequence of rolling chins combined to produce in Bradbury that instinctive feeling of being in the presence of a superior which we experience when meeting scratch golfers, headwaiters of fashionable restaurants, and traffic-policemen. A sudden pang of suspicion pierced him.

"Well?" he said, hoarsely. "What of him?"

"Bradbury, you must not judge me too harshly. We were thrown together and I was tempted——"

"Woman," thundered Bradbury Fisher, "who is this man?"

231

"His name is Vosper."

"And what is there between you and him, and when did it start, and why and how and where?"

Mrs. Fisher dabbed at her eyes with her handkerchief.

"It was at the Duke of Bootle's, Bradbury. I was invited there for the week-end."

"And this man was there?"

"Yes."

"Ha! Proceed!"

"The moment I set eyes on him, something seemed to go all over me."

"Indeed!"

"At first it was his mere appearance. I felt that I had dreamed of such a man all my life, and that for all these wasted years I had been putting up with the second-best."

"Oh, you did, eh? Really? Is that so? You did, did you?" snorted Bradbury Fisher.

"I couldn't help it, Bradbury. I know I have always seemed so devoted to Blizzard, and so I was. But honestly, there is no comparison between them—really there isn't. You should see the way Vosper stood behind the Duke's chair. Like a high priest presiding over some mystic religious ceremony. And his voice when he asks you if you will have sherry or hock! Like the music of some wonderful organ. I couldn't resist him. I approached him delicately, and found that he was willing to come to America. He had been eighteen years with the Duke, and he told me he couldn't stand the sight of the back of his head any longer. So——"

Bradbury Fisher reeled.

"This man—this Vosper. Who is he?"

"Why, I'm telling you, honey. He was the Duke's butler, and now he's ours. Oh, you know how impulsive I am. Honestly, it wasn't till we were half-way across the Atlantic that I suddenly said to myself, 'What about Blizzard?' What am I to do, Bradbury? I simply haven't the nerve to fire Blizzard. And yet what will happen when he walks into his pantry and finds Vosper there? Oh think, Bradbury, think!"

Bradbury Fisher was thinking—and for the first time in a week without agony.

"Evangeline," he said, gravely, "this is awkward."

"I know."

"Extremely awkward."

"I know, I know. But surely you can think of some way out of the muddle!"

"I may. I cannot promise, but I may." He pondered deeply. "Ha! I have it! It is just possible that I may be able to induce Gladstone Bott to take on Blizzard."

"Do you really think he would?"

"He may—if I play my cards carefully. At any rate, I will try to persuade him. For the moment you and Vosper had better remain in New York, while I go home and put the negotiations in train. If I am successful, I will let you know."

"Do try your very hardest."

"I think I shall be able to manage it. Gladstone and I are old friends, and he would stretch a point to oblige me. But let this be a lesson to you, Evangeline."

"Oh, I will."

"By the way," said Bradbury Fisher, "I am cabling my London agents to-day to instruct them to buy J. H. Taylor's shirt-stud for my collection."

"Quite right, Bradbury darling. And anything else you want in that way you will get, won't you?"

"I will," said Bradbury Fisher.

TWO WAYS OF . . .

"MISS BLAKE—Susan—Susie." He took her other hand in his. His voice rang out clear and unimpeded. "It cannot have escaped your notice that I have long entertained towards you sentiments warmer and deeper than those of ordinary friendship. It is love, Susan, that has been animating my bosom. Love, first a tiny seed, has burgeoned in my heart till, blazing into flame, it has swept away on the crest of its wave my diffidence, my doubt, my fears, and my foreboding, and now, like the topmost topaz of some ancient tower, it cries to all the world in a voice of thunder: 'You are mine! My mate! Predestined to me since Time first began!' As the star guides the mariner when, battered by boiling billows, he hies him home to the haven of hope and happiness, so do you gleam upon me along life's rough road and seem to say, 'Have courage, George! I am here!' Susan, I am not an eloquent man—I cannot speak fluently as I could wish—but these simple words which you have just heard come from the heart, from the unspotted heart of an English gentleman. Susan, I love you. Will you be my wife, married woman, matron, spouse, help-meet, consort, partner or better half?"

. . . SAYING THE SAME THING

"Ronnie sort of grunted and said 'I say!' and I said 'Hullo?' and he said 'Will you marry me?' and I said 'All right,' and he said 'I ought to warn you, I despise all women,' and I said 'And I loathe all men' and he said 'Right-ho, I think we shall be very happy.' "

ARCHIBALD GOES SLUMMING

My NEPHEW Archibald, like all the Mulliners, is of an honest and candid disposition, incapable of subterfuge, and there is no doubt that if you had asked him his opinion of Bottleton East as he paced its streets that night he would have confessed frankly that he was just a bit disappointed in the place. Too bright, would have been his verdict, too bally jovial. Arriving in the expectation of finding a sort of grey inferno, he appeared to have been plunged into a perfect maelstrom of gaiety.

On every side, merry matrons sat calling each other names on doorsteps. Cheery cats fought among the garbage-pails. From the busy public-houses came the sound of mouth-organ and song. While, as for the children, who were present in enormous quantities, so far from crying for bread, as he had been led to expect, they were playing hop-scotch all over the pavements. The whole atmosphere, in a word, was, he tells me, more like that of Guest Night at the National Liberal Club than anything he had ever encountered.

CONVERSATION PIECE

"I DON'T understand English titles," she said.

"No?" I said.

"No," she said. "There's nothing I enjoy more than curling up with a good English book, but the titles always puzzle me. That New York paper called you the Earl of Havershot. Is an Earl the same as a Duke?"

"Not quite. Dukes are a bit higher up."

"Is it the same as a Viscount?"

"No. Viscounts are a bit lower down. We Earls rather sneer at Viscounts. One is pretty haughty with them, poor devils."

"What is your wife? A Countess?"

"I haven't got a wife. If I had she would be a Countess."

A sort of far-away look came into her eyes.

"The Countess of Havershot," she murmured.

"That's right. The Countess of Havershot."

"What is Havershot? The place where you live?"

"No. I don't quite know where the Havershot comes in. The family doss-house is at Biddleford, in Norfolk."

"Is it a very lovely place?"

"Quite a goodish sort of shack."

"Battlements?"

"Lots of battlements."

"And deer?"

"Several deer."

"I love deer."

"Me, too. I've met some very decent deer."

PIG-HOO-O-O-O-EY!

THANKS to the publicity given to the matter by *The Bridgnorth, Shifnal and Albrighton Argus* (with which is incorporated *The Wheat-Growers' Intelligencer and Stock Breeders' Gazetteer*), the whole world to-day knows that the silver medal in the Fat Pigs class at the eighty-seventh annual Shropshire Agricultural Show was won by the Earl of Emsworth's black Berkshire sow, Empress of Blandings.

Very few people, however, are aware how near that splendid animal came to missing the coveted honour.

Now it can be told.

This brief chapter of Secret History may be said to have begun on the night of the eighteenth of July, when George Cyril Wellbeloved (twenty-nine), pig-man in the employ of Lord Emsworth, was arrested by Police-Constable Evans of Market Blandings for being drunk and disorderly in the tap-room of the Goat and Feathers. On July the nineteenth, after first offering to apologize, then explaining that it had been his birthday, and finally attempting to prove an alibi, George Cyril was very properly jugged for fourteen days without the option of a fine.

On July the twentieth, Empress of Blandings, always hitherto a hearty and even a boisterous feeder, for the first time on record declined all nourishment. And on the morning of July the twenty-first, the veterinary surgeon called in to diagnose and deal with this strange asceticism, was compelled to confess to Lord Emsworth that the thing was beyond his professional skill.

Let us just see, before proceeding, that we have got these dates correct:

July 18.—Birthday Orgy of Cyril Wellbeloved.
July 19.—Incarceration of Ditto.
July 20.—Pig Lays off the Vitamins.

July 21.—Veterinary Surgeon Baffled.
Right.

The effect of the veterinary surgeon's announcement on Lord Emsworth was overwhelming. As a rule, the wear and tear of our complex modern life left this vague and amiable peer unscathed. So long as he had sunshine, regular meals, and complete freedom from the society of his younger son Frederick, he was placidly happy. But there were chinks in his armour, and one of these had been pierced this morning. Dazed by the news he had received, he stood at the window of the great library of Blandings Castle, looking out with unseeing eyes.

As he stood there, the door opened. Lord Emsworth turned; and having blinked once or twice, as was his habit when confronted suddenly with anything, recognized in the handsome and imperious-looking woman who had entered his sister, Lady Constance Keeble. Her demeanour, like his own, betrayed the deepest agitation.

"Clarence," she cried, "an awful thing has happened!"

Lord Emsworth nodded dully.

"I know. He's just told me."

"What! Has he been here?"

"Only this moment left."

"Why did you let him go? You must have known I would want to see him."

"What good would that have done?"

"I could at least have assured him of my sympathy," said Lady Constance stiffly.

"Yes, I suppose you could," said Lord Emsworth, having considered the point. "Not that he deserves any sympathy. The man's an ass."

"Nothing of the kind. A most intelligent young man, as young men go."

"Young? Would you call him young? Fifty, I should have said, if a day."

"Are you out of your senses? Heacham fifty?"

"Not Heacham. Smithers."

As frequently happened to her when in conversation with her brother, Lady Constance experienced a swimming sensation in the head.

"Will you kindly tell me, Clarence, in a few simple words, what you imagine we are talking about?"

"I'm talking about Smithers. Empress of Blandings is refusing her food, and Smithers says he can't do anything about it. And he calls himself a vet!"

"Then you haven't heard? Clarence, a dreadful thing has happened. Angela has broken off her engagement to Heacham."

"And the Agricultural Show on Wednesday week!"

"What on earth has that got to do with it?" demanded Lady Constance, feeling a recurrence of the swimming sensation.

"What has it got to do with it?" said Lord Emsworth warmly. "My champion sow, with less than ten days to prepare herself for a most searching examination in competition with all the finest pigs in the country, starts refusing her food——"

"Will you stop maundering on about your insufferable pig and give your attention to something that really matters? I tell you that Angela—your niece Angela—has broken off her engagement to Lord Heacham and expresses her intention of marrying that hopeless ne'er-do-well, James Belford."

"The son of old Belford, the parson?"

"Yes."

"She can't. He's in America."

"He is not in America. He is in London."

"No," said Lord Emsworth, shaking his head sagely. "You're wrong. I remember meeting his father two years ago out on the road by Meeker's twenty-acre field, and he distinctly told me the boy was sailing for America next day. He must be there by this time."

"Can't you understand? He's come back."

"Oh? Come back? I see. Come *back*?"

240

"You know there was once a silly sentimental sort of affair between him and Angela; but a year after he left she became engaged to Heacham and I thought the whole thing was over and done with. And now it seems that she met this young man Belford when she was in London last week, and it has started all over again. She tells me she has written to Heacham and broken the engagement."

There was a silence. Brother and sister remained for a space plunged in thought. Lord Emsworth was the first to speak.

"We've tried acorns," he said. "We've tried skim milk. And we've tried potato-peel. But, no, she won't touch them."

Conscious of two eyes raising blisters on his sensitive skin, he came to himself with a start.

"Absurd! Ridiculous! Preposterous!" he said, hurriedly. "Breaking the engagement? Pooh! Tush! What nonsense! I'll have a word with that young man. If he thinks he can go about the place playing fast and loose with my niece and jilting her without so much as a——"

"Clarence!"

Lord Emsworth blinked. Something appeared to be wrong, but he could not imagine what. It seemed to him that in his last speech he had struck just the right note—strong, forceful, dignified.

"Eh?"

"It is Angela who has broken the engagement."

"Oh, Angela?"

"She is infatuated with this man Belford. And the point is, what are we to do about it?"

Lord Emsworth reflected.

"Take a strong line," he said firmly. "Stand no nonsense Don't send 'em a wedding-present."

There is no doubt that, given time, Lady Constance would have found and uttered some adequately corrosive comment on this imbecile suggestion; but even as she was swelling preparatory to giving tongue, the door opened and a girl came in.

She was a pretty girl, with fair hair and blue eyes which in their softer moments probably reminded all sorts of people of twin lagoons slumbering beneath a southern sky. This, however, was not one of those moments. To Lord Emsworth, as they met his, they looked like something out of an oxy-acetylene blow-pipe; and, as far as he was capable of being disturbed by anything that was not his younger son Frederick, he was disturbed. Angela, it seemed to him, was upset about something; and he was sorry. He liked Angela.

To ease a tense situation, he said:

"Angela, my dear, do you know anything about pigs?"

The girl laughed. One of those sharp, bitter laughs which are so unpleasant just after breakfast.

"Yes, I do. You're one."

"Me?"

"Yes, you. Aunt Constance says that, if I marry Jimmy, you won't let me have my money."

"Money? Money?" Lord Emsworth was mildly puzzled. "What money? You never lent me any money."

Lady Constance's feelings found vent in a sound like an overheated radiator.

"I believe this absent-mindedness of yours is nothing but a ridiculous pose, Clarence. You know perfectly well that when poor Jane died she left you Angela's trustee."

"And I can't touch my money without your consent till I'm twenty-five."

"Well, how old are you?"

"Twenty-one."

"Then what are you worrying about?" asked Lord Emsworth, surprised. "No need to worry about it for another four years. God bless my soul, the money is quite safe. It is in excellent securities."

Angela stamped her foot. An unladylike action, no doubt, but how much better than kicking an uncle with it, as her lower nature prompted.

"I have told Angela," explained Lady Constance, "that, while we naturally cannot force her to marry Lord Heacham, we can at least keep her money from being squandered by this wastrel on whom she proposes to throw herself away."

"He isn't a wastrel. He's got quite enough money to marry me on, but he wants some capital to buy a partnership in a——"

"He is a wastrel. Wasn't he sent abroad because——"

"That was two years ago. And since then——"

"My dear Angela, you may argue until——"

"I'm not arguing. I'm simply saying that I'm going to marry Jimmy, if we both have to starve in the gutter."

"What gutter?" asked his lordship, wrenching his errant mind away from thoughts of acorns.

"Any gutter."

"Now, please listen to me, Angela."

It seemed to Lord Emsworth that there was a frightful amount of conversation going on. He had the sensation of having become a mere bit of flotsam upon a tossing sea of female voices. Both his sister and his niece appeared to have much to say, and they were saying it simultaneously and fortissimo. He looked wistfully at the door.

It was smoothly done. A twist of the handle, and he was where beyond those voices there was peace. Galloping gaily down the stairs, he charged out into the sunshine.

His gaiety was not long-lived. Free at last to concentrate itself on the really serious issues of life, his mind grew sombre and grim. Once more there descended upon him the cloud which had been oppressing his soul before all this Heacham-Angela-Belford business began. Each step that took him nearer to the sty where the ailing Empress resided seemed a heavier step than the last. He reached the sty; and, draping himself over the rails, peered moodily at the vast expanse of pig within.

For, even though she had been doing a bit of dieting of late, Empress of Blandings was far from being an ill-nourished animal. She resembled a captive balloon with ears and a tail, and was as nearly circular as a pig can be without bursting.

Nevertheless, Lord Emsworth, as he regarded her, mourned and would not be comforted. A few more square meals under her belt, and no pig in all Shropshire could have held its head up in the Empress's presence. And now, just for lack of those few meals, the supreme animal would probably be relegated to the mean obscurity of an "Honourably Mentioned." It was bitter, bitter.

He became aware that somebody was speaking to him; and, turning, perceived a solemn young man in riding breeches.

"I say," said the young man.

Lord Emsworth, though he would have preferred solitude, was relieved to find that the intruder was at least one of his own sex. Women are apt to stray off into side-issues, but men are practical and can be relied on to stick to the fundamentals. Besides, young Heacham probably kept pigs himself and might have a useful hint or two up his sleeve.

"I say, I've just ridden over to see if there was anything I could do about this fearful business."

"Uncommonly kind and thoughtful of you, my dear fellow," said Lord Emsworth, touched. "I fear things look very black."

"It's an absolute mystery to me."

"To me, too."

"I mean to say, she was all right last week."

"She was all right as late as the day before yesterday."

"Seemed quite cheery and chirpy and all that."

"Entirely so."

"And then this happens—out of a blue sky, as you might say."

"Exactly. It is insoluble. We have done everything possible to tempt her appetite."

"Her appetite? Is Angela ill?"

"Angela? No, I fancy not. She seemed perfectly well a few minutes ago."

"You've seen her this morning, then? Did she say anything about this fearful business?"

"No. She was speaking about some money."

"It's all so dashed unexpected."

"Like a bolt from the blue," agreed Lord Emsworth. "Such a thing has never happened before. I fear the worst. According to the Wolff-Lehmann feeding standards, a pig, if in health, should consume daily nourishment amounting to fifty-seven thousand eight hundred calories, these to consist of proteids four pounds five ounces, carbohydrates twenty-five pounds——"

"What has that got to do with Angela?"

"Angela?"

"I came to find out why Angela has broken off our engagement."

Lord Emsworth marshalled his thoughts. He had a misty idea that he had heard something mentioned about that. It came back to him.

"Ah, yes, of course. She has broken off the engagement, hasn't she? I believe it is because she is in love with someone else. Yes, now that I recollect, that was distinctly stated. The whole thing comes back to me quite clearly. Angela has decided to marry someone else. I knew there was some satisfactory explanation. Tell me, my dear fellow, what are your views on linseed meal."

"What do you mean, linseed meal?"

"Why, linseed meal," said Lord Emsworth, not being able to find a better definition. "As a food for pigs."

"Oh, curse all pigs!"

"What!" There was a sort of astounded horror in Lord Emsworth's voice. He had never been particularly fond of young Heacham, for he was not a man who took much to his juniors, but he had not supposed him capable of anarchistic sentiments like this. "What did you say?"

"I said, 'Curse all pigs!' You keep talking about pigs. I'm not interested in pigs. I don't want to discuss pigs. Blast and damn every pig in existence!"

Lord Emsworth watched him, as he strode away, with an emotion that was partly indignation and partly relief—indignation that a landowner and a fellow son of Shropshire

245

could have brought himself to utter such words, and relief that one capable of such utterance was not going to marry into his family. He had always in his woollen-headed way been very fond of his niece Angela, and it was nice to think that the child had such solid good sense and so much cool discernment. Many girls of her age would have been carried away by the glamour of young Heacham's position and wealth; but she, divining with an intuition beyond her years that he was unsound on the subject of pigs, had drawn back while there was still time and refused to marry him.

A pleasant glow suffused Lord Emsworth's bosom, to be frozen out a few moments later as he perceived his sister Constance bearing down upon him. Lady Constance was a beautiful woman, but there were times when the charm of her face was marred by a rather curious expression; and from nursery days onward his lordship had learned that this expression meant trouble. She was wearing it now.

"Clarence," she said, "I have had enough of this nonsense of Angela and young Belford. The thing cannot be allowed to go drifting on. You must catch the two o'clock train to London."

"What! Why?"

"You must see this man Belford and tell him that, if Angela insists on marrying him, she will not have a penny for four years. I shall be greatly surprised if that piece of information does not put an end to the whole business."

Lord Emsworth scratched meditatively at the Empress's tank-like back. A mutinous expression was on his mild face.

"Don't see why she shouldn't marry the fellow," he mumbled.

"Marry James Belford?"

"I don't see why not. Seems fond of him and all that."

"You never have had a grain of sense in your head, Clarence. Angela is going to marry Heacham."

"Can't stand that man. All wrong about pigs."

"Clarence, I don't wish to have any more discussion and

argument. You will go to London on the two o'clock train. You will see Mr. Belford. And you will tell him about Angela's money. Is that quite clear?"

"Oh, all right," said his lordship moodily. "All right, all right, all right."

The emotions of the Earl of Emsworth, as he sat next day facing his luncheon-guest, James Bartholomew Belford, across a table in the main dining-room of the Senior Conservative Club, were not of the liveliest and most agreeable. It was bad enough to be in London at all on such a day of golden sunshine. To be charged, while there, with the task of blighting the romance of two young people for whom he entertained a warm regard was unpleasant to a degree.

For, now that he had given the matter thought, Lord Emsworth recalled that he had always liked this boy Belford. A pleasant lad, with, he remembered now, a healthy fondness for that rural existence which so appealed to himself. By no means the sort of fellow who, in the very presence and hearing of Empress of Blandings, would have spoken disparagingly and with oaths of pigs as a class. It occurred to Lord Emsworth, as it has occurred to so many people, that the distribution of money in this world is all wrong. Why should a man like pig-despising Heacham have a rent roll that ran into the tens of thousands, while this very deserving youngster had nothing?

These thoughts not only saddened Lord Emsworth—they embarrassed him. He hated unpleasantness, and it was suddenly borne in upon him that, after he had broken the news that Angela's bit of capital was locked up and not likely to get loose, conversation with his young friend during the remainder of lunch would tend to be somewhat difficult.

He made up his mind to postpone the revelation. During the meal, he decided, he would chat pleasantly of this and that; and then, later, while bidding his guest good-bye, he would spring the thing on him suddenly and dive back into the recesses of the club.

Considerably cheered at having solved a delicate problem with such adroitness, he started to prattle.

"The gardens at Blandings," he said, "are looking particularly attractive this summer. My head-gardener, Angus McAllister, is a man with whom I do not always find myself seeing eye to eye, notably in the matter of hollyhocks, on which I consider his views subversive to a degree; but there is no denying that he understands roses. The rose garden——"

"How well I remember that rose garden," said James Belford, sighing slightly and helping himself to brussels sprouts. "It was there that Angela and I used to meet on summer mornings."

Lord Emsworth blinked. This was not an encouraging start, but the Emsworths were a fighting clan. He had another try.

"I have seldom seen such a blaze of colour as was to be witnessed there during the month of June. Both McAllister and I adopted a very strong policy with the slugs and plant lice, with the result that the place was a mass of flourishing Damasks and Ayrshires and——"

"Properly to appreciate roses," said James Belford, "you want to see them as a setting for a girl like Angela. With her fair hair gleaming against the green leaves she makes a rose garden seem a veritable Paradise."

"No doubt," said Lord Emsworth. "No doubt. I am glad you liked my rose garden. At Blandings, of course, we have the natural advantage of loamy soil, rich in plant food and humus; but, as I often say to McAllister, and on this point we have never had the slightest disagreement, loamy soil by itself is not enough. You must have manure. If every autumn a liberal mulch of stable manure is spread upon the beds and the coarser parts removed in the spring before the annual forking——"

"Angela tells me," said James Belford, "that you have forbidden our marriage."

Lord Emsworth choked dismally over his chicken. Directness of this kind, he told himself with a pang of self-pity, was the sort of thing young Englishmen picked up in America. Diplomatic circumlocution flourished only in a more leisurely civilization, and in those energetic and forceful surroundings you learned to Talk Quick and Do It Now, and all sorts of uncomfortable things.

" Er—well, yes, now you mention it, I believe some informal decision of that nature was arrived at. You see, my dear fellow, my sister Constance feels rather strongly——"

"I understand. I suppose she thinks I'm a sort of prodigal."

"No, no, my dear fellow. She never said that. Wastrel was the term she employed."

"Well, perhaps I did start out in business on those lines. But you can take it from me that when you find yourself employed on a farm in Nebraska belonging to an applejack-nourished patriarch with strong views on work and a good vocabulary, you soon develop a certain liveliness."

"Are you employed on a farm?"

"I was employed on a farm."

"Pigs?" said Lord Emsworth in a low, eager voice.

"Among other things."

Lord Emsworth gulped. His fingers clutched at the table-cloth.

"Then perhaps, my dear fellow, you can give me some advice. For the last two days my prize sow, Empress of Blandings, has declined all nourishment. And the Agricultural Show is on Wednesday week. I am distracted with anxiety."

James Belford frowned thoughtfully.

"What does your pig-man say about it?"

"My pig-man was sent to prison two days ago. Two days!" For the first time the significance of the coincidence struck him. "You don't think that can have anything to do with the animal's loss of appetite?"

"Certainly. I imagine she is missing him and pining away because he isn't there."

Lord Emsworth was surprised. He had only a distant acquaintance with George Cyril Wellbeloved, but from what he had seen of him he had not credited him with this fatal allure.

"She probably misses his afternoon call."

Again his lordship found himself perplexed. He had had no notion that pigs were such sticklers for the formalities of social life.

"His call?"

"He must have had some special call that he used when he wanted her to come to dinner. One of the first things you learn on a farm is hog-calling. Pigs are temperamental. Omit to call them, and they'll starve rather than put on the nose-bag. Call them right, and they will follow you to the ends of the earth with their mouths watering."

"God bless my soul! Fancy that."

"A fact, I assure you. These calls vary in different parts of America. In Wisconsin, for example, the words, 'Poig, Poige, Poig,' bring home—in both the literal and the figurative sense —the bacon. In Illinois, I believe they call 'Burp, Burp, Burp,' while in Iowa the phrase 'Kus, Kus, Kus,' is preferred. Proceeding to Minnesota, we find 'Peega, Peega, Peega' or, alternatively, 'Oink, Oink, Oink,' whereas in Milwaukee, so largely inhabited by those of German descent, you will hear the good old Teuton 'Komm Schweine, Komm Schweine.' Oh, yes, there are all sorts of pig-calls, from the Massachusetts 'Phew, Phew, Phew' to the 'Loo-ey, Loo-ey, Loo-ey' of Ohio, not counting various local devices such as beating on tin cans with axes or rattling pebbles in a suit-case. I knew a man out in Nebraska who used to call his pigs by tapping on the edge of the trough with his wooden leg."

"Did he, indeed?"

"But a most unfortunate thing happened. One evening, hearing a woodpecker at the top of a tree, they started shinning up it; and when the man came out he found them all lying there in a circle with their necks broken."

"This is no time for joking," said Lord Emsworth, pained.

"I'm not joking. Solid fact. Ask anybody out there."

Lord Emsworth placed a hand to his throbbing forehead.

"But if there is this wide variety, we have no means of knowing which call Wellbeloved. . . ."

"Ah," said James Belford, "but wait. I haven't told you all. There is a master-word."

"A what?"

"Most people don't know it, but I had it straight from the lips of Fred Patzel, the hog-calling champion of the Western States. What a man! I've know him to bring pork chops leaping from their plates. He informed me that, no matter whether an animal has been trained to answer to the Illinois 'Burp' or the Minnesota 'Oink,' it will always give immediate service in response to this magic combination of syllables. It is to the pig world what the Masonic grip is to the human. 'Oink' in Illinois or 'Burp' in Minnesota, and the animal merely raises its eyebrows and stares coldly. But go to either state and call 'Pig-hoo-oo-ey!' . . ."

The expression on Lord Emsworth's face was that of a drowning man who sees a lifeline.

"Is that the master-word of which you spoke?"

"That's it."

"Pig—?"

"—hoo-oo-ey."

"Pig-hoo-o-ey?"

"You haven't got it quite right. The first syllable should be short and staccato, the second long and rising into a falsetto, high but true."

"Pig-hoo-o-o-ey."

"Pig-hoo-o-o-ey."

"Pig-hoo-o-o-ey!" yodelled Lord Emsworth, flinging his head back and giving tongue in a high, penetrating tenor which caused ninety-three Senior Conservatives, lunching in the vicinity, to congeal into living statues of alarm and disapproval.

"More body to the 'hoo,'" advised James Belford.

"Pig-hoo-o-o-ey!"

The Senior Conservative Club is one of the few places in London where lunchers are not accustomed to getting music with their meals. White-whiskered financiers gazed bleakly at bald-headed politicians as if asking silently what was to be done about this. Bald-headed politicians stared back at white-whiskered financiers, replying in the language of the eye that they did not know. The general sentiment prevailing was a vague determination to write to the Committee about it.

"Pig-hoo-o-o-o-ey!" carolled Lord Emsworth. And as he did so, his eye fell on the clock over the mantelpiece. Its hands pointed to twenty minutes to two.

He started convulsively. The best train in the day for Market Blandings was the one which left Paddington station at two sharp. After that there was nothing till the five-five.

He was not a man who often thought; but, when he did, to think was with him to act. A moment later he was scudding over the carpet, making for the door that led to the broad staircase.

Throughout the room which he had left, the decision to write in strong terms to the Committee was now universal; but from the mind, such as it was, of Lord Emsworth the past, with the single exception of the word "Pig-hoo-o-o-o-ey!" had been completely blotted.

Whispering the magic syllables, he sped to the cloak-room and retrieved his hat. Murmuring them over and over again, he sprang into a cab. He was still repeating them as the train moved out of the station; and he would doubtless have gone on repeating them all the way to Market Blandings, had he not, as was his invariable practice when travelling by rail, fallen asleep after the first ten minutes of the journey.

The stopping of the train at Swindon Junction woke him with a start. He sat up, wondering, after his usual fashion on these occasions, who and where he was. Memory returned to him, but a memory that was, alas, incomplete. He remembered his name. He remembered that he was on his way home from a visit to London. But what it was that you said to a pig when you invited it to drop in for a bite of dinner he had completely forgotten.

It was the opinion of Lady Constance Keeble, expressed verbally during dinner in the brief intervals when they were alone, and by means of silent telepathy when Beach, the butler, was adding his dignified presence to the proceedings, that her brother Clarence, in his expedition to London to put matters plainly to James Belford, had made an outstanding idiot of himself.

There had been no need whatever to invite the man Belford to lunch; but, having invited him to lunch, to leave him sitting, without having clearly stated that Angela would have no money for four years, was the act of a congenital imbecile. Lady Constance had been aware ever since their childhood days that her brother had about as much sense as a——

Here Beach entered, superintending the bringing-in of the savoury, and she had been obliged to suspend her remarks.

This sort of conversation is never agreeable to a sensitive man, and his lordship had removed himself from the danger zone as soon as he could manage it. He was now seated in the library, sipping port and straining a brain which Nature had never intended for hard exercise in an effort to bring back that word of magic of which his unfortunate habit of sleeping in trains had robbed him.

"Pig——"

He could remember as far as that; but of what avail was a single syllable? Besides, weak as his memory was, he could recall that the whole gist or nub of the thing lay in the syllable that followed. The "pig" was a mere preliminary.

Lord Emsworth finished his port and got up. He felt restless, stifled. The summer night seemed to call to him like some silver-voiced swineherd calling to his pig. Possibly, he thought, a breath of fresh air might stimulate his brain-cells. He wandered downstairs; and, having dug a shocking old slouch hat out of the cupboard where he hid it to keep his sister Constance from impounding and burning it, he strode heavily out into the garden.

He was pottering aimlessly to and fro in the parts adjacent to the rear of the castle when there appeared in his path a slender female form. He recognized it without pleasure. Any unbiased judge would have said that his niece Angela, standing there in the soft, pale light, looked like some dainty spirit of the Moon. Lord Emsworth was not an unbiased judge. To him Angela merely looked like Trouble. The march of civilization has given the modern girl a vocabulary and an ability to use it which her grandmother never had. Lord Emsworth would not have minded meeting Angela's grandmother a bit.

"Is that you, my dear?" he said nervously.

"Yes."

"I didn't see you at dinner."

"I didn't want any dinner. The food would have choked me. I can't eat."

"It's precisely the same with my pig," said his lordship. "Young Belford tells me——"

Into Angela's queenly disdain there flashed a sudden animation.

"Have you seen Jimmy? What did he say?"

"That's just what I can't remember. It began with the word 'Pig'——"

"But after he had finished talking about you, I mean. Didn't he say anything about coming down here?"

"Not that I remember."

"I expect you weren't listening. You've got a very annoying habit, Uncle Clarence," said Angela maternally, "of switching your mind off and just going blah when people are talking to you. It gets you very much disliked on all sides. Didn't Jimmy say anything about me?"

"I fancy so. Yes, I am nearly sure he did."

"Well, what?"

"I cannot remember."

There was a sharp clicking noise in the darkness. It was caused by Angela's upper front teeth meeting her lower front teeth; and was followed by a sort of wordless exclamation. It seemed only too plain that the love and respect which a niece should have for an uncle were in the present instance at a very low ebb.

"I wish you wouldn't do that," said Lord Emsworth plaintively.

"Do what?"

"Make clicking noises at me."

"I will make clicking noises at you. You know perfectly well, Uncle Clarence, that you are behaving like a bohunkus."

"A what?"

"A bohunkus," explained his niece coldly, "is a very inferior sort of worm. Not the kind of worm that you see on lawns, which you can respect, but a really degraded species."

"I wish you would go in, my dear," said Lord Emsworth. "The night air may give you a chill."

"I won't go in. I came out here to look at the moon and think of Jimmy. What are you doing out here, if it comes to that?"

"I came here to think. I am greatly exercised about my pig, Empress of Blandings. For two days she has refused her food and young Belford says she will not eat until she hears the proper call or cry. He very kindly taught it to me, but unfortunately I have forgotten it."

"I wonder you had the nerve to ask Jimmy to teach you pig-calls, considering the way you're treating him."

"But——"

"Like a leper, or something. And all I can say is that, if you remember this call of his, and it makes the Empress eat, you ought to be ashamed of yourself if you still refuse to let me marry him."

"My dear," said Lord Emsworth earnestly, "if through young Belford's instrumentality Empress of Blandings is induced to take nourishment once more, there is nothing I will refuse him—nothing."

"Honour bright?"

"I give you my solemn word."

"You won't let Aunt Constance bully you out of it?"

Lord Emsworth drew himself up.

"Certainly not," he said proudly. "I am always ready to listen to your Aunt Constance's views, but there are certain matters where I claim the right to act according to my own judgment." He paused and stood musing. "It began with the word 'Pig——'"

From somewhere near at hand music made itself heard. The servants' hall, its day's labours ended, was refreshing itself with the housekeeper's gramophone. To Lord Emsworth the strains were merely an additional annoyance. He was not fond of music. It reminded him of his younger son Frederick, a flat but persevering songster both in and out of the bath.

"Yes, I can distinctly recall as much as that. Pig—Pig——"

"WHO——"

Lord Emsworth leaped in the air. It was as if an electric shock had been applied to his person.

"WHO stole my heart away?" howled the gramophone. "WHO——?"

The peace of the summer night was shattered by a triumphant shout.

"Pig-HOO-o-o-o-ey!"

A window opened. A large, bald head appeared. A dignified voice spoke.

"Who is there? Who is making that noise?"

"Beach!" cried Lord Emsworth. "Come out here at once."

"Very good, your lordship."

And presently the beautiful night was made still more lovely by the added attraction of the butler's presence.

"Beach, listen to this."

"Very good, your lordship."

"Pig-hoo-o-o-o-ey!"

"Very good, your lordship."

"Now you do it."

"I, your lordship?"

"Yes. It's a way you call pigs."

"I do not call pigs, your lordship," said the butler coldly.

"What do you want Beach to do it for?" asked Angela.

"Two heads are better than one. If we both learn it, it will not matter should I forget it again."

"By Jove, yes! Come on, Beach. Push it over the thorax,"

urged the girl eagerly. "You don't know it, but this is a matter of life and death. At-a-boy, Beach! Inflate the lungs and go to it."

It had been the butler's intention, prefacing his remarks with the statement that he had been in service at the castle for eighteen years, to explain frigidly to Lord Emsworth that it was not his place to stand in the moonlight practising pig-calls. If, he would have gone on to add, his lordship saw the matter from a different angle, then it was his, Beach's, painful duty to tender his resignation, to become effective one month from that day.

But the intervention of Angela made this impossible to a man of chivalry and heart. A paternal fondness for the girl, dating from the days when he had stooped to enacting—and very convincingly, too, for his was a figure that lent itself to the impersonation—the *rôle* of a hippopotamus for her childish amusement, checked the words he would have uttered. She was looking at him with bright eyes, and even the rendering of pig-noises seemed a small sacrifice to make for her sake.

"Very good, your lordship," he said in a low voice, his face pale and set in the moonlight. "I shall endeavour to give satisfaction. I would merely advance the suggestion, your lordship, that we move a few steps farther away from the vicinity of the servants' hall. If I were to be overheard by any of the lower domestics, it would weaken my position as a disciplinary force."

"What chumps we are!" cried Angela, inspired. "The place to do it is outside the Empress's sty. Then, if it works, we'll see it working."

Lord Emsworth found this a little abstruse, but after a moment he got it.

"Angela," he said, "you are a very intelligent girl. Where you get your brains from, I don't know. Not from my side of the family."

The bijou residence of the Empress of Blandings looked very snug and attractive in the moonlight. But beneath even the beautiful things of life there is always an underlying sadness.

This was supplied in the present instance by a long, low trough, only too plainly full to the brim of succulent mash and acorns. The fast, obviously, was still in progress.

The sty stood some considerable distance from the castle walls, so that there had been ample opportunity for Lord Emsworth to rehearse his little company during the journey. By the time they had ranged themselves against the rails, his two assistants were letter-perfect.

"Now," said his lordship.

There floated out upon the summer night a strange composite sound that sent the birds roosting in the trees above shooting off their perches like rockets. Angela's clear soprano rang out like the voice of the village blacksmith's daughter. Lord Emsworth contributed a reedy tenor. And the bass notes of Beach probably did more to startle the birds than any other one item in the programme.

They paused and listened. Inside the Empress's boudoir there sounded the movement of a heavy body. There was an inquiring grunt. The next moment the sacking that covered the doorway was pushed aside, and the noble animal emerged.

"Now!" said Lord Emsworth again.

Once more that musical cry shattered the silence of the night. But it brought no responsive movement from the Empress of Blandings. She stood there motionless, her nose elevated, her ears hanging down, her eyes everywhere but on the trough where, by rights, she should now have been digging in and getting hers. A chill disappointment crept over Lord Emsworth, to be succeeded by a gust of petulant anger.

"I might have known it," he said bitterly. "That young scoundrel was deceiving me. He was playing a joke on me."

"He wasn't," cried Angela indignantly. "Was he, Beach?"

"Not knowing the circumstances, miss, I cannot venture an opinion."

"Well, why has it no effect, then?" demanded Lord Emsworth.

"You can't expect it to work right away. We've got her

stirred up, haven't we? She's thinking it over, isn't she? Once more will do the trick. Ready, Breach?"

"Quite ready, Miss."

"Then when I say three. And this time, Uncle Clarence, do please for goodness' sake not yowl like you did before. It was enough to put any pig off. Let it come out quite easily and gracefully. Now, then. One, two—three!"

The echoes died away. And as they did so a voice spoke.

"Community singing?"

"Jimmy!" cried Angela, whisking round.

"Hullo, Angela. Hullo, Lord Emsworth. Hullo, Beach."

"Good evening, sir. Happy to see you once more."

"Thanks. I'm spending a few days at the Vicarage with my father. I got down here by the five-five."

Lord Emsworth cut peevishly in upon these civilities.

"Young man," he said, "what do you mean by telling me that my pig would respond to that cry? It does nothing of the kind."

"You can't have done it right."

"I did it precisely as you instructed me. I have had, more-over, the assistance of Beach here and my niece Angela——"

"Let's hear a sample."

Lord Emsworth cleared his throat.

"Pig-hoo-o-o-o-ey!"

James Belford shook his head.

"Nothing like it," he said. "You want to begin the 'Hoo' in a low minor of two quarter notes in four-four time. From this build gradually to a higher note, until at last the voice is soaring in full crescendo, reaching F sharp on the natural scale and dwelling for two retarded half notes, then breaking into a shower of accidental grace-notes."

"God bless my soul!" said Lord Emsworth, appalled. "I shall never be able to do it."

"Jimmy will do it for you," said Angela. "Now that he's engaged to me, he'll be one of the family and always popping about here. He can do it every day till the show is over."

James Belford nodded.

"I think that would be the wisest plan. It is doubtful if an amateur would ever produce real results. You need a voice that has been trained on the open prairie and that has gathered richness and strength from competing with tornadoes. You need a manly, sunburned, wind-scorched voice with a suggestion in it of the crackling of corn husks and the whisper of evening breezes in the fodder. Like this!"

Resting his hands on the rail before him, James Belford swelled before their eyes like a young balloon. The muscles on his cheekbones stood out, his forehead became corrugated, his ears seemed to shimmer. Then, at the very height of the tension, he let it go like, as the poet beautifully puts it, the sound of a great Amen.

"Pig-HOOOOO-OOO-OOO-O-O-ey!"

They looked at him, awed. Slowly, fading off across hill and dale, the vast bellow died away. And suddenly, as it died, another, softer sound succeeded it. A sort of gulpy, gurgly, plobby, squishy, wofflesome sound, like a thousand eager men drinking soup in a foreign restaurant. And, as he heard it, Lord Emsworth uttered a cry of rapture.

The Empress was feeding.

*　　　*　　　*　　　*　　　*

It looked something like a pen-wiper and something like a piece of hearth-rug. A second and keener inspection revealed it as a Pekinese puppy.

THE IMPORTANCE OF A FELLOW'S FACE

"She wouldn't look at me," I repeated. The Cooley half-portion addressed Eggy.

"He's thinking of his face."

"Oh?" said Eggy. "Oh, ah, yes, of course."

"What does a fellow's face matter, anyway?" said Joey Cooley.

"Exactly."

"Looks don't mean a thing. Didn't Frankenstein get married?"

"Did he?" said Eggy. "I don't know. I never met him. Harrow man, I expect."

*   *   *   *   *

" Something of the gallant fire which was animating him seemed to pass out of Sir Aylmer Bostock. He blinked like some knight of King Arthur's court, who, galloping to perform a deed of derring-do, has had the misfortune to collide with a tree."

*   *   *   *   *

"He spoke with a certain what-is-it in his voice, and I could see that, if not actually disgruntled, he was far from being gruntled, so I tactfully changed the subject."

THE SOFTENING-UP OF AN UNCLE

The spectacle of an uncle, even if only an uncle by marriage, going down for the third time in a sea of dance-champagne can never be an agreeable one. But though I moaned as a nephew I am bound to say I found myself pretty bucked in my capacity as ambassador for Boko. Pie-eyed, even plastered, this man might be, but there was no mistaking his geniality. It was like something out of Dickens and I saw that he was going to be clay in my hands.

TO W. TOWNEND

DEAR BILL,—

I have never been much of a lad for the

TO ———

But For Whose Sympathy and Encouragement
This Book
Would Never Have Been Written

type of dedication. It sounds so weak-minded. But in the case
of *Love Among the Chickens* it is unavoidable. It is not so much
that you sympathised and encouraged—where you really
came out strong was that you gave me the stuff. I like people
who sympathise with me. I am grateful to those who en-
courage me. But the man to whom I raise the Wodehouse
hat—owing to the increased cost of living, the same old brown
one I had last year—it is being complained of on all sides, but
the public must bear it like men till the straw hat season comes

round—I say, the man to whom
I raise this venerable relic is the
man who gives me the material.

Sixteen years ago, my William,
when we were young and spritely
lads; when you were a tricky
centre-forward and I a fast
bowler; when your head was
covered with hair and my list
of "Hobbies" in *Who's Who* included Boxing; I received from
you one morning about thirty
closely-written foolscap pages
giving me the details of your
friend ———'s adventures on his

Devonshire chicken farm. Round these I wove as funny a plot as I could, but the book stands or falls by the stuff you gave me about "Ukridge"—the things that actually happened.

You will notice that I have practically re-written the book. There was some pretty bad work in it, and it had "dated." As an instance of the way in which the march of modern civilisation has left the 1906 edition behind, I may mention that on page twenty-one I was able to make Ukridge speak of selling eggs at six for fivepence!

Yours ever,

London, 1920.   P. G. WODEHOUSE.

BACK TO WHISKERS

It is probably generally agreed, I think—and what I think to-day Manchester thinks to-morrow—that something has got to be done to restore vigour and vitality to literary criticism. There was a time, not so long ago, when reviewers were reviewers. They lived on raw meat and spoke their minds, and an author who published a book did so at his own risk. If he got by without severe contusions of his self-respect, he knew that he must be pretty good. And if the reception of his first novel left him feeling as if he had been drawn through a wringer or forcibly unclothed in public, that was an excellent

thing for his art. It put him on his toes. If he had the stuff, he persevered. If he hadn't, he gave it up.

To-day the question *Have you read any good books lately?* is one which it is impossible to answer.

There are no good books nowadays—only superb books, astounding books, genuine masterpieces, books which we are not ashamed to say brought tears to our eyes.

Some people (who ought to be ashamed of themselves) say that the reason for this tidal wave of sweetness and amiability is the fact that reviewers to-day are all novelists themselves. Old Bill, they claim, who does the literary page of *The Scrutineer*, is not going to jump on Old Joe's *Sundered*

Souls when he knows that his own *Storm over Brixton* is coming out next week and that Joe runs the book column of *The Spokesman*.

This, of course, is not so.

Nobody who really knows novelists and their flaming integrity would believe it for a moment. It is with genuine surprise that William, having added *Sundered Souls* to the list of the world's masterpieces, finds that Joseph, a week later, has done the same by *Storm over Brixton*. An odd coincidence, he feels.

No, the root of the whole trouble is that critics to-day, with the exception of a few of the younger set who have a sort of unpleasant downy growth alongside the ears, are all clean-shaven.

Whether the great critics were bitter because they had beards or grew beards because they were bitter is beside the point. The fact remains that all the great literary rows you read about were between bearded men, whiskered men, critics who looked like bursting horsehair sofas, and novelists who had forgotten to shave for years. The Edinburgh reviewers were beavers to a man.

The connection between whiskers and caustic criticism is not hard to see.

There is probably nothing which so soothes a man and puts him in a frame of mind to see only good in everything as a nice, clean shave. He feels his smooth, pink cheeks, and the milk of human kindness begins to gurgle within him.

What a day! he says, as he looks out of the window. What a kipper! he says, as he starts his breakfast. And, if he is a literary critic, What a book! he feels as he takes up the latest ghastly effort of some author who ought to be selling coals instead of writing novels.

But let a man omit to shave, even for a single day, and mark the result. He feels hot and scrubby. Within twelve hours his outlook has become jaundiced and captious.

If his interests lie in the direction of politics, he goes out and throws a bomb at someone. If he is an employer of labour, he starts a lockout. If he is a critic, he sits down to write his criticism with the determination that by the time has finished reading it the author will know he has been in a fight.

You have only to look about you to appreciate the truth of this. All whiskered things are testy and short-tempered—pumas, wild cats, Bernard Shaw, and—in the mating season —shrimps. Would Ben Jonson have knifed a man on account of some literary disagreement if he had not been bearded to the eyebrows? Can you imagine a nation of spruce, clean-shaven Bolsheviks, smelling of bay rum?

There is only one thing to be done. We must go back to whiskers. And there must be no half-measures.

It is not enough for a critic to have a beard like Frank Swinnerton's, which, though technically a beard, is not bushy enough to sour the natural kindliness of his disposition. We must have the old Assyrian stuff, the sort of beards Hebrew minor prophets wore—great, cascading, spade-shaped things such as the great Victorians grew—whether under glass or not has never been ascertained.

I realise that I shall suffer myself from the change. There will be no more of those eulogies for my work like "Another Wodehouse" or "8 by 10½, 315 pp." which I have been pasting into my scrapbook for so many years. But I am prepared to sacrifice myself for the sake of literature, and I know that a sudden ebullition of whiskers among critics would raise the whole standard of writing.

A young author would think twice before starting his introspective novel of adolescence if he knew that quite probably it would be handed over for review to somebody who looked like W. G. Grace at the age of eighteen.

Nervous women would stop writing altogether, and what a break that would be for the reading public. The only novelists who would carry on would be a small, select group of tough eggs who had the stuff.

And it is useless for the critics to protest their inability to fall in with the idea. It is perfectly easy to grow whiskers. There is a whiskered all-in wrestler in America—Hairy Dean. He did it. Are our star reviewers going to tell me that they are inferior in will power and determination to an all-in wrestler?

Tush!

BURIED TREASURE

THE situation in Germany had come up for discussion in the bar parlour of the Angler's Rest, and it was generally agreed that Hitler was standing at the crossroads and would soon be compelled to do something definite. His present policy, said a Whisky and Splash, was mere shilly-shallying.

"He'll have to let it grow or shave it off," said the Whisky and Splash. "He can't go on sitting on the fence like this. Either a man has a moustache or he has not. There can be no middle course."

The thoughtful pause which followed these words was broken by a Small Bass.

"Talking of moustaches," he said, "you don't seem to see any nowadays, not what I call moustaches. What's become of them?"

"I've often asked myself the same question," said a Gin and Italian Vermouth. "Where, I've often asked myself, are the great sweeping moustaches of our boyhood? I've got a photograph of my grandfather as a young man in the album at home, and he's just a pair of eyes staring over a sort of quickset hedge."

"Special cups they used to have," said the Small Bass, "to

269

keep the vegetation out of their coffee. Ah, well, those days are gone for ever."

Mr. Mulliner shook his head.

"Not entirely," he said, stirring his hot Scotch and lemon. "I admit that they are rarer than they used to be, but in the remoter rural districts you will still find these curious growths flourishing. What causes them to survive is partly boredom and partly the good, clean spirit of amateur sport which has made us Englishmen what we are."

The Small Bass said he did not quite get that.

"What I mean," said Mr. Mulliner, "is that life has not much to offer in the way of excitement to men who are buried in the country all the year round, so for want of anything better to do they grow moustaches at one another."

"Sort of competitively, as it were?"

"Exactly. One landowner will start to try to surpass his neighbour in luxuriance of moustache, and the neighbour, inflamed, fights right back at him. There is often a great deal of very intense feeling about these contests, with not a little wagering on the side. So, at least, my nephew Brancepeth, the artist, tells me. And he should know, for his present affluence and happiness are directly due to one of them."

"Did he grow a moustache?"

"No. He was merely caught up in the whirlwind of the struggle for supremacy between Lord Bromborough, of Rumpling Hall, Lower Rumpling, Norfolk, and Sir Preston Potter, Bart., of Wapleigh Towers in the same county. Most of the vintage moustaches nowadays are to be found in Norfolk and Suffolk. I suppose the keen, moist sea air brings them on. Certainly it, or some equally stimulating agency, had brought on those of Lord Bromborough and Sir Preston Potter, for in the whole of England at that time there were probably no two finer specimens than the former's Joyeuse and the latter's Love in Idleness."

It was Lord Bromborough's daughter Muriel (said Mr. Mulliner) who had entitled these two moustaches in this

270

manner. A poetic, imaginative girl, much addicted to reading old sagas and romances, she had adapted to modern conditions the practice of the ancient heroes of bestowing names on their favourite swords. King Arthur, you will remember, had his Excalibur, Charlemagne his Flamberge, Doolin of Mayence the famous Merveilleuse: and Muriel saw no reason why this custom should be allowed to die out. A pretty idea, she thought and I thought it a pretty idea when my nephew Brancepeth told me of it, and he thought it a pretty idea when told of it by Muriel.

For Muriel and Brancepeth had made one another's acquaintance some time before this story opens. The girl, unlike her father, who never left the ancestral acres, came often to London, and on one of these visits my nephew was introduced to her.

With Brancepeth it seems to have been a case of love at first sight, and it was not long before Muriel admitted to returning his passion. She had been favourably attracted to him from the moment when she found that their dance steps fitted, and when some little while later he offered to paint her portrait for nothing there was a look in her eyes which it was impossible to mistake. As early as the middle of the first sitting he folded her in his arms, and she nestled against his waistcoat with a low, cooing gurgle. Both knew that in the other they had found a soul-mate.

Such, then, was the relationship of the young couple, when one summer morning Brancepeth's telephone rang and, removing the receiver, he heard the voice of the girl he loved.

"Hey, cocky," she was saying.

"What ho, reptile," responded Brancepeth. "Where are you speaking from?"

"Rumpling. Listen, I've got a job for you."

"What sort of job?"

"A commission. Father wants his portrait painted."

"Oh yes?"

"Yes. His sinister design is to present it to the local Men's Club. I don't know what he's got against them. A nasty jar it'll be for the poor fellows when they learn of it."

"Why, is the old dad a bit of a gargoyle?"

"You never spoke a truer word. All moustache and eye-brows. The former has to be seen to be believed."

"Pretty septic?"

"My dear! Suppurating. Well, are you on? I've told Father you're the coming man."

"So I am," said Brancepeth. "I'm coming this afternoon."

He was as good as his word. He caught the 3.15 train from Liverpool Street and at 7.20 alighted at the little station at Lower Rumpling, arriving at the Hall just in time to dress for dinner.

Always a rapid dresser, to-night Brancepeth excelled himself, for he yearned to see Muriel once more after their extended separation. Racing down to the drawing-room, however, tying his tie as he went, he found that his impetuosity had brought him there too early. The only occupant of the room at the moment of his entrance was a portly man whom, from the evidence submitted, he took to be his host. Except for a few outlying ears and the tip of a nose, the fellow was entirely moustache, and until he set eyes upon it, Brancepeth tells me, he had never really appreciated the full significance of those opening words of Longfellow's Evangeline, "This is the forest primeval."

He introduced himself courteously.

"How do you do, Lord Bromborough? My name is Mulliner."

The other regarded him—over the zareba—with displeasure, it seemed to Brancepeth.

"What do you mean—Lord Bromborough?" he snapped curtly.

Brancepeth said he had meant Lord Bromborough.

"I'm not Lord Bromborough," said the man.

Brancepeth was taken aback.

"Oh, aren't you?" he said. "I'm sorry."

"I'm glad," said the man. "Whatever gave you the silly idea that I was old Bromborough?"

"I was told that he had a very fine moustache."

"Who told you that?"

"His daughter."

The other snorted.

"You can't go by what a man's daughter says. She's biased. Prejudiced. Blinded by filial love, and all that sort of thing. If I wanted an opinion on a moustache, I wouldn't go to a man's daughter. I'd go to somebody who knew about moustaches. 'Mr. Walkinshaw,' I'd say, or whatever the name might be. . . . Bromborough's moustache a very fine moustache, indeed! Pshaw! Bromborough *has* a moustache—of a sort. He is not clean-shaven—I concede that . . . but fine? Pooh. Absurd. Ridiculous. Preposterous. Never heard such nonsense in my life."

He turned pettishly away, and so hurt and offended was his manner that Brancepeth had no heart to continue the conversation. Muttering something about having forgotten his handkerchief, he sidled from the room and hung about on the landing outside. And presently Muriel came tripping down the stairs, looking more beautiful than ever.

She seemed delighted to see him.

"Hullo, Brancepeth, you old bounder," she said cordially. "So you got here? What are you doing parked on the stairs? Why aren't you in the drawing-room?"

Brancepeth shot a glance at the closed door and lowered his voice.

"There's a hairy bird in there who wasn't any too matey. I thought it must be your father and accosted him as such, and he got extraordinary peevish. He seemed to resent my saying that I had heard your father had a fine moustache."

The girl laughed.

"Golly! You put your foot in it properly. Old Potter's madly jealous of Father's moustache. That was Sir Preston Potter, of Wapleigh Towers, one of our better-known local Barts. He and his son are staying here." She broke off to address the butler, a kindly, silver-haired old man who at this moment mounted the stairs. "Hullo, Phipps, are you ambling up to announce the tea and shrimps? You're a bit early. I don't think Father and Mr. Potter are down yet. Ah, here's Father," she said, as a brilliantly moustached man of middle age appeared. "Father, this is Mr. Mulliner."

Brancepeth eyed his host keenly as he shook hands and his heart sank a little. He saw that the task of committing this man to canvas was going to be a difficult one. The recent slurs of Sir Preston Potter had been entirely without justification. Lord Bromborough's moustache was an extraordinarily fine one, fully as lush as that which barred the public from getting a square view of the Baronet. It seemed to Brancepeth, indeed, that the job before him was more one for a landscape artist than a portrait painter.

Sir Preston Potter, however, who now emerged from the drawing-room, clung stoutly to his opinion. He looked sneeringly at his rival.

"You been clipping your moustache, Bromborough?"

"Of course I have not been clipping my moustache," replied Lord Bromborough shortly. It was only too plain that there was bad blood between the two men. "What the dooce would I clip my moustache for? What makes you think I've been clipping my moustache?"

"I thought it had shrunk," said Sir Preston Potter. "It looks very small to me, very small. Perhaps the moth's been at it."

Lord Bromborough quivered beneath the coarse insult, but his patrician breeding checked the hot reply which rose to his lips. He was a host. Controlling himself with a strong effort, he turned the conversation to the subject of early mangold-wurzels; and it was while he was speaking of these with eloquence and even fire that a young man with butter-coloured hair came hurrying down the stairs.

"Buck up, Edwin," said Muriel impatiently. "What's the idea of keeping us all waiting like this?"

"Oh, sorry," said the young man.

"So you ought to be. Well, now you're here, I'd like to introduce you to Mr. Mulliner. He's come to paint Father's portrait. Mr. Mulliner . . . Mr. Edwin Potter, my *fiancé*."

"Dinner is served," said Phipps the butler.

It was in a sort of trance that my nephew Brancepeth sat through the meal which followed. He toyed listlessly with his food and contributed so little to the conversation that a casual observer entering the room would have supposed him to be a deaf-mute who was on a diet. Nor can we fairly blame him for this, for he had had a severe shock. Few things are more calculated to jar an ardent lover and upset his poise than the sudden announcement by the girl he loves that she is engaged to somebody else, and Muriel's words had been like a kick in the stomach from an army mule. And in addition to suffering the keenest mental anguish, Brancepeth was completely bewildered.

It was not as if this Edwin Potter had been Clark Gable or somebody. Studying him closely, Brancepeth was unable to discern in him any of those qualities which win girls' hearts. He had an ordinary, meaningless face, disfigured by an eye-glass, and was plainly a boob of the first water. Brancepeth could make nothing of it. He resolved at the earliest possible moment to get hold of Muriel and institute a probe.

It was not until next day before luncheon that he found an opportunity of doing so. His morning had been spent in making preliminary sketches of her father. This task concluded, he came out into the garden and saw her reclining in a hammock slung between two trees at the edge of the large lawn.

He made his way towards her with quick, nervous strides. He was feeling jaded and irritated. His first impressions of Lord Bromborough had not misled him. Painting his portrait, he saw, was going to prove, as he had feared it would prove, a severe test of his courage and strength. There seemed so little about Lord Bromborough's face for an artist to get hold of. It was as if he had been commissioned to depict a client who, for reasons of his own, insisted on lying hid behind a haystack.

His emotions lent acerbity to his voice. It was with a sharp intonation that he uttered the preliminary "Hoy!"

The girl sat up.

"Oh, hullo," she said.

"Oh, hullo, yourself, with knobs on," retorted Brancepeth. "Never mind the 'Oh, hullo.' I want an explanation."

"What's puzzling you?"

"This engagement of yours."

"Oh, that?"

"Yes, that. A nice surprise that was to spring on a chap, was it not? A jolly way of saying 'Welcome to Rumpling Hall,' I don't think." Brancepeth choked. "I came here thinking that you loved me. . . ."

"So I do."

"What?"

"Madly. Devotedly."

"Then why the dickens do I find you betrothed to this blighted Potter?"

Muriel sighed.

"It's the old, old story."

"What's the old, old story?"

"This is. It's all so simple, if you'd only understand. I don't suppose any girl ever worshipped a man as I worship you, Brancepeth, but Father hasn't a bean . . . you know what it's like owning land nowadays. Between ourselves, while we're on the subject, I'd stipulate for a bit down in advance on that portrait, if I were you. . . ."

Brancepeth understood.

"Is this Potter rotter rich?"

"Rolling. Sir Preston was Potter's Potted Table Delicacies."

There was a silence.

"H'm," said Brancepeth.

"Exactly. You see now. Oh, Brancepeth," said the girl, her voice trembling, "why haven't you money? If you only had the merest pittance—enough for a flat in Mayfair and a little week-end place in the country somewhere and a couple of good cars and a villa in the South of France and a bit of trout fishing on some decent river, I would risk all for love. But as it is. . . ."

Another silence fell.

"What you ought to do," said Muriel, "is invent some good

animal for the movies. That's where the money is. Look at Walt Disney."

Brancepeth started. It was as if she had read his thoughts. Like all young artists nowadays, he had always held before him as a goal of his ambition the invention of some new comic animal for the motion pictures. What he burned to do, as Velasquez would have burned to do if he had lived to-day, was to think of another Mickey Mouse and then give up work and just sit back and watch the money roll in.

"It isn't so easy," he said sadly.

"Have you tried?"

"Of course I've tried. For years I have followed the gleam. I thought I had something with Hilda the Hen and Bertie the Bandicoot, but nobody would look at them. I see now that they were lifeless, uninspired. I am a man who needs the direct inspiration."

"Doesn't Father suggest anything to you?"

Brancepeth shook his head.

"No. I have studied your father, alert for the slightest hint. . . ."

"Walter the Walrus?"

"No. Lord Bromborough looks like a walrus, yes, but unfortunately not a funny walrus. That moustache of his is majestic rather than diverting. It arouses in the beholder a feeling of awe, such as one gets on first seeing the pyramids. One senses the terrific effort behind it. I suppose it must have taken a lifetime of incessant toil to produce a cascade like that?"

"Oh, no. Father hadn't a moustache at all a few years ago. It was only when Sir Preston began to grow one and rather flaunt it at him at District Council meetings that he buckled down to it. But why," demanded the girl passionately, "are we wasting time talking about moustaches? Kiss me, Brancepeth. We have just time before lunch."

Brancepeth did as directed, and the incident closed.

I do not propose (resumed Mr. Mulliner, who had broken off his narrative at this point to request Miss Postlethwaite, our able barmaid, to give him another hot Scotch and lemon) to dwell in detail on the agony of spirit endured by my nephew Brancepeth in the days that followed this poignant conversation. The spectacle of a sensitive artist soul on the rack is never a pleasant one. Suffice it to say that as each day came and went it left behind it an increased despair.

What with the brooding on his shattered romance and trying to paint Lord Bromborough's portrait and having his nerves afflicted by the incessant bickering that went on between Lord Bromborough and Sir Preston Potter and watching Edwin Potter bleating round Muriel and not being able to think of a funny animal for the movies, it is little wonder that his normally healthy complexion began to shade off to a sallow pallor and that his eyes took on a haunted look. Before the end of the first week he had become an object to excite the pity of the tender-hearted.

Phipps the butler was tender-hearted, and had been since a boy. Brancepeth excited his pity, and he yearned to do something to ameliorate the young man's lot. The method that suggested itself to him was to take a bottle of champagne to his room. It might prove a palliative rather than a cure, but he was convinced that it would, if only temporarily, bring the roses back to Brancepeth's cheeks. So he took a bottle of champagne to his room on the fifth night of my nephew's visit, and found him lying on his bed in striped pyjamas and a watered silk dressing-gown, staring at the ceiling.

The day that was now drawing to a close had been a particularly bad one for Brancepeth. The weather was unusually warm, and this had increased his despondency, so that he had found himself chafing beneath Lord Bromborough's moustache in a spirit of sullen rebellion. Before the afternoon sitting was over, he had become conscious of a vivid feeling of hatred for the thing. He longed for the courage to get at it with a hatchet after the manner of a pioneer in some wild country hewing a clearing in the surrounding jungle. When Phipps found him, his fists were clenched and he was biting his lower lip.

"I have brought you a little champagne, sir," said Phipps, in his kindly, silver-haired way. "It occurred to me that you might be in need of a restorative."

Brancepeth was touched. He sat up, the hard glare in his eyes softening.

"That's awfully good of you," he said. "You are quite right. I could do with a drop or two from the old bin. I am feeling rather fagged. The weather, I suppose."

A gentle smile played over the butler's face as he watched the young man put away a couple, quick.

"No, sir. I do not think it is the weather. You may be quite frank with me, sir. I understand. It must be a very wearing task, painting his lordship. Several artists have had to give it up. There was a young fellow here in the spring of last year who had to be removed to the cottage hospital. His manner had been strange and moody for some days, and one night we found him on a ladder, in the nude, tearing and tearing away at the ivy on the west wall. His lordship's moustache had been too much for him."

Brancepeth groaned and refilled his glass. He knew just how his brother brush must have felt.

"The ironical thing," continued the butler, "is that conditions would be just as bad, were the moustache non-existent. I have been in service at the Hall for a number of years, and I can assure you that his lordship was fully as hard on the eye when he was clean-shaven. Well, sir, when I tell you that I was actually relieved when he began to grow a moustache, you will understand."

"Why, what was the matter with him?"

"He had a face like a fish, sir."

"A fish?"

"Yes, sir."

Something resembling an electric shock shot through Brancepeth, causing him to quiver in every limb.

"A funny fish?" he asked in a choking voice.

"Yes, sir. Extremely droll."

Brancepeth was trembling like a saucepan of boiling milk at the height of its fever. A strange, wild thought had come into his mind. A funny fish . . .

There had never been a funny fish on the screen. Funny mice, funny cats, funny dogs . . . but not a funny fish. He stared before him with glowing eyes.

"Yes, sir, when his lordship began to grow a moustache, I was relieved. It seemed to me that it must be a change for the better. And so it was at first. But now . . . you know how it is, sir. . . . I often find myself wishing those old happy days were back again. We never know when we are well off, sir, do we?"

"You would be glad to see the last of Lord Bromborough's moustache?"

"Yes, sir. Very glad."

"Right," said Brancepeth. "Then I'll shave it off."

In private life, butlers relax that impassive gravity which the rules of their union compel them to maintain in public. Spring something sensational on a butler when he is chatting with you in your bedroom, and he will leap and goggle like any ordinary man. Phipps did so now.

"Shave it off, sir?" he gasped, quaveringly.

"Shave it off," said Brancepeth, pouring out the last of the champagne.

"Shave off his lordship's moustache?"

"This very night. Leaving not a wrack behind."

"But, sir . . ."

"Well?"

"The thought that crossed my mind, sir, was—how?"

Brancepeth clicked his tongue impatiently.

"Quite easy. I suppose he likes a little something last thing at night? Whisky or what not?"

"I always bring his lordship a glass of warm milk to the smoking-room."

"Have you taken it to him yet?"

"Not yet, sir. I was about to do so when I left you."

"And is there anything in the nature of a sleeping draught in the house?"

"Yes, sir. His lordship is a poor sleeper in the hot weather and generally takes a tablet of Slumberola in his milk."

280

"Then, Phipps, if you are the pal I think you are, you will slip into his milk to-night not one tablet but four tablets."

"But, sir. . . ."

"I know, I know. What you are trying to say, I presume, is —What is there in it for you? I will tell you, Phipps. There is a packet in it for you. If Lord Bromborough's face in its stark fundamentals is as you describe it, I can guarantee that in less than no time I shall be bounding about the place trying to evade super-tax. In which event, rest assured that you will get your cut. You are sure of your facts? If I make a clearing in the tangled wildwood, I shall come down eventually to a face like a fish?"

"Yes, sir."

"A fish with good comedy values?"

"Oh, yes, sir. Till it began to get me down, many is the laugh I have had at the sight of it."

"That is all I wish to know. Right. Well, Phipps, can I count on your co-operation? I may add, before you speak, that this means my life's happiness. Sit in, and I shall be able to marry the girl I adore. Refuse to do your bit, and I drift through the remainder of my life a soured, blighted bachelor."

The butler was plainly moved. Always kindly and silver-haired, he looked kindlier and more silver-haired than ever before.

"It's like that, is it, sir?"

"It is."

"Well, sir, I wouldn't wish to come between a young gentleman and his life's happiness. I know what it means to love."

"You do?"

"I do indeed, sir. It is not for me to boast, but there was a time when the girls used to call me Saucy George."

"And so——?"

"I will do as you request, sir."

"I knew it, Phipps," said Brancepeth with emotion. "I knew that I could rely on you. All that remains, then, is for you to show me which is Lord Bromborough's room." He

281

paused. A disturbing thought had struck him. "I say! Suppose he locks his door?"

"It is quite all right, sir," the butler reassured him. "In the later summer months, when the nights are sultry, his lordship does not sleep in his room. He reposes in a hammock slung between two trees on the large lawn."

"I know the hammock," said Brancepeth tenderly. "Well, that's fine, then. The thing's in the bag, Phipps," said Brancepeth, grasping his hand. "I don't know how to express my gratitude. If everything develops as I expect it to; if Lord Bromborough's face gives me the inspiration which I anticipate and I clean up big, you, I repeat, shall share my riches. In due season there will call at your pantry elephants laden with gold, and camels bearing precious stones and rare spices. Also apes, ivory and peacocks. And . . . you say your name is George?"

"Yes, sir."

"Then my eldest child shall be christened George. Or, if female, Georgiana."

"Thank you very much, sir."

"Not at all," said Brancepeth. "A pleasure."

Brancepeth's first impression on waking next morning was that he had had a strange and beautiful dream. It was a vivid, lovely thing, all about stealing out of the house in striped pyjamas and a watered silk dressing-gown, armed with a pair of scissors, and stooping over the hammock where Lord Bromborough lay and razing his great moustache Joyeuse to its foundations. And he was just heaving a wistful sigh and wishing it were true, when he found that it was. It all came back to him—the furtive sneak downstairs, the wary passage of the lawn, the snip-snip-snip of the scissors blending with a strong man's snores in the silent night. It was no dream. The thing had actually occurred. His host's upper lip had become a devastated area.

It was not Brancepeth's custom, as a rule, to spring from his bed at the beginning of a new day, but he did so now. He was consumed with a burning eagerness to gaze upon his handiwork, for the first time to see Lord Bromborough steadily and see him whole. Scarcely ten minutes had elapsed before he was in his clothes and on his way to the breakfast-room. The other, he knew, was an early riser, and even so great a bereavement as he had suffered would not deter him from getting at the coffee and kippers directly he caught a whiff of them.

Only Phipps, however, was in the breakfast-room. He was lighting wicks under the hot dishes on the sideboard. Brancepeth greeted him jovially.

"Good morning, Phipps. What ho, what ho, with a hey nonny nonny and a hot cha-cha."

The butler was looking nervous, like Macbeth interviewing Lady Macbeth after one of her visits to the spare room.

"Good morning, sir. Er—might I ask, sir. . . ."

"Oh, yes," said Brancepeth. "The operation was a complete success. Everything went according to plan."

"I am very glad to hear it, sir."

"Not a hitch from start to finish. Tell me, Phipps," said Brancepeth, helping himself buoyantly to a fried egg and a bit of bacon and seating himself at the table, "what sort of a fish did Lord Bromborough look like before he had a moustache?"

The butler reflected.

"Well, sir, I don't know if you have seen Sidney the Sturgeon?"

"Eh?"

"On the pictures, sir. I recently attended a cinematographic performance at Norwich—it was on my afternoon off last week—and," said Phipps, chuckling gently at the recollection, "they were showing a most entertaining new feature, 'The Adventures of Sidney the Sturgeon.' It came on before the big picture, and it was all I could do to keep a straight face. This sturgeon looked extremely like his lordship in the old days."

He drifted from the room and Brancepeth stared after him,

283

stunned. His air castles had fallen about him in ruins. Fame, fortune, and married bliss were as far away from him as ever. All his labour had been in vain. If there was already a funny fish functioning on the silver screen, it was obvious that it would be mere waste of time to do another. He clasped his head in his hands and groaned over his fried egg. And, as he did so, the door opened.

"Ha!" said Lord Bromborough's voice. "Good morning, good morning."

Brancepeth spun round with a sharp jerk which sent a piece of bacon flying off his fork as if it had been shot from a catapult. Although his host's appearance could not affect his professional future now, he was consumed with curiosity to see what he looked like. And, having spun round, he sat transfixed. There before him stood Lord Bromborough, but not a hair of his moustache was missing. It flew before him like a banner in all its pristine luxuriance.

"Eh, what?" said Lord Bromborough, sniffing. "Kedgeree? Capital, capital."

He headed purposefully for the sideboard. The door opened again, and Edwin Potter came in, looking more of a boob than ever.

In addition to looking like a boob, Edwin Potter seemed worried.

"I say," he said, "my father's missing."

"On how many cylinders?" asked Lord Bromborough. He was a man who liked his joke of a morning.

"I mean to say," continued Edwin Potter, "I can't find him. I went to speak to him about something just now, and his room was empty and his bed had not been slept in."

Lord Bromborough was dishing out kedgeree on to a plate.

"That's all right," he said. "He wanted to try my hammock last night, so I let him. If he slept as soundly as I did, he slept well. I came over all drowsy as I was finishing my glass of hot milk and I woke this morning in an arm-chair in the smoking-room. Ah, my dear," he went on, as Muriel entered, "come along and try this kedgeree. It smells excellent. I was just telling our young friend here that his father slept in my hammock last night."

Muriel's face was wearing a look of perplexity.

"Out in the garden, do you mean?"

"Of course I mean out in the garden. You know where my hammock is. I've seen you lying in it."

"Then there must be a goat in the garden."

"Goat?" said Lord Bromborough, who had now taken his place at the table and was shovelling kedgeree into himself like a stevedore loading a grain ship. "What do you mean, goat? There's no goat in the garden. Why should there be a goat in the garden?"

"Because something has eaten off Sir Preston's moustache."

"What!"

"Yes. I met him outside, and the shrubbery had completely disappeared. Here he is. Look."

What seemed at first to Brancepeth a total stranger was standing in the doorway. It was only when the newcomer folded his arms and began to speak in a familiar rasping voice that he recognized Sir Preston Potter, Bart., of Wapleigh Towers.

"So!" said Sir Preston, directing at Lord Bromborough a fiery glance full of deleterious animal magnetism.

Lord Bromborough finished his kedgeree and looked up.

"Ah, Potter," he said. "Shaved your moustache, have you? Very sensible. It would never have amounted to anything, and you will be happier without it."

Flame shot from Sir Preston Potter's eye. The man was plainly stirred to his foundations.

"Bromborough," he snarled, "I have only five things to say to you. The first is that you are the lowest, foulest fiend that ever disgraced the pure pages of Debrett; the second that your dastardly act in clipping off my moustache shows you a craven, who knew that defeat stared him in the eye and that only thus he could hope to triumph; the third that I intend to approach my lawyer immediately with a view to taking legal action; the fourth is good-bye for ever; and the fifth——"

"Have an egg," said Lord Bromborough.

"I will not have an egg. This is not a matter which can be lightly passed off with eggs. The fifth thing I wish to say——"

"But, my dear fellow, you seem to be suggesting that I had something to do with this. I approve of what has happened, yes. I approve of it heartily. Norfolk will be a sweeter and better place to live in now that this has occurred. But it was none of my doing. I was asleep in the smoking-room all night."

"The fifth thing I wish to say——"

"In an arm-chair. If you doubt me, I can show you the arm-chair."

"The fifth thing I wish to say is that the engagement between my son and your daughter is at an end."

"Like your moustache. Ha, ha!" said Lord Bromborough, who had many good qualities but was not tactful.

"Oh, but, Father!" cried Edwin Potter. "I mean, dash it!"

"And *I* mean," thundered Sir Preston, "that your engagement is at an end. You have my five points quite clear, Bromborough?"

"I think so," said Lord Bromborough, ticking them off on his fingers. "I am a foul fiend, I'm a craven, you are going to institute legal proceedings, you bid me good-bye for ever, and my daughter shall never marry your son. Yes, five in all."

"Add a sixth. I shall see that you are expelled from all your clubs."

"I haven't got any."

"Oh?" said Sir Preston, a little taken aback. "Well, if ever you make a speech in the House of Lords, beware. I shall be up in the gallery, booing."

He turned and strode from the room, followed by Edwin, protesting bleatingly. Lord Bromborough took a cigarette from his case.

"Silly old ass," he said. "I expect that moustache of his was clipped off by a body of public-spirited citizens. Like the Vigilantes they have in America. It is absurd to suppose that a man could grow a beastly, weedy caricature of a moustache like Potter's without inflaming popular feeling. No doubt they have been lying in wait for him for months. Lurking. Watching their opportunity. Well, my dear, so your wedding's off. A nuisance in a way of course, for I'd just bought a new pair of trousers to give you away in. Still it can't be helped."

"No, it can't be helped," said Muriel. "Besides there will be another one along in a minute."

She shot a tender smile at Brancepeth, but on his lips there was no answering simper. He sat in silence, crouched over his fried egg.

What did it profit him, he was asking himself bitterly, that the wedding was off? He himself could never marry Muriel. He was a penniless artist without prospects. He would never invent a comic animal for the movies now. There had been an instant when he had hoped that Sir Preston's uncovered face might suggest one, but the hope had died at birth. Sir Preston Potter, without his moustache, had merely looked like a man without a moustache.

He became aware that his host was addressing him.

"I beg your pardon?"

"I said, 'Got a light?'"

"Oh, sorry," said Brancepeth.

He took out his lighter and gave it a twiddle. Then, absently, he put the flame to the cigarette between his host's lips.

Or, rather, for preoccupation had temporarily destroyed his judgment of distance, to the moustache that billowed above and around it. And the next moment there was a sheet of flame and a cloud of acrid smoke. When this had cleared away, only a little smouldering stubble was left of what had once been one of Norfolk's two most outstanding eyesores.

A barely human cry rent the air, but Brancepeth hardly heard it. He was staring like one in a trance at the face that confronted him through the shrouding mists, fascinated by the short, broad nose, the bulging eyes, the mouth that gaped and twitched. It was only when his host made a swift dive across the table with bared teeth and clutching hands that Prudence returned to its throne. He slid under the table and came out on the other side.

"Catch him!" cried the infuriated peer. "Trip him up! Sit on his head!"

"Certainly not," said Muriel. "He is the man I love."

"Is he!" said Lord Bromborough, breathing heavily as he crouched for another spring. "Well, he's the man I am going to disembowel with my bare hands—when I catch him."

"I think I should nip through the window, darling," said Muriel gently.

Brancepeth weighed the advice hastily and found it good. The window, giving on to the gravel drive, was, he perceived, open at the bottom. The sweet summer air floated in, and an instant later he was floating out. As he rose from the gravel, something solid struck him on the back of the head. It was a coffee-pot.

But coffee-pots, however shrewdly aimed, mattered little to Brancepeth now. This one had raised a painful contusion, and he had in addition skinned both hands and one of his knees. His trousers, moreover, a favourite pair, had a large hole in them. Nevertheless, his heart was singing within him.

For Phipps had been wrong. Phipps was an ass. Phipps did not know a fish when he saw one. Lord Bromborough's face did not resemble that of a fish at all. It suggested something much finer, much fuller of screen possibilities, much more box-office than a fish. In that one blinding instant of illumination before he had dived under the table, Brancepeth had seen Lord Bromborough for what he was—Ferdinand the Frog.

He turned, to perceive his host in the act of hurling a cottage loaf.

"Muriel!" he cried.

"Hullo?" said the girl, who had joined her father at the window and was watching the scene with great interest.

"I love you, Muriel."

"Same here."

"But for the moment I must leave you."

"I would," said Muriel. She glanced over her shoulder. "He's gone to get the kedgeree." And Brancepeth saw that Lord Bromborough had left his butt. "He is now," she added, "coming back."

"Will you wait for me, Muriel?"

"To all eternity."

"It will not be necessary," said Brancepeth. "Call it six months or a year. By that time I shall have won fame and fortune."

He would have spoken further, but at this moment Lord Bromborough reappeared, poising the kedgeree. With a loving smile and a wave of the hand, Brancepeth leaped smartly to one side. Then, turning, he made his way down the drive, gazing raptly into a future of Rolls-Royces, caviare and silk underclothing made to measure.

*　　*　　*　　*　　*

A gaping chasm opened in the hillside. The air became full of a sort of macédoine of grass, dirt, flowers, and beetles. And dimly in the centre of this moving hash, one perceived the ball travelling well. Accompanied by about a pound of mixed solids, it cleared the brow and vanished from our sight.

THE DEFEAT OF A CRITIC

A CERTAIN critic—for such men, I regret to say, do exist—made the nasty remark about my last novel that it contained "all the old Wodehouse characters under different names." He has probably by now been eaten by bears, like the children who made mock of the prophet Elisha: but if he still survives he will not be able to make a similar charge against *Summer Lightning*. With my superior intelligence, I have outgeneralled the man this time by putting in all the old Wodehouse characters under the same names. Pretty silly it will make him feel, I rather fancy.

This story is a sort of Old Home Week of my—if I may coin a phrase—puppets. Hugo Carmody and Ronnie Fish appeared in *Money for Nothing*. Pilbeam was in *Bill the Conqueror*. And the rest of them, Lord Emsworth, the Efficient Baxter, Butler Beach and the others have all done their bit before in *Something Fresh* and *Leave it to Psmith*. Even Empress of Blandings, that pre-eminent pig, is coming up for the second time, having made her debut in a short story called "Pig-hoo-o-o-o-ey!" which, with other Blandings Castle stories, too fascinating to mention, will eventually appear in volume form.

The fact is, I cannot tear myself away from Blandings Castle. The place exercises a sort of spell over me. I am always popping down to Shropshire and looking in there to hear the latest news, and there always seems to be something to interest me. It is in the hope that it will also interest My Public that I have jotted down the bit of gossip from the old spot which I have called *Summer Lightning*.

A word about the title. It is related of Thackeray that, hitting upon "Vanity Fair" after retiring to rest one night, he leaped out of bed and ran seven times round the room, shouting at the top of his voice. Oddly enough, I behaved in exactly the same way when I thought of *Summer Lightning*. I recognised it immediately as the ideal title for a novel. My exuberance has been a little diminished since by the discovery that I am not the only one who thinks highly of it. Already I have been informed that two novels with the same name have been published in England, and my agent in America cables to say that three have recently been placed on the market in the United States. As my story has appeared in serial form under its present label, it is too late to alter it now. I can only express the modest hope that this story will be considered worthy of inclusion in the list of the Hundred Best Books Called *Summer Lightning*.

Author's Preface, "*Summer Lightning*."

THE CLICKING OF CUTHBERT

THE YOUNG man came into the smoking-room of the club-house, and flung his bag with a clatter on the floor. He sank moodily into an arm-chair and pressed the bell.

"Waiter!"

"Sir?"

The young man pointed at the bag with every evidence of distaste.

"You may have these clubs," he said. "Take them away. If you don't want them yourself, give them to one of the caddies."

Across the room the Oldest Member gazed at him with a grave sadness through the smoke of his pipe. His eye was deep and dreamy,—the eye of a man who, as the poet says, has seen Golf steadily and seen it whole.

"You are giving up golf?" he said.

He was not altogether unprepared for such an attitude on the young man's part: for from his eyrie on the terrace above the ninth green he had observed him start out on the afternoon's round and had seen him lose a couple of balls in the lake at the second hole after taking seven strokes at the first.

"Yes!" cried the young man fiercely. "For ever, dammit! Footling game! Blanked infernal fat-headed silly ass of a game! Nothing but a waste of time."

The Sage winced.

"Don't say that, my boy."

"But I do say it. What earthly good is golf? Life is stern and life is earnest. We live in a practical age. All round us we see foreign competition making itself unpleasant. And we Spend our time playing golf! What do we get out of it? Is golf any *use*? That's what I'm asking you. Can you name me a single case where devotion to this pestilential pastime has done a man any practical good?"

292

The Sage smiled gently.

"I could name a thousand."

"One will do."

"I will select," said the Sage, "from the innumerable memories that rush to my mind, the story of Cuthbert Banks."

"Never heard of him."

"Be of good cheer," said the Oldest Member. "You are going to hear of him now."

*　　*　　*　　*　　*

It was in the picturesque little settlement of Wood Hills (said the Oldest Member) that the incidents occurred which I am about to relate. Even if you have never been in Wood Hills, that suburban paradise is probably familiar to you by name. Situated at a convenient distance from the city, it combines in a notable manner the advantages of town life with the pleasant surroundings and healthful air of the country. Its inhabitants live in commodious houses, standing in their own grounds, and enjoy so many luxuries—such as gravel soil, main drainage, electric light, telephone, baths (h. and c.), and company's own water, that you might be pardoned for imagining life to be so ideal for them that no possible improvement could be added to their lot. Mrs. Willoughby Smethurst was under no such delusion. What Wood Hills needed to make it perfect, she realized, was Culture. Material comforts are all very well, but, if the *summum bonum* is to be achieved, the Soul also demands a look in, and it was Mrs. Smethurst's unfaltering resolve that never while she had her strength should the Soul be handed the loser's end. It was her intention to make Wood Hills a centre of all that was most cultivated and refined, and, golly! how she had succeeded. Under her presidency the Wood Hills Literary and Debating Society had tripled its membership.

But there is always a fly in the ointment, a caterpillar in the salad. The local golf club, an institution to which Mrs. Smethurst strongly objected, had also tripled its membership; and the division of the community into two rival camps, the

293

Golfers and the Cultured, had become more marked than ever. This division, always acute, had attained now to the dimensions of a Schism. The rival sects treated one another with a cold hostility.

Unfortunate episodes came to widen the breach. Mrs. Smethurst's house adjoined the links, standing to the right of the fourth tee: and, as the Literary Society was in the habit of entertaining visiting lecturers, many a golfer had foozled his drive owning to sudden loud outbursts of applause coinciding with his down-swing. And not long before this story opens a sliced ball, whizzing in at the open window, had come within an ace of incapacitating Raymond Parsloe Devine, the rising young novelist (who rose at that moment a clear foot and a half) from any further exercise of his art. Two inches, indeed, to the right and Raymond must inevitably have handed in his dinner-pail.

To make matters worse, a ring at the front-door bell followed almost immediately, and the maid ushered in a young man of pleasing appearance in a sweater and baggy knickerbockers who apologetically but firmly insisted on playing his ball where it lay, and what with the shock of the lecturer's narrow escape and the spectacle of the intruder standing on the table and working away with a niblick, the afternoon's session had to be classed as a complete frost. Mr. Devine's determination, from which no argument could swerve him, to deliver the rest of his lecture in the coal-cellar gave the meeting a jolt from which it never recovered.

I have dwelt upon this incident, because it was the means of introducing Cuthbert Banks to Mrs. Smethurst's niece, Adeline. As Cuthbert, for it was he who had so nearly reduced the muster-roll of rising novelists by one, hopped down from the table after his stroke, he was suddenly aware that a beautiful girl was looking at him intently. As a matter of fact, everyone in the room was looking at him intently, none more so that Raymond Parsloe Devine, but none of the others were beautiful girls. Long as the members of Wood Hills Literary Society were on brain, they were short on looks, and, to Cuthbert's excited eye, Adeline Smethurst stood out like a jewel in a pile of coke.

He had never seen her before, for she had only arrived at her aunt's house on the previous day, but he was perfectly certain that life, even when lived in the midst of gravel soil, main drainage, and company's own water, was going to be a pretty poor affair if he did not see her again. Yes, Cuthbert was in love: and it is interesting to record, as showing the effect of the tender emotion on a man's game, that twenty minutes after he had met Adeline he did the short eleventh in one, and as near as a toucher got a three on the four-hundred-yard twelfth.

I will skip lightly over the intermediate stages of Cuthbert's courtship and come to the moment when—at the annual ball in aid of the local Cottage Hospital, the only occasion during the year on which the lion, so to speak, lay down with the lamb, and the Golfers and the Cultured met on terms of easy comradeship, their differences temporarily laid aside—he proposed to Adeline and was badly stymied.

That fair, soulful girl could not see him with a spy-glass.

"Mr. Banks," she said, "I will speak frankly."

"Charge right ahead," assented Cuthbert.

"Deeply sensible as I am of——"

"I know. Of the honour and the compliment and all that. But, passing lightly over all that guff, what seems to be the trouble? I love you to distraction——"

"Love is not everything."

"You're wrong," said Cuthbert, earnestly. "You're right off it. Love——" And he was about to dilate on the theme when she interrupted him.

"I am a girl of ambition."

"And very nice, too," said Cuthbert.

"I am a girl of ambition," repeated Adeline, "and I realise that the fulfilment of my ambitions must come through my husband. I am very ordinary myself——"

"What!" cried Cuthbert. "You ordinary? Why, you are a pearl among women, the queen of your sex. You can't have been looking in a glass lately. You stand alone. Simply alone. You make the rest look like battered repaints."

"Well," said Adeline, softening a trifle, "I believe I am fairly good-looking——"

"Anybody who was content to call you fairly good-looking would describe the Taj Mahal as a pretty nifty tomb."

"But that is not the point. What I mean is, if I marry a nonentity I shall be a nonentity myself for ever. And I would sooner die than be a nonentity."

"And, if I follow your reasoning, you think that that lets *me* out?"

"Well, really, Mr. Banks, *have* you done anything, or are you likely ever to do anything worth while?"

Cuthbert hesitated.

"It's true," he said, "I didn't finish in the first ten in the open, and I was knocked out in the semi-final of the Amateur, but I won the French Open last year."

"The—what?"

"The French Open Championship. Golf, you know."

"Golf! You waste all your time playing golf. I admire a man who is more spiritual, more intellectual."

A pang of jealousy rent Cuthbert's bosom.

"Like What's-his-name Devine?" he said, sullenly.

"Mr. Devine," replied Adeline, blushing faintly, "is going to be a great man. Already he has achieved much. The critics say that he is more Russian than any other young English writer."

"And is that good?"

"Of course it's good."

"I should have thought the wheeze would be to be more English than any other young English writer."

"Nonsense! Who wants an English writer to be English? You've got to be Russian or Spanish or something to be a real success. The mantle of the great Russians has descended on Mr. Devine."

"From what I've heard of Russians, I should hate to have that happen to *me*."

"There is no danger of that," said Adeline, scornfully.

"Oh! Well, let me tell you that there is a lot more in me than you think."

"That might easily be so."

"You think I'm not spiritual and intellectual," said Cuthbert, deeply moved. "Very well. To-morrow I join the Literary Society."

Even as he spoke the words his leg was itching to kick himself for being such a chump, but the sudden expression of pleasure on Adeline's face soothed him; and he went home that night with the feeling that he had taken on something rather attractive. It was only in the cold, grey light of the morning that he realised what he had let himself in for.

I do not know if you have had any experience of suburban literary societies, but the one that flourished under the eye of Mrs. Willoughby Smethurst at Wood Hills was rather more so than the average. With my feeble powers of narrative, I cannot hope to make clear to you all that Cuthbert Banks endured in the next few weeks. And, even if I could, I doubt if I should do so. It is all very well to excite pity and terror, as Aristotle recommends, but there are limits. In the ancient Greek tragedies it was an ironclad rule that all the real rough stuff should take place off-stage, and I shall follow this admirable principle. It will suffice if I say merely that J. Cuthbert Banks had a thin time. After attending eleven debates and fourteen lectures on *vers libre* Poetry, the Seventeenth-Century Essayists, the Neo-Scandinavian Movement in Portuguese Literature, and other subjects of a similar nature, he grew so enfeebled that, on the rare occasions when he had time for a visit to the links, he had to take a full iron for his mashie shots.

It was not simply the oppressive nature of the debates and lectures that sapped his vitality. What really got right in amongst him was the torture of seeing Adeline's adoration of Raymond Parsloe Devine. The man seemed to have made the deepest possible impression upon her plastic emotions. When he spoke, she leaned forward with parted lips and looked at him. When he was not speaking—which was seldom—she leaned back and looked at him. And when he happened to take the next seat to her, she leaned sideways and looked at him. One glance at Mr. Devine would have been more than enough for Cuthbert; but Adeline found him a spectacle that never palled. She could not have gazed at him with a more rapturous intensity if she had been a small child and he a saucer of icecream. All this Cuthbert had to witness while still endeavouring to retain the possession of his faculties sufficiently to enable him to duck and back away if somebody suddenly asked him what he thought of the sombre realism of Vladimir Brusiloff. It is little wonder that he tossed in bed, picking at the coverlet, through sleepless nights, and had to have all his waistcoats taken in three inches to keep them from sagging.

This Vladimir Brusiloff to whom I have referred was the famous Russian novelist, and, owing to the fact of his being in the country on a lecturing tour at the moment, there had been something of a boom in his works. The Wood Hills Literary Society had been studying them for weeks, and never since his first entrance into intellectual circles had Cuthbert Banks come nearer to throwing in the towel. Vladimir specialized in grey studies of hopeless misery, where nothing happened till page three hundred and eighty, when the moujik decided to commit suicide. It was tough going for a man whose deepest reading hitherto had been Vardon on the Push-Shot, and there can be no greater proof of the magic of love than the fact that Cuthbert stuck it without a cry. But the strain was terrible and I am inclined to think that he must have cracked, had it not been for the daily reports in the papers of the internecine strife which was proceeding so briskly in Russia. Cuthbert was an optimist at heart, and it seemed to him that, at the rate at which the inhabitants of that interesting country were murdering one another, the supply of Russian novelists must eventually give out.

One morning, as he tottered down the road for the short walk which was now almost the only exercise to which he was equal, Cuthbert met Adeline. A spasm of anguish flitted through all his nerve-centres as he saw that she was accompanied by Raymond Parsloe Devine.

"Good morning, Mr. Banks," said Adeline.

"Good morning," said Cuthbert, hollowly.

"Such good news about Vladimir Brusiloff."

"Dead?" said Cuthbert, with a touch of hope.

"Dead? Of course not. Why should he be? No. Aunt Emily met his manager after his lecture at Queen's Hall yesterday, and he has promised that Mr. Brusiloff shall come to her next Wednesday reception."

"Oh, ah!" said Cuthbert, dully.

"I don't know how she managed it. I think she must have told him that Mr. Devine would be there to meet him."

"But you said he was coming," argued Cuthbert.

"I shall be very glad," said Raymond Devine, "of the opportunity of meeting Brusiloff."

"I'm sure," said Adeline, "he will be very glad of the opportunity of meeting you."

"Possibly," said Mr. Devine. "Possibly. Competent critics have said that my work closely resembles that of the great Russian Masters."

"Your psychology is so deep."

"Yes, yes."

"And your atmosphere."

"Quite."

Cuthbert, in a perfect agony of spirit, prepared to withdraw from this love-feast. The sun was shining brightly, but the world was black to him. Birds sang in the tree-tops, but he did not hear them. He might have been a moujik for all the pleasure he found in life.

"You will be there, Mr. Banks?" said Adeline, as he turned away.

"Oh, all right," said Cuthbert.

When Cuthbert had entered the drawing-room on the following Wednesday and had taken his usual place in a distant corner where, while able to feast his gaze on Adeline, he had a sporting chance of being overlooked or mistaken for a piece of furniture, he perceived the great Russian thinker seated in the midst of a circle of admiring females. Raymond Parsloe Devine had not yet arrived.

His first glance at the novelist surprised Cuthbert. Doubtless with the best motives, Vladimir Brusiloff had permitted his face to become almost entirely concealed behind a dense zareba of hair, but his eyes were visible through the undergrowth, and it seemed to Cuthbert that there was an expression in them not unlike that of a cat in a strange backyard surrounded by small boys. The man looked forlorn and hopeless, and Cuthbert wondered whether he had had bad news from home.

This was not the case. The latest news which Vladimir Brusiloff had had from Russia had been particularly cheering. Three of his principal creditors had perished in the last massacre of the *bourgeoisie*, and a man whom he owed for five years for a samovar and a pair of overshoes had fled the country, and had not been heard of since. It was not bad news from home that was depressing Vladimir. What was wrong with him was the fact that this was the eighty-second suburban literary reception he had been compelled to attend since he had landed in the country on his lecturing tour, and he was sick to death of it. When his agent had first suggested the trip, he had signed on the dotted line without an instant's hesitation. Worked out in roubles, the fees offered had seemed just about right. But now, as he peered through the brushwood at the faces round him, and realised that eight out of ten of those present had manuscripts of some sort concealed on their persons, and were only waiting for an opportunity to whip them out and start reading, he wished that he had stayed at his quiet home in Nijni-Novgorod, where the worst thing that could happen to a fellow was a brace of bombs coming in through the window and mixing themselves up with his breakfast egg.

At this point in his meditations he was aware that his hostess was looming up before him with a pale young man in horn-rimmed spectacles at her side. There was in Mrs. Smethurst's demeanour something of the unction of the master-of-ceremonies at the big fight who introduces the earnest gentleman who wishes to challenge the winner.

"Oh, Mr. Brusiloff," said Mrs. Smethurst, "I do so want you to meet Mr. Raymond Parsloe Devine, whose work I expect you know. He is one of our younger novelists."

The distinguished visitor peered in a wary and defensive manner through the shrubbery, but did not speak. Inwardly he was thinking how exactly like Mr. Devine was to the eighty-one other younger novelists to whom he had been introduced at various hamlets throughout the country. Raymond Parsloe Devine bowed courteously, while Cuthbert wedged into his corner, glowered at him.

"The critics," said Mr. Devine, "have been kind enough to say that my poor efforts contain a good deal of the Russian spirit. I owe much to the great Russians. I have been greatly influenced by Sovietski."

Down in the forest something stirred. It was Vladimir Brusiloff's mouth opening, as he prepared to speak. He was not a man who prattled readily, especially in a foreign tongue. He gave the impression that each word was excavated from his interior by some up-to-date process of mining. He glared bleakly at Mr. Devine, and allowed three words to drop out of him.

"Sovietski no good!"

He paused for a moment, set the machinery working again, and delivered five more at the pit-head.

"I spit me of Sovietski!"

There was a painful sensation. The lot of a popular idol is in many ways an enviable one, but it has the drawback of uncertainty. Here to-day and gone to-morrow. Until this moment Raymond Parsloe Devine's stock had stood at something considerably over par in Wood Hills intellectual circles, but now there was a rapid slump. Hitherto he had been greatly admired for being influenced by Sovietski, but it appeared now that this was not a good thing to be. It was evidently a rotten thing to be. The law could not touch you for being influenced by Sovietski, but there is an ethical as well as a legal code, and this it was obvious that Raymond Parsloe Devine had transgressed. Women drew away from him slightly, holding their skirts. Men looked at him censoriously. Adeline Smethurst started violently, and dropped a tea-cup. And Cuthbert Banks, doing his popular imitation of a sardine in his corner, felt for the first time that life held something of sunshine.

Raymond Parsloe Devine was plainly shaken, but he made an adroit attempt to recover his lost prestige.

"When I say I have been influenced by Sovietski, I mean, of course, that I was once under his spell. A young writer commits many follies. I have long since passed through that phase. The false glamour of Sovietski has ceased to dazzle me. I now belong whole-heartedly to the school of Nastikoff."

There was a reaction. People nodded at one another sympathetically. After all, we cannot expect old heads on young shoulders, and a lapse at the outset of one's career should not be held against one who has eventually seen the light.

"Nastikoff no good," said Vladimir Brusiloff, coldly. He paused, listening to the machinery.

"Nastikoff worse than Sovietski."

He paused again.

"I spit me of Nastikoff!" he said.

This time there was no doubt about it. The bottom had dropped out of the market, and Raymond Parsloe Devine Preferred were down in the cellar with no takers. It was clear to the entire assembled company that they had been all wrong about Raymond Parsloe Devine. They had allowed him to play on their innocence and sell them a pup. They had taken him at his own valuation, and had been cheated into admiring him as a man who amounted to something, and all the while he had belonged to the school of Nastikoff. You never can tell. Mrs. Smethurst's guests were well-bred, and there was consequently no violent demonstration, but you could see by

302

their faces what they felt. Those nearest Raymond Parsloe jostled to get further away. Mrs. Smethurst eyed him stonily through a raised lorgnette. One or two low hisses were heard, and over at the other end of the room somebody opened the window in a marked manner.

Raymond Parsloe Devine hesitated for a moment, then, realising his situation, turned and slunk to the door. There was an audible sigh of relief as it closed behind him.

Vladimir Brusiloff proceeded to sum up.

"No novelists any good except me. Sovietski—yah! Nastikoff—bah! I spit me of zem all. No novelists anywhere any good except me. P. G. Wodehouse and Tolstoi not bad. Not good, but not bad. No novelists any good except me."

And, having uttered this dictum, he removed a slab of cake from a near-by plate, steered it through the jungle, and began to champ.

It is too much to say that there was a dead silence. There could never be that in any room in which Vladimir Brusiloff was eating cake. But certainly what you might call the general chit-chat was pretty well down and out. Nobody liked to be the first to speak. The members of the Wood Hills Literary Society looked at one another timidly. Cuthbert, for his part, gazed at Adeline; and Adeline gazed into space. It was plain that the girl was deeply stirred. Her eyes were opened wide, a faint flush crimsoned her cheeks, and her breath was coming quickly.

Adeline's mind was in a whirl. She felt as if she had been walking gaily along a pleasant path and had stopped suddenly on the very brink of a precipice. It would be idle to deny that Raymond Parsloe Devine had attracted her extraordinarily. She had taken him at his own valuation as an extremely hot potato, and her hero-worship had gradually been turning into love. And now her hero had been shown to have feet of clay. It was hard, I consider, on Raymond Parsloe Devine, but that is how it goes in this world. You get a following as a celebrity, and then you run up against another bigger celebrity and your admirers desert you. One could moralise on this at considerable length, but better not, perhaps. Enough to say that the glamour of Raymond Devine ceased abruptly in that moment for Adeline, and her most coherent thought at this juncture was the resolve, as soon as she got up to her room, to burn the three signed photographs he had sent her and to give the autographed presentation set of his books to the grocer's boy.

Mrs. Smethurst, meanwhile, having rallied somewhat, was endeavouring to set the feast of reason and flow of soul going again.

" And how do you like England, Mr. Brusiloff?" she asked.

The celebrity paused in the act of lowering another segment of cake.

"Dam' good," he replied, cordially.

"I suppose you have travelled all over the country by this time?"

"You said it," agreed the Thinker.

"Have you met many of our great public men?"

"Yais—Yais—Quite a few of the nibs—Lloyd George, I meet him. But——" Beneath the matting a discontented expression came into his face, and his voice took on a peevish note. " But I not meet your *real* great men—your Arbmishel, your Arreevadon—I not meet them. That's what gives me the pipovitch. Have *you* ever met Arbmishel and Arreevadon?"

A strained, anguished look came into Mrs. Smethurst's face and was reflected in the faces of the other members of the circle. The eminent Russian had sprung two entirely new ones on them, and they felt that their ignorance was about to be exposed. What would Vladimir Brusiloff think of the Wood Hills Literary Society? The reputation of the Wood Hills Literary Society was at stake, trembling in the balance, and coming up for the third time. In dumb agony Mrs. Smethurst rolled her eyes about the room searching for someone capable of coming to the rescue. She drew blank.

And then, from a distant corner, there sounded a deprecating cough, and those nearest Cuthbert Banks saw that he had stopped twisting his right foot round his left ankle and his left foot round his right ankle and was sitting up with a light of almost human intelligence in his eyes.

"Er——" said Cuthbert, blushing as every eye in the room seemed to fix itself on him, "I think he means Abe Mitchell and Harry Vardon."

"Abe Mitchell and Harry Vardon?" repeated Mrs. Smethurst, blankly. "I never heard of——"

"Yais! Yais! Most! Very!" shouted Vladimir Brusiloff, enthusiastically. "Arbmishel and Arreevadon. You know them, yes, what, no, perhaps?"

"I've played with Abe Mitchell often, and I was partnered with Harry Vardon in last year's Open."

The great Russian uttered a cry that shook the chandelier.

"You play in ze Open? Why," he demanded reproachfully of Mrs. Smethurst, "was I not been introduced to this young man who plays in opens?"

"Well, really," faltered Mrs. Smethurst. "Well, the fact is, Mr. Brusiloff——"

She broke off. She was unequal to the task of explaining, without hurting anyone's feelings, that she had always regarded Cuthbert as a piece of cheese and a blot on the landscape.

"Introduce me!" thundered the Celebrity.

"Why, certainly, certainly, of course. This is Mr.——"

She looked appealingly at Cuthbert.

"Banks," prompted Cuthbert.

"Banks!" cried Vladimir Brusiloff. "Not Cootaboot Banks?"

"*Is* your name Cootaboot?" asked Mrs. Smethurst, faintly.

"Well, it's Cuthbert."

"Yais! Yais! Cootaboot!" There was a rush and swirl as the effervescent Muscovite burst his way through the throng and rushed to where Cuthbert sat. He stood for a moment eyeing him excitedly, then, stooping swiftly, kissed him on both cheeks before Cuthbert could get his guard up. "My dear young man, I saw you win ze French Open. Great! Great! Grand! Superb! Hot stuff, and you can say so! Will you permit one who is but eighteen at Nijni-Novgorod to salute you once more?"

And he kissed Cuthbert again. Then, brushing aside one or two intellectuals who were in the way, he dragged up a chair and sat down.

"You are a great man!" he said.

"Oh, no," said Cuthbert modestly.

"Yais! Great. Most! Very! The way you lay your approach-putts dead from anywhere!"

"Oh, I don't know."

Mr. Brusiloff drew his chair closer.

"Let me tell you one vairy funny story about putting. It was one day I play at Nijni-Novgorod with the pro against Lenin and Trotsky, and Trotsky had a two-inch putt for the hole. But, just as he addressed the ball, some one in the crowd he tries to assassinate Lenin with a rewolwer—you know that is our great national sport, trying to assassinate Lenin with rewolwers—and the bang puts Trotsky off his stroke and he goes five yards past the hole, and then Lenin, who is rather shaken, you understand, he misses again himself, and we win the hole and match and I clean up three hundred and ninety-six thousand roubles, or fifteen shillings in your money. Some gameovitch! And now let me tell you one other vairy funny story——"

Desultory conversation had begun in murmurs over the rest of the room, as the Wood Hills intellectuals politely endeavoured to conceal the fact that they realised that they were about as much out of it at this re-union of twin souls as cats at a dog-show. From time to time they started as Vladimir Brusiloff's laugh boomed out. Perhaps it was a consolation to them to know that he was enjoying himself.

As for Adeline, how shall I describe her emotions? She was stunned. Before her very eyes the stone which the builders had rejected had become the main thing, the hundred-to-one shot had walked away with the race. A rush of tender admiration for Cuthbert Banks flooded her heart. She saw that she had been all wrong. Cuthbert, whom she had always treated with a patronising superiority, was really a man to be looked up to and worshipped. A deep, dreamy sigh shook Adeline's fragile form.

Half an hour later Vladimir and Cuthbert Banks rose.

"Goot-a-bye, Mrs. Smet-thirst," said the Celebrity. "Zank you for a most charming visit. My friend Cootaboot and me we go now to shoot a few holes. You will lend me clobs, friend Cootaboot?"

"Any you want."

"The noblicksy is what I use most. Goot-a-bye, Mrs. Smet-thirst."

They were moving to the door, when Cuthbert felt a light touch on his arm. Adeline was looking up at him tenderly.

"May I come, too, and walk round with you?"

Cuthbert's bosom heaved.

"Oh," he said, with a tremor in his voice, "that you would walk round with me for life!"

Her eyes met his.

"Perhaps," she whispered, softly, "it could be arranged."

.   .   .   .   .

"And so," (concluded the Oldest Member), "you see that golf can be of the greatest practical assistance to a man in Life's struggle. Raymond Parsloe Devine, who was no player, had to move out of the neighbourhood immediately, and is now, I believe, writing scenarios out in California for the Flicker Film Company. Adeline is married to Cuthbert, and it was only his earnest pleading which prevented her from having their eldest son christened Abe Mitchell Ribbed-Faced Mashie Banks, for she is now as keen a devotee of the great game as her husband. Those who know them say that theirs is a union so devoted, so——"

.   .   .   .   .

The Sage broke off abruptly, for the young man had rushed to the door and out into the passage. Through the open door he could hear him crying passionately to the waiter to bring back his clubs.

To my daughter Leonora,
Queen of her species.

Author's Dedication, "Leave it to Psmith."

" *She knows how many times everybody in Hollywood has been divorced and why, how much every picture for the last twenty years has grossed, and how many Warner brothers there are. She even knows how many times Artie Shaw has been married, which I bet he couldn't tell you himself. She asked if I had ever married Artie Shaw, and when I said no, seemed to think I was pulling her leg or must have done it without noticing. I tried to explain that when a girl goes to Hollywood she doesn't have to marry Artie Shaw, it's optional, but I don't think I convinced her....* "

* * * * *

"He was stung. Like most young men whose thoughts are an open book to the populace, he supposed that if there were anything more than another for which he was remarkable, it was his iron inscrutability."

* * * * *

" *I hated her mixing with all that seedy crowd in Chelsea. Bounders with beards,*" said Pongo with an austere shudder. " *I've been in her studio sometimes and the blighters were crawling out of the woodwork in hundreds, bearded to the eyebrows.*"

* * * * *

" He looked like a dictator on the point of starting a purge."

THE SAGA HABIT

EXCEPT FOR the tendency to write articles about the Modern Girl and allow his side-whiskers to grow, there is nothing an author to-day has to guard himself against more carefully than the Saga habit. The least slackening of vigilance and the thing has gripped him. He writes a story. Another story dealing with the same characters occurs to him, and he writes that. He feels that just once more won't hurt him, and he writes a third. And before he knows where he is, he is down with a Saga, and no cure in sight.

This is what happened to me with Bertie Wooster and Jeeves, and it has happened again with Lord Emsworth, his son Frederick, his butler Beach, his pig the Empress and the other residents of Blandings Castle. Beginning with *Something Fresh*, I went on to *Leave it to Psmith*, then to *Summer Lightning*, after that to *Heavy Weather*, and now to the volume which you have just borrowed. And, to show the habit-forming nature of the drug, while it was eight years after *Something Fresh* before the urge for *Leave it to Psmith* gripped me, only eighteen months elapsed between *Summer Lightning* and *Heavy Weather*. In a word, once a man who could take it or leave it alone, I had become an addict.

The stories in the first part of this book represent what I may term the short snorts in between the solid orgies. From time to time I would feel the Blandings Castle craving creeping over me, but I had the manhood to content myself with a small dose.

In point of time, these stories come after *Leave it to Psmith* and before *Summer Lightning*. *Pig-hoo-o-o-o-ey*, for example, shows Empress of Blandings winning her first silver medal in the Fat Pigs class at the Shropshire Agricultural Show. In *Summer Lightning* and *Heavy Weather* she is seen struggling to repeat in the following year.

The Custody of the Pumpkin shows Lord Emsworth passing through the brief pumpkin phase, which preceded the more lasting pig seizure.

And so on.

Bobbie Wickham, of *Mr. Potter Takes a Rest Cure*, appeared in three of the stories in a book called *Mr. Mulliner Speaking.*

The final section of the volume deals with the secret history of Hollywood, revealing in print some of those stories which are whispered over the frosted malted milk when the boys get together in the commissary.

Author's Preface, "Blandings Castle."

"*Haven't you heard of Sister Lora Luella Stott?*"

"*No, who is she?*"

"*She is the woman who is leading California out of the swamp of alcohol.*"

"*Good God!*" *I could tell by Eggy's voice that he was interested.* "*Is there a swamp of alcohol in these parts? What an amazing country America is! Talk about every modern convenience. Do you mean you can simply go there and lap?*"

GALLANT RESCUE BY WELL-DRESSED YOUNG MAN

THE WHITE Star liner "Atlantic" lay at her pier with steam up and gangway down, ready for her trip to Southampton. The hour of departure was near, and there was a good deal of mixed activity going on. Sailors fiddled about with ropes. Junior officers flitted to and fro. White-jacketed stewards wrestled with trunks. Probably the captain, though not visible, was also employed on some useful work of a nautical nature and not wasting his time. Men, women, boxes, rugs, dogs, flowers, and baskets of fruit were flowing on board in a steady stream.

The usual drove of citizens had come to see the travellers off. There were men on the passenger-list who were being seen off by fathers, by mothers, by sisters, by cousins, and by aunts. In the steerage, there was an elderly Jewish lady who was being seen off by exactly thirty-seven of her late neighbours in Rivington Street. And two men in the second cabin were being seen off by detectives, surely the crowning compliment a great nation can bestow. The cavernous Customs sheds were congested with friends and relatives, and Sam Marlowe, heading for the gang-plank, was only able to make progress by employing all the muscle and energy which Nature had bestowed upon him, and which during the greater part of his life he had developed by athletic exercise. However, after some minutes of silent endeavour, now driving his shoulder into the midriff of some obstructing male, now courteously lifting some stout female off his feet, he had succeeded in struggling to within a few yards of his goal, when suddenly a sharp pain shot through his right arm, and he spun round with a cry.

It seemed to Sam that he had been bitten, and this puzzled

him, for New York crowds, though they may shove and jostle, rarely bite.

He found himself face to face with an extraordinarily pretty girl.

She was a red-haired girl, with the beautiful ivory skin which goes with red hair. Her eyes, though they were under the shadow of her hat, and he could not be certain, he diagnosed as green, or maybe blue, or possibly grey. Not that it mattered, for he had a catholic taste in feminine eyes. So long as they were large and bright, as were the specimens under his immediate notice, he was not the man to quibble about a point of colour. Her nose was small, and on the very tip of it there was a tiny freckle. Her mouth was nice and wide, her chin soft and round. She was just about the height which every girl ought to be. Her figure was trim, her feet tiny, and she wore one of those dresses of which a man can say no more than that they look pretty well all right.

Nature abhors a vacuum. Samuel Marlowe was a susceptible young man, and for many a long month his heart had been lying empty, all swept and garnished, with "Welcome" on the mat. This girl seemed to rush in and fill it. She was not the prettiest girl he had ever seen. She was the third prettiest. He had an orderly mind, one capable of classifying and docketing girls. But there was a subtle something about her, a sort of how-shall-one-put-it, which he had never encountered before. He swallowed convulsively. His well-developed chest swelled beneath its covering of blue flannel and invisible stripe. At last, he told himself, he was in love, really in love, and at first sight, too, which made it all the more impressive. He doubted whether in the whole course of history anything like this had ever happened before to anybody. Oh, to clasp this girl to him and. . . .

But she had bitten him in the arm. That was hardly the right spirit. That, he felt, constituted an obstacle.

"Oh, I'm so sorry!" she cried.

Well, of course, if she regretted her rash act. . . . After all, an impulsive girl might bite a man in the arm in the excitement of the moment and still have a sweet, womanly nature. . . .

"The crowd seems to make Pinky-Boodles so nervous."

Sam might have remained mystified, but at this juncture there proceeded from a bundle of rugs in the neighbourhood of the girl's lower ribs, a sharp yapping sound, of such a calibre as to be plainly audible over the confused noise of Mamies who were telling Sadies to be sure and write, of Bills who were instructing Dicks to look up old Joe in Paris and give him their best, and of all the fruit-boys, candy-boys, magazine-boys, American-flag-boys, and telegraph boys who were honking their wares on every side.

"I hope he didn't hurt you much. You're the third person he's bitten to-day." She kissed the animal in a loving and congratulatory way on the tip of his black nose. "Not counting waiters at the hotel, of course," she added. And then she was swept from him in the crowd, and he was left thinking of all the things he might have said—all those graceful, witty, ingratiating things which just make a bit of difference on these occasions.

He had said nothing. Not a sound, exclusive of the first sharp yowl of pain, had proceeded from him. He had just goggled. A rotten exhibition! Perhaps he would never see this girl again. She looked the sort of girl who comes to see friends off and doesn't sail herself. And what memory of him would she retain? She would mix him up with the time when she went to visit the deaf-and-dumb hospital.

Extract from an early chapter of "The Girl on the Boat."

*　　　*　　　*　　　*　　　*

The sun shone down from a sky of cornflower blue, and what one would really like would be to describe in leisurely detail the ancient battlements, the smooth green lawns, the rolling parkland, the majestic trees, the well-bred bees and the gentlemanly birds on which it shone.

NO WEDDING BELLS FOR HIM

To UKRIDGE, as might be expected from one of his sunny optimism, the whole affair has long since come to present itself in the light of yet another proof of the way in which all things in this world of ours work together for good. In it, from start to finish, he sees the finger of Providence; and, when marshalling evidence to support his theory that a means of escape from the most formidable perils will always be vouchsafed to the righteous and deserving, this is the episode which he advances as Exhibit A.

The thing may be said to have had its beginning in the Haymarket one afternoon towards the middle of the summer. We had been lunching at my expense at the Pall Mall Restaurant, and as we came out a large and shiny car drew up beside the kerb, and the chauffeur, alighting, opened the bonnet and began to fiddle about in its interior with a pair of pliers. Had I been alone, a casual glance in passing would have contented me, but for Ukridge the spectacle of somebody else working always had an irresistible fascination, and, gripping my arm, he steered me up to assist him in giving the toiler moral support. About two minutes after he had started to breathe earnestly on the man's neck, the latter, seeming to become aware that what was tickling his back hair was not some wandering June zephyr, looked up with a certain petulance.

"'Ere!" he said, protestingly. Then his annoyance gave place to something which—for a chauffeur—approached cordiality. "'Ullo!" he observed.

"Why, hallo, Frederick," said Ukridge. "Didn't recognise you. Is this the new car?"

"Ah," nodded the chauffeur.

"Pal of mine," explained Ukridge to me in a brief aside.

"Met him in a pub." London was congested with pals whom Ukridge had met in pubs. "What's the trouble?"

"Missing," said Frederick the chauffeur. "Soon 'ave her right."

His confidence in his skill was not misplaced. After a short interval he straightened himself, closed the bonnet, and wiped his hands.

"Nice day," he said.

"Terrific," agreed Ukridge. "Where are you off to?"

"Got to go to Addington. Pick up the guvnor, playin' golf there." He seemed to hesitate for a moment, then the mellowing influence of the summer sunshine asserted itself. "Like a ride as far as East Croydon? Get a train back from there."

It was a handsome offer, and one which neither Ukridge nor myself felt disposed to decline. We climbed in, Frederick trod on the self-starter, and off we bowled, two gentlemen of fashion taking their afternoon airing. Speaking for myself I felt tranquil and debonair, and I have no reason to suppose that Ukridge was otherwise. The deplorable incident which now occurred was thus rendered doubly distressing. We had stopped at the foot of the street to allow the north-bound traffic to pass, when our pleasant after-luncheon torpidity was shattered by a sudden and violent shout.

"Hi!"

That the shouter was addressing us there was no room for doubt. He was standing on the pavement not four feet away, glaring unmistakably into our costly tonneau—a stout, bearded man of middle age, unsuitably clad, considering the weather and the sartorial prejudices of Society, in a frock-coat and a bowler hat. "Hi! You!" he bellowed, to the scandal of all good passers-by.

Frederick the chauffeur, after one swift glance of god-like disdain out of the corner of his left eye, had ceased to interest himself in this undignified exhibition on the part of one of the lower orders, but I was surprised to observe that Ukridge was betraying all the discomposure of some wild thing taken in a trap. His face had turned crimson and assumed a bulbous expression, and he was staring straight ahead of him with a piteous effort to ignore what manifestly would not be ignored.

"I'd like a word with you," boomed the bearded one.

And then matters proceeded with a good deal of rapidity. The traffic had begun to move on now, and as we moved with it, travelling with increasing speed, the man appeared to realise that if 'twere done 'twere well 'twere done quickly. He executed a cumbersome leap and landed on our running-board; and Ukridge, coming suddenly to life, put out a large flat hand and pushed. The intruder dropped off, and the last I saw of him he was standing in the middle of the road, shaking his fist, in imminent danger of being run over by a number three omnibus.

"Gosh!" sighed Ukridge, with some feverishness.

"What was it all about?" I enquired.

"Bloke I owe a bit of money to," explained Ukridge, tersely.

"Ah!" I said, feeling that all had been made clear. I had never before actually seen one of Ukridge's creditors in action, but he had frequently given me to understand that they lurked all over London like leopards in the jungle, waiting to spring on him. There were certain streets down which he would never walk for fear of what might befall.

"Been trailing me like a bloodhound for two years," said Ukridge. "Keeps bobbing up when I don't expect him and turning my hair white to the roots."

I was willing to hear more, and even hinted as much, but he relapsed into a moody silence. We were moving at a brisk clip into Clapham Common when the second of the incidents occurred which were to make this drive linger in the memory. Just as we came in sight of the Common, a fool of a girl loomed up right before our front wheels. She had been crossing the road, and now, after the manner of her species, she lost her head. She was a large, silly-looking girl, and she darted to and fro like a lunatic hen; and as Ukridge and I rose simultaneously from our seats, clutching each other in agony,

318

she tripped over her feet and fell. But Frederick, master of his craft, had the situation well in hand. He made an inspired swerve, and when we stopped a moment later, the girl was picking herself up, dusty, but still in one piece.

These happenings affect different men in different ways. In Frederick's cold grey eye as he looked over his shoulder and backed the car there was only the weary scorn of a superman for the never-ending follies of a woollen-headed proletariat. I, on the other hand, had reacted in a gust of nervous profanity. And Ukridge, I perceived as I grew calmer, the affair had touched on his chivalrous side. All the time we were backing he was mumbling to himself, and he was out of the car, bleating apologies, almost before we had stopped.

"Awfully sorry. Might have killed you. Can't forgive myself."

The girl treated the affair in still another way. She giggled. And somehow that brainless laugh afflicted me more than anything that had gone before. It was not her fault, I suppose. This untimely mirth was merely due to disordered nerves. But I had taken a prejudice against her at first sight.

"I do hope," babbled Ukridge, "you aren't hurt? Do tell me you aren't hurt."

The girl giggled again. And she was at least twelve pounds too heavy to be a giggler. I wanted to pass on and forget her.

"No, reely, thanks."

"But shaken, what?"

"I did come down a fair old bang," chuckled this repellent female.

"I thought so. I was afraid so. Shaken. Ganglions vibrating. You must let me drive you home."

"Oh, it doesn't matter."

"I insist. Positively I insist!"

" 'Ere!" said Frederick the chauffeur, in a low, compelling voice.

"Eh?"

"Got to get on to Addington."

"Yes, yes, yes," said Ukridge, with testy impatience, quite

the seigneur resenting interference from an underling. "But there's plenty of time to drive this lady home. Can't you see she's shaken? Where can I take you?"

"It's only just round the corner in the next street. Balbriggan the name of the house is."

"Balbriggan, Frederick, in the next street," said Ukridge, in a tone that brooked no argument.

I suppose the spectacle of the daughter of the house rolling up to the front door in a Daimler is unusual in Peabody Road, Clapham Common. At any rate, we had hardly drawn up when Balbriggan began to exude its occupants in platoons. Father, mother, three small sisters, and a brace of brothers were on the steps in the first ten seconds. They surged down the garden path in a solid mass.

Ukridge was at his most spacious. Quickly establishing himself on the footing of a friend of the family, he took charge of the whole affair. Introductions sped to and fro, and in a few moving words he explained the situation, while I remained mute and insignificant in my corner and Frederick the chauffeur stared at his oil-gauge with a fathomless eye.

"Couldn't have forgiven myself, Mr. Price, if anything had happened to Miss Price. Fortunately my chauffeur is an excellent driver and swerved just in time. You showed great presence of mind, Frederick," said Ukridge, handsomely, "great presence of mind."

Frederick continued to gaze aloofly at his oil-gauge.

"What a lovely car, Mr. Ukridge!" said the mother of the family.

"Yes," said Ukridge, airily. "Yes, quite a good old machine."

"Can you drive yourself?" asked the smaller of the two small brothers, reverently.

"Oh, yes. Yes. But I generally use Frederick for town work."

"Would you and your friend care to come in for a cup of tea?" said Mrs. Price.

I could see Ukridge hesitate. He had only recently finished

an excellent lunch, but there was that about the offer of a free meal which never failed to touch a chord in him. At this point, however, Frederick spoke.

" 'Ere!" said Frederick.

"Eh?"

"Got to get on to Addington," said Frederick, firmly.

Ukridge started as one waked from a dream. I really believe he had succeeded in persuading himself that the car belonged to him.

"Of course, yes. I was forgetting. I have to be at Addington almost immediately. Promised to pick up some golfing friends. Some other time, eh?"

"Any time you're in the neighbourhood, Mr. Ukridge," said Mr. Price, beaming upon the popular pet.

"Thanks, thanks."

"Tell me, Mr. Ukridge," said Mrs. Price. "I've been wondering ever since you told me your name. It's such an unusual one. Are you any relation to the Miss Ukridge who writes books?"

"My aunt," beamed Ukridge.

"No, really? I do love her stories so. Tell me——"

Frederick, whom I could not sufficiently admire, here broke off what promised to be a lengthy literary discussion by treading on the self-starter, and we drove off in a flurry of good wishes and invitations. I rather fancy I heard Ukridge, as he leaned over the back of the car, promising to bring his aunt round to Sunday supper some time. He resumed his seat as we turned the corner and at once began to moralise.

"Always sow the good seed, laddie. Absolutely nothing to beat the good seed. Never lose the chance of establishing yourself. It is the secret of a successful life. Just a few genial words, you see, and here I am with a place I can always pop into for a bite when funds are low."

I was shocked at his sordid outlook, and said so. He rebuked me out of his larger wisdom.

"It's all very well to take that attitude, Corky, my boy, but do you realise that a family like that has cold beef, baked potatoes, pickles, salad, blanc-mange, and some sort of cheese every Sunday night after Divine service? There are moments in a man's life, laddie, when a spot of cold beef with blanc-mange to follow means more than words can tell."

It was about a week later that I happened to go to the British Museum to gather material for one of those brightly informative articles of mine which appeared from time to time in the weekly papers. I was wandering through the place, accumulating data, when I came upon Ukridge with a small boy attached to each hand. He seemed a trifle weary, and he welcomed me with something of the gratification of the shipwrecked mariner who sights a sail.

"Run along and improve your bally minds, you kids," he said to the children. "You'll find me here when you've finished."

"All right, Uncle Stanley," chorused the children.

"Uncle Stanley?" I said, accusingly.

He winced a little. I had to give him credit for that.

"Those are the Price kids. From Clapham."

"I remember them."

"I'm taking them out for the day. Must repay hospitality, Corky, my boy."

"Then you have really been inflicting yourself on those unfortunate people?"

"I have looked in from time to time," said Ukridge, with dignity.

"It's just over a week since you met them. How often have you looked in?"

"Couple of times, perhaps. Maybe three."

"To meals?"

"There was a bit of browsing going on," admitted Ukridge.

"And now you're Uncle Stanley!"

"Fine warm-hearted people," said Ukridge, and it seemed to me that he spoke with a touch of defiance. "Made me one of the family right from the beginning. Of course, it cuts both ways. This afternoon, for instance, I got landed with those kids. But, all in all, taking the rough with the smooth, it has worked out distinctly on the right side of the ledger. I own I'm not over keen on the hymns after Sunday supper, but the supper, laddie, is undeniable. As good a bit of cold beef," said Ukridge, dreamily, "as I ever chewed."

"Greedy brute," I said, censoriously.

"Must keep body and soul together, old man. Of course, there are one or two things about the business that are a bit embarrassing. For instance, somehow or other they seem to have got the idea that that car we turned up in that day belongs to me, and the kids are always pestering me to take them for a ride. Fortunately I've managed to square Frederick, and he thinks he can arrange for a spin or two during the next few days. And then Mrs. Price keeps asking me to bring my aunt round for a cup of tea and a chat, and I haven't the heart to tell her that my aunt absolutely and finally disowned me the day after that business of the dance."

"You didn't tell me that."

"Didn't I? Oh, yes. I got a letter from her saying that as far as she was concerned I had ceased to exist. I thought it showed a nasty, narrow spirit, but I can't say I was altogether surprised. Still, it makes it awkward when Mrs. Price wants to get matey with her. I've had to tell her that my aunt is a chronic invalid and never goes out, being practically bed-ridden. I find all this a bit wearing, laddie."

"I suppose so."

"You see," said Ukridge, "I dislike subterfuge."

There seemed no possibility of his beating this, so I left the man and resumed my researches.

After this I was out of town for a few weeks, taking my annual vacation. When I got back to Ebury Street, Bowles, my landlord, after complimenting me in a stately way on my sunburned appearance, informed me that George Tupper had called several times while I was away.

"Appeared remarkably anxious to see you, sir."

I was surprised at this. George Tupper was always glad—or seemed to be glad—to see an old school friend when I called upon him, but he rarely sought me out in my home.

"Did he say what he wanted?"

"No, sir. He left no message. He merely enquired as to the probable date of your return and expressed a desire that you would visit him as soon as convenient."

"I'd better go and see him now."

"It might be advisable, sir."

I found George Tupper at the Foreign Office, surrounded by important-looking papers.

"Here you are at last!" cried George, resentfully, it seemed to me. "I thought you were never coming back."

"I had a splendid time, thanks very much for asking," I replied. "Got the roses back to my cheeks."

George, who seemed far from his usual tranquil self, briefly cursed my cheeks and their roses.

"Look here," he said, urgently, "something's got to be done. Have you seen Ukridge yet?"

"Not yet. I thought I would look him up this evening."

"You'd better. Do you know what has happened? That poor ass has gone and got himself engaged to be married to a girl at Clapham!"

"What?"

"Engaged! Girl at Clapham. Clapham Common," added George Tupper, as if in his opinion that made the matter even worse.

"You're joking!"

"I'm not joking," said George peevishly. "Do I look as if I were joking? I met him in Battersea Park with her, and he introduced me. She reminded me," said George Tupper, shivering slightly, for that fearful evening had seared his soul deeply, "of that ghastly female in pink he brought with him the night I gave you two dinner at the Regent Grill—the one who talked at the top of her voice all the time about her aunt's stomach-trouble."

Here I think he did Miss Price an injustice. She had struck me during my brief acquaintance as something of a blister, but I had never quite classed her with Battling Billson's Flossie.

"Well, what do you want me to do?" I asked, not, I think, unreasonably.

"You've got to think of some way of getting him out of it. I can't do anything. I'm busy all day."

"So am I busy."

"Busy my left foot!" said George Tupper, who in moments of strong emotion was apt to relapse into the phraseology of school days and express himself in a very un-Foreign Official manner. "About once a week you work up energy enough to write a rotten article for some rag of a paper on 'Should Curates Kiss?' or some silly subject, and the rest of the time you loaf about with Ukridge. It's obviously your job to disentangle the poor idiot."

"But how do you know he wants to be disentangled? It seems to me you're jumping pretty readily to conclusions. It's all very well for you bloodless officials to sneer at the holy passion, but it's love, as I sometimes say, that makes the world go round. Ukridge probably feels that until now he never realised what true happiness could mean."

"Does he?" snorted George Tupper. "Well, he didn't look it when I met him. He looked like—well, do you remember when he went in for the heavyweights at school and that chap in Seymour's house hit him in the wind in the first round? That's how he looked when he was introducing the girl to me."

I am bound to say the comparison impressed me. It is odd how these little incidents of one's boyhood linger in the memory. Across the years I could see Ukridge now, half doubled up, one gloved hand caressing his diaphragm, a stunned and horrified bewilderment in his eyes. If his bearing as an engaged man had reminded George Tupper of that occasion, it certainly did seem as if the time had come for his friends to rally round him.

"You seem to have taken on the job of acting as a sort of unofficial keeper to the man," said George. "You'll have to help him now."

"Well, I'll go and see him."

325

"The whole thing is too absurd," said George Tupper. "How can Ukridge get married to anyone? He hasn't a bob in the world."

"I'll point that out to him. He's probably overlooked it."

It was my custom when I visited Ukridge at his lodgings to stand underneath his window and bellow his name—upon which, if at home and receiving, he would lean out and drop me down his latchkey, thus avoiding troubling his landlady to come up from the basement to open the door. A very judicious proceeding, for his relations with that autocrat were usually in a somewhat strained condition. I bellowed now, and his head popped out.

"Hallo, laddie!"

It seemed to me, even at this long range, that there was something peculiar about his face, but it was not till I had climbed the stairs to his room that I was able to be certain. I then perceived that he had somehow managed to acquire a black eye, which, though past its first bloom, was still of an extraordinary richness.

"Great Scott!" I cried, staring at this decoration. "How and when?"

Ukridge drew at his pipe moodily.

"It's a long story," he said. "Do you remember some people named Price at Clapham——"

"You aren't going to tell me your *fiancée* has biffed you in the eye already?"

"Have you heard?" said Ukridge, surprised. "Who told you I was engaged?"

"George Tupper. I've just been seeing him."

"Oh, well, that saves a lot of explanation. Laddie," said Ukridge, solemnly, "let this be a warning to you. Never——"

I wanted facts, not moralisings.

"How did you get the eye?" I interrupted.

Ukridge blew out a cloud of smoke and his other eye glowed sombrely.

"That was Ernie Finch," he said, in a cold voice.

"Who is Ernie Finch? I've never heard of him."

326

"He's a sort of friend of the family, and as far as I can make out was going rather strong as regards Mabel till I came along. When we got engaged he was away, and no one apparently thought it worth while to tell him about it and he came along one night and found me kissing her good-bye in the front garden. Observe how these things work out, Corky. The sight of him coming along suddenly gave Mabel a start, and she screamed; the fact that she screamed gave this man Finch a totally wrong angle on the situation; and this caused him, blast him, to rush, yank off my glasses with one hand, and hit me with the other right in the eye. And before I could get at him the family were roused by Mabel's screeches and came out and separated us and explained that I was engaged to Mabel. Of course, when he heard that, the man apologised. And I wish you could have seen the beastly smirk he gave when he was doing it. Then there was a bit of a row and old Price forbade him the house. A fat lot of good that was! I've had to stay indoors ever since waiting for the colour-scheme to dim a bit."

"Of course," I urged, "one can't help being sorry for the chap in a way."

"*I* can," said Ukridge, emphatically. "I've reached the conclusion that there is not room in this world for Ernie Finch and myself, and I'm living in the hope of meeting him one of these nights down in a dark alley."

"You sneaked his girl," I pointed out.

"I don't want his beastly girl," said Ukridge, with ungallant heat.

"Then you really do want to get out of this thing?"

"Of course I want to get out of it."

"But if you feel like that, how on earth did you ever let it happen?"

"I simply couldn't tell you, old horse," said Ukridge, frankly. "It's all a horrid blur. The whole affair was the most ghastly shock to me. It came absolutely out of a blue sky. I have never so much as suspected the possibility of such a thing. All I know is that we found ourselves alone in the drawing-room after Sunday supper, and all of a sudden the room became full of Prices of every description babbling blessings. And there I was!"

"But you must have given them something to go on."

"I was holding her hand. I admit that."

"Ah!"

"Well, my gosh, I don't see why there should have been such a fuss about that. What does a bit of hand-holding amount to? The whole thing, Corky, my boy, boils down to the question, Is any man safe? It's got so nowadays," said Ukridge, with a strong sense of injury, "that you've only to throw a girl a kindly word, and the next thing you know you're in the Lord Warden Hotel at Dover, picking the rice out of your hair."

"Well, you must own that you were asking for it. You rolled up in a new Daimler and put on enough dog for half a dozen millionaires. And you took the family for rides, didn't you?"

"Perhaps a couple of times."

"And talked about your aunt, I expect, and how rich she was?"

"I may have touched on my aunt occasionally."

"Well, naturally these people thought you were sent from heaven. The wealthy son-in-law." Ukridge projected himself from the depths sufficiently to muster up the beginnings of a faint smile of gratification at the description. Then his troubles swept him back again. "All you've got to do, if you want to get out of it, is to confess to them that you haven't a bob."

"But, laddie, that's the difficulty. It's a most unfortunate thing, but, as it happens, I am on the eve of making an immense fortune, and I'm afraid I hinted as much to them from time to time."

"What do you mean?"

"Since I saw you last I've put all my money in a bookmaker's business."

"How do you mean—all your money? Where did you get any money?"

"You haven't forgotten the fifty quid I made selling tickets for my aunt's dance? And then I collected a bit more here and there out of some judicious bets. So there it is. The firm is in a small way at present, but with the world full of mugs shoving and jostling one another to back losers, the thing is a potential gold-mine, and I'm a sleeping partner. It's no good my trying to make these people believe I'm hard up. They would simply laugh in my face and rush off and start breach-of-promise actions. Upon my Sam, it's a little hard! Just when I have my foot firmly planted on the ladder of success, this has to happen." He brooded in silence for a while. "There's just one scheme that occurred to me," he said at length. "Would you have any objection to writing an anonymous letter?"

"What's the idea?"

"I was just thinking that, if you were to write them an anonymous letter, accusing me of all sorts of things—— Might say I was married already."

"Not a bit of good."

"Perhaps you're right," said Ukridge, gloomily, and after a few minutes more of thoughtful silence I left him. I was standing on the front steps when I heard him clattering down the stairs.

"Corky, old man!"

"Hallo?"

"I think I've got it," said Ukridge, joining me on the steps. "Came to me in a flash a second ago. How would it be if someone were to go down to Clapham and pretend to be a detective making enquiries about me? Dashed sinister and mysterious, you know. A good deal of meaning nods and shakes of the head. Give the impression that I was wanted for something or other. You get the idea? You would ask a lot of questions and take notes in a book——"

"How do you mean—*I* would?"

Ukridge looked at me in pained surprise.

"Surely, old horse, you wouldn't object to doing a trifling service like this for an old friend?"

329

"I would, strongly. And in any case, what would be the use of my going? They've seen me."

"Yes, but they wouldn't recognise you. Yours," said Ukridge, ingratiatingly, "is an ordinary, meaningless sort of face. Or one of those theatrical costumier people would fit you out with a disguise——"

"No!" I said, firmly. "I'm willing to do anything in reason to help you out of this mess, but I refuse to wear false whiskers for you or anyone."

"All right then," said Ukridge, despondently; "in that case, there's nothing to be——"

At this moment he disappeared. It was so swiftly done that he seemed to have been snatched up to heaven. Only the searching odour of his powerful tobacco lingered to remind me that he had once been at my side, and only the slam of the front door told me where he had gone. I looked about, puzzled to account for this abrupt departure, and as I did so heard galloping footsteps and perceived a stout, bearded gentleman of middle age, clad in a frock coat and a bowler hat. He was one of those men who, once seen, are not readily forgotten; and I recognised him at once. It was the creditor, the bloke Ukridge owed a bit of money to, the man who had tried to board our car in the Haymarket. Halting on the pavement below me, he removed the hat and dabbed at his forehead with a large coloured silk handkerchief.

"Was that Mr. Smallweed you were talking to?" he demanded, gustily. He was obviously touched in the wind.

"No," I replied, civilly. "No. Not Mr. Smallweed."

"You're lying to me, young man!" cried the creditor, his voice rising in a too-familiar shout. And at the words, as if they had been some magic spell, the street seemed suddenly to wake from slumber. It seethed with human life. Maids popped out of windows, areas disgorged landladies, the very stones seemed to belch forth excited spectators. I found myself the centre of attraction—and, for some reason which was beyond me, cast for the *rôle* of the villain of the drama. What I had actually done to the poor old man, nobody appeared to know; but the school of thought which held that I had picked his pocket and brutally assaulted him had the largest number of adherents, and there was a good deal of informal talk of lynching me. Fortunately a young man in a blue flannel suit, who had been one of the earliest arrivals on the scene, constituted himself a peacemaker.

"Come along, o' man," he said, soothingly, his arm weaving itself into that of the fermenting creditor. "You don't want to make yourself conspicuous, do you?"

"In there!" roared the creditor, pointing at the door.

The crowd seemed to recognise that there had been an error in its diagnosis. The prevalent opinion now was that I had kidnapped the man's daughter and was holding her prisoner behind that sinister door. The movement in favour of lynching me became almost universal.

"Now, now!" said the young man, whom I was beginning to like more every minute.

"I'll kick the door in!"

"Now, now! You don't want to go doing anything silly or foolish," pleaded the peacemaker. "There'll be a policeman along before you know where you are, and you'll look foolish if he finds you kicking up a silly row."

I must say that, if I had been in the bearded one's place and had had right so indisputably on my side, this argument would not have influenced me greatly, but I suppose respectable citizens with a reputation to lose have different views on the importance of colliding with the police, however right they may be. The creditor's violence began to ebb. He hesitated. He was plainly trying to approach the matter in the light of pure reason.

"You know where the fellow lives," argued the young man. "See what I mean? Meantersay, you can come and find him when ever you like."

This, too, sounded thin to me. But it appeared to convince the injured man. He allowed himself to be led away, and presently, the star having left the stage, the drama ceased to attract. The audience melted away. Windows closed, areas emptied themselves, and presently the street was given over once more to the cat lunching in the gutter and the coster hymning his Brussels Sprouts.

A hoarse voice spoke through the letter-box.

"Has he gone, laddie?"

I put my mouth to the slit, and we talked together like Pyramus and Thisbe.

"Yes."

"You're sure?"

"Certain."

"He isn't lurking round the corner somewhere, waiting to pop out?"

"No. He's gone."

The door opened and an embittered Ukridge emerged.

"It's a little hard!" he said, querulously. "You would scarcely credit it, Corky, but all that fuss was about a measly one pound two and threepence for a rotten little clockwork man that broke the first time I wound it up. Absolutely the first time, old man! It's not as if it had been a tandem bicycle, an enlarging camera, a Kodak, and magic lantern."

I could not follow him.

"Why should a clockwork man be a tandem bicycle and the rest of it?"

"It's like this," said Ukridge. "There was a bicycle and photograph shop down near where I lived a couple of years ago, and I happened to see a tandem bicycle there which I rather liked the look of. So I ordered it provisionally from this cove. Absolutely provisionally, you understand. Also an enlarging camera, a Kodak, and a magic lantern. The goods were to be delivered when I had made up my mind about them. Well, after about a week the fellow asks if there are any further particulars I want to learn before definitely buying the muck. I say I am considering the matter, and in the meantime will he be good enough to let me have that little clockwork man in his window which walks when wound up?"

"Well?"

"Well, damme," said Ukridge, aggrieved, "it didn't walk.

It broke the first time I tried to wind it. Then a few weeks went by and this bloke started to make himself dashed unpleasant. Wanted me to pay him money! I reasoned with the blighter. I said: 'Now look here, my man, need we say any more about this? Really, I think you've come out of the thing extremely well. Which,' I said, 'would you rather be owed for? A clockwork man or a tandem bicycle, an enlarging camera, a Kodak, and a magic lantern?' You'd think that would have been simple enough for the meanest intellect, but no, he continued to make a fuss, until finally I had to move out of the neighbourhood. Fortunately, I had given him a false name——"

"Why?"

"Just an ordinary business precaution," explained Ukridge.

"I see."

"I looked on the matter as closed. But ever since then he has been bounding out at me when I least expect him. Once, by gad, he nearly nailed me in the middle of the Strand, and I had to leg it like a hare up Burleigh Street and through Covent Garden. I'd have been collared to a certainty, only he tripped over a basket of potatoes. It's persecution, damme, that's what it is—persecution!"

"Why don't you pay the man?" I suggested.

"Corky, old horse," said Ukridge, with evident disapproval of these reckless fiscal methods, "talk sense. How can I pay the man? Apart from the fact that at this stage of my career it would be madness to start flinging money right and left, there's the principle of the thing!"

The immediate result of this disturbing episode was that Ukridge, packing his belongings in a small suit-case and reluctantly disgorging a week's rent in lieu of notice, softly and silently vanished away from his own lodgings and came to dwell in mine, to the acute gratification of Bowles, who greeted his arrival with a solemn joy and brooded over him at dinner the first night like a father over a long-lost son. I had often given him sanctuary before in his hour of need, and he settled down with the easy smoothness of an old campaigner. He was good enough to describe my little place as a home from home, and said that he had half a mind to stay on and end his declining years there.

I cannot say that this suggestion gave me the rapturous pleasure it seemed to give Bowles, who nearly dropped the potato dish in his emotion; but still I must say that on the whole the man was not an exacting guest. His practice of never rising before lunch-time ensured me those mornings of undisturbed solitude which are so necessary to the young writer if he is to give *Interesting Bits* of his best; and if I had work to do in the evenings he was always ready to toddle downstairs and smoke a pipe with Bowles, whom he seemed to find as congenial a companion as Bowles found him. His only defect, indeed, was the habit he had developed of looking in on me in my bedroom at all hours of the night to discuss some new scheme designed to relieve him of his honourable obligations to Miss Mabel Price, of Balbriggan, Peabody Road, Clapham Common. My outspoken remarks on this behaviour checked him for forty-eight hours, but at three o'clock on the Sunday morning that ended the first week of his visit light flashing out above my head told me that he was in again.

"I think, laddie," I heard a satisfied voice remark, as a heavy weight descended on my toes, "I think, laddie, that at last I have hit the bull's-eye and rung the bell. Hats off to Bowles, without whom I would never have got the idea. It was only when he told me the plot of that story he is reading that I began to see daylight. Listen, old man," said Ukridge, settling himself more comfortably on my feet, "and tell me if you don't think I am on to a good thing. About a couple of days before Lord Claude Tremaine was to marry Angela Bracebridge, the most beautiful girl in London——"

"What the devil are you talking about? And do you know what the time is?"

"Never mind the time, Corky, my boy. To-morrow is the day of rest and you can sleep on till an advanced hour. I was telling you the plot of this Primrose Novelette thing that Bowles is reading."

"You haven't woken me up at three in the morning to tell me the plot of a rotten novelette!"

"You haven't been listening, old man," said Ukridge, with gentle reproach. "I was saying that it was this plot that gave me my big idea. To cut it fairly short, as you seem in a strange mood, this Lord Claude bloke, having had a rummy pain in his left side, went to see a doctor a couple of days before the wedding, and the doc. gave him the start of his young life by telling him that he had only six months to live. There's a lot more of it, of course, and in the end it turns out that the fool of a doctor was all wrong; but what I'm driving at is that this development absolutely put the bee on the wedding. Everybody sympathised with Claude and said it was out of the question that he could dream of getting married. So it suddenly occurred to me, laddie, that here was the scheme of a lifetime. I'm going to supper at Balbriggan to-morrow, and what I want you to do is simply to——"

"You can stop right there," I said, with emotion. "I know what you want me to do. You want me to come along with you, disguised in a top-hat and a stethoscope, and explain to these people that I am a Harley Street specialist, and have been sounding you and have discovered that you are in the last stages of heart-disease."

"Nothing of the kind, old man, nothing of the kind. I wouldn't dream of asking you to do anything like that."

"Yes, you would, if you had happened to think of it."

"Well, as a matter of fact, since you mention it," said Ukridge, thoughtfully, "it wouldn't be a bad scheme. But if you don't feel like taking it on——"

"I don't."

"Well, then, all I want you to do is to come to Balbriggan at about nine. Supper will be over by then. No sense," said Ukridge, thoughtfully, "in missing supper. Come to Balbriggan at about nine, ask for me, and tell me in front of the gang that my aunt is dangerously ill."

"What's the sense in that?"

"You aren't showing that clear, keen intelligence of which

335

I have often spoken so highly, Corky. Don't you see? The news is a terrible shock to me. It bowls me over. I clutch at my heart——"

"They'll see through it in a second."

"I ask for water——"

"Ah, that's a convincing touch. That'll make them realise you aren't yourself."

"And after a while we leave. In fact, we leave as quickly as we jolly well can. You see what happens? I have established the fact that my heart is weak, and in a few days I write and say I've been looked over and the wedding must unfortunately be off because——"

"Damned silly idea!"

"Corky, my boy," said Ukridge gravely, "to a man as up against it as I am no idea is silly that looks as if it might work. Don't you think this will work?"

"Well, it might, of course," I admitted.

"Then I shall have a dash at it. I can rely on you to do your part?"

"How am I supposed to know that your aunt is ill?"

"Perfectly simple. They 'phone from her house, and you are the only person who knows where I'm spending the evening."

"And will you swear that this is really all you want me to do?"

"Absolutely all."

"No getting me there and letting me in for something foul?"

"My dear old man!"

"All right," I said. "I feel in my bones that something's going to go wrong, but I suppose I've got to do it."

"Spoken like a true friend," said Ukridge.

At nine o'clock on the following evening I stood on the steps of Balbriggan waiting for my ring at the bell to be answered. Cats prowled furtively in the purple dusk, and from behind a lighted window on the ground floor of the house came the tinkle of a piano and the sound of voices raised in one of the more mournful types of hymn. I recognised Ukridge's above the rest. He was expressing with a vigour which nearly cracked the glass a desire to be as a little child washed clean of sin, and it somehow seemed to deepen my already substantial gloom. Long experience of Ukridge's ingenious schemes had given me a fatalistic feeling with regard to them. With whatever fair prospects I started out to co-operate with him on these occasions, I almost invariably found myself entangled sooner or later in some nightmare imbroglio.

The door opened. A maid appeared.

"Is Mr. Ukridge here?"

"Yes, sir."

"Could I see him for a moment?"

I followed her into the drawing-room.

"Gentleman to see Mr. Ukridge, please," said the maid and left me to do my stuff.

I was aware of a peculiar feeling. It was a sort of dry-mouthed panic, and I suddenly recognised it as the same helpless stage-fright which I had experienced years before on the occasion when, the old place presumably being short of talent, I had been picked on to sing a solo at the annual concert at school. I gazed upon the roomful of Prices, and words failed me. Near the bookshelf against the wall was a stuffed seagull of blackguardly aspect, suspended with outstretched wings by a piece of string. It had a gaping, gamboge beak and its eye was bright and sardonic. I found myself gazing at it in a hypnotised manner. It seemed to see through me at a glance.

It was Ukridge who came to the rescue. Incredibly at his ease in this frightful room, he advanced to welcome me, resplendent in a morning-coat, patent-leather shoes, and tie, all of which I recognised as my property. As always when he looted my wardrobe, he exuded wealth and respectability.

"Want to see me, laddie?"

His eye met mine meaningly, and I found speech. We had rehearsed this little scene with a good deal of care over the luncheon-table, and the dialogue began to come back to me. I was able to ignore the seagull and proceed.

"I'm afraid I have serious news, old man," I said, in a hushed voice.

"Serious news?" said Ukridge trying to turn pale.

"Serious news!"

I had warned him during rehearsals that this was going to sound uncommonly like a vaudeville cross-talk act of the Argumentative College Chums type, but he had ruled out the objection as far-fetched. Nevertheless, that is just what it did sound like, and I found myself blushing warmly.

"What is it?" demanded Ukridge, emotionally, clutching me by the arm in a grip like the bite of a horse.

"Ouch!" I cried. "Your aunt!"

"My aunt?"

"They telephoned from the house just now," I proceeded, warming to my work, "to say that she had had a relapse. Her condition is very serious. They want you there at once. Even now it may be too late."

"Water!" said Ukridge, staggering back and clawing at his waistcoat—or rather at my waistcoat, which I had foolishly omitted to lock up. "Water!"

It was well done. Even I, much as I wished that he would stop wrenching one of my best ties all out of shape, was obliged to admit that. I suppose it was his lifelong training in staggering under the blows of Fate that made him so convincing. The Price family seemed to be shaken to its foundations. There was no water in the room, but a horde of juvenile Prices immediately rushed off in quest of some, and meanwhile the rest of the family gathered about the stricken man, solicitous and sympathetic.

"My aunt! Ill!" moaned Ukridge.

"I shouldn't worry, o' man," said a voice at the door.

So sneering and altogether unpleasant was this voice that for a moment I almost thought that it must have been the seagull that had spoken. Then, turning, I perceived a young man in a blue flannel suit. A young man whom I had seen before. It was the Peacemaker, the fellow who had soothed and led away the infuriated bloke to whom Ukridge owed a bit of money.

338

"I shouldn't worry," he said again, and looked malevolently upon Ukridge. His advent caused a sensation. Mr. Price, who had been kneading Ukridge's shoulder with a strong man's silent sympathy, towered as majestically as his five foot six would permit him.

"Mr. Finch," he said, "may I enquire what you are doing in my house?"

"All right, all right——"

"I thought I told you——"

"All right, all right," repeated Ernie Finch, who appeared to be a young man of character. "I've only come to expose an impostor."

"Impostor!"

"Him!" said young Mr. Finch, pointing a scornful finger at Ukridge.

I think Ukridge was about to speak, but he seemed to change his mind. As for me, I had edged out of the centre of things, and was looking on as inconspicuously as I could from behind a red plush sofa. I wished to dissociate myself entirely from the proceedings.

"Ernie Finch," said Mrs. Price, swelling, "what do you mean?"

The young man seemed in no way discouraged by the general atmosphere of hostility. He twirled his small moustache and smiled a frosty smile.

"I mean," he said, feeling in his pocket and producing an envelope, "that this fellow here hasn't got an aunt. Or, if he has, she isn't Miss Julia Ukridge, the well-known and wealthy novelist. I had my suspicions about this gentleman right from the first, I may as well tell you, so ever since he came to this house I've been going round making a few enquiries about him. The first thing I did was to write his aunt—the lady he says is his aunt—making out I wanted her nephew's address, me being an old school chum of his. Here's what she writes back—you can see it for yourselves if you want to: 'Miss Ukridge acknowledges receipt of Mr. Finch's letter, and in reply wishes to state that she has no nephew.' No nephew!

339

That's plain enough, isn't it?" He raised a hand to check comment. "And here's another thing," he proceeded. "That motor-car he's been swanking about in. It doesn't belong to him at all. It belongs to a man named Fillimore. I noted the number and made investigations. This fellow's name isn't Ukridge at all. It's Smallweed. He's a penniless impostor who's been pulling all your legs from the moment he came into the house; and if you let Mabel marry him you'll be making the biggest bloomer of your lives!"

There was an awestruck silence. Price looked upon Price in dumb consternation.

"I don't believe you," said the master of the house at length, but he spoke without conviction.

"Then, perhaps," retorted Ernie Finch, "you'll believe this gentleman. Come in, Mr. Grindlay."

Bearded, frock-coated, and sinister beyond words, the Creditor stalked into the room.

"You tell 'em," said Ernie Finch.

The Creditor appeared more than willing. He fixed Ukridge with a glittering eye, and his bosom heaved with pent-up emotion.

"Sorry to intrude on a family on Sunday evening," he said, "but this young man told me I should find Mr. Smallweed here, so I came along. I've been hunting for him high and low for two years and more about a matter of one pound two and threepence for goods supplied."

"He owes you money?" faltered Mr. Price.

"He bilked me," said the Creditor, precisely.

"Is that true?" said Mr. Price, turning to Ukridge.

Ukridge had risen and seemed to be wondering whether it was possible to sidle unobserved from the room. At this question he halted, and a weak smile played about his lips.

"Well——" said Ukridge.

The head of the family pursued his examination no further. His mind appeared to be made up. He had weighed the evidence and reached a decision. His eyes flashed. He raised a hand and pointed to the door.

"Leave my house!" he thundered.

"Right-o!" said Ukridge, mildly.

"And never enter it again!"

"Right-o!" said Ukridge.

Mr. Price turned to his daughter.

"Mabel," he said, "this engagement of yours is broken. Broken, do you understand? I forbid you ever to see this scoundrel again. You hear me?"

"All right, pa," said Miss Price, speaking for the first and last time. She seemed to be of a docile and equable disposition. I fancied I caught a not-displeased glance on its way to Ernie Finch.

"And now, sir," cried Mr. Price, "go!"

"Right-o!" said Ukridge.

But here the Creditor struck a business note.

"And what," he enquired, "about my one pound two and threepence?"

It seemed for a moment that matters were about to become difficult. But Ukridge, ever ready-witted, found the solution.

"Have you got one pound two and threepence on you, old man?" he said to me.

And with my usual bad luck I had.

We walked together down Peabody Road. Already Ukridge's momentary discomfiture had passed.

"It just shows, laddie," he said, exuberantly, "that one should never despair. However black the outlook, old horse, never, never despair. That scheme of mine might or might not have worked—one cannot tell. But, instead of having to go to all the bother of subterfuge, to which I always object, here we have a nice, clean-cut solution of the thing without any trouble at all." He mused happily for a moment. "I never thought," he said, "that the time would come when I would feel a gush of kindly feeling towards Ernie Finch; but, upon my Sam, laddie, if he were here now, I would embrace the fellow. Clasp him to my bosom, dash it!" He fell once more into a reverie. "Amazing, old horse," he proceeded, "how things work out. Many a time I've been on the very point of

341

paying that blighter Grindlay his money, merely to be rid of the annoyance of having him always popping up, but every time something seemed to stop me. I can't tell you what it was—a sort of feeling. Almost as if one had a guardian angel at one's elbow guiding one. My gosh, just think where I would have been if I had yielded to the impulse. It was Grindlay blowing in that turned the scale. By Gad, Corky, my boy, this is the happiest moment of my life."

"It might be the happiest of mine," I said, churlishly, "if I thought I should ever see that one pound two and threepence again."

"Now, laddie, laddie," protested Ukridge, "these are not the words of a friend. Don't mar a moment of unalloyed gladness. Don't you worry, you'll get your money back. A thousandfold!"

"When?"

"One of these days," said Ukridge, buoyantly. "One of these days."

GOOD GNUS
(*A Vignette in Verse*)
BY
CHARLOTTE MULLINER

When cares attack and life seems black
How sweet it is to pot a yak,
   Or puncture hares and grizzly bears,
      And others I could mention:
But in my Animals "Who's Who"
No name stands higher than the Gnu:
   And each new gnu that comes in view
      Receives my prompt attention.

When Afric's sun is sinking low,
And shadows wander to and fro,
   And everywhere there's in the air
      A hush that's deep and solemn;
Then is the time good men and true
With View Halloo pursue the gnu:
   (The safest spot to put your shot
      Is through the spinal column).

To take the creature by surprise
We must adopt some rude disguise,
   Although deceit is never sweet,
      And falsehoods don't attract us:
So, as with gun in hand you wait,
Remember to impersonate
   A tuft of grass, a mountain-pass,
      A kopje or a cactus.

A brief suspense, and then at last
The waiting's o'er, the vigil past:

A careful aim. A spurt of flame.
It's done. You've pulled the trigger,
And one more gnu, so fair and frail,
Has handed in its dinner-pail:
(The females all are rather small,
The males are somewhat bigger).

*　　　*　　　*　　　*　　　*

"*My mother died when I was born. I never knew my father.*"

"*I sometimes wish I didn't know mine,*" *said the Biscuit.* "*The sixth Earl has his moments, but he can on occasion be more than a bit of a blister. Why didn't you know your father? A pretty exclusive kid, were you?*"

THE PINHEADEDNESS OF ARCHIBALD

PEOPLE who enjoyed a merely superficial acquaintance with my nephew Archibald (said Mr. Mulliner) were accustomed to set him down as just an ordinary pinheaded young man. It was only when they came to know him better that they discovered their mistake. Then they realised that his pinheadedness, so far from being ordinary, was exceptional. Even at the Drones Club, where the average of intellect is not high, it was often said of Archibald that, had his brain been constructed of silk, he would have been hard put to it to find sufficient material to make a canary a pair of cami-knickers. He sauntered through life with a cheerful insouciance, and up to the age of twenty-five had only once been moved by anything in the nature of a really strong emotion—on the occasion when, in the heart of Bond Street and at the height of the London season, he discovered that his man, Meadowes, had carelessly sent him out with odd spats on.

THE SINISTER CUDSTER

It was a silver cow. But when I say "cow" don't go running away with the idea of some decent, self-respecting cudster such as you may observe loading grass into itself in the nearest meadow. This was a sinister, leering, Underworld sort of animal, the kind that would spit out of the side of its mouth for twopence.

IN WHICH A MOTHER PLEADS FOR HER SON AND A NEPHEW GETS THE BIRD

Sunshine pierced the haze that enveloped London. It came down Fleet Street, turned to the right, stopped at the premises of the Mammoth Publishing Company, and, entering through an upper window, beamed pleasantly upon Lord Tilbury, founder and proprietor of that vast factory of popular literature as he sat reading the batch of weekly papers which his secretary had placed on the desk for his inspection. Among the secrets of this great man's success was the fact that he kept a personal eye on all the firm's products.

Considering what a pleasing rarity sunshine in London is, one might have expected the man behind the Mammoth to beam back. Instead, he merely pressed the buzzer. His secretary appeared. He pointed silently. The secretary drew the shade, and the sunshine, having called without an appointment, was excluded.

"I beg your pardon, Lord Tilbury. . . ."

"Well?"

"A Lady Julia Fish has just rung up on the telephone."

"Well?"

"She says she would like to see you this morning."

Lord Tilbury frowned. He remembered Lady Julia Fish as an agreeable hotel acquaintance during his recent holiday at Biarritz. But this was Tilbury House, and at Tilbury House he did not desire the company of hotel acquaintances, however agreeable.

"Did she say what she wanted?"

"No, Lord Tilbury."

"All right."

The secretary withdrew. Lord Tilbury returned to his reading.

The particular periodical which had happened to come to

hand was the current number of that admirable children's paper, "Tiny Tots," and for some moments he scanned its pages with an attempt at his usual conscientious thoroughness. But it was plain that his heart was not in his work. The Adventures of Pinky, Winky, and Pop in Slumberland made little impression upon him. He passed on to a thoughtful article by Laura J. Smedley on what a wee girlie can do to help mother, but it was evident that for once Laura J. had failed to grip. Presently with a grunt he threw the paper down and for the third time since it had arrived by the morning post picked up a letter which lay on the desk. He already knew it by heart, so there was no real necessity for him to read it again, but the human tendency to twist the knife in the wound is universal.

It was a brief letter. Its writer's eighteenth century ancestors who believed in filling their twelve sheets when they took pen in hand, would have winced at the sight of it. But for all its brevity it had ruined Lord Tilbury's day.

It ran as follows:—

> *Blandings   Castle,*
> *Shropshire.*
>
> *Dear Sir,*
> *Enclosed find cheque for the advance you paid me on those Reminiscences of mine.*
> *I have been thinking it over, and have decided not to publish them after all.*
>
> *Yours truly,*
> *G. Threepwood.*

"Cor!" said Lord Tilbury, an ejaculation to which he was much addicted in times of mental stress.

He rose from his chair and began to pace the room. Always Napoleonic of aspect, being short and square and stumpy and about twenty-five pounds overweight, he looked now like a Napoleon taking his morning walk at St. Helena.

And yet, oddly enough, there were men in England who would have whooped with joy at the sight of that letter. Some of them might even have gone to the length of lighting bonfires and roasting oxen whole for the tenantry about it. Those few words over that signature would have spread happiness in every county from Cumberland to Cornwall. So true is it that in this world everything depends on the point of view.

When, some months before, the news had got about that the Hon. Galahad Threepwood, brother of the Earl of Emsworth and as sprightly an old gentleman as was ever thrown out of a Victorian music-hall, was engaged in writing the recollections of his colourful career as a man about town in the 'nineties, the shock to the many now highly respectable members of the governing classes who in their hot youth had shared it was severe. All over the country decorous Dukes and steady Viscounts, who had once sown wild oats in the society of the young Galahad, sat quivering in their slippers at the thought of what long-cupboarded skeletons those Reminiscences might disclose.

They knew their Gally, and their imagination allowed them to picture with a crystal clearness the sort of book he would be likely to produce. It would, they felt in their ageing bones, be essentially one of those of which the critics say "A veritable storehouse of diverting anecdote." To not a few—Lord Emsworth's nearest neighbour, Sir Gregory Parsloe-Parsloe of Matchingham Hall, was one of them—it was as if the Recording Angel had suddenly decided to rush into print.

Lord Tilbury, however, had looked on the thing from a different angle. He knew—no man better—what big money there was in this type of literature. The circulation of his nasty little paper, "Society Spice," proved that. Even though Percy Pilbeam, its nasty little editor, had handed in his portfolio and gone off to start a Private Enquiry Agency, it was still a gold-mine. He had known Gally Threepwood in the old days—not intimately, but quite well enough to cause him now to hasten to acquire all rights to the story of his life, sight unseen. It seemed to him that the book could not fail to be the *succès de scandale* of the year.

Acute, therefore, as had been the consternation of the Dukes and Viscounts on learning that the dead past was about to be disinterred, it paled in comparison with that of Lord Tilbury on suddenly receiving this intimation that it was not. There is a tender spot in all great men. Achilles had his heel. With Lord Tilbury it was his pocket. He hated to see money get away from him, and out of this book of Gally Threepwood's he had been looking forward to making a small fortune.

Little wonder, then, that he mourned and was unable to concentrate on "Tiny Tots." He was still mourning when his secretary entered bearing a slip of paper.

Name—Lady Julia Fish. *Business*—Personal.

Lord Tilbury snorted irritably. At a time like this!

"Tell her I'm . . ."

And then there flashed into his mind a sudden recollection of something he had heard somebody say about this Lady Julia Fish. The words "Blandings Castle" seemed to be connected with it. He turned to the desk and took up Debrett's Peerage, searching among the E's for "Emsworth, Earl of."

Yes, there it was. Lady Julia Fish had been born Lady Julia Threepwood. She was a sister of the perjured Galahad.

That altered things. Here, he perceived, was an admirable opportunity of working off some of his stored-up venom. His knowledge of life told him that the woman would not be calling unless she wanted to get something out of him. To inform her in person that she was most certainly not going to get it would be balm to his lacerated feelings.

"Ask her to come up," he said.

Lady Julia Fish was a handsome middle-aged woman of the large, blonde type, of a personality both breezy and commanding. She came into the room a few moments later like a galleon under sail, her resolute chin and her china-blue eyes proclaiming a supreme confidence in her ability to get anything she wanted out of anyone. And Lord Tilbury, having bowed stiffly, stood regarding her with a pop-eyed hostility. Even setting aside her loathsome family connections there was a patronizing good humour about her manner which he resented. And certainly, if Lady Julia Fish's manner had a fault, it was that it resembled a little too closely that of the great lady of a village amusedly trying to make friends with the backward child of one of her tenants.

"Well, well, well," she said, not actually patting Lord Tilbury on the head but conveying the impression that she might see fit to do so at any moment, "you're looking very bonny. Biarritz did you good."

Lord Tilbury, with the geniality of a trapped wolf, admitted to being in robust health.

"So this is where you get out all those jolly little papers of yours, is it? I must say I'm impressed. Quite awe-inspiring, all that ritual on the threshold. Admirals in the Swiss Navy making you fill up forms with your name and business, and small boys in buttons eyeing you as if anything you said might be used in evidence against you."

"What *is* your business?" asked Lord Tilbury.

"The practical note!" said Lady Julia, with indulgent approval. "How stimulating that is! Time is money, and all that. Quite. Well, cutting the preamble, I want a job for Ronnie."

Lord Tilbury looked like a trapped wolf who had thought as much.

"Ronnie?" he said coldly.

"My son. Didn't you meet him at Biarritz? He was there. Small and pink."

Lord Tilbury drew in breath for the delivery of the nasty blow.

"I regret . . . "

"I know what you're going to say. You're very crowded here. Fearful congestion, and so on. Well, Ronnie won't take up much room. And I shouldn't think he could do any actual harm to a solidly established concern like this. Surely you could let him mess about at *something*? Why, Sir Gregory Parsloe, our neighbour down in Shropshire, told me that you were employing his nephew, Monty. And while I would be the last woman to claim that Ronnie is a mental giant, at least he's brighter than young Monty Bodkin."

A quiver ran through Lord Tilbury's stocky form. This woman had unbared his secret shame. A man who prided himself on never letting himself be worked for jobs, he had had a few weeks before a brief moment of madness when, under the softening influence of a particularly good public dinner, he had yielded to the request of the banqueter on his left that he should find a place at Tilbury House for his nephew.

He had regretted the lapse next morning. He had regretted it more on seeing the nephew. And he had not ceased to regret it now.

"That," he said tensely, "has nothing to do with the case."

"I don't see why. Swallowing camels and straining at gnats is what I should call it."

"Nothing," repeated Lord Tilbury, "to do with the case."

He was beginning to feel that this interview was not working out as he had anticipated. He had meant to be strong, brusque, decisive—the man of iron. And here this woman had got him arguing and explaining—almost in a position of defending himself. Like so many people who came in contact with her, he began to feel that there was something disagreeably hypnotic about Lady Julia Fish.

"But what do you want your son to work here *for?*" he asked, realizing as he spoke that a man of iron ought to have scorned to put such a question.

Lady Julia considered.

"Oh, a pittance. Whatever the dole is you give your slaves."

Lord Tilbury made himself clearer.

"I mean, why? Has he shown any aptitude for journalism?"

This seemed to amuse Lady Julia.

"My dear man," she said, tickled by the quaint conceit, "no member of my family has ever shown any aptitude for anything except eating and sleeping."

"Then why do you want him to join my staff?"

"Well, primarily, to distract his mind."

"What!"

"To distract his . . . well, yes, I suppose in a loose way you could call it a mind."

"I don't understand you."

"Well, it's like this. The poor half-wit is trying to marry a chorus-girl, and it seemed to me that if he were safe at Tilbury House, inking his nose and getting bustled about by editors and people, it might take his mind off the tender passion."

Lord Tilbury drew a long, deep, rasping breath. The weakness had passed. He could be strong now. This outrageous insult to the business he loved had shattered the spell which those china-blue eyes and that confident manner had been weaving about him. He spoke curtly, placing his thumbs in the armholes of his waistcoat to lend emphasis to his remarks.

"I fear you have mistaken the functions of Tilbury House, Lady Julia."

"I beg your pardon?"

"We publish newspapers, magazines, weekly journals. We are not a Home for the Lovelorn."

There was a brief silence.

"I see," said Lady Julia. She looked at him inquiringly. "You sound very stuffy," she went on. "Not your old merry Biarritz self at all. Did your breakfast disagree with you this morning?"

"Cor!"

"Something's the matter. Why, at Biarritz you were known as Sunny Jim."

Lord Tilbury was ill attuned to badinage.

"Yes," he said. "Something is the matter. If you really wish to know, I am scarcely in a frame of mind to-day to go out of my way to oblige members of your family. After what has occurred."

"What has occurred?"

"Your brother Galahad . . . . " Lord Tilbury choked.

He extended the letter rather in the manner of one anxious

to rid himself of a snake which has somehow come into his possession. Lady Julia scrutinized it with languid interest.

"It's monstrous. Abominable. He accepted the contract, and he ought to fulfil it. At the very least, in common decency, he might have given his reasons for behaving in this utterly treacherous and unethical way. But does he? Not at all. Explanations? None. Apologies? Regrets? Oh dear, no. He merely 'decides not to publish.' In all my thirty years of. . . . "

Lady Julia was never a very good listener.

"Odd," she said, handing the letter back. "My brother Galahad is a man who moves in a mysterious way his wonders to perform. A quite unaccountable mentality. I knew he was writing this book, of course, but I have no notion whatever why he has had this sudden change of heart. Perhaps some Duke who doesn't want to see himself in the 'Peers I Have Been Thrown Out Of Public Houses With' chapter has been threatening to take him for a ride."

"Cor!"

"Or some Earl with a guilty conscience. Or a Baronet. 'Society Scribe Bumped Off By Baronets'—that would make a good head-line for one of your papers."

"This is not a joking matter."

"Well, at any rate, my dear man, it's no good savaging *me*. I'm not responsible for Galahad's eccentricities. I'm simply an innocent widow-woman trying to wangle a cushy job for her only son. Coming back to which, I rather gather from what you said just now that you do not intend to set Ronnie punching the clock?"

Lord Tilbury shook from stem to stern. His eyes gleamed balefully. Nature in the raw is seldom mild.

"I absolutely and positively refuse to employ your son at Tilbury House in any capacity whatsoever."

"Well, that's a fair answer to a fair question, and seems to close the discussion."

Lady Julia rose.

"Too bad about Gally's little effort," she said silkily. "You'll lose a lot of money, won't you? There's a mint of it in a really

354

indiscreet book of Reminiscences. They tell me that Lady Wensleydale's 'Sixty Years Near the Knuckle In Mayfair,' or whatever it was called, sold a hundred thousand copies. And, knowing Gally, I'll bet he would have started remembering where old Jane Wensleydale left off. *Good* morning, Lord Tilbury. So nice to have seen you again."

The door closed. The proprietor of the Mammoth sat staring before him. His agony was too keen to permit him even to say "Cor!"

The spasm passed. Presently life seemed to steal back to that rigid form. It would be too much to say that Lord Tilbury became himself, but at least he began to function once more. Though pain and anguish rack the brow, the world's work has to be done. Like a convalescent reaching for his barley-water, he stretched out a shaking hand and took up "Tiny Tots" again.

And here it would be agreeable to leave him—the good man restoring his *moral* with refreshing draughts at the fount of wholesome literature. But this happy ending was not to be. Once more it was to be proved that this was not Lord Tilbury's lucky morning. Scarcely had he begun to read, when his eyes suddenly protruded from their sockets, his stout body underwent a strong convulsion, and from his parted lips there proceeded a loud snort. It was as if a viper had sprung from between the pages and bitten him on the chin.

And this was odd, because "Tiny Tots" is a journal not as a rule provocative of violent expressions of feeling. Ably edited by that well-known writer of tales for the young, the Rev. Aubrey Sellick, it strives always to take the sane middle course. Its editorial page, in particular, is a model of non-partisan moderation. And yet, amazingly, it was this same editorial page which had just made Lord Tilbury's blood-pressure hit a new high.

It occurred to him that mental strain might have affected his eyesight. He blinked and took another look.

No, there it was, just as before.

Well, chickabiddies, how are you all? Minding what Nursie says and eating your spinach like good little men? That's right. I know the stuff tastes like a motor-man's glove, but they say there's iron in it, and that's what puts hair on the chest.

Lord Tilbury, having taken time out to make a noise like a leaking siphon, resumed his reading.

Well, now let's get down to it. This week, my dear little souls, Uncle Woggly is going to put you on to a good thing. We all want to make a spot of easy money these hard times, don't we? Well, here's the low-down, straight from the horse's mouth. All you have to do is to get hold of some mug and lure him into betting that a quart whisky bottle holds a quart of whisky.

Sounds rummy, what? I mean, that's what you would naturally think it would hold. So does the mug. But it isn't. It's really more, and I'll tell you why.

First you fill the bottle. This gives you your quart. Then you shove the cork in. And then—follow me closely here— you turn the bottle upside down and you find there's a sort of bulging-in part at the bottom. Well, slosh some whisky into that, and there you are. Because the bot. is now holding more than a quart and you scoop the stakes.

I have to acknowledge a sweet little letter from Frankie Kendon (Hendon) about his canary which goes tweet-tweet-tweet. Also one from Muriel Poot (Stow-in-the-Wold), who is going to lose her shirt if she ever bets any-one she knows how to spell "tortoise".

Lord Tilbury had read enough. There was some good stuff further on about Willi Waters (Ponders End) and his cat Miggles, but he did not wait for it. He pressed the buzzer emotionally.

"Tots!" he cried, choking. "'Tiny Tots'! Who is editing 'Tiny Tots' now?"

"Mr. Sellick is the regular editor, Lord Tilbury," replied his secretary, who knew everything and wore horn-rimmed spectacles to prove it, "but he is away on his vacation. In his absence, the assistant editor is in charge of the paper. Mr. Bodkin."

"Bodkin!"

So loud was Lord Tilbury's voice and so sharply did his eyes bulge that the secretary recoiled a step, as if something had hit her.

"That popinjay!" said Lord Tilbury, in a strange, low, grating voice. "I might have guessed it. I might have foreseen something like this. Send Mr. Bodkin here at once."

It was a judgment, he felt. This was what came of going to public dinners and allowing yourself to depart from the principles of a lifetime. One false step, one moment of weakness when there were wheedling snakes of Baronets at your elbow, and what a harvest, what a reckoning!

He leaned back in his chair, tapping the desk with a paper-knife. He had just broken this, when there was a knock at the door and his young subordinate entered.

"Good morning, good morning, good morning," said the latter affably. "Want to see me about something?"

Monty Bodkin was rather an attractive popinjay, as popinjays go. He was tall and slender and lissom, and many people considered him quite good-looking. But not Lord Tilbury. He had disapproved of his appearance from their first meeting, thinking him much too well dressed, much too carefully groomed, and much too much like what he actually was, a member in good standing of the Drones Club. The proprietor of the Mammoth Publishing Company could not have put into words his ideal of a young journalist, but it would have been something rather shaggy, preferably with spectacles, certainly not wearing spats. And while Monty Bodkin was not actually spatted at the moment, there did undoubtedly hover about him a sort of spat aura.

"Ha!" said Lord Tilbury, sighting him.

He stared bleakly. His demeanour now was that of a Napoleon who, suffering from toothache, sees his way to taking it out of one of his minor marshals.

"Come in," he growled.

"Shut the door," he grunted.

"And don't grin like that," he snarled. "What the devil are you grinning for?"

The words were proof of the deeps of misunderstanding which yawned between the assistant editor of "Tiny Tots" and himself. Certainly something was splitting Monty Bodkin's face in a rather noticeable manner, but the latter could have taken his oath it was an ingratiating smile. He had intended it for an ingratiating smile, and unless something had gone extremely wrong with the works in the process of assembling it, that is what it should have come out as.

However, being a sweet-tempered popinjay and always anxious to oblige, he switched it off. He was feeling a little puzzled. The atmosphere seemed to him to lack chumminess, and he was at a loss to account for it.

"Nice day," he observed tentatively.

"Never mind the day."

"Right ho. Heard from Uncle Gregory lately?"

"Never mind your Uncle Gregory."

"Right ho."

"And don't say 'Right-ho.'"

"Right ho," said Monty dutifully.

"Read this."

Monty took the proffered copy of "Tots."

"You want me to read aloud to you?" he said, feeling that this was matier.

"You need not trouble. I have already seen the passage in question. Here, where I am pointing."

"Oh, ah, yes. Uncle Woggly. Right ho."

"Will you stop saying 'Right ho'! . . . Well?"

"Eh?"

"You wrote that, I take it?"

"Oh, rather."

"Cor!"

Monty was now definitely perplexed. He could conceal from himself no longer that there was ill-will in the air. Lord Tilbury's had never been an elfin personality, but he had always been a good deal more winsome than this.

A possible solution of his employer's emotion occurred to him.

"You aren't worrying about it not being accurate, are you? Because that's quite all right. I had it on the highest authority —from an old boy called Galahad Threepwood. Lord Emsworth's brother. You wouldn't have heard of him, of course, but he was a great lad about the metropolis at one time, and you can reply absolutely on anything he says about whisky bottles."

He broke off, puzzled once more. He could not understand what had caused his companion to strike the desk in that violent manner.

"What the devil do you mean, you wretched imbecile," demanded Lord Tilbury, speaking a little indistinctly, for he was sucking his fist, "by putting stuff of this sort in 'Tiny Tots'?"

"You don't like it?" said Monty, groping.

"How do you suppose the mothers who read that drivel to their children will feel?"

Monty was concerned. This opened up a new line of thought.

"Wrong tone, do you think?"

"Mugs . . . Betting . . . Whisky. . . . You have probably lost us ten thousand subscribers."

"I say, that never occurred to me. Yes, by Jove, I see what you mean now. Unfortunate slip, what? May quite easily cause alarm and despondency. Yes, yes, yes, to be sure. Oh, yes, indeed. Well, I can only say I'm sorry."

"You can not only say you are sorry," said Lord Tilbury, correcting this view, "you can go to the cashier, draw a month's salary, get to blazes out of here, and never let me see your face in the building again."

Monty's concern increased.

"But this sounds like the sack. Don't tell me that what you are hinting at is the sack?"

Speech failed Lord Tilbury. He jerked a thumb doorwards. And such was the magic of his personality that Monty found himself a moment later with his fingers on the handle. Its cold hardness seemed to wake him from a trance. He halted, making a sort of Custer's Last Stand.

"Reflect!" he said.

Lord Tilbury busied himself with his papers.

"Uncle Gregory won't like this," said Monty reproachfully.

Lord Tilbury quivered for an instant as if somebody had stuck a bradawl into him, but preserved an aloof silence.

"Well, he won't, you know." Monty had no wish to be severe, but he felt compelled to point this out. "He takes all the trouble to get me a job, I mean to say, and now this happens. Oh, no, don't deceive yourself, Uncle Gregory will be vexed."

"Get out," said Lord Tilbury.

Monty fondled the door-handle for a space, marshalling his thoughts. He had that to say which he rather fancied would melt the other's heart a goodish bit, but he was not quite sure how to begin.

"Haven't you gone?" said Lord Tilbury.

Monty reassured him.

"Not yet. The fact is, there's something I rather wanted to call to your attention. You don't know it, but for private and personal reasons I particularly want to hold this 'Tiny Tots' job for a year. There are wheels within wheels. It's a sort of bet, as a matter of fact. Have you ever met a girl called Gertrude Butterwick? . . . However, it's a long story and I won't bother you with it now. But you can take it from me that there definitely are wheels within wheels and unless I continue in your employment, till somewhere around the middle of next June, my life will be a blank and all my hopes and dreams shattered. So how about it? Would you, on second thoughts, taking this into consideration, feel disposed to postpone the rash act till then? If you've any doubts as to my doing my bit, dismiss them. I would work like the dickens. First at the office, last to come away, and solid, selfless, service all the time—no clock-watching, no folding of the hands in . . . "

"Get OUT!" said Lord Tilbury.

There was a silence.

"You will not reconsider?"

"No."

"You are not to be moved?"

"No."

Monty Bodkin drew himself up.

"Oh, right ho," he said stiffly. "Now we know where we are. Now we know where we stand. If that is the attitude you take, I suppose there is nothing to be done about it. Since you have no heart, no sympathy, no feeling, no bowels—of compassion, I mean—I have no alternative but to shove off. I have only two things to say to you, Lord Tilbury. One is that you have ruined a man's life. The other is Pip-pip."

He passed from the room, erect and dignified, like some young aristocrat of the French Revolution stepping into the tumbril. Lord Tilbury's secretary removed her ear from the door just in time to avoid a nasty flesh-wound.

Extract from the first two chapters of "Heavy Weather."

CHESTER FORGETS HIMSELF

THE afternoon was warm and heavy. Butterflies loafed languidly in the sunshine, birds panted in the shady recesses of the trees.

The Oldest Member, snug in his favourite chair, had long since succumbed to the drowsy influence of the weather. His eyes were closed, his chin sunk upon his breast. The pipe which he had been smoking lay beside him on the turf, and ever and anon there proceeded from him a muffled snore.

Suddenly the stillness was broken. There was a sharp, cracking sound as of splitting wood. The Oldest Member sat up, blinking. As soon as his eyes had become accustomed to the glare, he perceived that a foursome had holed out on the ninth and was disintegrating. Two of the players were moving with quick, purposeful steps in the direction of the side door which gave entrance to the bar; a third was making for the road that led to the village, bearing himself as one in profound dejection; the fourth came on to the terrace.

"Finished?" said the Oldest Member.

The other stopped, wiping a heated brow. He lowered himself into the adjoining chair and stretched his legs out.

"Yes. We started at the tenth. Golly, I'm tired. No joke playing in this weather."

"How did you come out?"

"We won on the last green. Jimmy Fothergill and I were playing the vicar and Rupert Blake."

"What was that sharp, cracking sound I heard?" asked the Oldest Member.

"That was the vicar smashing his putter. Poor old chap, he had rotten luck all the way round, and it didn't seem to make it any better for him that he wasn't able to relieve his feelings in the ordinary way."

"I suspected some such thing," said the Oldest Member,

"from the look of his back as he was leaving the green. His walk was the walk of an overwrought soul."

His companion did not reply. He was breathing deeply and regularly.

"It is a moot question," proceeded the Oldest Member, thoughtfully, "whether the clergy, considering their peculiar position, should not be more liberally handicapped at golf than the laymen with whom they compete. I have made a close study of the game since the days of the feather ball, and I am firmly convinced that to refrain entirely from oaths during a round is almost equivalent to giving away three bisques. There are certain occasions when an oath seems to be so imperatively demanded that the strain of keeping it in must inevitably affect the ganglions or nerve-centres in such a manner as to diminish the steadiness of the swing."

The man beside him slipped lower down in his chair. His mouth had opened slightly.

"I am reminded in this connection," said the Oldest Member, "of the story of young Chester Meredith, a friend of mine whom you have not, I think, met. He moved from this neighbourhood shortly before you came. There was a case where a man's whole happiness was very nearly wrecked purely because he tried to curb his instincts and thwart nature in this very respect. Perhaps you would care to hear the story?"

A snore proceeded from the next chair.

"Very well, then," said the Oldest Member, "I will relate it."

Chester Meredith (said the Oldest Member) was one of the nicest young fellows of my acquaintance. We had been friends ever since he had come to live here as a small boy, and I had watched him with a fatherly eye through all the more important crises of a young man's life. It was I who taught him to drive, and when he had all that trouble in his twenty-first year with shanking his short approaches, it was to me that he came for sympathy and advice. It was an odd coincidence, therefore, that I should have been present when he fell in love.

I was smoking my evening cigar out here and watching the last couples finishing their rounds, when Chester came out of the club-house and sat by me. I could see that the boy was perturbed about something, and wondered why, for I knew that he had won his match.

"What," I inquired, "is on your mind?"

"Oh, nothing," said Chester. "I was only thinking that there are some human misfits who ought not to be allowed on any decent links."

"You mean——?"

"The Wrecking Crew," said Chester, bitterly. "They held us up all the way round, confound them. Wouldn't let us through. What can you do with people who don't know enough of the etiquette of the game to understand that a single has right of way over a four-ball foursome? We had to loaf about for hours on end while they scratched at the turf like a lot of crimson hens. Eventually all four of them lost their balls simultaneously at the eleventh and we managed to get by. I hope they choke."

I was not altogether surprised at his warmth. The Wrecking Crew consisted of four retired business men who had taken up the noble game late in life because their doctors had ordered them air and exercise. Every club, I suppose, has a cross of this kind to bear, and it was not often that our members rebelled; but there was undoubtedly something particularly irritating in the methods of the Wrecking Crew. They tried so hard that it seemed almost inconceivable that they should be so slow.

"They are all respectable men," I said, "and were, I believe, highly thought of in their respective businesses. But on the links I admit that they are a trial."

"They are the direct lineal descendants of the Gadarene swine," said Chester firmly. "Every time they come out I expect to see them rush down the hill from the first tee and hurl themselves into the lake at the second. Of all the——"

"Hush!" I said.

Out of the corner of my eye I had seen a girl approaching, and I was afraid lest Chester in his annoyance might use strong

364

language. For he was one of those golfers who are apt to express themselves in moments of emotion with a good deal of generous warmth.

"Eh?" said Chester.

I jerked my head, and he looked round. And, as he did so, there came into his face an expression which I had seen there only once before, on the occasion when he won the President's Cup on the last green by holing a thirty-yard chip with his mashie. It was a look of ecstasy and awe. His mouth was open, his eyebrows raised, and he was breathing heavily through his nose.

"Golly!" I heard him mutter.

The girl passed by. I could not blame Chester for staring at her. She was a beautiful young thing, with a lissom figure and a perfect face. Her hair was a deep chestnut, her eyes blue, her nose small and laid back with about as much loft as a light iron. She disappeared, and Chester, after nearly dislocating his neck trying to see her round the corner of the club-house, emitted a deep, explosive sigh.

"Who is she?" he whispered.

I could tell him that. In one way and another I get to know most things around this locality.

"She is a Miss Blakeney. Felicia Blakeney. She has come to stay for a month with the Waterfields. I understand she was at school with Jane Waterfield. She is twenty-three, has a dog named Joseph, dances well, and dislikes parsnips. Her father is a distinguished writer on sociological subjects; her mother is Wilmot Royce, the well-known novelist, whose last work, *Sewers of the Soul*, was, you may recall, jerked before a tribunal by the Purity League. She has a brother, Crispin Blakeney, an eminent young reviewer and essayist, who is now in India studying local conditions with a view to a series of lectures. She only arrived here yesterday, so this is all I have been able to find out about her as yet."

Chester's mouth was still open when I began speaking. By the time I had finished it was open still wider. The ecstatic look in his eyes had changed to one of dull despair.

"My God!" he muttered. "If her family is like that, what chance is there for a rough-neck like me?"

"You admire her?"

"She is the alligator's Adam's apple," said Chester simply.

I patted his shoulder.

"Have courage, my boy," I said. "Always remember that the love of a good man, to whom the pro. can give only a couple of strokes in eighteen holes is not to be despised."

"Yes, that's all very well. But this girl is probably one solid mass of brain. She will look on me as an uneducated warthog."

"Well, I will introduce you, and we will see. She looked a nice girl."

"You're a great describer, aren't you?" said Chester. "A wonderful flow of language you've got, I don't think! Nice girl! Why, she's only the girl in the world. She's a pearl among women. She's the most marvellous, astounding, beautiful, heavenly thing that ever drew perfumed breath." He paused, as if his train of thought had been interrupted by an idea. "Did you say that her brother's name was Crispin?"

"I did. Why?"

Chester gave vent to a few manly oaths.

"Doesn't that just show you how things go in this rotten world?"

"What do you mean?"

"I was at school with him."

"Surely that should form a solid basis for friendship?"

"Should it? Should it, by gad? Well, let me tell you that I probably kicked that blighted worm Crispin Blakeney a matter of seven hundred and forty-six times in the few years I knew him. He was the world's worst. He could have walked straight into the Wrecking Crew and no questions asked. Wouldn't it jar you? I have the luck to know her brother, and it turns out that we couldn't stand the sight of each other."

"Well, there is no need to tell her that."

366

"Do you mean——?" He gazed at me wildly. "Do you mean I might pretend we were pals?"

"Why not? Seeing that he is in India, he can hardly contradict you."

"My gosh!" He mused for a moment. I could see that the idea was beginning to sink in. It was always thus with Chester. You had to give him time. "By Jove, it mightn't be a bad scheme at that. I mean, it would start me off with a rush, like being one up on bogey in the first two. And there's nothing like a good start. By gad, I'll do it."

"I should."

"Reminiscences of the dear old days when we were lads together, and all that sort of thing."

"Precisely."

"It isn't going to be easy, mind you," said Chester, meditatively. "I'll do it because I love her, but nothing else in this world would make me say a civil word about the blister. Well, then, that's settled. Get on with the introduction stuff, will you? I'm in a hurry."

One of the privileges of age is that it enables a man to thrust his society on a beautiful girl without causing her to draw herself up and say "Sir!" It was not difficult for me to make the acquaintance of Miss Blakeney, and, this done, my first act was to unleash Chester on her.

"Chester," I said, summoning him as he loafed with an overdone carelessness on the horizon, one leg almost inextricably entwined about the other, "I want you to meet Miss Blakeney. Miss Blakeney, this is my young friend Chester Meredith. He was at school with your brother Crispin. You were great friends, were you not?"

"Bosom," said Chester, after a pause.

"Oh, really?" said the girl. There was a pause. "He is in India now."

"Yes," said Chester.

There was another pause.

"Great chap," said Chester, gruffly.

"Crispin is very popular," said the girl, "with some people."

367

"Always been my best pal," said Chester.

"Yes?"

I was not altogether satisfied with the way matters were developing. The girl seemed cold and unfriendly, and I was afraid that this was due to Chester's repellent manner. Shyness, especially when complicated by love at first sight, is apt to have strange effects on a man, and the way it had taken Chester was to make him abnormally stiff and dignified. One of the most charming things about him, as a rule, was his delightful boyish smile Shyness had caused him to iron this out of his countenance till no trace of it remained. Not only did he not smile, he looked like a man who never had smiled and never would. His mouth was a thin, rigid line. His back was stiff with what appeared to be contemptuous aversion. He looked down his nose at Miss Blakeney as if she were less than the dust beneath his chariot-wheels.

I thought the best thing to do was to leave them alone together to get acquainted. Perhaps, I thought, it was my presence that was cramping Chester's style. I excused myself and receded.

It was some days before I saw Chester again. He came round to my cottage one night after dinner and sank into a chair, where he remained silent for several minutes.

"Well?" I said at last.

"Eh?" said Chester, starting violently.

"Have you been seeing anything of Miss Blakeney lately?"

"You bet I have."

"And how do you feel about her on further acquaintance?"

"Eh?" said Chester, absently.

"Do you still love her?"

Chester came out of his trance.

"Love her?" he cried, his voice vibrating with emotion. "Of course I love her. Who wouldn't love her? I'd be a silly chump not loving her. Do you know," the boy went on, a look in his eyes like that of some young knight seeing the Holy Grail in a vision, "do you know, she is the only woman I ever met who didn't overswing. Just a nice, crisp, snappy half-slosh, with a good follow-through. And another thing. You'll hardly believe me, but she waggles almost as little as George Duncan. You know how women waggle as a rule, fiddling about for a minute and a half like kittens playing with a ball of wool. Well, she just makes one firm pass with the club and then *bing!* There is none like her, none."

"Then you have been playing golf with her?"

"Nearly every day."

"How is your game?"

"Rather spotty. I seem to be mistiming them."

I was concerned.

"I do hope, my dear boy," I said, earnestly, "that you are taking great care to control your feelings when out on the links with Miss Blakeney. You know what you are like. I trust you have not been using the sort of language you generally employ on occasions when you are not timing them right?"

"Me?" said Chester, horrified. "Who, me? You don't imagine for a moment that I would dream of saying a thing that would bring a blush to her dear cheek, do you? Why, a bishop could have gone round with me and learned nothing new."

I was relieved.

"How do you find you manage the dialogue these days?" I asked. "When I introduced you, you behaved—you will forgive an old friend for criticising—you behaved a little like a stuffed frog with laryngitis. Have things got easier in that respect?"

"Oh yes. I'm quite the prattler now. I talk about her brother mostly. I put in the greater part of my time boosting the tick. It seems to be coming easier. Willpower, I suppose. And, then, of course, I talk a good deal about her mother's novels."

"Have you read them?"

" Every damned one of them—for her sake. And if there's a greater proof of love than that, show me! My gosh, what muck that woman writes! That reminds me, I've got to send to the bookshop for her latest—out yesterday. It's called *The Stench of Life*. A sequel, I understand, to *Grey Mildew*."

"Brave lad," I said, pressing his hand. "Brave, devoted lad!"

"Oh, I'd do more than that for her." He smoked for awhile in silence. "By the way, I'm going to propose to her to-morrow."

"Already?"

"Can't put it off a minute longer. It's been as much as I could manage, bottling it up till now. Where do you think would be the best place? I mean, it's not the sort of thing you can do while you're walking down the street or having a cup of tea. I thought of asking her to have a round with me and taking a stab at it on the links."

"You could not do better. The links—Nature's cathedral."

"Right-o, then! I'll let you know how I come out."

"I wish you luck, my boy," I said.

And what of Felicia, meanwhile? She was, alas, far from returning the devotion which scorched Chester's vital organs.

He seemed to her precisely the sort of man she most disliked. From childhood up Felicia Blakeney had lived in an atmosphere of highbrowism, and the type of husband she had always seen in her daydreams was the man who was simple and straightforward and earthy and did not know whether Artbashiekeff was a suburb of Moscow or a new kind of Russian drink. A man like Chester, who on his own statement would rather read one of her mother's novels than eat, revolted her. And his warm affection for her brother Crispin set the seal on her distaste.

Felicia was a dutiful child, and she loved her parents. It took a bit of doing, but she did it. But at her brother Crispin she drew the line. He wouldn't do, and his friends were worse than he was. They were high-voiced, super-cilious, pince-nezed young men who talked patronisingly of Life and Art, and Chester's unblushing confession that he was one of them had put him ten down and nine to play right away.

You may wonder why the boy's undeniable skill on the links had no power to soften the girl. The unfortunate fact was that all the good effects of his prowess were neutralised by his behaviour while playing. All her life she had treated golf with a proper reverence and awe, and in Chester's attitude towards the game she seemed to detect a horrible shallowness. The fact is, Chester, in his efforts to keep himself from using strong language, had found a sort of relief in a girlish giggle, and it made her shudder every time she heard it.

His deportment, therefore, in the space of time leading up to the proposal could not have been more injurious to his cause. They started out quite happily, Chester doing a nice two-hundred-yarder off the first tee, which for a moment awoke the girl's respect. But at the fourth, after a lovely brassie-shot, he found his ball deeply embedded in the print of a woman's high heel. It was just one of those rubs of the green which normally would have caused him to ease his bosom with a flood of sturdy protest, but now he was on his guard.

"Tee-hee!" simpered Chester, reaching for his niblick. "Too bad, too bad!" and the girl shuddered to the depths of her soul.

Having holed out, he proceeded to enliven the walk to the next tee with a few remarks on her mother's literary style, and it was while they were walking after their drives that he proposed.

His proposal, considering the circumstances, could hardly have been less happily worded. Little knowing that he was rushing upon his doom, Chester stressed the Crispin note. He gave Felicia the impression that he was suggesting this marriage more for Crispin's sake than anything else. He conveyed the idea that he thought how nice it would be for brother Crispin to have his old chum in the family. He drew a picture of their little home, with Crispin for ever popping in and out like a rabbit. It is not to be wondered at that, when at length he had finished and she had time to speak, the horrified girl turned him down with a thud.

It is at moments such as these that a man reaps the reward of a good upbringing.

In similar circumstances those who have not had the benefit of a sound training in golf are too apt to go wrong. Goaded by the sudden anguish, they take to drink, plunge into dissipation, and write *vers libre*. Chester was mercifully saved from this. I saw him the day after he had been handed the mitten, and was struck by the look of grim determination in his face. Deeply wounded though he was, I could see that he was the master of his fate and the captain of his soul.

"I am sorry, my boy," I said, sympathetically, when he had told me the painful news.

"It can't be helped," he replied, bravely.

"Her decision was final?"

"Quite."

"You do not contemplate having another pop at her?"

"No good. I know when I'm licked."

I patted him on the shoulder and said the only thing it seemed possible to say.

"After all, there is always golf."

He nodded.

"Yes. My game needs a lot of tuning up. Now is the time to do it. From now on I go at this pastime seriously. I make it my life-work. Who knows?" he murmured, with a sudden gleam in his eyes. "The Amateur Championship——"

"The Open!" I cried, falling gladly into his mood.

"The American Amateur," said Chester, flushing.

"The American Open," I chorused.

"No one has ever copped all four."

"No one."

"Watch me!" said Chester Meredith, simply.

It was about two weeks after this that I happened to look in on Chester at his house one morning. I found him about to start for the links. As he had foreshadowed in the conversation

372

which I have just related, he now spent most of the daylight hours on the course. In these two weeks he had gone about his task of achieving perfection with a furious energy which made him the talk of the club. Always one of the best players in the place, he had developed an astounding brilliance. Men who had played him level were now obliged to receive two and even three strokes. The pro. himself, conceding one, had only succeeded in halving their match. The struggle for the President's Cup came round once more, and Chester won it for the second time with ridiculous ease.

When I arrived, he was practising chip-shots in his sitting-room. I noticed that he seemed to be labouring under some strong emotion, and his first words gave me the clue.

"She's going away to-morrow," he said, abruptly, lofting a ball over the whatnot on to the Chesterfield.

I was not sure whether I was sorry or relieved. Her absence would leave a terrible blank, of course, but it might be that it would help him to get over his infatuation.

"Ah!" I said, non-committally.

Chester addressed his ball with a well-assumed phlegm, but I could see by the way his ears wiggled that he was feeling deeply. I was not surprised when he topped his shot into the coal-scuttle.

"She has promised to play a last round with me this morning," he said.

Again I was doubtful what view to take. It was a pretty, poetic idea, not unlike Browning's "Last Ride Together," but I was not sure if it was altogether wise. However, it was none of my business, so I merely patted him on the shoulder and he gathered up his clubs and went off.

Owing to motives of delicacy I had not offered to accompany him on his round, and it was not till later that I learned the actual details of what occurred. At the start, it seems, the spiritual anguish which he was suffering had a depressing effect on his game. He hooked his drive off the first tee and was only enabled to get a five by means of a strong niblick shot out of the rough. At the second, the lake hole, he lost a ball in the water and got another five. It was only at the third that he began to pull himself together.

The test of a great golfer is his ability to recover from a bad start. Chester had this quality to a pre-eminent degree. A lesser man, conscious of being three over bogey for the first two holes, might have looked on his round as ruined. To Chester it simply meant that he had to get a couple of "birdies" right speedily, and he set about it at once. Always a long driver, he excelled himself at the third. It is, as you know, an uphill hole all the way, but his drive could not have come far short of two hundred and fifty yards. A brassie-shot of equal strength and unerring direction put him on the edge of the green, and he holed out with a long putt two under bogey. He had hoped for a "birdie" and he had achieved an "eagle."

I think that this splendid feat must have softened Felicia's heart, had it not been for the fact that misery had by this time entirely robbed Chester of the ability to smile. Instead, therefore, of behaving in the wholesome, natural way of men who get threes at bogey five holes, he preserved a drawn, impassive countenance; and as she watched him tee up her ball, stiff, correct, polite, but to all outward appearance absolutely inhuman, the girl found herself stifling that thrill of what for a moment had been almost adoration. It was, she felt, exactly how her brother Crispin would have comported himself if he had done a hole in two under bogey.

And yet she could not altogether check a wistful sigh when, after a couple of fours at the next two holes, he picked up another stroke on the sixth and with an inspired spoon-shot brought his medal-score down to one better than bogey by getting a two at the hundred-and-seventy-yard seventh. But the brief spasm of tenderness passed, and when he finished the first nine with two more fours she refrained from anything warmer than a mere word of stereotyped congratulation.

"One under bogey for the first nine," she said. "Splendid!"

"One under bogey!" said Chester, woodenly.

"Out in thirty-four. What is the record for the course?"

Chester started. So great had been his pre-occupation that he had not given a thought to the course record. He suddenly realised now that the pro., who had done the lowest medal-score to date—the other course record was held by Peter Willard with a hundred and sixty-one, achieved in his first season—had gone out in only one better than his own figures that day.

"Sixty-eight," he said.

"What a pity you lost those strokes at the beginning!"

"Yes," said Chester.

He spoke absently—and, as it seemed to her, primly and without enthusiasm—for the flaming idea of having a go at the course record had only just occurred to him. Once before he had done the first nine in thirty-four, but on that occasion he had not felt that curious feeling of irresistible force which comes to a golfer at the very top of his form. Then he had been aware all the time that he had been putting chancily. They had gone in, yes, but he had uttered a prayer per putt. To-day he was superior to any weak doubtings. When he tapped the ball on the green, he knew it was going to sink. The course record? Why not? What a last offering to lay at her feet! She would go away, out of his life for ever; she would marry some other bird; but the memory of that supreme round would remain with her as long as she breathed. When he won the Open and Amateur for the second—the third—the fourth time, she would say to herself, "I was with him when he dented the record for his home course!" And he had only to pick up a couple of strokes on the last nine, to do threes at holes where he was wont to be satisfied with fours. Yes, by Vardon, he would take a whirl at it.

You, who are acquainted with these links, will no doubt say that the task which Chester Meredith had sketched out for himself—cutting two strokes off thirty-five for the second nine —was one at which Humanity might well shudder. The pro. himself, who had finished sixth in the last Open Championship, had never done better than a thirty-five, playing perfect

375

golf and being one under par. But such was Chester's mood that, as he teed up on the tenth, he did not even consider the possibility of failure. Every muscle in his body was working in perfect co-ordination with its fellows, his wrists felt as if they were made of tempered steel, and his eyes had just that hawk-like quality which enables a man to judge his short approaches to the inch. He swung forcefully, and the ball sailed so close to the direction-post that for a moment it seemed as if it had hit it.

"Ooo!" cried Felicia.

Chester did not speak. He was following the flight of the ball. It sailed over the brow of the hill, and with his knowledge of the course he could tell almost the exact patch of turf on which it must have come to rest. An iron would do the business from there, and a single putt would give him the first of the "birdies" he required. Two minutes later he had holed out a six-foot putt for a three.

"Oo!" said Felicia again.

Chester walked to the eleventh tee in silence.

"No, never mind," she said, as he stooped to put her ball on the sand. "I don't think I'll play any more. I'd much rather just watch you."

"Oh, that you could watch me through life!" said Chester, but he said it to himself. His actual words were "Very well!" and he spoke them with a stiff coldness which chilled the girl.

The eleventh is one of the trickiest holes on the course, as no doubt you have found out for yourself. It looks absurdly simple, but that little patch of wood on the right that seems so harmless is placed just in the deadliest position to catch even the most slightly sliced drive. Chester's lacked the austere precision of his last. A hundred yards from the tee it swerved almost imperceptibly, and, striking a branch, fell in the tangled undergrowth. It took him two strokes to hack it out and put it on the green, and then his long putt, after quivering on the edge of the hole, stayed there. For a swift instant red-hot words rose to his lips, but he caught them just as they were coming out and crushed them back. He looked at his ball and he looked at the hole.

"Tut!" said Chester.

Felicia uttered a deep sigh. The niblick-shot out of the rough had impressed her profoundly. If only, she felt, this superb golfer had been more human! If only she were able to be constantly in this man's society, to see exactly what it was that he did with his left wrist that gave that terrific snap to his drives, she might acquire the knack herself one of these days. For she was a clearthinking, honest girl, and thoroughly realised that she did not get the distance she ought to with her wood. With a husband like Chester beside her to stimulate and advise, of what might she not be capable? If she got wrong in her stance, he could put her right with a word. If she had a bout of slicing, how quickly he would tell her what caused it. And she knew that she had only to speak the word to wipe out the effects of her refusal, to bring him to her side for ever.

But could a girl pay such a price? When he had got that "eagle" on the third, he had looked bored. When he had missed this last putt, he had not seemed to care. "Tut!" What a word to use at such a moment! No, she felt sadly, it could not be done. To marry Chester Meredith, she told herself, would be like marrying a composite of Soames Forsyte, Sir Willoughby Patterne, and all her brother Crispin's friends. She sighed and was silent.

Chester, standing on the twelfth tee, reviewed the situation swiftly, like a general before a battle. There were seven holes to play, and he had to do these in two better than bogey. The one that faced him now offered few opportunities. It was a long, slogging, dog-leg hole, and even Ray and Taylor, when they had played their exhibition game on the course, had taken fives. No opening there.

The thirteenth—up a steep hill with a long iron-shot for one's second and a blind green fringed with bunkers? Scarcely practicable to hope for better than a four. The fourteenth—into the valley with the ground sloping sharply down to the ravine? He had once done it in three, but it had been a fluke. No; on these three holes he must be content to play for a steady par and trust to picking up a stroke on the fifteenth.

The fifteenth, straightforward up to the plateau green with its circle of bunkers, presents few difficulties to the finished golfer who is on his game. A bunker meant nothing to Chester in his present conquering vein. His mashie-shot second soared almost contemptuously over the chasm and rolled to within a foot of the pin. He came to the sixteenth with the clear-cut problem before him of snipping two strokes off par on the last three holes.

To the unthinking man, not acquainted with the layout of our links, this would no doubt appear a tremendous feat. But the fact is, the Green Committee, with perhaps an unduly sentimental bias towards the happy ending, have arranged a comparatively easy finish to the course. The sixteenth is a perfectly plain hole with broad fairway and a down-hill run; the seventeenth, a one-shot affair with no difficulties for the man who keeps them straight; and the eighteenth, though its up-hill run makes it deceptive to the stranger and leads the un-wary to take a mashie instead of a light iron for his second, has no real venom in it. Even Peter Willard has occasionally come home in a canter with a six, five, and seven, conceding himself only two eight-foot putts. It is, I think, this mild conclusion to a tough course that makes the refreshment-room of our club so noticeable for its sea of happy faces. The bar every day is crowded with rejoicing men who, forgetting the agonies of the first fifteen, are babbling of what they did on the last three. The seventeenth, with its possibilities of holing out a topped second, is particularly soothing.

Chester Meredith was not the man to top his second on any hole, so this supreme bliss did not come his way; but he laid a beautiful mashie-shot dead and got a three; and when with his iron he put his first well on the green at the seventeenth and holed out for a two, life, for all his broken heart, seemed pretty tolerable. He now had the situation well in hand. He had only to play his usual game to get a four on the last and lower the course record by one stroke.

It was at this supreme moment of his life that he ran into the Wrecking Crew.

You doubtless find it difficult to understand how it came about that if the Wrecking Crew were on the course at all he had not run into them long before. The explanation is that, with a regard for the etiquette of the game unusual in these miserable men, they had for once obeyed the law that enacts that foursomes shall start at the tenth. They had begun their dark work on the second nine, accordingly, at almost the exact moment when Chester Meredith was driving off at the first, and this had enabled them to keep ahead until now. When Chester came to the eighteenth tee, they were just leaving it, moving up the fairway with their caddies in mass formation and looking to his exasperated eye like one of those great race-migrations of the Middle Ages. Wherever Chester looked he seemed to see human, so to speak, figures. One was doddering about in the long grass fifty yards from the tee, others debouched to left and right. The course was crawling with them.

Chester sat down on the bench with a weary sigh. He knew these men. Self-centred, remorseless, deaf to all the promptings of their better nature, they never let anyone through. There was nothing to do but wait.

The Wrecking Crew scratched on. The man near the tee rolled his ball ten yards, then twenty, then thirty—he was improving. Ere long he would be out of range. Chester rose and swished his driver.

But the end was not yet. The individual operating in the rough on the left had been advancing in slow stages, and now finding his ball teed up on a tuft of grass, he opened his shoulders and let himself go. There was a loud report, and the ball, hitting a tree squarely, bounded back almost to the tee, and all the weary work was to do again. By the time Chester was able to drive, he was reduced by impatience, and the necessity of refraining from commenting on the state of affairs as he would have wished to comment, to a frame of mind in which no man could have kept himself from pressing. He pressed, and topped. The ball skidded over the turf for a meagre hundred yards.

"D-d-d-dear me!" said Chester.

The next moment he uttered a bitter laugh. Too late a miracle had happened. One of the foul figures in front was waving its club. Other ghastly creatures were withdrawing to the side of the fairway. Now, when the harm had been done, these outcasts were signalling to him to go through. The hollow mockery of the thing swept over Chester like a wave. What was the use of going through now? He was a good three hundred yards from the green, and he needed bogey at this hole to break the record. Almost absently he drew his brassie from his bag; then, as the full sense of his wrongs bit into his soul, he swung viciously.

Golf is a strange game. Chester had pressed on the tee and foozled. He pressed now, and achieved the most perfect shot of his life. The ball shot from its place as if a charge of powerful explosive were behind it. Never deviating from a straight line, never more than six feet from the ground, it sailed up the hill, crossed the bunker, eluded the mounds beyond, struck the turf, rolled, and stopped fifty feet from the hole. It was a brassie-shot of a lifetime, and shrill senile yippings of excitement and congratulation floated down from the Wrecking Crew. For, degraded though they were, these men were not wholly devoid of human instincts.

Chester drew a deep breath. His ordeal was over. That third shot, which would lay the ball right up to the pin, was precisely the sort of thing he did best. Almost from boyhood he had been a wizard at the short approach. He could hole out in two now on his left ear. He strode up the hill to his ball. It could not have been lying better. Two inches away there was a nasty cup in the turf; but it had avoided this and was sitting nicely perched up, smiling an invitation to the mashie-niblick. Chester shuffled his feet and eyed the flag keenly. Then he stooped to play, and Felicia watched him breathlessly. Her whole being seemed to be concentrated on him. She had forgotten everything save that she was seeing a course record get broken. She could not have been more wrapped up in his success if she had had large sums of money on it.

The Wrecking Crew, meanwhile, had come to life again. They had stopped twittering about Chester's brassie-shot and were thinking of resuming their own game. Even in foursomes where fifty yards is reckoned a good shot somebody must be away, and the man whose turn it was to play was the one who had acquired from his brother-members of the club the nickname of the First Grave-Digger.

A word about this human wen. He was—if there can be said to be grades in such a sub-species—the star performer of the Wrecking Crew. The lunches of fifty-seven years had caused his chest to slip down into the mezzanine floor, but he was still a powerful man, and had in his youth been a hammer-thrower of some repute. He differed from his colleagues—the Man With the Hoe, Old Father Time, and Consul, the Almost Human—in that, while they were content to peck cautiously at the ball, he never spared himself in his efforts to do it a violent injury. Frequently he had cut a blue dot almost in half with his niblick. He was completely muscle-bound, so that he seldom achieved anything beyond a series of chasms in the turf, but he was always trying, and it was his secret belief that, given two or three miracles happening simultaneously, he would one of these days bring off a snifter. Years of disappointment had, however, reduced the flood of hope to a mere trickle, and when he took his brassie now and addressed the ball he had no immediate plans beyond a vague intention of rolling the thing a few yards farther up the hill.

The fact that he had no business to play at all till Chester had holed out did not occur to him; and even if it had occurred he would have dismissed the objection as finicking. Chester, bending over his ball, was nearly two hundred yards away—or the distance of three full brassie-shots. The First Grave-Digger did not hesitate. He whirled up his club as in distant days he had been wont to swing the hammer, and, with the grunt which this performance always wrung from him, brought it down.

Golfers—and I stretch this term to include the Wrecking Crew—are a highly imitative race. The spectacle of a flubber flubbering ahead of us on the fairway inclines to make us flub as well; and, conversely, it is immediately after we have seen a magnificent shot that we are apt to eclipse ourselves. Consciously the Grave-Digger had no notion how Chester had made that superb brassie-biff of his, but all the while I suppose his subconscious self had been taking notes. At any rate, on this one occasion he, too, did the shot of a lifetime. As he opened his eyes, which he always shut tightly at the moment of impact, and started to unravel himself from the complicated tangle in which his follow-through had left him, he perceived the ball breasting the hill like some untamed jack-rabbit of the Californian prairie.

For a moment his only emotion was one of dreamlike amazement. He stood looking at the ball with a wholly impersonal wonder, like a man suddenly confronted with some terrific work of Nature. Then, as a sleepwalker awakens, he came to himself with a start. Directly in front of the flying ball was a man bending to make an approach-shot.

Chester, always a concentrated golfer when there was man's work to do, had scarcely heard the crack of the brassie behind him. Certainly he had paid no attention to it. His whole mind was fixed on his stroke. He measured with his eye the distance to the pin, noted the down-slope of the green, and shifted his stance a little to allow for it. Then, with a final swift waggle, he laid his club-head behind the ball and slowly raised it. It was just coming down when the world became full of shouts of "Fore!" and something hard smote him violently on the seat of his plus-fours.

The supreme tragedies of life leave us momentarily stunned. For an instant which seemed an age Chester could not understand what had happened. True, he realised that there had been an earthquake, a cloud-burst, and a railway accident, and that a high building had fallen on him at the exact moment when somebody had shot him with a gun, but these happenings would account for only a small part of his sensations. He blinked several times, and rolled his eyes wildly. And it was while rolling them that he caught sight of the gesticulating Wrecking Crew on the lower slopes and found enlightenment. Simultaneously, he observed his ball only a yard and a half from where it had been when he addressed it.

Chester Meredith gave one look at his ball, one look at the flag, one look at the Wrecking Crew, one look at the sky. His lips writhed, his forehead turned vermilion. Beads of perspiration started out on his forehead. And then, with his whole soul seething like a cistern struck by a thunderbolt, he spoke.

"! ! ! ! ! ! ! ! ! ! ! ! ! ! !" cried Chester.

Dimly he was aware of a wordless exclamation from the girl beside him, but he was too distraught to think of her now. It was as if all the oaths pent up within his bosom for so many weary days were struggling and jostling to see which could get out first. They cannoned into each other, they linked hands and formed parties, they got themselves all mixed up in weird vowel-sounds, the second syllable of some red-hot verb forming a temporary union with the first syllable of some blistering noun.

"——! ——!! ——!!! ——!!!! ——!!!!!" cried Chester.

Felicia stood staring at him. In her eyes was the look of one who sees visions.

"★★★!!! ★★★!!! ★★★!!! ★★★!!!" roared Chester, in part.

A great wave of emotion flooded over the girl. How she had misjudged this silver-tongued man! She shivered as she thought that, had this not happened, in another five minutes they would have parted for ever, sundered by seas of misunderstanding, she cold and scornful, he with all his music still within him.

"Oh, Mr. Meredith!" she cried faintly.

With a sickening abruptness Chester came to himself. It

was as if somebody had poured a pint of ice-cold water down his back. He blushed vividly. He realised with horror and shame how grossly he had offended against all the canons of decency and good taste. He felt like the man in one of those "What Is Wrong With This Picture?" things in the advertisements of the etiquette-books.

"I beg—I beg your pardon!" he mumbled, humbly. "Please, please, forgive me. I should not have spoken like that."

"You should! You should!" cried the girl, passionately. "You should have said all that and a lot more. That awful man ruining your record round like that! Oh, why I am a poor weak woman with practically no vocabulary that's any use for anything!"

Quite suddenly, without knowing that she had moved, she found herself at his side, holding his hand.

"Oh, to think how I misjudged you!" she wailed. "I thought you cold, stiff, formal, precise. I hated the way you sniggered when you foozled a shot. I see it all now! You were keeping it in for my sake. Can you ever forgive me?"

Chester, as I have said, was not a very quick-minded young man, but it would have taken a duller youth than he to fail to read the message in the girl's eyes, to miss the meaning of the pressure of her hand on his.

"My gosh!" he exclaimed wildly. "Do you mean——? Do you think——? Do you really——? Honestly, has this made a difference? Is there any chance for a fellow, I mean?"

Her eyes helped him on. He felt suddenly confident and masterful.

"Look here—no kidding—will you marry me?" he said.

"I will! I will!"

"Darling!" cried Chester.

He would have said more, but at this point he was interrupted by the arrival of the Wrecking Crew, who panted up full of apologies; and Chester, as he eyed them, thought that he had never seen a nicer, cheerier, pleasanter lot of fellows in his life. His heart warmed to them. He made a mental resolve to hunt them up some time and have a good long talk. He waved the Grave-Digger's remorse airily aside.

"Don't mention it," he said. "Not at all. Faults on both sides. By the way, my *fiancée*, Miss Blakeney."

The Wrecking Crew puffed acknowledgment.

"But, my dear fellow," said the Grave-Digger, "it was—really it was—unforgivable. Spoiling your shot. Never dreamed I would send the ball that distance. Lucky you weren't playing an important match."

"But he was," moaned Felicia. "He was trying for the course record, and now he can't break it."

The Wrecking Crew paled behind their whiskers, aghast at this tragedy, but Chester, glowing with the yeasty intoxication of love, laughed lightly.

"What do you mean, can't break it?" he cried, cheerily. "I've one more shot."

And, carelessly addressing the ball, he holed out with a light flick of his mashie-niblick.

"Chester, darling!" said Felicia.

They were walking slowly through a secluded glade in the quiet evenfall.

"Yes, precious?"

Felicia hesitated. What she was going to say would hurt him, she knew, and her love was so great that to hurt him was agony.

"Do you think——" she began. "I wonder whether—— It's about Crispin."

"Good old Crispin!"

Felicia sighed, but the matter was too vital to be shirked. Cost what it might, she must speak her mind.

"Chester, darling, when we are married, would you mind very, *very* much if we didn't have Crispin with us *all* the time?"

Chester started.

"Good Lord!" he exclaimed. "Don't you like him?"

"Not very much," confessed Felicia. "I don't think I'm clever enough for him. I've rather disliked him ever since we were children. But I know what a friend he is of yours——"

Chester uttered a joyous laugh.

"Friend of mine! Why, I can't stand the blighter! I loathe the worm! I abominate the excrescence! I only pretended we were friends because I thought it would put me in solid with you. The man is a pest and should have been strangled at birth. At school I used to kick him every time I saw him. If your brother Crispin tries so much as to set foot across the threshold of our little home, I'll set the dog on him."

"Darling!" whispered Felicia. "We shall be very, very happy." She drew her arm through his. "Tell me, dearest," she murmured, "all about how you used to kick Crispin at school."

And together they wandered off into the sunset.

*　　*　　*　　*　　*

Big chap with a small moustache and the sort of eye that can open an oyster at sixty paces.

"Man and boy, Jeeves, I have been in some tough spots in my time, but this one wins the mottled oyster."

"Certainly a somewhat sharp crisis in your affairs would appear to have been precipitated, sir."

A DAMSEL IN DISTRESS

"A ROTTEN world," George mused, as the cab, after proceeding a couple of yards, came to a standstill in a block of the traffic. "A dull, flat bore of a world, in which nothing happens or ever will happen. Even when you take a cab it just sticks and doesn't move."

At this point the door of the cab opened, and the girl in brown jumped in.

"I'm so sorry," she said breathlessly, "but would you mind hiding me, please."

$$*\qquad*\qquad*\qquad*\qquad*$$

George hid her. He did it, too, without wasting precious time by asking questions. In a situation which might well have thrown the quickest-witted of men off his balance, he acted with promptitude, intelligence and despatch. The fact is, George had for years been an assiduous golfer; and there is no finer school for teaching concentration and a strict attention to the matter in hand. Few crises, however unexpected, have the power to disturb a man who has so conquered the weakness of the flesh as to have trained himself to bend his left knee, raise his left heel, swing his arms well out from the body, twist himself into the shape of a corkscrew and use the muscle of the wrist, at the same time keeping his head still and his eye on the ball. It is estimated that there are twenty-three important points to be borne in mind simultaneously while making a drive at golf; and to the man who has mastered the art of remembering them all the task of hiding girls in taxicabs is mere child's play. To pull down the blinds on the side of the vehicle nearest the kerb was with George the work of a moment. Then he leaned out of the centre window in such a manner as completely to screen the interior of the cab from public view.

"Thank you so much," murmured a voice behind him. It seemed to come from the floor.

"Not at all," said George, trying a sort of vocal chip-shot out of the corner of his mouth, designed to lift his voice backwards and lay it dead inside the cab.

He gazed upon Piccadilly with eyes from which the scales had fallen. Reason told him that he was still in Piccadilly. Otherwise it would have seemed incredible to him that this could be the same street which a moment before he had passed judgment upon and found flat and uninteresting. True, in its salient features it had altered little. The same number of stodgy-looking people moved up and down. The buildings retained their air of not having had a bath since the days of the Tudors. The east wind still blew. But, though superficially the same, in reality Piccadilly had altered completely. Before it had been just Piccadilly. Now it was a golden street in the City of Romance, a main thoroughfare of Baghdad, one of the principal arteries of the capital of Fairyland. A rose-coloured mist swam before George's eyes. His spirits, so low but a few moments back, soared like a good niblick shot out of the bunker of Gloom. The years fell away from him till, in an instant, from being a rather poorly preserved, liverish greybeard of sixty-five or so, he became a sprightly lad of twenty-one in a world of springtime and flowers and laughing brooks. In other words, taking it by and large, George felt pretty good. The impossible had happened; Heaven had sent him an adventure, and he didn't care if it snowed.

It was possibly the rose-coloured mist before his eyes that prevented him from observing the hurried approach of a faultlessly-attired young man, aged about twenty-one, who during George's preparations for ensuring privacy in his cab had been galloping in pursuit in a resolute manner that suggested a well-dressed bloodhound somewhat overfed and out of condition. Only when this person stopped and began to pant within a few inches of his face did he become aware of his existence.

"You, sir!" said the bloodhound, removing a gleaming silk hat, mopping a pink forehead, and replacing the luminous superstructure once more in position. "You, sir!"

Whatever may be said of the possibility of love at first sight, in which theory George was now a confirmed believer, there can be no doubt that an exactly opposite phenomenon is of frequent occurrence. After one look at some people even friendship is impossible. Such a one, in George's opinion, was this gurgling excrescence underneath the silk hat. He comprised in his single person practically all the qualities which George disliked most. He was, for a young man, extraordinarily obese. Already a second edition of his chin had been published, and the perfectly-cut morning coat which encased his upper section bulged out in an opulent semicircle. He wore a little moustache, which to George's prejudiced eye seemed more a complaint than a moustache. His face was red, his manner dictatorial, and he was touched in the wind. Take him for all in all he looked like a bit of bad news.

George had been educated at Lawrenceville and Harvard, and had subsequently had the privilege of mixing socially with many of New York's most prominent theatrical managers; so he knew how to behave himself. No Vere de Vere could have exhibited greater repose of manner.

"And what," he inquired suavely, leaning a little further out of the cab, "is eating *you*, Bill?"

A messenger boy, two shabby men engaged in nonessential industries, and a shop girl paused to observe the scene. Time was not of the essence to these confirmed sightseers. The shop girl was late already, so it didn't matter if she was any later; the messenger boy had nothing on hand except a message marked "Important: Rush"; and as for the two shabby men, their only immediate plans consisted of a vague intention of getting to some public house and leaning against the wall; so George's time was their time. One of the pair put his head on one side and said: "What ho!" the other picked up a cigar stub from the gutter and began to smoke.

"A young lady got into your cab," said the stout young man.

"Surely not?" said George.

"What the devil do you mean—surely not?"

"I've been in the cab all the time, and I should have noticed it."

At this juncture the block in the traffic was relieved, and the cab bowled smartly on for some fifty yards when it was again halted. George, protruding from the window like a snail, was entertained by the spectacle of the pursuit. The hunt was up. Short of throwing his head up and baying, the stout young man behaved exactly as a bloodhound in similar circumstances would have conducted itself. He broke into a jerky gallop, attended by his self-appointed associates; and, considering that the young man was so stout, that the messenger boy considered it unprofessional to hurry, that the shop girl had doubts as to whether sprinting was quite lady-like, and that the two Bohemians were moving at a quicker gait than a shuffle for the first occasion in eleven years, the cavalcade made good time. The cab was still stationary when they arrived in a body.

"Here he is, guv'nor," said the messenger boy, removing a bead of perspiration with the rush message.

"Here he is, guv'nor," said the non-smoking Bohemian. "What oh!"

"Here I am!" agreed George affably. "And what can I do for you?"

The smoker spat appreciatively at a passing dog. The point seemed to him well taken. Not for many a day had he so enjoyed himself. In an arid world containing too few goes of gin and too many policemen, a world in which the poor were oppressed and could seldom even enjoy a quiet cigar without having their fingers trodden upon, he found himself for the moment contented, happy, and expectant. This looked like a row between toffs, and of all things which most intrigued him a row between toffs ranked highest.

"R!" he said approvingly. "Now you're torking!"

The shop girl had espied an acquaintance in the crowd. She gave tongue.

"Mordee! Cummere! Cummere quick! Sumfin' hap'nin'!"

Maudie, accompanied by perhaps a dozen more of London's millions, added herself to the audience. These all belonged to the class which will gather round and watch silently while a motorist mends a tyre. They are not impatient. They do not call for rapid and continuous action. A mere hole in the ground, which of all sights is perhaps the least vivid and dramatic, is enough to grip their attention for hours at a time. They stared at George and George's cab with unblinking gaze. They did not know what would happen or when it would happen, but they intended to wait till something did happen. It might be for years or it might be for ever, but they meant to be there when things began to occur.

Speculations became audible.

"Wot is it? 'Naccident?"

"Nah! Gent 'ad 'is pocket picked!"

"Two toffs 'ad a scrap!"

"Feller bilked the cabman!"

A sceptic made a cynical suggestion.

"They're doin' of it for the pictures."

The idea gained instant popularity.

"'Jear that? It's a fillum!"

"Wot o', Charlie!"

"The kemerer's 'idden in the keb."

"Wot'll they be up to next!"

A red-nosed spectator with a tray of collar-studs harnessed to his stomach started another school of thought. He spoke with decision as one having authority.

"Nothin' of the blinkin' kind! The fat 'un's bin 'avin' one or two around the corner, and it's gorn and got into 'is 'ead!"

The driver of the cab, who till now had been ostentatiously unaware that there was any sort of disturbance among the lower orders, suddenly became humanly inquisitive.

"What's it all about?" he asked, swinging round and addressing George's head.

"Exactly what I want to know," said George. He indicated the collar-stud merchant. "The gentleman over there with the portable Woolworth-bargain-counter seems to me to have the best theory."

The stout young man, whose peculiar behaviour had drawn all this flattering attention from the many-headed and who appeared considerably ruffled by the publicity, had been puffing noisily during the foregoing conversation. Now, having recovered sufficient breath to resume the attack, he addressed himself to George once more.

"Damn you, sir, will you let me look inside that cab?"

"Leave me," said George, "I would be alone."

"There is a young lady in that cab. I saw her get in, and I have been watching ever since, and she has not got out, so she is there now."

George nodded approval of this close reasoning.

"Your argument seems to be without a flaw. But what then? We applaud the Man of Logic, but what of the Man of Action? What are you going to do about it?"

"Get out of my way!"

"I won't."

"Then I'll force my way in!"

"If you try it, I shall infallibly bust you one on the jaw."

The stout young man drew back a pace.

"You can't do that sort of thing, you know."

"I know I can't," said George, "but I shall. In this life, my dear sir, we must be prepared for every emergency. We must distinguish between the unusual and the impossible. It would be unusual for a comparative stranger to lean out of a cab window and sock you one, but you appear to have laid your plans on the assumption that it would be impossible. Let this be a lesson to you!"

"I tell you what it is——"

"The advice I give to every young man starting life is 'Never confuse the unusual with the impossible!' Take the present case, for instance. If you had only realized the possibility of somebody some day busting you on the jaw when you tried to get into a cab, you might have thought out dozens of crafty schemes for dealing with the matter. As it is, you are unprepared. The thing comes on you as a surprise. The whisper flies around the clubs: 'Poor old What's-his-name has been taken unawares. He cannot cope with the situation!' "

The man with the collar-studs made another diagnosis. He was seeing clearer and clearer into the thing every minute.

"Looney!" he decided. "This 'ere one's bin moppin' of it up, and the one in the keb's orf 'is bloomin' onion. That's why 'e 's standin' up instead of settin'. 'E won't set down 'cept you bring 'im a bit o' toast, 'cos he thinks 'e 's a poached egg."

George beamed upon the intelligent fellow.

"Your reasoning is admirable, but——"

He broke off here, not because he had not more to say, but for the reason that the stout young man, now in quite a Berserk frame of mind, made a sudden spring at the cab door and clutched the handle, which he was about to wrench when George acted with all the promptitude and decision which had marked his behaviour from the start.

It was a situation which called for the nicest judgment. To allow the assailant free play with the handle or even to wrestle with him for its possession entailed the risk that the door might open and reveal the girl. To bust the young man on the jaw, as promised, on the other hand, was not in George's eyes a practical policy. Excellent a deterrent as the threat of such a proceeding might be, its actual accomplishment was not to be thought of. Gaols yawn and actions for assault lie in wait for those who go about the place busting their fellows on the jaw. No. Something swift, something decided and immediate was indicated, but something that stopped short of technical battery.

George brought his hand round with a sweep and knocked the stout young man's silk hat off.

The effect was magical. We all of us have our Achilles' heel, and—paradoxically enough—in the case of the stout young man that heel was his hat. Superbly built by the only hatter in London who can construct a silk hat that is a silk hat, and freshly ironed by loving hands but a brief hour before at the only shaving-parlour in London where ironing is ironing and not a brutal attack, it was his pride and joy. To lose it was like losing his trousers. It made him feel insufficiently clad. With a passionate cry like that of some wild creature deprived of its young, the erstwhile Berserk released the handle and sprang in pursuit. At the same moment the traffic moved on again.

The last George saw was a group scene with the stout young man in the middle of it. The hat had been popped up into the infield, where it had been caught by the messenger boy. The stout young man was bending over it and stroking it with soothing fingers. It was too far off for anything to be audible, but he seemed to George to be murmuring words of endearment to it. Then, placing it on his head, he darted out into the road and George saw him no more. The audience remained motionless, staring at the spot where the incident had happened. They would continue to do this till the next policeman came along and moved them on.

With a pleasant wave of farewell, in case any of them might be glancing in his direction, George drew in his body and sat down.

The girl in brown had risen from the floor, if she had ever been there, and was now seated composedly at the further end of the cab.

Extract from an early chapter in: "A Damsel in Distress."

*A confirmed recluse you would have called him,
if you had happened to know the word.*

FORE!

THIS BOOK marks an epoch in my literary career. It is written in blood. It is the outpouring of a soul as deeply seared by Fate's unkindness as the pretty on the dog-leg hole of the second nine was ever seared by my iron. It is the work of a very nearly desperate man, an eighteen-handicap man, who has got to look extremely slippy if he doesn't want to find himself in the twenties again.

As a writer of light fiction, I have always till now been handicapped by the fact that my disposition was cheerful, my heart intact, and my life unsoured. Handicapped, I say, because the public likes to feel that a writer of farcical stories is piquantly miserable in his private life, and that, if he turns out anything amusing, he does it simply in order to obtain relief from the most insupportable weight of an existence which he has long since realised to be a wash-out. Well, to-day I am just like that.

Two years ago, I admit, I was a shallow *farceur*. My work lacked depth. I wrote flippantly simply because I was having a thoroughly good time. Then I took up golf, and now I can smile through the tears and laugh, like Figaro, that I may not weep, and generally hold my head up and feel that I am entitled to respect.

If you find anything in this volume that amuses you, kindly bear in mind that it was probably written on my return home after losing three balls in the gorse or breaking the head off a favourite driver: and, with a murmured, "Brave fellow! Brave fellow!" recall the story of the clown jesting while his child lay dying at home. That is all. Thank you for your sympathy. It means more to me than I can say. Do you think that if I tried the square stance for a bit . . . But, after all, this cannot interest you. Leave me to my misery.

Postscript.—In the second chapter I allude to Stout Cortez staring at the Pacific. Shortly after the appearance of this narrative in serial form in America, I received an anonymous letter containing the words, "You big stiff, it wasn't Cortez, it was Balboa." This, I believe, is historically accurate. On the other hand, if Cortez was good enough for Keats, he is good enough for me. Besides, even if it *was* Balboa, the Pacific was open for being stared at about that time, and I see no reason why Cortez should not have had a look at it as well.

Author's Preface, "Clicking of Cuthbert."

HOLLYWOOD INTERLUDE

WHETHER BY pure spontaneous combustion, or because I had inadvertently taken aboard too large a segment of ice-cream, the old Havershot wisdom tooth had begun to assert its personality.

I had had my eye on this tooth for some time, and I suppose I ought to have taken a firm line with it before. But you know how it is when you're travelling. You shrink from entrusting the snappers to a strange dentist. You say to yourself: "Stick it out, old cock, till you get back to London and can toddle round to the maestro who's been looking after you since you were so high." And then, of course, you cop it unexpectedly, as I had done. So next day I was in the dentist's waiting-room, about to keep my tryst with I. J. Zizzbaum, the man behind the forceps.

Across the room in an arm-chair, turning the pages of the National Geographic Magazine, was a kid of the Little Lord Fauntleroy type. His left cheek, like mine, was bulging, and I deduced that we were both awaiting the awful summons.

He was, I observed, a kid of singular personal beauty. Not even the bulge in his cheek could conceal that. He had large, expressive eyes and golden ringlets. Long lashes hid these eyes as he gazed down at his National Geographic Magazine.

I never know what's the correct course to pursue on occasions like this. Should one try to help things along with a friendly word or two, if only about the weather? Or is silence best? I was just debating this question in my mind, when he opened the conversation himself.

He lowered his National Geographic Magazine and looked across at me.

"Where," he asked, "are the rest of the boys?"

His meaning eluded me. I didn't get him. A cryptic kid. One of those kids, who, as the expression is, speak in riddles.

He was staring at me enquiringly, and I stared at him, also enquiringly.

Then I said, going straight to the point and evading all side issues:

"What boys?"

"The newspaper boys."

"The newspaper boys?"

An idea seemed to strike him.

"Aren't you a reporter?"

"No, not a reporter."

"Then what are you doing here?"

"I've come to have a tooth out."

This appeared to surprise and displease him. He said, with marked acerbity:

"You can't have come to have a tooth out."

"Yes, I have."

"But I've come to have a tooth out."

I spotted a possible solution.

"Perhaps," I said, throwing out the suggestion for what it was worth, "we've both come to have a tooth out, what? I mean to say, you one and me another. Tooth A, and Tooth B., as it were."

He still seemed ruffled. He eyed me searchingly.

"When's your appointment?"

"Three-thirty."

"It can't be. Mine is."

"So is mine. I. J. Zizzbaum was most definite about that. We arranged it over the 'phone, and his words left no loophole for misunderstanding. 'Three-thirty,' said I. J. Zizzbaum, as plain as I see you now."

The kid became calmer. His alabaster brow lost its frown, and he ceased to regard me as if I were some hijacker or bandit. It was as if a great light had shone upon him.

"Oh, I. J. Zizzbaum?" he said. "B. K. Burwash is doing mine."

And, looking about me, I now perceived that on either side of the apartment in which we sat was a door.

On one of these doors was imprinted the legend:

I. J. ZIZZBAUM.

And on the other:

B. K. BURWASH.

The mystery was solved. Possibly because they were old dental college chums, or possibly from motives of economy, these two fang-wrenchers shared a common waiting-room.

Convinced now that no attempt was being made to jump his claim, the kid had become affability itself. Seeing in me no rival for first whack at the operating-chair, but merely a fellow human being up against the facts of life just as he was, he changed his tone to one of kindly interest.

"Does your tooth hurt?"

"Like the dickens."

"So does mine. Coo!"

"Coo here, too."

"Where does it seem to catch you most?"

"Pretty well all the way down to the toenails."

"Me, too. This tooth of mine is certainly fierce. Yessir."

"So is mine."

"I'll bet mine's worse than yours."

"It couldn't be."

He made what he evidently considered a telling point.

"I'm having gas."

I came right back at him.

"So am I."

"I'll bet I need more gas than you."

"I'll bet you don't."

"I'll bet you a trillion dollars I do."

It seemed to me that rancour was beginning to creep into the conversation once more, and that pretty soon we would be descending to a common wrangle. So, rather than allow the harmony of the proceedings to be marred by a jarring note, I dropped the theme and switched off to an aspect of the matter which had been puzzling me from the first. You will remember that I had thought this kid to have spoken in riddles, and I still wanted an explanation of those rather mystic opening words of his.

"You're probably right," I said pacifically. "But, be that as it may, what made you think I was a reporter?"

"I'm expecting a flock of them here."

"You are?"

"Sure. There'll be camera men, too, and human interest writers."

"What, to see you have a tooth out?"

"Sure. When I have a tooth out, that's news."

"What?"

"Sure. This is going to make the front page of every paper in the country."

"What, your tooth?"

"Yay, my tooth. Listen, when I had my tonsils extracted last year, it rocked civilization. I'm some shucks, I want to tell you."

"Somebody special, you mean?"

"I'll say that's what I mean. I'm Joey Cooley."

Owing to the fact that one of my unswerving rules in life is never to go to a picture if I am informed by my spies that there is a child in it, I had never actually set eyes on this stripling. But of course I knew the name. Ann, if you remember, had spoken of him. So had April June.

"Oh, ah," I said. "Joey Cooley, eh?"

"Joey Cooley is correct."

"Yes, I've heard of you."

"So I should think."

"I know your nurse."

"My what?"

"Well, your female attendant or whatever she is. Ann Bannister."

"Oh, Ann? She's an all-right guy, Ann is."

"Quite."

"A corker, and don't let anyone tell you different."

"I won't."

"Ann's a peach. Yessir, that's what Ann is."

"And April June was talking about you the other day."

"Oh, yeah? And what did she have to say?"

"She told me you were in her last picture."

"She did, did she?" He snorted with not a little violence, and his brow darkened. It was plain that he was piqued. Meaning nothing but to pass along a casual item of information, I appeared to have touched some exposed nerve. "The crust of that dame! In *her* last picture, eh? Let me tell you that *she* was in *my* last picture!"

He snorted a bit more. He had taken up the National Geographic Magazine again, and I noted that it quivered in his hands, as if he were wrestling with some powerful emotion. Presently the spasm passed, and he was himself again.

"So you've met that pill, have you?" he said.

It was my turn to quiver, and I did so like a jelly.

"That what?"

"That pill."

"Did you say 'pill'?"

" 'Pill' was what I said. Slice her where you like, she's still boloney."

I drew myself up.

"You are speaking," I said, "of the woman I love."

He started to say something, but I raised my hand coldly and said "Please," and silence supervened. He read his National Geographic Magazine. I read mine. And for some minutes matters proceeded along these lines. Then I thought to myself: "Oh, well, dash it," and decided to extend the olive branch. Too damn silly, I mean, a couple of fellows on the brink of having teeth out simply sitting reading the National Geographic Magazine at one another instead of trying to forget by means of pleasant chit-chat the ordeal which lay before them.

"So you're Joey Cooley?" I said.

He accepted the overture in the spirit in which it was intended.

"You never spoke a truer word," he replied agreeably. "That's about who I am, if you come right down to it. Joey Cooley, the Idol of American Motherhood. Who are you?"

"Havershot's my name."

"English, aren't you?"

"That's right."

"Been in Hollywood long?"

"About a week."

"Where are you staying?"

"I've a bungalow at the Garden of the Hesperides."

"Do you like Hollywood?"

"Oh, rather. Topping spot."

"You ought to see Chillicothe, Ohio."

"Why?"

"That's where I come from. And that's where I'd like to be now. Yessir, right back there in little old Chillicothe."

"You're homesick, what?"

"You betcher."

"Still, I suppose you have a pretty good time here?"

His face clouded. Once more, it appeared, I had said the wrong thing.

"Who, me? I do not."

"Why not?"

"I'll tell you why not. Because I'm practically a member of a chain gang. I couldn't have it much tougher if this was Devil's Island or the Foreign Legion or sump'n. Do you know what?"

"What?"

"Do you know what old Brinkmeyer did when the contract was being drawn up?"

"No, what?"

"Slipped in a clause that I had to live at his house, so that I could be under his personal eye."

"Who is this Brinkmeyer?"

"The boss of the corporation I work for."

"And you don't like his personal eye?"

"I don't mind him. He's a pretty good sort of old stiff. It's

404

his sister Beulah. She was the one who put him up to it. She's the heavy in the sequence. As tough as they come. Ever hear of Simon Legree?"

"Yes."

"Beulah Brinkmeyer. Know what a serf is?"

"What you swim in, you mean."

"No, I don't mean what you swim in. I mean what's downtrodden and oppressed and gets the dirty end of the stick all the time. That's me. Gosh, what a life! Shall I tell you something?"

"Do."

"I'm not allowed to play games, because I might get hurt. I'm not allowed to keep a dog, because it might bite me. I'm not allowed in the swimming-pool, because I might get drowned. And, listen, get this one. No candy, because I might put on weight."

"You don't mean that?"

"I do mean that. It's in my contract. 'The party of the second part, hereinafter to be called the artist, shall abstain from all ice-creams, chocolate-creams, nut sundaes, fudge, and all-day suckers, hereinafter to be called candy, this is be understood to comprise doughnuts, marshmallows, pies in their season, all starchy foods and twice of chicken.' Can you imagine my lawyer letting them slip that over."

I must say I was a bit appalled. We Havershots have always been good trenchermen, and it never fails to give me a grey feeling when I hear of somebody being on a diet. I know how I should have felt at his age if some strong hand had kept me from the sock-shop.

"I wonder you don't chuck it."

"I can't."

"You love your Art too much?"

"No, I don't."

"You like bringing sunshine into drab lives in Pittsburgh and Cincinnati?"

"I don't care if Pittsburgh chokes. And that goes for Cincinnati, too."

"Then perhaps you feel that all the money and fame make up for these what you might call hideous privations?"

He snorted. He seemed to have as low an opinion of money and fame as April June.

"What's the good of money and fame? I can't eat them, can I? There's nothing I'd like better than to tie a can to the whole outfit and go back to where hearts are pure and men are men in Chillicothe, Ohio. I'd like to be home with mother right now. You should taste her fried chicken, southern style. And she'd be tickled pink to have me, too. But I can't get away. I've a five-year contract, and you can bet they're going to hold me to it."

"I see."

"Oh, yes, I'm Uncle Tom, all right. But listen, shall I tell you something? I'm biding my time. I'm waiting. Some day I'll grow up. And when I do, oh, baby!"

"Oh what?"

"I said 'Oh, baby!' I'm going to poke Beulah Brinkmeyer right in the snoot."

"What! Would you strike a woman?"

"You betcher I'd strike a woman. Yessir, she'll get hers. And there's about six directors I'm going to poke in the snoot, and a whole raft of supervisors and production experts. And that press agent of mine. I'm going to poke him in the snoot, all right. Yessir! Matter of fact," he said, summing up, "you'd have a tough time finding somebody I'm not going to poke in the snoot, once I'm big enough. I've got all their names in a little notebook."

He relapsed into a moody silence, and I didn't quite know what to say. No words of mine, I felt, could cheer this stricken child. The iron had plainly entered a dashed sight too deep into his soul for a mere "Buck up, old bird!" to do any good.

However, as it turned out, I would have had no time to deliver anything in the nature of pep talk, for at this moment the door opened and in poured a susurration of blighters, some male, some female, some with cameras, some without, and the air became so thick with interviewing and picture-talking that it would have been impossible to get a word in. I just sat reading my National Geographic Magazine. And presently a white-robed attendant appeared and announced that B. K. Burwash was straining at the forceps, and the gang passed through into his room, interviewing to the last.

And not long after that another white-robed attendant came and said that I. J. Zizzbaum would be glad if I would look in, so I commended my soul to God, and followed her into the operating theatre.

Extract from "Laughing Gas."

BRIEFLY

"THEY SAY fish are good for the brain. Have a go at the sardines and come back and report."

*   *   *   *   *

"I've always treated the man with unremitting kindness, and if he won't do a little thing like this for me, I'll kick his spine through his hat."

*   *   *   *   *

Blair Eggleston seemed to pull himself together with a strong effort.

"Well, I went in and he was standing there, and before I could get a word out he said, 'Are you honest and sober?'"

"Honest and sober?" squeaked Jane.

"The first thing fathers ask prospective sons-in-laws," Packy assured her. "Pure routine."

"And what did you say?"

"I said I was."

"That sounds like the right answer," said Packy critically.

"And then he asked me if I knew how to take care of clothes. And I said I did. And then he said, 'Well, you don't look like much, but I suppose I've got to give you a trial.' And I suddenly discovered he had engaged me as his valet."

CONCERNING

Events Which Preceded the Episode
Narrated in the Following Chapter

It was the supreme virtuosity of Ben Bloom and his Sixteen Baltimore Buddies that fired Bertram Wooster to make a study of the banjolele and devote many hours to assiduous, if discordant, practice. Immediately, complaints from the other residents of Berkeley Mansions descended upon him and an ultimatum from the manager resulted.

Unconcerned, Bertie announced to Jeeves his intention of taking a cottage in the country there to resume his studies. But, respectful as ever, Jeeves issued a further ultimatum—that if it was Mr. Wooster's intention to play "that instrument" within the narrow confines of a country cottage he would reluctantly have to tender his resignation.

Well, the Woosters have their pride . . .

Thus it is that we find Bertie and his banjolele installed in a cottage at Chuffnell Regis, and Jeeves in the employment of J. Washburn Stoker whose great white yacht is lying off the Chuffnell foreshore. A peaceful setting, you would say, but already the storm clouds have begun to gather. Last night Pauline Stoker who was once engaged to Bertie, paid an ill-timed visit to Bertie's cottage: Chuffy, her fiancé, also appeared on the scene and harsh words ensued. No sooner had the couple departed on their separate ways than Old Man Stoker arrived breathing fire and insisting on searching the house for his errant daughter.

It was a trying night for Bertram.

SINISTER BEHAVIOUR OF A YACHT-OWNER[1]

It was not until I had finished breakfast and was playing the banjolele in the front garden that something seemed to whisper reproachfully in my ear that I had no right to be feeling as perky as this on what was so essentially the morning after. Dirty work had been perpetrated overnight. Tragedy had stalked through the home. Scarcely ten hours earlier I had been a witness of a scene which, if I were the man of fine fibre I like to think myself, should have removed all the sunshine from my life. Two loving hearts, one of which I had been at school and Oxford with, had gone to the mat together in my presence and having chewed holes in one another had parted in anger, never—according to present schedule—to meet again. And here I was, care-free and callous, playing "I Lift Up My Finger And I Say Tweet-Tweet" on the banjolele.

All wrong. I switched to "Body and Soul," and a sober sadness came upon me.

Something, I felt, must be done. Steps must be taken and avenues explored.

But I could not conceal from myself that the situation was complex. Usually, in my experience, when one of my pals has broken off diplomatic relations with a girl or vice versa they have been staying in a country house together or at least living in London; where it wasn't so dashed difficult to arrange a meeting and join their hands with a benevolent smile. But in this matter of Chuffy and Pauline Stoker, consider the facts. She was on the yacht, virtually in irons. He was at the Hall, three miles inland. And anybody who wanted to do any hand-joining had got to be a much more mobile force than I was. True, my standing with old Stoker had improved a bit overnight, but there had been no hint on his part of any disposition to give me the run of his yacht. I seemed to have about as

[1] An Episode from the Novel *Thank You, Jeeves*. See preceding page.

much chance of getting in touch with Pauline and endeavouring to reason with her as if she had never come over from America at all.

Quite a prob., I mean to say, and I was still brooding on it when the garden gate clicked and I perceived Jeeves walking up the path.

"Ah, Jeeves," I said.

My manner probably seemed to him a little distant, and I jolly well meant it to. What Pauline had told me about his loose and unconsidered remarks with reference to my mentality had piqued me considerably. It was not the first time he had said that sort of thing, and one has one's feelings.

But if he sensed the hauteur, he affected to ignore it. His bearing continued placid and unmoved.

"Good morning, sir."

"Have you come from the yacht?"

"Yes, sir."

"Was Miss Stoker there?"

"Yes, sir. She appeared at the breakfast table. I was somewhat surprised to see her. I had assumed that it was her intention to remain ashore and establish communication with his lordship."

I laughed shortly.

"They established communication, all right!"

"Sir?"

I put down the banjolele and looked at him sternly.

"A nice thing you let all and sundry in for last night!" I said.

"Sir?"

"You can't get out of it by saying 'Sir?' Why on earth didn't you stop Miss Stoker from swimming ashore yestreen?"

"I could scarcely take the liberty, sir, of thwarting the young lady in an enterprise on which her heart was so plainly set."

"She says you urged her on with word and gesture."

"No, sir. I merely expressed sympathy with her stated aims."

"You said I would be delighted to put her up for the night."

"She had already decided to seek refuge in your house, sir. I did nothing more than hazard the opinion that you would do all that lay in your power to assist her."

"Well, do you know what the outcome was—the upshot, if I may use the term? I was pursued by the police."

"Indeed, sir?"

"Yes. Naturally I couldn't sleep in the house, with every nook and cranny bulging with blighted girls, so I withdrew to the garage. I had hardly been there ten minutes before Sergeant Voules arrived."

"I have not met Sergeant Voules, sir."

"With him Constable Dobson."

"I am acquainted with Constable Dobson. A nice young fellow. He is keeping company with Mary, the parlourmaid at the Hall. A red-haired girl, sir."

"Resist the urge to talk about the colour of parlourmaids' hair, Jeeves," I said coldly. "It is not germane to the issue. Stick to the point. Which is that I spent a sleepless night, chased to and fro by the gendarmerie."

"I am sorry to hear that, sir."

"Eventually Chuffy arrived. Forming a totally erroneous diagnosis of the case, he insisted on helping me to my room, removing my boots, and putting me to bed. He was thus occupied when Miss Stoker strolled in, wearing my heliotrope pyjamas."

"Most disturbing, sir."

"It was. They had the dickens of a row, Jeeves."

"Indeed, sir?"

"Eyes flashed, voices were raised. Eventually Chuffy fell downstairs and went moodily out into the night. And the point is—the nub of the thing is—what is to be done about it?"

"It is a situation that will require careful thought, sir."

"You mean you have not had any ideas yet?"

"I have only this moment heard what transpired, sir."

"True. I was forgetting that. Have you had speech with Miss Stoker this morning?"

"No, sir."

"Well, I can see no point in your going to the Hall and tackling Chuffy. I have given this matter a good deal of thought, Jeeves, and it is plain to me that Miss Stoker is the one who will require the persuasive word, the nicely reasoned argument—in short, the old oil. Last night Chuffy wounded her deepest feelings, and it's going to take a lot of spadework to bring her round. In comparison, the problem of Chuffy is simple. I shouldn't be surprised if even now he was kicking himself soundly for having behaved so like a perfect chump. One day of quiet meditation, at the outside, should be enough to convince him that he wronged the girl. To go and reason with Chuffy is simply a waste of time. Leave him alone, and Nature will effect the cure. You had better go straight back to the yacht and see what you can do at the other end."

"It was not with the intention of interviewing his lordship that I came ashore, sir. Once more I must reiterate that, until you informed me just now, I was not aware that anything in the nature of a rift had occurred My motive in coming here was to hand you a note from Mr. Stoker."

I was puzzled.

"A note?"

"Here it is, sir."

I opened it, still fogged, and read contents. I can't say I felt much clearer when I had done so.

"Rummy, Jeeves."

"Sir?"

"This is a letter of invitation."

"Indeed, sir?"

"Absolutely. Bidding me to the feast. 'Dear Mr. Wooster,' writes Pop Stoker. 'I shall be frightfully bucked if you will come and mangle a spot of garbage on the boat to-night. Don't dress.' I give you the gist of the thing. Peculiar, Jeeves."

"Certainly unforeseen, sir."

"I forgot to tell you that among my visitors last night was this same Stoker. He bounded in, shouting that his daughter was on the premises, and searched the house."

"Indeed, sir?"

"Well, of course, he didn't find any daughter, because she was already on her way back to the yacht, and he seemed conscious of having made rather an ass of himself. His manner on departing was chastened. He actually spoke to me civilly— a thing I'd have taken eleven to four on that he didn't know how to do. But does that explain this sudden gush of hospitality? I don't think so. Last night he seemed apologetic rather than matey. There was no indication whatever that he wished to start one of those great friendships."

"I think it is possible that a conversation which I had this morning with the gentleman, sir . . ."

"Ah! It was you, was it, who caused this pro-Bertram sentiment?"

"Immediately after breakfast, sir, Mr. Stoker sent for me and inquired if I had once been in your employment. He said that he fancied that he recalled having seen me at your apartment in New York. On my replying in the affirmative, he proceeded to question me with regard to certain incidents in the past."

"The cats in the bedroom?"

"And the hot-water bottle episode."

"The purloined hat?"

"And also the matter of your sliding down pipes, sir."

"And you said——?"

"I explained that Sir Roderick Glossop had taken a biased view of these occurrences, sir, and proceeded to relate their inner history."

"And he——?"

"—seemed pleased, sir. He appeared to think that he had misjudged you. He said that he ought to have known better than to believe information proceeding from Sir Roderick— to whom he alluded as a bald-headed old son of a something which for the moment has escaped my memory. It was, I imagine, shortly after this that he must have written this letter inviting you to dinner, sir."

I was pleased with the man. When Bertram Wooster finds

the old feudal spirit flourishing, he views it with approval and puts that approval into words.

"Thank you, Jeeves."

"Not at all, sir."

"You have done well. Regarding the matter from one aspect, of course, it is negligible whether Pop Stoker thinks I'm a loony or not. I mean to say, a fellow closely connected by ties of blood with a man who used to walk about on his hands is scarcely in a position, where the question of sanity is concerned, to put on dog and set himself up as an . . ."

"*Arbiter elegantiarum,* sir?"

"Quite. It matters little to me, therefore, from one point of view, what old Stoker thinks about my upper storey. One shrugs the shoulders. But, setting that aside, I admit that this change of heart is welcome. It has come at the right time. I shall accept his invitation. I regard it as . . ."

"The *amende honorable,* sir?"

"I was going to say olive branch."

"Or olive branch. The two terms are virtually synonymous. The French phrase I would be inclined to consider perhaps slightly the more exact in the circumstances—carrying with it, as it does, the implication of remorse, of the desire to make restitution. But if you prefer the expression 'olive branch,' by all means employ it, sir."

"Thank you, Jeeves."

"Not at all, sir."

"I suppose you know that you have made me completely forget what I was saying?"

"I beg your pardon, sir. I should not have interrupted. If I recollect, you were observing that it was your intention to accept Mr. Stoker's invitation."

"Ah, yes. Very well, then. I shall accept his invitation— whether as an olive branch or an *amende honorable* is wholly immaterial and doesn't matter a single, solitary damn, Jeeves. . . ."

"No, sir."

"And shall I tell you why I shall accept his invitation? Because it will enable me to get together with Miss Stoker and plead Chuffy's cause."

"I understand, sir."

"Not that it's going to be easy. I hardly know what line to take."

"If I might make the suggestion, sir, I should imagine that the young lady would respond most satisfactorily to the statement that his lordship was in poor health."

"She knows he's as fit as a fiddle."

"Poor health induced since her parting from him by distress of mind."

"Ah! I get you, Distraught?"

"Precisely, sir."

"Contemplating self-destruction?"

"Exactly, sir."

"Her gentle heart would be touched by that, you think?"

"Very conceivably, sir."

"Then that is the vein I shall work. I see this invitation says dinner at seven. A bit on the early side, what?"

"I presume that the arrangements have been made with a view to the convenience of Master Dwight, sir. This would be the birthday party of which I informed you yesterday."

"Of course, yes. With nigger minstrel entertainment to follow. They are coming all right, I take it?"

"Yes, sir. The Negroes will be present."

"I wonder if there would be any chance of a word with the one who plays the banjo. There are certain points in his execution I would like to consult him about."

"No doubt it could be arranged, sir."

He seemed to speak with a certain reserve, and I could see that he felt that the conversation had taken an embarrassing turn. Probing the old sore, I mean.

Well, the best thing to do on these occasions, I've always found, is to be open and direct.

"I'm making great progress with the banjolele, Jeeves."

"Indeed, sir?"

"Would you like me to play you 'What Is This Thing Called Love'?"

"No, sir."

"Your views on the instrument are unchanged?"

"Yes, sir."

"Ah, well! A pity we could not see eye to eye on that matter."

"Yes, sir."

"Still it can't be helped. No hard feelings."

"No, sir."

"Unfortunate, though."

"Most unfortunate, sir."

"Well, tell old Stoker that I shall be there at seven prompt with my hair in a braid."

"Yes, sir."

"Or should I write a brief, civil note?"

"No, sir. I was instructed to bring back a verbal reply."

"Right ho, then."

"Very good, sir."

At seven on the dot, accordingly, I stepped aboard the yacht and handed the hat and light overcoat to a passing salt. It was with mixed feelings that I did so, for conflicting emotions were warring in the bosom. On the one hand, the keen ozone of Chuffnell Regis had given me a good appetite, and I knew from recollections of his hosp. in New York that J. Washburn Stoker did his guests well. On the other, I had never been what you might call tranquil in his society, and I was not looking forward to it particularly now. You might put it like this if you cared to—The fleshly or corporeal Wooster was anticipating the binge with pleasure, but his spiritual side rather recoiled a bit.

In my experience, there are two kinds of elderly American. One, the stout and horn-rimmed, is matiness itself. He greets you as if you were a favourite son, starts agitating the cocktail shaker before you know where you are, slips a couple into you with a merry laugh, claps you on the back, tells you a dialect story about two Irishmen named Pat and Mike, and, in a word, makes life one grand, sweet song.

The other, which runs a good deal to the cold, grey stare and the square jaw, seems to view the English cousin with concern. It is not Elfin. It broods. It says little. It sucks in its breath in a pained way. And every now and again you catch its eye, and it is like colliding with a raw oyster.

Of this latter class or species J. Washburn Stoker had always been the perpetual vice-president.

It was with considerable relief, therefore, that I found that to-night he had eased off a bit. While not precisely affable, he gave a distinct impression of being as nearly affable as he knew how.

"I hope you have no objection to a quiet family dinner, Mr. Wooster?" he said, having shaken the hand.

"Rather not. Dashed good of you to ask me," I replied, not to be outdone in the courtesies.

"Just you and Dwight and myself. My daughter is lying down. She has a headache."

This was something of a jar. In fact, it seemed to me to take what you might describe as the whole meaning out of this expedition.

"Oh?" I said.

"I am afraid she found her exertions last night a little too much for her," said Pop Stoker, with something of the old fishlike expression in the eye: and, reading between the lines, I rather gathered that Pauline had been sent to bed without her supper, in disgrace. Old Stoker was not one of your broad-minded, modern parents. There was, as I had had occasion to notice before, a distinct touch of the stern and rockbound old Pilgrim Father about him. A man, in short, who, in his dealings with his family, believed in the firm hand.

Observing that eye, I found it a bit difficult to shape the kindly inquiries.

"Then you—er . . . she—er——?"

"Yes. You were quite right, Mr. Wooster. She had gone for a swim."

And once more, as he spoke, I caught a flash of the fish-like. I could see that Pauline's stock was far from high this p.m., and I would have liked to put in a word for the poor young blighter. But beyond an idea of saying that girls would be girls, which I abandoned, I could think of nothing.

At this moment, however, a steward of sorts announced dinner, and we pushed in.

I must say that there were moments during that dinner when I regretted that occurrences which could not be over-looked had resulted in the absence from the board of the Hall party. You will question this statement, no doubt, inclining to the view that all a dinner party needs to make it a success is for Sir Roderick Glossop, the Dowager Lady Chuffnell, and the latter's son, Seabury, not to be there. Nevertheless, I stick to my opinion. There was a certain uncomfortable something about the atmosphere which more or less turned the food to ashes in my mouth. If it hadn't been that this man, this Stoker, had gone out of his way to invite me, I should have said that I was giving him a pain in the neck. Most of the time he just sat and champed in a sort of dark silence, like a man with something on his mind. And when he did speak it was with a marked what-d'you-call-it. I mean to say, not actually out of the corner of his mouth, but very near it.

I did my best to promote a flow of conversation. But it was not till young Dwight had left the table and we were lighting the cigars that I seemed to hit on a topic that interested, elevated, and amused.

"A fine boat, this, Mr. Stoker," I said.

For the first time, something approaching animation came into the face.

"Not many better."

"I've never done much yachting. And, except at Cowes one year, I've never been on a boat this size."

He puffed at his cigar. An eye came swivelling round in my direction, then pushed off again.

"There are advantages in having a yacht."

"Oh, rather."

"Plenty of room to put your friends up."

"Heaps."

"And, when you've got 'em, they can't get away so easy as they could ashore."

It seemed a rummy way of looking at it, but I supposed a man like Stoker would naturally have a difficulty in keeping guests. I mean, I took it that he had had painful experiences in the past. And nothing, of course, makes a host look sillier than to have somebody arrive at his country house for a long visit and then to find, round about lunch-time the second day, that he has made a quiet sneak for the railway station.

"Care to look over the boat?" he asked.

"Fine," I said.

"I'd be glad to show it to you. This is the main saloon we're in."

"Ah," I said.

"I'll show you the state-rooms."

He rose, and went along passages and things. We came to a door. He opened it and switched on the light.

"This is one of our larger guest-rooms."

"Very nice, too."

"Go in and take a look round."

Well, there wasn't much to see that I couldn't focus from the threshold, but one has to do the civil thing on these occasions. I toddled over and gave the bed a prod.

And, as I did so, the door slammed. And when I nipped round, the old boy had disappeared.

Rather rummy, was my verdict. In fact, distinctly rummy. I went across and gave the handle a twist.

The bally door was locked.

"Hoy!" I called.

No answer.

"Hey!" I said. "Mr. Stoker."

Only silence, and lots of it.

I went and sat down on the bed. This seemed to me to want thinking out.

I can't say I liked the look of things. In addition to being at a loss and completely unable to follow the scenario, I was also distinctly on the uneasy side. I don't know if you ever read a book called "The Masked Seven?" It's one of those goose-fleshers and there's a chap in it, Drexdale Yeats, a private investigator, who starts looking for clues in a cellar one night, and he's hardly collected a couple when—*bingo*—there's a metallic clang and there he is with the trapdoor shut and some-one sniggering nastily on the other side. For a moment his heart stood still, and so did mine. Excluding the nasty snigger (which Stoker might quite well have uttered without my hear-ing it), it seemed to me that my case was more or less on all fours with his. Like jolly old Drexdale, I sensed some lurking peril.

Of course, mark you, if something on these lines had occurred at some country house where I was staying, and the hand that had turned the key had been that of a pal of mine, a ready explanation would have presented itself. I should have set it down as a spot of hearty humour. My circle of friends is crammed with fellows who would consider it dashed diverting to bung you into a room and lock the door. But on the present occasion I could not see this being the solution. There was nothing roguish about old Stoker. Whatever view you might take of this fishy-eyed man, you would never call him playful. If Pop Stoker put his guests in cold storage, his motive in so doing was sinister.

Little wonder, then, that as he sat on the edge of the bed pensively sucking at his cigar, Bertram was feeling uneasy. The thought of Stoker's second cousin, George, forced itself upon the mind. Dotty, beyond a question. And who knew but what that dottiness might not run in the family? It didn't seem such a long step, I mean to say, from a Stoker locking people in state-rooms to a Stoker with slavering jaws and wild, animal eyes coming back and doing them a bit of no good with the meat axe.

When, therefore, there was a click and the door opened, revealing mine host on the threshold, I confess that I rather drew myself together somewhat and pretty well prepared myself for the worst.

His manner, however, was reassuring. Puff-faced, yes, but not fiend-in-human-shape-y. The eyes were steady and the mouth lacked foam. And he was still smoking his cigar, which I felt was promising. I mean, I've never met any homicidal loonies, but I should imagine that the first thing they would do before setting about a fellow would be to throw away their cigars.

"Well, Mr. Wooster?"

I never have know quite what to answer when blokes say "Well?" to me, and I didn't now.

"I must apologize for leaving you so abruptly," proceeded the Stoker, "but I had to get the concert started."

"I'm looking forward to the concert," I said.

"A pity," said Pop Stoker. "Because you're going to miss it."

He eyed me musingly.

"There was a time, when I was younger, when I would have broken your neck," he said.

I didn't like the trend the conversation was taking. After all, a man is as young as he feels, and there was no knowing that he wouldn't suddenly get one of these—what do you call them?—illusions of youth. I had an uncle once, aged seventy-six, who, under the influence of old crusted port, would climb trees.

"Look here," I said civilly but with what you might call a certain urgency, "I know it's trespassing on your time, but could you tell me what all this is about?"

"You don't know?"

"No, I'm hanged if I do."

"And you can't guess?"

"No, I'm dashed if I can."

"Then I had best tell you from the beginning. Perhaps you recall my visiting you last night?"

I said I hadn't forgotten.

"I thought my daughter was in your cottage. I searched it. I did not find her."

I twiddled a hand magnanimously.

"We all make mistakes."

He nodded.

"Yes. So I went away. And do you know what happened after I left you, Mr. Wooster? I was coming out of the garden gate when your local police sergeant stopped me. He seemed suspicious."

I waved my cigar sympathetically.

"Something will have to be done about Voules," I said. "The man is a pest. I hope you were pretty terse with him."

"Not at all. I suppose he was only doing his duty. I told him who I was and where I lived. On learning that I came from this yacht, he asked me to accompany him to the police station."

I was amazed.

"What bally cheek! You mean he pinched you?"

"No, he was not arresting me. He wished me to identify someone who was in custody."

"Bally cheek, all the same. What on earth did he bother you with that sort of job for? Besides, how on earth could you identify anyone? I mean, a stranger in these parts, and all that sort of thing."

"In this instance it was simple. The prisoner happened to be my daughter, Pauline."

"What!"

"Yes, Mr. Wooster. It seems that this man Voules was in his back garden late last night—it adjoins yours, if you recollect—and he saw a figure climbing out of one of the lower windows of your house. He ran down the garden and caught this individual. It was my daughter Pauline. She was wearing a swimming suit and an overcoat belonging to you. So, you see, you were right when you told me she had probably gone for a swim."

He knocked the ash carefully off his cigar. I didn't need to do it to mine.

"She must have been with you a few moments before I arrived. Now, perhaps, Mr. Wooster, you can understand what I meant when I said that, when I was a younger man, I would have broken your neck."

I hadn't anything much to say. One hasn't sometimes.

"Nowadays, I'm more sensible," he proceeded. "I take the easier way. I say to myself that Mr. Wooster is not the son-in-law I would have chosen personally, but if my hand has been forced that is all there is to it. Anyway, you're not the gibbering idiot I thought you at one time, I'm glad to say. I have heard since that those stories which caused me to break off Pauline's engagement to you in New York were untrue. So we can consider everything just as it was three months ago. We will look upon that letter of Pauline's as unwritten."

You can't reel when you're sitting on a bed. Otherwise, I would have done so, and right heartily. I was feeling as if a hidden hand had socked me in the solar plexus.

"Do you mean——?"

He let me have an eye squarely in the pupil. A beastly sort of eye, cold and yet hot, if you follow me. If this was the Boss's Eye you read so much about in the advertisements in American magazines, I was dashed if I could see why any ambitious young shipping clerk should be so bally anxious to catch it. It went clean through me, and I lost the thread of my remarks.

"I am assuming that you wish to marry my daughter?"

Well, of course . . . I mean, dash it . . . I mean, there isn't much you can say to an observation like that. I just weighed in with a mild "Oh, ah."

"I am not quite sure if I understand the precise significance of the expression 'Oh, ah!'" he said, and, by Jove, I wonder if you notice a rather rummy thing. I mean to say, this man had had the advantage of Jeeves's society for only about twenty-four hours, and here he was—except that Jeeves would have said "wholly" instead of "quite" and stuck in a "Sir" or two—

talking just like him. I mean, it just shows. I remember putting young Catsmeat Potter-Pirbright up at the flat for a week once, and the very second day he said something to me about gauging somebody's latent potentialities. And Catsmeat a fellow who had always thought you were kidding him when you assured him that there were words in the language that had more than one syllable. As I say, it simply goes to show. . . .

However, where was I?

"I am not quite sure if I understand the precise significance of the expression 'Oh, ah!'" said this Stoker, "but I will take it to mean that you do. I won't pretend that I'm delighted, but one can't have everything. What are your views upon engagements, Mr. Wooster?"

"Engagements?"

"Should they be short or long?"

"Well . . ."

"I prefer them short. I feel that we had best put this wedding through as quickly as possible. I shall have to find out how soon that is on this side. I believe you cannot simply go to the nearest minister, as in my country. There are formalities. While there are being attended to, you will, of course, be my guest. I'm afraid I can't offer you the freedom of the boat, because you are a pretty slippery young gentleman and might suddenly remember a date elsewhere—some unfortunate appointment which would necessitate your leaving. But I shall do my best to make you comfortable in this room for the next few days. There are books on that shelf—I assume you can read?—and cigarettes on the table. I will send my man along in a few minutes with some pyjamas and so on. And now I will wish you good night, Mr. Wooster. I must be getting back to the concert. I can't stay away from my son's birthday party, can I, even for the pleasure of talking to you?"

He slipped through the door and oozed out, and I was alone.

Now, it so happened that twice in my career I had had the experience of sitting in a cell and listening to keys turning in locks. The first time was the one to which Chuffy had alluded, when I had been compelled to assure the magistrate that I was one of the West Dulwich Plimsolls. The other—and both, oddly enough, had occurred on Boat Race night—was when I had gone into partnership with my old friend, Oliver Sipperley, to pick up a policeman's helmet as a souvenir, only to discover that there was a policeman inside it. On both these occasions I had ended up behind the bars, and you might suppose that an old lag like myself would have been getting used to it by now.

But this present binge was something quite different. Before, I had been faced merely with the prospect of a moderate fine. Now, a life sentence stared me in the eyeball.

A casual observer, noting Pauline's pre-eminent pulchritude and bearing in mind the fact that she was heiress to a sum amounting to more than fifty million fish, might have considered that in writhing, as I did, in agony of spirit at the prospect of having to marry her, I was making a lot of fuss about nothing. Such an observer, no doubt, would have wished that he had half my complaint. But the fact remains that I did writhe, and writhe pretty considerably.

Apart from the fact that I didn't want to marry Pauline Stoker, there was the dashed serious snag that I knew jolly well that she didn't want to marry me. She might have ticked him off with great breadth and freedom at their recent parting, but I was certain that deep down in her the old love for Chuffy still persisted and only needed a bit of corkscrew work to get it to the surface again. And Chuffy, for all that he had hurled himself downstairs and stalked out into the night, still loved her. So that what it amounted to, when you came to tot up the pros and cons, was that by marrying this girl I should not only be landing myself in the soup but breaking both her heart and that of the old school friend. And if that doesn't justify a fellow in writhing, I should very much like to know what does.

Only one gleam of light appeared in the darkness—viz. that old Stoker had said that he was sending his man along with the necessaries for the night. It might be that Jeeves would find the way.

Though how even Jeeves could get me out of the current jam was more than I could envisage. It was with the feeling that no bookie would hesitate to lay a hundred to one against that I finished my cigar and threw myself on the bed.

I was still picking at the coverlet when the door opened and a respectful cough informed me that he was in my midst. His arms were full of clothing of various species. He laid these on a chair and regarded me with what I might describe as commiseration.

"Mr. Stoker instructed me to bring your pyjamas, sir."

I emitted a hollow g.

"It is not pyjamas I need, Jeeves, but the wings of a dove. Are you abreast of the latest development?"

"Yes, sir."

"Who told you?"

"My informant was Miss Stoker, sir."

"You've been having a talk with her?"

"Yes, sir. She related to me an outline of the plans which Mr. Stoker had made."

The first spot of hope I had had since the start of this ghastly affair now shot through my bosom.

"By Jove, Jeeves, an idea occurs to me. Things aren't quite as bad as I thought they were."

"No, sir?"

"No. Can't you see? It's all very well for old Stoker to talk—er——"

"Glibly, sir?"

"Airily."

"Airily or glibly, sir, whichever you prefer."

"It's all very well for old Stoker to talk with airy glibness about marrying us off, but he can't do it, Jeeves. Miss Stoker will simply put her ears back and refuse to co-operate. You can lead a horse to the altar, Jeeves, but you can't make it drink."

427

"In my recent conversation with the young lady, sir, I did not receive the impression that she was antagonistic to the arrangements."

"What!"

"No, sir. She seemed, if I may say so, resigned and defiant."

"She couldn't be both."

"Yes, sir. Miss Stoker's attitude was partly one of listlessness, as if she felt that nothing mattered now, but I gathered that she was also influenced by the thought that in contracting a matrimonial alliance with you, she would be making—shall I say, a defiant gesture at his lordship."

"A defiant gesture?"

"Yes, sir."

"Scoring off him, you mean?"

"Precisely, sir."

"What a damn silly idea. The girl must be cuckoo."

"Feminine psychology is admittedly odd, sir. The poet Pope . . ."

"Never mind about the poet Pope, Jeeves."

"No, sir."

"There are times when one wants to hear all about the poet Pope and times when one doesn't."

"Very true, sir."

"The point is, I seem to be up against it. If that's the way she feels, nothing can save me. I am a pipped man."

"Yes, sir. Unless——"

"Unless?"

"Well, I was wondering, sir, if on the whole it would not be best if you were to obviate all unpleasantness and embarrassment by removing yourself from the yacht."

"What!"

"Yacht, sir."

"I know you said 'Yacht.' And I said 'What!' Jeeves," I went on, and there was a quiver in the voice, "it is not like you to come in here at a crisis like this with straws in your hair and talk absolute drip. How the devil can I leave the yacht?"

428

"The matter could be readily arranged, if you are agreeable, sir. It would, of course, involve certain inconveniences . . ."

"Jeeves," I said, "short of squeezing through the port-hole, which can't be done, I am ready to undergo any little passing inconvenience if it will get me off this bally floating dungeon and restore me to terra firma." I paused and regarded him anxiously. "This is not mere gibbering, is it? You really have a scheme?"

"Yes, sir. The reason I hesitated to advance it was that I feared you might not approve of the idea of covering your face with boot polish."

"What!"

"Time being of the essence, sir, I think it would not be advisable to employ burnt cork."

I turned my face to the wall. It was the end.

"Leave me, Jeeves," I said. "You've been having a couple."

And I'm not sure that what cut me like a knife, more even than any agony at my fearful predicament, was not the realization that my original suspicions had been correct and that, after all these years, that superb brain had at last come unstuck. For, though I had tactfully affected to set all this talk of burnt cork and boot polish down to mere squiffiness, in my heart I was convinced that the fellow had gone off his onion.

He coughed.

"If you will permit me to explain, sir. The entertainers are just concluding their performance. In a short time they will be leaving the boat."

I sat up. Hope dawned once more, and remorse gnawed me like a bull-pup worrying a rubber bone at the thought that I should have so misjudged this man. I saw what that giant brain was driving at.

"You mean——?"

"I have a small tin of boot polish here, sir. I brought it with me in anticipation of this move. It would be a simple task to apply it to your face and hands in such a manner as to create the illusion, should you encounter Mr. Stoker, that you were a member of this troupe of negroid entertainers."

"Jeeves!"

"The suggestion I would make, sir, is that, if you are amenable to what I propose, we should wait until these black-faced persons have left for the shore. I could then inform the captain that one of them, a personal friend of mine, had lingered behind to talk with me and so had missed the motor launch. I have little doubt that he would accord me permission to row you ashore in one of the smaller boats."

I stared at the man. Years of intimate acquaintance, the memory of swift ones he had pulled in the past, the knowledge that he lived largely on fish, thus causing his brain to be about as full of phosphorus as the human brain can jolly well stick, had not prepared me for this supreme effort.

"Jeeves," I said, "as I have so often had occasion to say before, you stand alone."

"Thank you, sir."

"Others abide our question. Thou art free."

"I endeavour to give satisfaction, sir."

"You think it would work?"

"Yes, sir."

"The scheme carries your personal guarantee?"

"Yes, sir."

"And you say you have the stuff handy?"

"Yes, sir."

I flung myself into a chair and turned the features ceiling-wards.

"Then start smearing, Jeeves," I said, "and continue to smear till your trained senses tell you that you have smeared enough."

'Had P.G. Wodehouse's only contribution to literature been Lord Emsworth and Blandings Castle, his place in history would have been assured. Had he written of none but Mike and Psmith, he would be cherished today as the best and brightest of our comic authors. If Jeeves and Wooster had been his solitary theme, still he would be hailed as The Master. If he had given us only Ukridge, or nothing but the recollections of the Mulliner family, or a pure diet of golfing stories, Wodehouse would never the less be considered immortal. That he gave us all those and more – so much more – is our good fortune and a testament to the most industrious, prolific and beneficent author ever to have sat down, scratched his head and banged out a sentence.'   Stephen Fry

We hope you have enjoyed this book. With over ninety novels and around 300 short stories to choose from, you may be wondering which Wodehouse to choose next. It is our pleasure to introduce...

UNCLE FRED

Uncle Dynamite

Meet Frederick Altamount Cornwallis Twistleton, Fifth Earl of Ickenham. Better known as Uncle Fred, an old boy of such a sunny and youthful nature that explosions of sweetness and light detonate all around him.

Cocktail Time

Frederick, Earl of Ickenham, remains young at heart. So his jape of using a catapult to ping to silk top hat off his grumpy half-brother-in-law, is nothing out of the ordinary but the consequences abound with possibilities.

UKRIDGE

Ukridge

Money makes the world go round for Stanley Featherstonehaugh Ukridge – looking like an animated blob of mustard in his bright yellow raincoat – and when there isn't enough of it, the world just has to spin a bit faster.

MR MULLINER

Meet Mr Mulliner

Sitting in the Angler's Rest, drinking hot scotch and lemon, Mr Mulliner has fabulous stories to tell of the extraordinary behaviour of his far flung family. This includes Wilfred, whose formula for Buck-U-Uppo enables elephants to face tigers with the necessary nonchalance.

Mr Mulliner Speaking

Holding court in the bar-parlour of the Angler's Rest, Mr Mulliner reveals what happened to The Man Who Gave Up Smoking, what the Something Squishy was that the butler on a silver salver, and what caused the dreadful Unpleasantness at Bludleigh Court.

MONTY BODKIN

The Luck of the Bodkins

Monty Bodkin, besotted with 'precious dream-rabbit' Gertrude Butterwick, Reggie and Ambrose Tennyson (the latter mistaken for the late Poet Laureate), and Hollywood starlet Lotus Blossom, complete with pet alligator, all embark on a voyage of personal discovery aboard the luxurious liner S. S. Atlantic.

JEEVES
The Novels

Thank You, Jeeves

Bertie disappears to the country as a guest of his chum Chuffy – only to find his peace shattered by the arrival of his ex-fiancée Pauline Stoker, her formidable father and the eminent loony-doctor Sir Roderick Glossop. When Chuffy falls in love with Pauline and Bertie seems to be caught in flagrante, a situation boils up which only Jeeves (whether employed or not) can simmer down . . .

Jeeves and the Feudal Spirit

A moustachioed Bertie must live up to 'Stilton' Cheesewright's expectations in the Drones Club darts tournament, or risk being beaten to a pulp by 'Stilton', jealous of his fiancée Florence's affections . . .

Much Obliged, Jeeves

What happens when the Book of Revelations, the Junior Ganymede Club's recording of their masters' less than perfect habits falls into potentially hostile hands?

Aunts Aren't Gentlemen

Under doctor's orders, Bertie moves with Jeeves to a countryside cottage. But Jeeves can cope with anything – even Aunt Dahlia.

Jeeves in the Offing

When Jeeves goes on holiday to Herne Bay, Bertie's life collapses; finding his mysterious engagement announced in The Times and encountering his nemesis Sir Roderick Glossop in disguise, Bertie hightails it to Herne Bay. Then the fun really starts . . .

The Code of the Woosters

Purloining an antique cow creamer under the instruction of the indomitable Aunt Dahlia is the least of Bertie's tasks, for he has to play Cupid while feuding with Spode.

The Mating Season

In an idyllic Tudor manor in a picture-perfect English village, Bertie is in disguise as Gussie Fink-Nottle, Gussie is in disguise as Bertram Wooster and Jeeves, also in disguise, is the only one who can set things right . . .

Ring for Jeeves

Patch Perkins and his clerk are not the 'honest bookies' they seem, but Bill, the rather impoverished 9th Earl of Rowcester, and his temporary butler Jeeves. When they abscond with the freak winnings of Captain Biggar, Jeeves's resourcefulness is put to the test . . .

Stiff Upper Lip, Jeeves

Bertie Wooster visits Major Plank in an attempt to return a work of art which Stiffy had told Bertie had been effectively stolen from Plank by Sir Watkyn Bassett. Thank goodness for Chief Inspector Witherspoon – but is he all he seems?

Right Ho, Jeeves

Bertie assumes his alter-ego of Cupid and arranges the engagement of Gussie Fink-Nottle to Tuppy Glossop. Thankfully, Jeeves is ever present to correct the blundering plans hatched by his master.

Joy in the Morning

Trapped in rural Steeple Bumpleigh with old flame Florence Craye, her new and suspicious fiancé Stilton Cheesewright, and two-faced Edwin the Boy Scout, Bertie desperately needs Jeeves to save him . . .

JEEVES

The Collections

Carry on, Jeeves

In his new role as valet to Bertie Wooster, Jeeves's first duty is to create a miracle hangover cure. From that moment, the partnership that is Jeeves and Wooster never looks back ...

Very Good, Jeeves

Endeavouring to give satisfaction, Jeeves embarks on a number of rescue missions, including rescuing Bingo Little and Tuppy Glossop from the soup ... Twice each.

The Inimitable Jeeves

In pages stalked by the carnivorous Aunt Agatha, Bingo Little embarks on a relationship rollercoaster and Bertie needs Jeeves's help to narrowly evade the clutches of terrifying Honoria Glossop ...

The World of Jeeves

A complete collection of the Jeeves and Wooster short stories, described by Wodehouse as 'the ideal paperweight'.

BLANDINGS

Something Fresh

The first Blandings novel, featuring the delightfully dotty Lord Emsworth and introducing the first of many impostors who are to visit the Castle.

Pigs Have Wings

Can the Empress of Blandings avoid a pignapping to win the Fat Pigs class at the Shropshire Show for the third year running?

Leave it to Psmith

Lady Constance Keeble, sister of Lord Emsworth of Blandings Castle, has both an imperious manner and a valuable diamond necklace. The precarious peace of Blandings is shattered when her necklace becomes the object of dark plottings, for within the castle lurk some well-connected jewel thieves – among them a pair of American crooks, Lord Emsworth's younger son Freddie, desperate for money to establish a bookie's business, and Psmith, hoping to use a promised commission to finance his old school friend Mike's purchase of a farm to secure his future happiness.

Service with a Smile

When Clarence, Ninth Earl of Emsworth, must travel to London for the opening of Parliament, he grudgingly leaves beloved pig, the Empress of Blandings, at home. When he returns, he must call upon Uncle Fred to restore normality to the chaos instilled during his absence . . .

Summer Lightning

The first appearance in a novel of The Empress of Blandings, the prize-winning pig and all-consuming passion of Clarence, Ninth Earl of Emsworth, which has disappeared. Suspects within the Castle abound . . . Did the butler do it?

Full Moon

When the moon is full at Blandings, strange things happen. Including a renowned painter being miraculously revivified to paint a portrait of the beloved pig The Empress of Blandings, decades after his death . . .

Uncle Fred in the Springtime

Uncle Fred believes he can achieve anything in the springtime, however disguised as a loony-doctor and trying to prevent prize pig, the Empress of Blandings from falling into the hands of the unscrupulous Duke of Dunstable, he is stretched to his limit . . .

A Pelican at Blandings

Skulduggery is afoot, involving the sale of a modern nude painting, which in Lord Emsworth's eyes, resembles a pig. Inundated with unwelcome guests, Clarence is embarking on the short journey to the end of his wits. Fortunately Galahad Threepwood is on hand to solve all the mysteries . . .

The World of Blandings (Omnibus)

This wonderfully fat omnibus (containing three short stories and two full novels) spans the dimensions of the Empress of Blandings herself, surely the fattest pig in England . . .

Blandings Castle

The Empress of Blandings, potential silver medal winner in the Fat Pigs Class at the Shropshire Agricultural show, is off her food. Clarence, absent-minded Ninth Earl of Emsworth, is engaged in a feud with Head Gardener McAllister. But first of all, the vexed matter of the custody of the pumpkin must be resolved. This collection also includes Mr Mulliner's stories about Hollywood.

And Some Other Treats...

What Ho!

Introduced by Stephen Fry, this is a bumper anthology, providing the cream of the crop of Wodehouse's hilarious stories, together with verse, articles and all manner of treasures.

The Heart of a Goof

From his favourite chair on the terrace above the ninth hole, the Oldest Member reveals the stories behind his club's players, from notorious 'golfing giggler' Evangeline to poor, inept Rollo Podmarsh.

The Clicking of Cuthbert

A collection of stories, including that of Cuthbert, golfing ace, hopelessly in love with Adeline, who only cares for rising young writers. But enter a Great Russian Novelist with a strange passion, and Cuthbert's prospects might be looking up . . .

Big Money

Berry Conway, employee of dyspeptic American millionaire Torquil Patterson Frisby, has inherited a large number of shares in the Dream Come True copper mine. Of course they're worthless . . . aren't they?

Hot Water

In the heady atmosphere of a 1930s French Château, J Wellington Gedge only wants to return to his life in California, where everything is as it seems . . .

Laughing Gas

Joey Cooley, golden-curled Hollywood child film star, and Reginald, six-foot tall boxer Earl of Havershot, are both under anaesthetic in the dentist's when their identities are swapped in the fourth dimension.

The Small Bachelor

It's Prohibition America and shy young George Finch is setting out as an artist – without the encumbrance of a shred of talent. Will George triumph over the social snob Mrs Waddington and successfully woo her stepdaughter?

Money for Nothing

Two households, both alike in dignity, in fair Rudge-in-the-Vale, where we lay our scene . . . Will the love of John Carmody and Pat Wyvern survive the bitter feud between their fathers, miserly Lester Carmody and peppery Colonel Wyvern?

Summer Moonshine

Poor Sir Buckstone Abbott owns in Walsingford Hall one of the least attractive stately homes in the country, so when a rich continental princess seems willing to buy it, he's overjoyed. But will the deal be completed?

The Adventures of Sally

When Sally Nicholas inherits some money, her life becomes increasingly complicated; with a needy brother, a handsome fiancé, who is not all he seems, and a naive generosity of spirit, Sally must turn to doting, clueless Ginger Kemp to set things right . . .

Young Men in Spats

Meet the Young Men in Spats – all innocent members of the Drones Club, all hopeless suitors, and all busy betting their sometimes non-existent fortunes on highly improbable outcomes. That is when they're not recovering from driving their sports cars *through* Marble Arch . . .

Piccadilly Jim

It takes a lot of effort for Jimmy Crocker to become Piccadilly Jim – nights on the town roistering, and a string of broken hearts. When he eventually succeeds, Jimmy ends up having to pretend he's himself, possibly the hardest pretence of all …

A Damsel in Distress

The Earl of Marshmoreton just wants a quiet life pottering around his garden, supported by his portly butler Keggs. However when his spirited daughter Lady Maud is placed under house-arrest due to an unfortunate infatuation, and American George Bevan determines to claim her heart, the Earl is allowed no such reprieve …

The Girl in Blue

Young Jerry West has a few problems, including uncles with butlers who aren't all they seem, and a love for the woman he is not due to marry … When his uncle's miniature Gainsborough, *The Girl in Blue*, is stolen, Jerry sets out on a mission to find her … Will everything come right in the process?

Join the P G Wodehouse community!

Visit the official website:
www.wodehouse.co.uk

Become a fan on facebook:
 **/wodehousepage**

Join the P G Wodehouse Society:
www.pgwodehousesociety.org.uk